To
Eric Ulmer —
best wishes,
I hope you enjoy the

Charles Daubert
7-7-99

MW01106668

HANSA-HEWLETT
PUBLISHING COMPANY

# The Temptation

## of

## St. Rosalie

# The Temptation Of St. Rosalie

## PORTRAIT OF A BLACK SLAVE OWNER

By

# Charles Daudert

Hansa-Hewlett  Publishing Company
Kalamazoo

*For All God's Children*

# Acknowledgement & Forward

I am deeply indebted to Andrew Durnford, free man of color, who lived from 1800 to 1859. Without Andrew Durnford, the black slave-owner, this book would not have been possible. It is his story. During his life he built one of the most successful sugar plantations on the Mississippi.

There are more surviving records of Durnford's plantation than any other of its time. Andrew Durnford's close friend and mentor was John McDonogh, the richest man in Louisiana. Almost every school in New Orleans bears McDonogh's name and was built with money bequeathed by him to the Crescent City. Since McDonogh's entire estate was given in trust for educational purposes, every scrap of paper in his possession was saved by the trustees. And McDonogh had saved everything. He saved all the letters to and from his protege, Andrew Durnford. Those letters are now under the care of the Historical Center of the Louisiana State Museum. All the records of business transactions with Durnford, which were numerous, have survived with the papers of the McDonogh estate, most of which are at Tulane University. Durnford also kept meticulous journals of his plantation which were saved by his granddaughters, and are now under the care of the Historic New Orleans Collection and Tulane University. I thank all three of those institutions for allowing me to review and copy the original documents and letters, still in excellent condition.

For my discovery of the black plantation owner and the key to original source materials, I am forever indebted to David Whitten, the author of *ANDREW DURNFORD, Free Man of Color*. Those interested in reading further are advised to obtain a copy of his well-documented book.

Much of the speech and setting of the era is from *THE COTTON KINGDOM, A Traveler's Observations on Cotton and Slavery in the American Slave States,* by Frederick Law Olmstead. Additional sources of information which I have used in writing the book are: *LIFE ON THE MISSISSIPPI,* by Mark Twain, *BEFORE FREEDOM, WHEN I JUST CAN REMEMBER,* oral histories of former slaves edited by Belinda Hurmence, *THE CREOLES OF COLOR OF NEW ORLEANS,* by James Haskins, *THE FORGOTTEN PEOPLE, CANE RIVER CREOLES OF COLOR,* by Gary B. Mills, and *THE WORLD FROM JACKSON SQUARE, a New Orleans Reader,* edited by Etolia S. Basso, and many, many other works too numerous to mention.

Finally, a great deal of material came from the pages of the newspapers of the time; *The Courier* for the years 1835 & 1836, *The Louisiana Courier* for the year 1850, and *The Daily Picayune* for the years 1835, 1850, 1860, and 1862.

To truly understand the history of slavery, I believe one must understand Andrew Durnford. And to truly understand the relations between black and white Americans today, I believe one must listen to what Andrew Durnford had to tell us.

Andrew Durnford was a well-educated black man who spoke and wrote in both French and English. Trained as a physician, he treated without charge both black and white citizens of Plaquemines Parish while building a small financial empire on the backs of slave labor. He was a philosopher with a library the equal of many colleges of the time, and far more extensive than on any other plantation on the banks of the Mississippi. He knew well the history of slavery throughout the world and throughout time. And he knew that slavery was wrong. But he continued to expand his holdings, always rationalizing his position, always insisting that God knew that in his heart, Andrew Durnford wanted the best for his people, and that in the end he would do what was right.

# Chapter One

His clothes were not the coarse wear of the seaman who rushed about, or even the broadcloth of the ship's officers who huddled at the stern. He wore the slick dress of the leisure class; a well-tailored cashmere coat and linen pants with a sharp crease that pointed down to soft leather shoes. And by the tenth day of his journey, Andrew Durnford believed he could become his father's son.

Pacing the deck into the night, Durnford smoked black cigars and spat over the rail. He could not face his old friend, that throbbing head pain, in the cabin's quiet. Toward midnight he went to the ship's saloon in the center of the vessel. It was elaborately decorated and reserved for the social use of the passengers. Deserted glass bowls with spoons in them slid lazily back and forth on fiddle-lined tables. The last man reading shut up his book and blew out his candle, leaving only the dim flicker of a whale lamp over the table.

Andrew Durnford slid onto a bench near the door.

The man who had been reading pushed spectacles into his coat pocket and rubbed his chin. His face was ghost-white and lined. The swaying lantern over the table splashed shadows about his sunken eyes. "Evening, Doctor," the man said at last in a high-pitched, hesitating voice.

"Yes. And good evening to you, sir. I've seen you about the ship, but I'm sorry to say I don't know your name."

"Thomas Hollingsworth. From New Bedford. Parson there, you should know, and I belong to the Massachusetts legislature as well. You are the sugar planter we picked up along the river."

Durnford sat up straight on the cushioned bench. His dark face flushed. He'd hoped to find the saloon empty. "Yes. I'm the plantation man."

"You...Durnford, are capable of the greatest understatements. You are the richest man on this ship. The hold contains nothing but barrels and hogsheads of your sugar and molasses. A small fortune. Took most of the day to hoist it aboard. Might I ask what you intend to do with it?"

"Why, I intend to sell it, Mr. Hollingsworth. That's why we are carrying it to Philadelphia." With that statement, Durnford rose from the bench and turned to the door. He intended to bring the conversation to an end as quickly as possible.

"And what will you do then, Durnford?"

Durnford paused with his hand on the doorknob and looked over his shoulder. "I'll take a little holiday with my family, Parson. We'll see the State of Virginia, and a little of Washington City. Then maybe we'll travel north and look at New York. But if you'll excuse me now, I must retire to my quarters."

"Virginia is a slave-breeding state, Durnford. I saw slaves on your plantation, Negro slaves. A man of your race wouldn't be traveling to Virginia to buy slaves, would he, Durnford?"

Durnford slipped out of the saloon and shut the door as the familiar pain slammed to his head. He staggered along the rolling deck until he came to the small officer's cabin on the port side assigned to him for quarters. Inside was a washstand with a small, oval mirror over it. He splashed water over his face and rubbed his head with a towel, hoping to wash away the terrible smell of musk which always came with the pain that crushed his temples.

Next to the mirror was a candle which swung in a gimbals. Durnford lit the candle with a shaking hand. He sat down on his mattress and absently boxed his pillow. In the bunk over his head, reached by climbing up half-opened drawers, slept Thomas, Durnford's son, nine years old.

Durnford ran his thick hand along the rough timbers at the back of his bunk. On the other side of the wall, in a cabin with a door opening to the ship's starboard deck, lay his wife, Marie-Charlotte Remy Durnford. Above her, in the top bunk, slept their daughter, Rosella.

Durnford thought of tapping on the wall, but he knew there would be no response. Marie-Charlotte had been asleep for hours. So Andrew sat on his bunk in the rolling ship and listened to the howling wind and the water crashing along the hull, and sighed. He had built St. Rosalie Plantation because that was what he thought he had to do for his family. Now they expected him to keep on with the plantation, Marie Charlotte, his mother, even the children. No one talked about the lawsuit brought by his English cousins, claiming title to the land.

Durnford had left the care of the plantation to Noel, a young slave who at the age of twenty-five was the accountant and undisputed master of the plantation ledgers. To assist Noel, Durnford had secured the services of Baptiste, the white overseer from the plantation to the north of St. Rosalie.

Andrew Durnford sat on his cabin bunk, watched the candle swing in its gimbals, thought about his plantation and wondered how long it would last. For a hundred years, perhaps two hundred years or more the family would prosper and the plantation would grow. That was what his father had said. That was what Andrew believed. And he was proud to be the founder of a dynasty. Proud to be the founder of St. Rosalie. Proud to be his father's son.

Durnford was a member of a third class of people in Louisiana. He was a free man of color, a class accorded special privileges, opportunities, and citizenship not granted to Negroes in other states. He could sue in courts. He could not serve on the jury, but he could, and did, win, even against whites.

In 1835, the year of Andrew Durnford's voyage to Philadelphia, over half the population of New Orleans was black. Half of those blacks were slaves and half were free people of color. A thousand of the free people themselves owned slaves. In the parishes and on plantations along the Mississippi, and up the Red River in the Cane Colony, well educated, cultured, wealthy men of color like Andrew Durnford owned their brothers and sisters as slaves.

Durnford fumbled around in his medical bag. The pounding in his head was unbearable. The sour-sweet smell of musk was nauseating. When his hand glided over a smooth glass jar, he lifted it to the light. Inside the small jar were several layers of packed, wet, grass. And writhing in the wet grass were a dozen perfect specimens. They were from three to four inches long, dark black with smooth, segmented fat bodies. At each extremity of the silky body was a large suction disk. And in the middle of the sucking disk were three small white teeth. With these sharp, saw-like projections the large worms made a deep wound which produced a fresh flow of blood. The fat, shiny, ringed worms were medical leeches, carefully selected by Andrew Durnford from the best imported stock available in New Orleans. He placed the glass jar between his legs and unscrewed the perforated lid. With wooden tweezers, he carefully removed five of the biggest black leeches and dropped them on his left arm. The worms quickly attached themselves, and with shiny bodies pulsating in the dim candlelight, began sucking blood from

Durnford's arm.

He watched with fascination as the black bodies fed on his blood. This rich fluid from his body was the only nourishment the worms received. He alone, through his life-giving sustenance, kept the dark leeches from death.

Durnford waited. He knew it was impossible to tear the smooth worms from his flesh until they had completed their mission. And as the segmented bodies swelled with their meals, he picked them up and dropped them into the jar. After a few lazy turns, the fat worms, gorged with blood, settled down to sleep in the upper layers of wet grass. Durnford's mind cleared as he watched the leeches in peaceful repose. The throbbing pain disappeared from his temples. The nauseous taste of musk receded. Perhaps it was an excess of pressure from too much blood in his system that caused his condition. Or perhaps by some magic method, the worms withdrew only the poisonous blood. Or perhaps this business with the leeches was no more than witchcraft. Nevertheless, it was witchcraft that worked for him. Outside the cabin the ship's bell struck eight bells to toll the midnight hour and was answered by a cheerful "All's well" of the deck watch.

After changing to his night clothes and blowing out the candle, Durnford settled into his bunk and wedged in the wooden board which protected him from violent rolls of the steam-powered sailing brig. He lay for a long time listening to the pagan chant of the water babbling along the ship's side. Then for a moment he thought the pagan voice in the water was calling to him: "Andrew...what is a man of your race doing with slaves?"

He sat boldly upright. There was no voice in the water. He had only imagined it while falling asleep. And it was all the fault of that damned parson from New Bedford. Durnford had little doubt the parson was an abolitionist, one of those badly informed intellectuals who swept through the South every year or so, and then returned North to write hot-tempered books about the people who'd been so gracious to them.

In the morning, Durnford was awakened by the splash and clang of the galley boy washing last night's dinner plates on deck. He stepped from his bunk and slid back his inner window which had been closed during the night by the watch. Then he reopened his outer deadlight and looked at the slow-rolling, lead-colored waves with dirty-white tops, over which the dawn struggled up the sky on a cold morning off the entrance to Delaware Bay. The boilers had been fired sometime during the night and black smoke rolled up the sails as the steam engine below deck hissed and pumped, churning the paddle wheels at each side of the ship to help speed it on its way to Philadelphia.

Thomas was still soundly asleep in his bunk. Durnford lay down again and waited for the passenger call to breakfast, which was always broiled ham, biscuits with gravy and tea or coffee.

The Durnfords had their own table in the saloon, and on the voyage they ate with the children and their servant, Barba. Barba, Durnford's short, stout, and obedient body servant, had come with him on the trip and slept in the ship's forecastle. Barely three years older than Durnford and lacking in all education, Barba was the equal of his owner as a philosopher. He had been Andrew's playmate when they were very young. And Durnford always respected Barba's opinions, even after Durnford went to Paris and earned a medical degree at the academy there. At breakfast, Andrew Durnford sat next to Barba, across from Marie-Charlotte and the children. He looked only briefly into his wife's smoldering eyes, and knew her passion for him was as great as his desire for her. But the voyage had been a voyage of celibacy, necessitated by the sleeping arrangements with the children. He smiled quickly and she nodded. Perhaps later that day, when the children were playing on deck, they would find an opportunity to slip into her cabin and leave the troubles of the world behind.

The children's skin was a darker tone than the copper color of their mulatto mother, but they both had her fine features. Andrew had the rough and rugged features of his English father and the walnut skin of his mother, Rosaline Mercier, who remained behind on the plantation. Durnford's mother, Rosaline, was quite safe on the plantation. She was watched day and night by Noel and the servants. Andrew had left the plantation in good hands. If something came up that neither Noel nor the overseer could handle, John McDonogh, Andrew's mentor and the richest man in Louisiana, would see that all was put in proper order. With the exception of Barba, the plantation group had all been seasick for the first three days, but by now, the eleventh day of the voyage, they felt quite comfortable, even though the ship was rolling in heavier weather.

The remaining passengers, numbering about ten or twelve, crowded the other table in the saloon. The parson, Hollingsworth, led the passengers in prayer each meal, paying little attention to the two businessmen from New Orleans who respectfully bowed their heads. Durnford smiled. The parson had not the sharp eye that Durnford had in matters of race, and did not realize the businessmen were Jews.

Except for the parson from New Bedford, all the other passengers on the ship were from New Orleans. They had lined the rail as the ship landed at the dock at St. Rosalie to pick up the Durnfords and the cargo of sugar and molasses from the plantation.

"Lord Almighty and eternal God," the parson launched into the breakfast prayer that morning, "your goodness is beyond what we could dream of, your benevolence extends beyond the boundaries of race and nation. Give us the courage to stand before your truth, and may the walls which prejudice raises between us crumble beneath the shadow of your spirit. Amen."

The two Jews responded with a polite nod. The other passengers waved a hand, which was supposed to be the sign of the cross but was more in the nature of a protest, and murmured a barely audible, "Amen."

The Durnfords were Catholics, as were the other passengers, except for the two Jewish businessmen and the parson. The Durnfords were Catholics and the passengers were Catholics simply because they were from New Orleans. And being Catholics the Durnfords had upon occasion attended mass at St. Louis Cathedral on the public square in the city, the only church where black and white knelt together, side by side, without thought of segregation. And the only church in which free people of color owned half of the pews while whites owned the other half, all fully integrated.

Barba's smokey, black face scowled, and he spoke quietly as the normal hum of breakfast noise followed the parson's prayer. "Nothin' aggravate more dan a moral man wid a mean mind, Massa Andrew," Barba said. "You'd tink dis Methodist minister hab none o' dat feelin' 'gainst color. Surely him and his brothers was among de first to renounce dat unholy attertude. But no, dey disowns der' black brothers and sisters 'fore de world, and only afters all de white members ob der congregation has been served wid bread and wine, do dey beckons to de black sheep on de back benches to come up for de Lord's Sup."

"Really, Barba?" It was the high-pitched, earnest voice of Rosella. "You know that for sure, Barba? Barba, have you been North?"

"Hush, child," Marie-Charlotte said. "We don't talk about these matters at the table." Then she turned and looked directly at Barba. "Nor do we discuss such things in front of the children before they are old enough to understand some of the ways of this world."

Andrew Durnford knew his wife did not want, ever, to bring up the fact that Barba had once, long ago, run away from slavery.

And Barba knew not to further incur the wrath of his mistress. In silence, he ladled out portions of broiled ham, biscuits and gravy for the family, and poured coffee for the adults and tea for the children.

The children ate quickly, as they did at every meal on the ship, drained their weak tea, and sat patiently.  As soon as the adults at the table had finished their breakfast, Andrew said, "Look out for your sister, Thomas.  And keep free of the men working the ship."  It was the same thing he said to them every morning.  The children jumped up from the table and left the room at a run.

The children had been gone only a moment when Andrew Durnford felt a presence at his elbow.  He sat down his coffee mug and looked up.

"Good morning, Doctor Durnford," Thomas Hollingsworth, the methodist minister from New Bedford said.  "Good morning Mrs. Durnford."  Hollingsworth then turned from Marie-Charlotte to Barba and nodded.

Andrew Durnford rose slowly, and Barba at his side did the same.  "Good morning, sir."

"Do not rise on my account, Dr. Durnford."  Hollingsworth rested a hand gently on Andrew's shoulder.  Durnford eased back into his chair, but Barba remained standing.

Hollingsworth gestured to Barba's chair.  "Please, boy, take your seat as well."

"It would be a violation of his training," Andrew said hesitantly.  "Only when you are seated may he sit as well."  But Andrew had no intention of offering Hollingsworth a seat at their table, and by the tone of his voice, he made sure Hollingsworth understood that.

"I...I overheard your servant's earlier statement."  Hollingsworth said.  Then looking around Andrew at Barba, he continued.  "I am sorry to hear you felt mistreated at one of our churches.  Which church was it, may I ask?"

"Allow me to introduce my wife," Andrew said quickly, rising from his chair again.  He and Marie-Charlotte had seen Hollingsworth many times at breakfast and other meals, but, as was the case with the other passengers, they had never formally met.  "You of course know her by association with me; my wife, Marie-Charlotte Remy Durnford.  And this man, Miss Remy, is Thomas Hollingsworth, a Methodist minister from New Bedford.  I spoke with him for the first time last night."

Marie-Charlotte neither rose nor offered her hand, but simply nodded.  The tone of Andrew's voice clearly told her that Hollingsworth was an unwelcome intruder upon their coffee hour.

"It bin de Elm Street Methodist Church," Barba said in response to

Hollingsworth's earlier question to him.

Hollingsworth smiled broadly at Barba, then Marie-Charlotte and Andrew. "You are surely speaking of Reverend Bonney."

"Yassuh, dat be de man."

"I have been in his church many, many times, and he in mine." Hollingsworth smiled and nodded and bounced around. "I can hear him singing now, very sweetly, in that lovely voice of his, *Salvation 'Tis a Joyful Sound* and then he would administer the sacrament, isn't that right?"

"Dat be right, suh. Oh dem whites, dey went up to de alter by de benches full...and when all dem whites taken ob de bread and de wine, den Brother Bonney—after a long pause—he looks around and he spies de black folks a sittin' way back der—and he say—"

Hollingsworth raised a hand and interrupted. "Come forward, colored friends! Come forward! You too have an interest in the Blood of Christ. God is no respecter of persons. Come forward, and take this holy sacrament to your comfort." Hollingsworth clapped his hands together joyfully. "You speak of the sacrament of the Lord's Supper, that most sacred and most solemn of all the ordinances of the Christian Church, lovingly offered to our colored friends as well. And did you partake of the holy sacrament?"

"No, suh. I went out and neber back. And den I went home—to Massa Andrew, where I belongs."

Hollingsworth stepped back and shook his head. "You are not a free man? You are a slave?"

"Yassuh. And I be better slave o' Massa Andrew den a black sheep in dat church."

And when a rolling chuckle broke out in the dinning room of the ship, Hollingsworth staggered back, turned on his heel, and marched from the saloon.


The next night found the three-masted bark running up the Chesapeake under full sail and full steam. It was too dark for Durnford to see much of the sky beyond the cloud of smoke that rose from the steamship's single stack, but the sea below was a brilliant phosphorescent. There were no other passengers on deck at that late hour. Durnford was there because he could sleep no longer. The musty smell and throbbing of his temples had again driven him from the small cabin. A double lookout stood at the bow. Durnford nodded his approval. No doubt a necessary precaution because of the great way on the ship. The smoother waters of Delaware Bay had enabled the captain to make good on his promise to Durnford to recover some of the time lost off Cape Hatteras.

The second officer stood by the quartermaster at the compass. The third officer was at the stern with a lantern, busily making ready rockets. The two deck hands at the wheel were quiet and steady, and prompt to answer the captain's orders. The third officer at the stern fired a rocket, then a second. Durnford checked his pocket watch. It was a few minutes after 2:00 a.m. Just faintly, far off in the black sky where the bay narrowed into the Delaware River, Durnford saw a single, glum light. The third officer fired two more rockets from the stern. The answer was a flash of blue on the horizon, followed by a pencil line of white light and a burst of red in the sky. The captain calmly instructed the helmsman to change course ten degrees to starboard.

A short time later they came upon and passed the dim light at the entrance to the Delaware River, leaving the light astern. "We'll be landing around noon, Durnford," the captain said. It was the first time the captain had spoken to him in several days. "And your cargo will be on the dock before the banks close."

Without waiting for a response, the captain abruptly turned his back and walked away.

Durnford had chartered the entire ship for this voyage. The captain and crew were to be at his disposal. But the captain had breached the contract. He'd be damned before he'd sail back to New Orleans with Durnford, the captain said. No one had told him the return cargo would be slaves. And pointing a finger at Durnford, he told him plainly that never would he be the master of a slaver.

A small steam packet came alongside spewing a shower of sparks, picked up the mail and dropped off a pilot while the ship pushed steadily up the Delaware against the current.

The pilot gave Durnford a quizzical look as he climbed over the rail with a lantern in one hand. "Where be the captain?" the pilot asked.

Durnford waved a hand in the direction of the gimbals where the captain talked in low tones with the helmsman.

Durnford had liked the captain since first meeting him at New Orleans. He was a man with admirable characteristics. Firm, competent, a master at his trade, meticulous in all matters of navigation and management of the ship. And he had treated Durnford as an equal. Although Durnford expected such treatment from a citizen of Louisiana in purely business matters, he was, nevertheless surprised by the captain's attitude, because the captain was from Baltimore. The citizens of that area were not accustomed to dealing with free men of color who were also men of considerable wealth.

So when the captain breached the agreement and refused the return trip to New Orleans Durnford did not feel personally scorned. The captain was a principled man, Durnford assured himself. And the issue upon which the captain stood so firmly was one which quickly brought the blood of otherwise reasonable men to a boil.

Durnford had simply shrugged his shoulders. There were other ships and other captains, and any loss he might incur because of this unfortunate breach of a business agreement would be covered by the captain's superiors once Durnford returned to New Orleans. Resort to the courts might become necessary, but then Durnford had been taught well by his mentor, John McDonogh, the mysteries of the legal universe.

# Chapter Two

As the Durnfords turned on to bustling Market Street under an overcast sky, they were met by the finest carriage Marie-Charlotte had seen since leaving her home in the Cane River colony. The carriage was drawn by two chestnut-colored sorrels with white manes and tails. The horses' heads were high and their nostrils steamed in the cool air. Moisture stood out on the horses flanks. Marie-Charlotte knew they had been driven hard.

The carriage had a white leather extension top, and its seats were upholstered with dark-green English leather. The high, delicate wheels were covered with fenders which were full and wide, and lacquered dark green with gold trim. At the front on each side of the carriage were silver-plated French beveled glass lamps.

"Dr. Durnford, Dr. Andrew Durnford, how very, very pleased I am to meet you at last." Elliott Cresson, a large-headed fat man with a fat face and crimson complexion leapt from the carriage with outstretched hand before the conveyance came to a stop. He introduced himself as Chairman of the Young Men's Colonization Society of Pennsylvania, and was in turn introduced to Marie-Charlotte, then the Durnford children, and the slave, Barba.

"A warm welcome to you and your family in our beloved City of Philadelphia." He bowed to Marie-Charlotte, then reached out to the children as if to pat them on the head, and thinking better of that, withdrew his hand to his side, as Rosella was wearing her best bonnet, and Thomas his best hat, a blue cloth cap with a glazed bill.

Elliot Cresson continued in his high-pitched voice, "Now you know that a protege of John McDonogh is most welcome among our family, and simply put, you must come to our house for your stay in this fine city."

"We have made arrangements with Naylor's," Andrew Durnford replied, meaning the small hotel on Dock Street.

Marie-Charlotte winced. Naylor's was not one of the better hotels in Philadelphia, but it was on the waterfront, extremely reasonable, which pleased her husband, and was willing to accept a family of color.

"No, no, that will never do," Cresson said. "Of course you must stay with us." He smiled at Marie-Charlotte. "However could I justify to Mr. McDonogh your putting up in public accommodations."

Cresson, dressed in a large great coat and a tall wool hat, flapped his arms as he spoke, and looked, Marie-Charlotte thought, like a large bird, a fat crow, even his voice was nearer that of crow than man. And he was insistent. So Marie-Charlotte knew at once that there could be no acceptable protest.

"Mr. William McKenney has come down from Baltimore to meet you and your family, Dr. Durnford. You know of course that he is the business agent for the Maryland State Colonization Society?"

"No," Andrew Durnford said, "I'm afraid I know nothing of Mr. McKenney."

"A fine man he is, Dr. Durnford, a most astute man. He alone is responsible for the first expedition to Africa, just two years ago now. And he waits at my humble house to meet you and your delightful family with far more queries than anyone should bear, considering, you know, your peculiar circumstances."

"Perhaps then he will find my peculiar circumstances disturbing, Mr. Cresson."

"Ah, Dr. Durnford. We already know of your fine heart from our most noble friend and supporter, Mr. John McDonogh. Nay, disturbing never. Nor shall you find Mr. McKenney uncomfortable, or he you. Most interesting, rather. We are an enlightened people, Dr. Durnford. And we think too that it is in the nature of equality that a person of your race be found sooner or later in your position. So, it is settled then, is it not? You will stay with us?"

Andrew Durnford took once again the outstretched hand of Elliot Cresson. "We gratefully accept your invitation, sir. But I'm afraid I've sent our trunks on to the hotel. You see, we planned on sending you a message later in the day. It is a surprise to find you coming to the wharf so quickly."

"The answer to that, Dr. Durnford, is that the pilot who came aboard your ship last night is a member of our Colonization Society. We have been on the watch for you for the past few days. So if you and your family will board the coach—servant by the driver—I will send my man with a truck to pick up your baggage."

"Sir, your hospitality warms my heart. And with your permission, my family shall accompany you to your house, and I will come later. It is a business matter I must attend to, the sale of my sugar and molasses to Messrs. Lippincott, Richards & Co."

Mr. Cresson waved to the driver, a Negro lad wearing a soiled top hat with a crimson band and a dirty white coat with tails. The young driver quickly dismounted and helped Marie-Charlotte and Rosella into the carriage. Thomas, sprang up to sit by the driver, and Cresson heaved himself aboard and waved to Durnford. "Supper is at eight, sir."

"I will be there long before that."

"You have the address, Dr. Durnford?"

"Surely I do, sir." And waving in return, Andrew Durnford, with Barba at his side, turned and proceeded toward the offices of Lippincott, Richards & Co.

The Philadelphia streets were graded to a remarkable smoothness and paved with wooden blocks, and as the coach's iron wheels clinked into the city Rosella leaned her thin body over the side of the carriage, and asked over her shoulder, "Mr. Cresson, sir, are all of these buildings owned by the same man?"

"Please don't mind the child, Mr. Cresson, she's always so curious—a bother, really." And turning to Rosella, her mother continued, "Rosella, sit down. You mustn't speak until spoken to. Now take notice."

"Mrs. Durnford, the child is no bother at all. And you will find my family not so reticent either. We are all rather liberal in that regard here." Mr. Cresson chuckled and leaned toward Rosella, who had again sat down beside her mother on the opposite seat in the coach. "Why, no child. The buildings are all individually owned by citizens of this fair city."

"But they all have the same coat of arms." She pointed high up on the brick buildings where a cast iron plaque adorned the fourth floor of each row house.

Mr. Cresson put a hand on his tall hat to keep it from falling off as he leaned his bulk out the side of the carriage and looked up. "That my dear Rosella is an identification marker for the firemen. Each house covered by insurance bears on its top story the iron plate of the Philadelphia Contributionship for the Insurance of Houses. That is a company founded by Benjamin Franklin. If you look closely, you will see that it is not a coat of arms, but four hands in a square, each hand clasps the wrist of the other. A unique design by the City's best-known and best-loved son. Perhaps you have heard of Dr. Franklin, the creator of *Poor Richard*, the scientist who drew electricity from lightning, the spokesman for the American Colonies, signer of the Declaration of Independence, wily diplomat, framer of the Constitution?"

"We have read much about your Benjamin Franklin," Marie-Charlotte said. "The children are well schooled in his philosophy.  In his earlier years he owned two slaves.  Later in life, when he became more closely associated with Philadelphia's Quakers, he was somewhat embarrassed by his ownership of people. Although rather than free them, I do think he sold his slaves.  And, as I recall, he was in favor of imposing large duties on the importation of Negroes because the traffic impeded the increase of whites.  But that was a long time before he became President of the Pennsylvania Abolition Society."  She paused for a moment as Mr. Cresson ran a finger between his shirt collar and the fat rolls of his neck. Then she smiled and spoke again. "And I believe if we continue in this direction we shall pass the library, which he founded, as well as the building of the American Philosophical Society adjoining the State House, also organized by Dr. Franklin."

"Yes, yes. Of course we shall." Mr. Cresson moved his hand to his chin and leaned back on the leather seat as Rosella suppressed a giggle. From his expression, Marie-Charlotte knew that the Chairman of the American Colonization Society was unsure whether he had just been upstaged, mimicked, ridiculed, or honored. It was a state Marie-Charlotte enjoyed immensely.

They eventually arrived at what Marie-Charlotte thought was a rather vulgar, large brown house with a green door.  The windows were all covered with wooden jalousies, adjustable horizontal slats for letting in light and closing out the rain, painted a bright yellow.

The rail on either side of a short flight of steps leading up to the door was made of thin iron, much too delicate for the structure, she thought, and at the street level the rail posts were adorned with large wooden monkeys, painted yellow to match the jalousies. The front door at the top of the stairs appeared to be much too small for the size of the house, and had in its middle a very large iron knocker in the form of a black crow.  And when Marie-Charlotte saw the knocker, the crow so much reminded her of Mr. Cresson that she clasped her mouth to keep from laughing out loud.  The name **CRESSON** was engraved on a brass plate below the crow-shaped knocker.

They were met in the hall by a large, florid girl, whom, Mr. Cresson explained, was the daughter of a Russian count who had left that terrible country for New York to better his economic circumstances.  They hung their coats on pegs along the wall while Mr. Cresson took Thomas with him to assist the coachman at the stable in unhitching the carriage and putting the horses over into the harness of a small wagon for the purpose of fetching the Durnford trunks from the hotel.

The Russian girl spoke hardly an understandable word, but led Marie-Charlotte down the hall to a room in the far back of the house. Inside the stale room, the servant-girl muttered a few indistinct words of introduction to the sole occupant of the room, and left.

The room was large and painted all light gray. A large dinning table stood in the center upon a worn carpet. A mixed assembly of chairs, a third of which had cane bottoms, surrounded the dining table. On the other side of the table was a Franklin stove, which looked like an iron bell stacked on a squat barrel. And on one side of the stove stood a gaunt old man with long, dirty gray hair and a grizzly, jagged beard. He was all wrapped up in a large travelling coat with big silver buttons and huge cuffs ornamented with dirty lace.

It was very hot in the room, and the old man, who smelled distinctly of stale tobacco and unwashed body, collapsed back into his rocking chair before introductions were completed. The old man announced in a harsh and gravely voice, that he was William McKenney, agent for the Maryland State Colonization Society, and that he had come to Philadelphia to meet the Durnfords. He was interested in the St. Rosalie operation and the relationship between the black master, Dr. Andrew Durnford, and the black slaves. Marie-Charlotte explained that her husband had gone with Barba to complete the sale of sugar and molasses from the ship, and would come to the Cresson house before supper. After leaning forward and demonstrating his accuracy with the spittoon, McKenney asked whether Barba was a slave. Marie-Charlotte explained that Barba was indeed a slave, the personal body servant of Dr. Durnford.

"And even here he is not free," Mr. McKenney said, "our legal system continues to recognize property rights in other people. But if he ran away it would be difficult to recover him. Does that cause you some concern?"

The air in the room was intensely hot and stifling from the stove, and the aroma of tobacco and the old man's unwashed body was almost more than Marie-Charlotte could bear. A sickly smell of cabbage soup came from the kitchen and mixed with the tobacco from the spittoons. At the direction of the old man, she had taken a seat in one of the sturdier-looking cane chairs, and Rosella had sat down beside her. "Barba would never run away," she explained. She had decided not to tell the old man about the one time Barba had run away and been gone for over a year. The stocky slave had been miserable in the cold New England climate, where he was treated much worse as a colored person than he had ever been treated by his masters, Barba's first master having been John McDonogh and his second master being his former playmate, Andrew Durnford. "Our people are very loyal to Dr. Durnford. But these are matters we do not discuss in the company of the children, Mr. McKenney."

Elliot Cresson came puffing into the room with the boy, Thomas Durnford close behind him. "I see you've met our other guest," Cresson said. "Please accept my apology for abandoning you, but our new driver has a terrible time with the horses, and I knew Mr. McKenney would put you at ease. Now, would you care for an afternoon tea, Mrs. Durnford? Or perhaps a little cabbage soup left over from our noon meal?"

Marie-Charlotte shook her head politely. "No, Sir. Thank you for your kindness. We ate a fine meal just before leaving the ship." Marie-Charlotte was afraid that she would become sick if food or drink were brought into the stifling room.

McKenney coughed and spat into the spittoon.

Cresson pulled a gold watch from his vest pocket, glanced at it, and said, "I expect Mrs. Cresson shall return momentarily from market. She has gone by foot, you see, which is her custom, and taken cook and the girls with her. She should be back by the time our coachman returns with your trunks. So perhaps you would like to go to your rooms now?"

The rooms reserved for the Durnfords were on the third floor of the house. Each room was a very little narrow room, with a half-window at the far end overlooking a courtyard below. The room assigned to Andrew and Marie-Charlotte contained one bed, which looked like a huge trunk without a lid, and held drawers in its side for their clothing. A small washstand with a porcelain bowel stood to one side of the window, and over it was a small mirror nailed to the wall. There were two plain and unpainted wooden chairs in the room, and a small piece of carpet which looked to Marie-Charlotte like it had served its better years elsewhere.

The children's room contained a similar half-window, washstand and mirror and two small beds placed against the walls. There was no other furniture in the room and no carpet on the rough boards which made up the floor. All in all, Marie-Charlotte thought, the house was indeed not what she had expected considering the fine carriage which had brought them there.

After explaining that the "servant," Barba, would sleep over the stable, Elliott

Cresson told Marie-Charlotte that the maid would bring up some water for freshening up, and he would now leave her to some peace and quiet after what must have been a tiring voyage.

In a short while, the Russian girl brought a little water to wash in and small towels for Marie-Charlotte and the children. After the children had washed, Marie-Charlotte sent them to bed for an afternoon nap, and then sat down herself on one of the old chairs in her room before the washstand and small mirror. She had bathed that morning in a tin tub on the ship, and so she dipped her towel into the water and dabbed at her face.

Marie-Charlotte was not a beautiful woman in the classical sense. But there was a pertness and smartness about her fine features that men found attractive. Certainly Andrew Durnford had been attracted to her from the time she first saw him when he came to visit Isle Brevelle on the Cane River. Marie-Charlotte was a twig of a girl, barely thirteen years old then, and Andrew Durnford was ten years older. Her mouth dropped open when she first saw him. He was a bronze god. He had been educated in Paris, spoke the language of the Cane River Colony, which was French, fluently, as that was also the language of his mother's household. In addition, he spoke enough Spanish to master business transactions, and reasonably good English. Andrew was a physician by profession, she learned from her mother, but still much indebted for his maintenance to his father. And his father always wanted Andrew to abandon his medical practice and apply his time to business matters in New Orleans for the reason that his patients were slow to pay and one shrewd business transaction in those boom times could earn Andrew more than he could expect from a lifetime in a medical practice.

The details of Andrew's heritage were explained to her by Andrew himself at the time of his proposal when Marie-Charlotte reached the age of sixteen.

Andrew's father was an Englishman, Thomas Durnford, who had landed in Pensacola at the age of fourteen to clerk for his uncle, the Lt. Governor. After the Spanish drove the English out of West Florida, Thomas Durnford stayed on and looked after the business affairs of his uncle. After his uncle died, Thomas eventually moved to New Orleans where he entered into a wholesale business and later took in a younger partner, John McDonogh, a crafty Scotsman.

Andrew's father chose as his life companion a creole woman of color in New Orleans who was a refugee from the slave revolt of San Domingo.

Marie-Charlotte knew the history of San Domingo well. It was a history studied carefully by slave owners. And it was the fear of another such revolt that led to many repressive measures. The colony of Saint Dominique, or San Domingo, the western part of the island of Hispaniola, had become the richest colony of France by the time of the outbreak of the French Revolution in 1789. Revolutionary fever spread to the island and in August the slaves rose up against their masters. By 1801, the slaves had driven out both the whites and the free blacks, and were masters of the island. The French came back briefly under Napoleon, but were defeated by the former slaves and yellow fever, and the victorious Negroes founded the independent Republic of Haiti. The creole woman, Rosaline, who became Andrew's mother, came from a black family that had owned extensive holdings and slaves on the island, and although forced to abandon their plantation, had nevertheless brought some of the slaves and considerable wealth to Spanish New Orleans.

It was only natural, Marie-Charlotte thought, that Andrew Durnford would seek a wife among the creoles of color of the Cane River Colony. The Cane River people had consistently refused to identify themselves as Negro, and the term *mullato* was particularly detested by them since the word was derived from the French and Spanish word for mule. Like the free blacks from San Domingo, the Cane River people were descendants of whites and Negroes. They were raised to believe that they were a race apart from the blacks—the more white blood the better and more superior they were.

Isle Brevelle, the plantation Marie-Charlotte knew as home and where she was born, was formed from soil deposits of the Red and Cane Rivers, and was the richest cotton-growing land in the entire South. It was a land of bounty, a Garden of Eden. Every tree and flower native to the South grew in profusion in the balmy air. And although Marie-Charlotte believed there might have been a larger and more beautiful house in Louisiana, she had never seen, in her travels on the Mississippi and her visits to New Orleans, a manor larger or with a greater veranda or more style than the house she was born in. Nor did it seem to her that the homes of her uncles and grandfather and cousins, and all the creoles of color of the Cane River Colony were any less sumptuous than the finest of homes in that lovely state.

She had now been the wife of Andrew Durnford for more than ten years. And although Andrew's mother often contested her, Marie-Charlotte was now the mistress of her own plantation, St. Rosalie, Andrew Durnford's holdings on the West side of the Mississippi River just thirty-five miles south of New Orleans.

There was no cotton at St. Rosalie. Instead there were acres and acres of sugar cane. Sugar was the road to riches. And one needed land to plant and slaves to harvest and grind the cane. Andrew had the land now. It had belonged to his father, Thomas Durnford, who purchased the land on the Mississippi and named it St. Rosalie. Andrew's father had bought the land to please Andrew's mother, Rosaline Mercier, and to honor a promise to her that one day she would have a plantation and a great house to replace the one her family left behind on San Domingo. But Thomas Durnford had no real interest in developing the plantation. He always thought that the easiest and surest money was in the mercantile trade, a trade he knew and exploited well. Then Andrew's father died suddenly, without a will. Andrew, the illegitimate son, received nothing from his father's estate. Neither did Andrew's mother, Rosaline Mercier, the life-long companion of Thomas Durnford, inherit anything from the old man. Rosaline had her own small plantation south of the city worked by six slaves and a large house on Tivoli Square with two house servants, old Ned and Charlotte, all from her parents. But her debts far exceeded her modest income and the sumptuous life she had enjoyed with Thomas Durnford and her dream for St. Rosalie came to an end upon his sudden death.

John McDonogh, Andrew's godfather and the business partner of Andrew's father, filed for administration of the Thomas Durnford estate less than two hours after the old man died. John McDonogh was a man of sharp contrast to his senior partner, Thomas Durnford. He was by far the better businessman, and knew that without any heirs in Louisiana, the first creditor to apply for administration of the Thomas Durnford Estate would gain control of it. So the day Thomas died, even before the funeral plans were made, the wily Scotsman filed papers in probate court at the Cabildo on the basis of an unpaid loan.

And it was John McDonogh who insisted that Rosaline file a claim against the estate for services rendered to Thomas Durnford for his care over the years. The amount of $2,500 was quickly approved and paid in installments.

But Rosaline's dream of a fine planation had died with her unacknowledged husband, Thomas Durnford, the man who would have married her if the law had permitted marriage between the races. She knew that many problems could have been avoided if Andrew's father had simply done what she begged him to do many times and gone down to the Cabildo and acknowledged paternity of Andrew and then written a will. Of course if Andrew's father had married a white woman and had white children, he could have left Andrew nothing. But with no other children, he could have passed on one-third of his wealth to Andrew, his child of color. But having done nothing, the only heirs of record were the white Durnfords, Andrew's cousins, living in England, who had no interest in the old man until he died. Now they were seeking to destroy Andrew and steal his plantation.

At the time of his father's death, Andrew still received a modest allowance to supplement his medical practice, and with a wife and small child of his own, was in no position to assume support of his mother. John McDonogh suggested an answer to the dilemma. As administrator of the Estate of Thomas Durnford, he would sell to Andrew the plantation land on the Mississippi River. Nothing could be given away, McDonogh had explained. But if Andrew wanted to build the plantation, he would sell him the land for nothing down with interest at only six percent. In addition, McDonogh agreed to personally lend his godson, Andrew Durnford, enough money to purchase machinery and equipment and a few slaves.

Perhaps it was a mistake, Marie-Charlotte thought. But when Andrew told her about the plan, she could think of nothing else than the big house they would build. And Andrew's mother, Rosaline, cried when Andrew said yes.

Well it was done and over with now. Andrew had gotten around that terrible law which gave the unacknowledged son nothing. Andrew bought the land. And it was a magic formula. Land plus slaves plus sugar equaled great wealth.

Andrew was brilliant. He made cane grow where no one else could. He knew how to handle the work force and got the most out of a day. All Andrew needed was his mother and Marie-Charlotte to keep his attentions from wandering. She knew Andrew was a physician first and a planter by necessity, and he was always ready to sell the sugar estate and return to his beloved practice of medicine. Why, he had even been so silly as to talk about moving to New York. But the plantation was where they belonged. Andrew's mother knew it. Marie-Charlotte knew it. And some day Andrew would come to the truth as well. St. Rosalie was the endeavor where Andrew would prosper and his race would not be an issue. Whether you were white or black, the land produced sugar cane. And that meant riches.

But the growing plantation needed more slaves. And slaves were no longer cheap in Louisiana. That is why Andrew decided to come to the East Coast. They were going to Virginia. They would return with the finest cargo of slaves money could buy.

They had brought with them a wealth of sugar and molasses. Andrew was as much a genius in business dealings as his mentor, John McDonogh. Andrew eliminated middlemen and wholesalers and shippers. Marie-Charlotte knew he would get for the sugar and molasses being unloaded that very day enough money to buy a hundred carriages like the one owned by Elliott Cresson.

Then finally, with the children tucked away for a nap, Marie-Charlotte sat down on her bed and read a poem. She had found the poem on Andrew's desk and copied it the year before. It was in his handwriting. From the style and choice of words she knew it had been composed by Andrew. He had written many poems, most of them to her. Andrew was an educated man, not just in matters of medicine, but in other fields as well. He spent hours reading volumes of philosophy. He knew history and had a familiarity with literature surpassing anyone she had known. He had mastered everything to be known in the field of science. There was nothing Andrew's curiosity had not led him to explore. He was also a reasonably good artist, although his attempts at her portrait made her laugh. But it was poetry that seemed to capture Andrew's imagination. His poems would make her smile or cry or sometimes simply gasp at the beauty of his thoughts. But this poem did not make her laugh or cry. It made her fear. She did not understand it. And she knew from its message she must watch Andrew and guard against his melancholy. Now she put down the paper and recited the poem from memory:

> I am the fool of time and terror.
> Days steal o'er me and steal from me;
> Yet I live,
> Loathing my life,
> Yet dreading still to die.

> Knowledge is not happiness; and science
> But an exchange of ignorance for that
> Which is another kind of ignorance.

> To give birth to those
> Who can but suffer many years and die,
> Is merely propagating death
> And multiplying an unforgivable lie.

> I know what I could have been; and feel
> I am not what I should be. Let it end.

> There lurks a wish within my breast

Not to feel the consciousness of rest.
Soon shall my fate that wish fulfil,
And I shall sleep without the dream
      Of what I was and would be still!

# Chapter Three

The oak-paneled parlor of the Cresson house was dimly but comfortably lit by candles along the walls and a large brick fireplace. The Cresson family and their house guests, Mr. McKenney and the Durnfords, settled into the ancient furniture of that room for a social evening.

"It seems to me, my dear sir," Elliot Cresson said addressing Andrew Durnford, "that the day has dawned which is to witness a most rapid expansion of those grand principles of the Gospel which contemplate the happiness of our fallen race." Cresson sat on the very edge of a horsehair upholstered chair and leaned forward. He waved first his right hand and then his left hand as he spoke. "Old fashioned prejudices, deeply rooted habits, especially in regard to the children of Africa in America, and the mode of treating them, are both yielding to the sweetly constraining power of the Gospel of Peace."

Next to Cresson near the fireplace sat his wife, Sally. Her face glowed as much from the eloquence of her husband as it did from the light of the fire. And her expression was mirrored in the faces of the Cresson daughters, both in their early twenties with the round and rosy features of their mother.

"It needs no prophetic vision," Elliott Cresson continued, "to foretell events of the most cheering and ennobling character in regard to Africa's long degraded race in our midst."

William McKenney coughed. Then he ran a hand through his long, dirty gray hair, and fired a salvo into the spittoon near his foot. Marie Charlotte, seated on a sofa next to Andrew in the bay window, looked abstractly at the curlicue pattern of the carpeting. Andrew stared politely at the fire, nodding in a serious manner now and then as Cresson spoke.

"The great and glorious truth, Dr. Durnford, is that Africa and her children in America are to be made a great people. Amidst them the Gospel shall shed its light." Cresson leaned back and smiled a look of satisfaction.

Talk of the Gospel always made Andrew Durnford uncomfortable. He was even more uncomfortable now because he thought he should say something. The extent of his religious demonstrations consisted of an occasional mass at the St. Louis Cathedral in New Orleans where blacks and whites knelt upon the cold granite floor together. His trips to that church were of necessity occasional, because it took a day to travel up to the city and another day to return. He went reluctantly at the insistence of his mother whenever she was certain she would die that week. They usually stayed overnight at John McDonogh's mansion on the West Bank, before returning home. The Protestant religion with its emotional embrace of the Gospel had never interested him. He preferred his portion of superstition in the form of something more remote, mysterious, and without concrete reason.

The old man, McKenney, continued where Elliot Cresson had left off, saying in his gravely voice, "Yes, even the South Carolina slave owners finally saw that religious teaching produced more cheerful submission on the part of the slaves than the stripes and blows of the overseer." He paused and spat into the spittoon. And pointing a bony finger continued, "Now Dr. Durnford, what say you about religion among your slaves?"

"As to religion, sir, I have nothing to say. I do not impose my views upon our work force. Many, as you know, have the Christian religion and receive instruction from John McDonogh's slaves on Sunday morning. Others have no religion at all. And some have mysterious African religions of which I understand very little."

"Have you seen Mr. McDonogh's church? " asked Charity, the older Cresson daughter. "I understand it is a most imposing structure."

"It is a large building, Miss Charity. Forty feet by eighty feet. All brick. Attached to the rear of the mansion itself. Mr. McDonogh has a great number of slaves."

"Happy slaves. Contented slaves, I might add," said Cresson. "Could the zealots of the North but know what is silently though effectually doing in the South at the McDonogh plantations they would be ashamed and no longer keep up their war of words against the Colonizationists."

"Now Dr. Durnford," said William McKenney, "I did not quite understand the nature of your plan."

"That may be because I have no plan, Mr. McKenney. As you know, I am not a member of the Colonization movement. To be more specific, I am not in favor of freeing slaves and shipping them off to Africa. Some day, I am sure, the slaves will all be freed, perhaps one or two hundred years from now. And whether that will be to their benefit I am not willing to say. In the meantime, I have no problems with our system. Certainly the Russian serfs are no better off." There was a prevailing and deep silence in the room when Durnford paused. "Yours is a noble experiment, sir. I wish for you success. And as in all things, time will give us the answer. My people, however, are not ready for such freedoms. They do not know responsibility. Any money that comes to hand is quickly spent. Whether they are that way by nature or because of their condition matters little. The fact is they could not live independently."

Elliot Cresson stood up with a disturbed look on his face. "But surely, Dr. Durnford, you do not think Mr. McDonogh is in error."

"I am much indebted to John McDonogh. I admire him greatly. His methods have made him very unpopular in the South, and he has great courage to continue. But in this manner of allowing slaves credits toward purchase of their freedom, I am not certain."

"But you would allow a slave of yours to purchase his freedom, would you not Dr. Durnford?" asked William McKenney.

"My slaves could do that. They have Sundays and Saturday afternoons during which they can work for money of their own." Durnford paused and smiled as Elliott Cresson, with a sigh of relief, sat back down in his chair. "But I need not fear any of them buying their freedom. So far not one has any savings. The money goes for liquor and tobacco and frivolous items."

"But what about your Noel?" asked Cresson. "He is a man of great expertise and responsibility...and your personal servant, Barba?"

"Barba does not want to be free. He would rather work for me under our present arrangement. And as for Noel, he is a shrewd one. He is the exception. His personal accounts far exceed his value, but the wily fellow enjoys his life the way it is, and he told me that he will wait until old age and then decide, when his value is much less, whether to buy his freedom."

What Andrew Durnford told his host was, for the most part, true. Durnford believed the slaves belonged to a different class. He was a paternalistic master. It had nothing to do with color or race, for some of his slaves had lighter skins than he, and Durnford knew his history well. He knew the dark-skinned Romans had light, blond English and some Germanic as slaves. He knew that many accomplished Greeks of the classical era had once been slaves. And he planned to keep his slaves until they could stand on their own. What was the sense in asking them to buy their freedom. They weren't slaves by choice. No one asked him, Andrew Durnford, to buy his freedom. That was an affront to humanity. When any of his slaves matured enough to deserve freedom, he would give it to them. His feelings were as simple as that. But he also did not think many would ever reach that point. Why that was so, he had not positively decided. Perhaps it was a matter of experience, or rather the lack of experience in being free. The real problem now was the amount of work and time it took to run the plantation. His time. His work. And the total time and work of the slaves. Nevertheless, Andrew Durnford, plantation owner, former practitioner of the healing arts, knew that some day he would find a way out, even if it meant giving the plantation to his slaves along with their freedom and moving North with Marie-Charlotte who so strongly opposed such silly ideas. But to ship them off to Africa, a country they knew nothing about when their real home was on the plantation, to ship them out of America, a country that belonged to them as much as anyone, that was total nonsense.

"When did you determine to be a planter?" William Mckenney asked, his thin, bony hands folded in his lap.

Andrew Durnford looked up startled. He had heard the voice but not the words and his mind was on his plantation, St. Rosalie. "I'm sorry." He shook his head.

"You studied in Paris, practiced medicine for some time, when did you decide for the plantation life, Dr. Durnford?"

"Decide? I don't think I did exactly decide."

The Cresson daughters leaned forward in their hard chairs. Elliot Cresson raised a hand to his chin, and McKenney straightened up with a sudden look of interest.

"You did not inherit the plantation, I believe." McKenney's eyes then narrowed. "Nor was your father the owner of slaves. Please excuse our brashness, but you are an interesting case, and Mr. McDonogh has always been rather circumspect in regard to your history. His letters disclose very little."

"My English cousins have a court case against us now concerning my lands," Durnford said slowly. "That may be the reason Mr. McDonogh is reluctant to put much to writing. We are both defendants."

Elliot Cresson leaned quickly forward and stretched out both arms. "Be certain of one thing, Dr. Durnford, you can be assured of our confidentiality, and I speak for my wife and daughters in this as well." The three women nodded earnestly. McKenney settled back in his chair and scowled.

"There is no need for concern," Durnford said. "I do not believe my English cousins can make a case. It is their claim that I did, indirectly, receive my lands and some slaves from my father, and since I am a man of color, that is forbidden under Louisiana law. But it is not true. I purchased, that is to say, I am purchasing my lands from Mr. McDonogh. He in turn purchased them from my father's estate." Durnford smiled at McKenney. "And my father did not own slaves. He rented Barba and Noel from John McDonogh. And I bought them from Mr. McDonogh after my father died. I paid cash for both those people. My mother owned slaves, eight altogether including the two house servants, and a small plantation we sold to obtain capital for St. Rosalie." Durnford looked first at Elliot Cresson and then McKenney. "Does that answer your questions?"

"We didn't mean to be impolite," Elliott Cresson said.

"Nothing was taken so," Durnford answered. "You are a gracious host, Mr. Cresson, and we feel comfortable here. I am sorry if I appeared offended."

Marie-Charlotte raised her voice in a more lively tone. "Goodness, let's not be so serious. We understand your interest. Everywhere we go we seem to be the center of conversation because of who we are and what we are, and the truth be known, we rather enjoy it all." Then she told in great detail how the plantation grew through the years and how the lumber for the big house was taken from keel boats put up for sale in New Orleans after coming down the Mississippi, and that the bricks were made on the land, and that Andrew had been his own architect and that the house was one of the biggest and finest in Louisiana.

In response to eager questions from the Cresson girls, Marie-Charlotte explained the social life in Louisiana, a social life which included them among the more liberal minded citizens of New Orleans, but rarely plantation people, who were not well educated and rather dull.

The Russian servant girl awkwardly made the rounds with claret for all, and the conversation soon sparkled. Andrew Durnford finally sighed in relief, thinking that perhaps his visit with the abolitionists would not be what he feared after all.

"I must tell you about the flea," Marie-Charlotte said with great delight. She was on her third glass of claret and had become quite animated in her language and gestures. "An English lady had married one of our Creole planters..."

"You refer to another Negro gentleman?" asked the older of the Cresson daughters.

"Oh, no, dear. The word 'Creole' in New Orleans means a person of French and Spanish ancestry. Creoles are always white people, although I do believe that in the North the word is meant to include mixed blood as well.

"Well the English lady had married the Creole planter in London when he was there on holiday. He took her back to Louisiana and to his plantation, about six miles below the city on the East bank. And it seems that, although the planter was quite a successful man, he lacked much in culture, had no books and could barely read and write, and had done little to establish himself in society, although he spoke French fluently, which is the mother tongue among the Creoles. His friends were all planters and of the same rough character. To remedy this situation, the lady, shortly after her arrival, announced a magnificent party to celebrate their marriage. She invited us, the Durnfords, as she had been terribly impressed with our plantation when she first came up the river past it.

"The poor lady had an attack of apoplexy when we arrived and she realized we were free people of color. We were seated as far as possible from the American business families, who could not make up their mind whether to leave or stay and remained entirely out of the conversation because they understood little French.

"It was a large dinner party, as great and elegant a display as her husband's plantation, one of the larger ones, could furnish. And so that there would be no lack of servants, a great clod of a lad who had been employed only in the fields, was trimmed, scrubbed, fitted out, and told to take his stand behind his mistress's chair, with strict instructions not to stir from the place. This lad was ordered not to do anything unless the lady directed him, as not much could be expected of the poor soul and the only safe place for him was under her firm control.

"Accordingly, the lad, whose name was Pitot, took his post at the head of the table behind his mistress, and for a while amused himself in looking at the assembled guests and watching their reactions to us, the Durnfords. Well into the second or third course of the evening, when everyone seemed to accept the situation and some sense of normalcy descended upon the dinner, Pitot lost interest in watching the guests and turned his attention to the back of his mistress. The lady was wearing a fine gown, low cut in the back, almost beyond the limit of decency. The guests were by that time engaged with the business of trying not to pay too much or too little attention to the Durnfords and with the requisite courtesies of the table and did not notice a sudden and dramatic change come over the face of Pitot. He was staring with delight down the naked back of his mistress, at a place where I assumed nakedness and clothing must meet, and my heart caught in my mouth for fear this poor wretch would be spotted in his silly foolery and prove to all at the table the despicable nature of the black man.

"But what I did not know was that Pitot's countenance shown with glee not for the wrong reasons, but for the reason he suddenly saw an opportunity of showing himself attentive and making himself useful. The lady was too much occupied with her company to feel the flea, but to her horror she felt the great finger and thumb of Pitot upon her back, and to her greater horror heard him exclaim in exultation, to the still greater amusement of the party: 'A flea, a flea, Missy Lisbeth. By Gawd I's cautched em!'

"The lady turned crimson from head to toe and stumbled from the room in tears, followed by her husband. Since it was evident that neither host nor hostess would return that night, the guests left that brilliantly lit dining room in silence and took their chances on the dark road with horse and carriage. Andrew and I left as silently as the rest, as no one knew quite what to say.

"Within a month the lady, who never made contact with Louisiana society again, sailed for England, vowing never to return."

Before Marie-Charlotte had finished, the Cresson women, mother and daughters, were convulsed with laughter and rocked back and forth in their chairs with tears streaming down their cheeks. Mr. Cresson grabbed his knees with locked hands and seemed to bounce up and down in his chair with mirth. William McKenney, obviously less prone to frivolity scratched in his long gray beard and looked sullenly at Marie-Charlotte.

"Left in their carriages in the dark," the younger Cresson daughter exclaimed, wiping the tears from her face with a lace handkerchief.

"Is it a dangerous road?" Mrs. Cresson asked.

"More dangerous than you might think," Marie-Charlotte answered. "The road runs along the levee." She sipped her claret. "That is because everything in Louisiana is backwards. Most rivers run through valleys and the land slants down to the water. But the delta was formed when the river overflowed its banks as it ran south. The highest part of all the land along the river is right at the river's edge. The only usable land runs for about a mile and a half or so back from the river, where it becomes mostly cyprus trees and swamp. So the driver must keep the carriage in the road by watching the edge of the dike. If he goes too far left, the carriage will tumble down into the river. If he goes too far right, the carriage will fall off the road and likely hit a tree. And in places there are trees on both sides, and so dark the driver must walk in front and lead the horses. Dinner parties usually last all night, with the men ending up at cards and the women gossiping, while the drivers sleep in the carriages until the sun comes up. Fortunately for us, we did not come by carriage. Our plantation is another thirty miles down the river on the west bank. We came up in our steamboat, a small vessel Andrew purchased at a Marshall's sale. We had docked at the plantation wharf and so we slept on the boat until dawn."

William McKenney shifted a spittoon with his foot and spat into it. "You tell entertaining stories, Mrs. Durnford. And if you were not colored I'd say that was one of the more blatantly racist stories I've heard."

Andrew Durnford stood up slowly. "I beg your pardon, sir!"

"Well Dr. Durnford, would your wife be telling the story of that poor slave Pitot if he were a mere white boy working on a farm and had done the same thing?"

"If I understand, Mr. McKenney, you are implying that we are racially prejudiced."

Elliott Cresson bolted from his chair as Durnford, feeling the effects of his claret, stepped forward to confront William McKenney. "Now, now gentlemen. Let us not be rash. We are here to learn from each other," Cresson said.

"I have learned enough," McKenney said. "These people are of a narrow intellect, indeed. They are colored people who are not true to their ancestry and mock everything we fight for by embracing the very worst of slavery." Now McKenney stood up and stepped forward, and Elliot Cresson wedged himself between the two antagonists.

"These people," McKenney continued in a louder voice, "are the daily robbers of their equal brothers and sisters. They come to us with the product of the blood and sweat of their brethren and turn it into riches. They go on vacation here, while their slaves at home toil in the heat. Slavery is wicked, pure and simple. It defaces the image of God just as the backs of the poor souls on the Durnford lands are defaced by the whip. Do not tell me, Dr. Durnford, that your work force can be maintained without brutal chastisement and enormous cruelty!"

"Enough! Enough!" Cresson shouted. "The Durnfords are our guests."

Mrs. Cresson at this point grabbed the arms of her daughters and rushed them from the room.

Andrew Durnford pressed forward. "You have, sir, insulted my honor and the honor of my wife. I demand satisfaction!"

"You are a silly man, indeed, Durnford. What satisfaction would you have in killing an old man like me who can but barely see. And I would die knowing you would hang for it. You are in Philadelphia, Durnford."

"Please, please gentlemen. Be civilized. Dr. Durnford, please forgive us. We see things quite differently, true. Our hearts unite in detestation of the tyranny of slavery. But gentlemen, Mr. McKenney, we must understand how those familiar with the system, accustomed to its injustice, and corrupted..."

"Corrupted!" Now Durnford exploded in anger. "It is the American Colonization society that is corrupted! What do you do for the thousands of free blacks in the North and South? Nothing! Every day laws are passed which restrict them in jobs and in housing. And do you oppose those laws? No. You agree we should not vote. We should not compete with whites for skilled jobs. You petition the government for ships to send us to Africa. You accept the proposition we are less than you. And you do it all in the name of God. Now when we come along, really your equal, the truth is more than you can hold, and your baseness spills out against us."

"Oh merciful God!" Cresson clutched his chest and fell back in his chair. Durnford was immediately at his side, checked his pulse, and loosened his cravat.

"This man suffers heart weakness," Durnford said. "Quickly, Miss Remy, fetch my bag."

As Marie-Charlotte dashed upstairs for Andrew's medical bag, Durnford said to Elliot Cresson. "I suspect you have experienced these distressing attacks before. Is that correct?"

Elliot Cresson nodded. Then Durnford looked up at Mr. McKenney. "You, sir, seem to be a vigorous man for your age. Perhaps you will assist me in getting our host to his bed."

They supported Elliot Cresson between them and steered his huge bulk to his bedroom where Andrew stretched the owner of the house out upon his mattress. When Mrs. Cresson rushed in, Andrew quickly explained to her what had happened.

Marie-Charlotte returned with the medical bag, and Durnford took from it a clear glass bottle containing a gray, powdered drug. He removed a portion of the powder with a small wooden spoon and instructed Cresson to place it under his tongue. "You will feel much better shortly," Durnford said.

Soon Cresson acknowledged that he was much improved and wished to return to the parlor.

"No, I think you have had enough excitement for this evening, sir. And I also think our discussions have come to an end," Durnford said.  "We shall leave in the morning."

# Chapter Four

Morning came to Philadelphia gray and drizzling. Andrew Durnford went down the narrow dark stairway of the Cresson house by candlelight. In the courtyard behind the house, Barba, along with Cresson's driver and Elliott Cresson himself, struggled to harness the horses.

"Good morning," Andrew said quietly to Cresson as he stepped into the packed dirt yard. "I trust you are improved."

"Thanks to you, Dr. Durnford, I can say I slept well indeed."

"Nevertheless," Durnford said, seizing the bridle of one of the unruly sorrels, "you should be careful for a few days. No straining. Ah, this horse does indeed have a contrary streak." Durnford stood his ground and backed the horse into Cresson's rig next to its mate, where the young driver, again wearing his dirty white coat and white top hat with a crimson band, buckled and strapped everything in place.

"I apologize for the conduct of Mr. McKenney," Cresson said. "I am sorry for the grief he caused you and Mrs. Durnford."

Andrew Durnford ran a hand down the smooth, muscular neck of the sorrel. "Never apologize for a person who is in the right, Mr. Cresson."

"Are you admitting your position on slavery is wrong?"

"What do we really know of wrong or right? I understand how you feel about the colonization movement. But I could also say that you are exporting a problem simply to get rid of it while you placate your race by insisting blacks are not entitled to vote or to compete in jobs. You believe I am wrong in the system of forced labor of my own people. But the system has its origins in history, has nothing to do with race, and has become self-perpetuating. By that I simply mean there is no solution. In our parish we have fifty slaves for every white man. Those slaves are like children. They can not think for themselves, nor can they provide for themselves. If they were freed tomorrow they would all die of starvation."

"I can not accept that, Dr. Durnford. With due respect to your experience at first hand, I still can not accept your hopeless conclusion."

"Let me give you an example, Mr. Cresson. The butterfly struggles in its cocoon, and as it struggles to free itself, it gains strength. Now if we were to free the young butterfly, to cut open its prison with a pocket knife, the butterfly would fall to the ground and die because it would be too weak to survive. Kindness to the butterfly in its cocoon would kill it. So it is with the slaves. They must struggle and gain strength before freedom. Otherwise they too will die. It may take a hundred years, it may take two hundred years. But now is not the time to free them."

"You choose an interesting example, Dr. Durnford. But the butterfly in its cocoon is a natural condition. The enslavement of one man by another is not his natural condition."

"That is true. And had we never brought slaves to this land, we would not now have the system which is both their prison and their cocoon. But I speak of things as they are, not as we might wish them to be. And each slave I buy comes to a better life. That is my small contribution. It is all that I can do for now. In the meantime, God knows that I mean well, and that perhaps someday I can do more."

Vapor from the nervous breathing of the two horses enveloped Durnford as he spoke, and he patted the horse next to him to calm it. "Can I have your word of honor, Mr. Cresson, that what I tell you shall pass no farther?"

"You may, Dr. Durnford. You may indeed."

Durnford leaned close to Cresson, and in a low, halting voice said, "The truth is, sir, that I know I am doing wrong. But I do it still. My rationale is that the poor souls are slaves already and the system will exist, they will be slaves to someone anyway. But then I realize we are, John McDonogh and I, creating a demand for slaves. McDonogh sends a slave to Africa and buys another. Down the line, another slave is bred to fill the gap. I put a few more acres into cane and buy a few more slaves with the same result, though I may intend to educate and free them later."

"Well, Dr. Durnford, all I can say is that the Lord is at work on your conscience and you already know that. Anyway, God bless you and help you find the courage to do what you believe is right."

Now Durnford was suddenly embarrassed. He had talked too much and said things he had told no one else before. And he didn't understand why he had done that. So Durnford took Cresson's hand and shook it. "Mr. Cresson this damp weather can do no good. I know you would accompany us to the hotel, but please abide my judgment and remain in the warmth of your house. We shall find our way with the assistance of your driver."

The Durnfords went directly to Naylor's Hotel on the waterfront, where Andrew deposited his wife, the two children, and Barba. From there, he went in the carriage to the offices of Lippencott, Richards & Co., where he dismissed the coach. From Lippencott, Richards & Co., Andrew recieved a bank check in the amount of $8,312.36, the net amount from the sale of his sugar and molasses after deducting freight and agent's commission. He intended to take the check to Richmond, where he would deposit it in a bank, and draw upon it for the purchase of slaves.

Andrew Durnford had told Thomas Hollingsworth, the parson on the ship, that he intended to go on a sight-seeing trip, and that was partly true. For the next two days the Durnford's stayed at Naylor's Hotel and toured the birthplace of American freedom, the city of Quakers and abolitionists. By Sunday, a day of rest and religious services at the segregated Catholic church, their feet were sore and blistered, the children were bored, and Marie-Charlotte was exhausted from her search of the stores and shops which contained nothing as fashionable or exotic as New Orleans. No one complained when Andrew announced they would sail for Washington City the next day.

Since the steam packet for Baltimore did not sail until 2:00 o'clock the next afternoon, the Durnfords lounged at Naylor's, where they had their usual lunch of watery bean soup, biscuits, from which they scrapped the mold, and salt pork.

The steamboat was slow, and even with a favorable current, the trip down river to Baltimore took the afternoon and night, and the Durnfords finally arrived early in the morning. Except for the children who found a cozy spot among bales of old hay, the Durnford party slept little on the trip.

With Barba pulling a rented hand truck and Andrew balancing their trunks and baggage upon it, the Durnfords left the wharf and hurried to the Baltimore train station where Andrew purchased tickets for passage to Washington City. The train to Washington was made up of a locomotive pulling a short open car loaded with wood and water barrels.  Behind the service car were connected five coaches, similar to stage coaches, but longer and higher.  The locomotive itself was a four-wheeled contraption, with very large wheels in front, to which steam cylinders were connected on each side, and smaller wheels at the rear.  The long boiler lay on its side between the wheels.  The furnace was at the rear and a smoke stack at the front.  Two men, one black and one white, stood upon the small iron platform at the rear of the locomotive and tossed chunks of wood into the firebox.

After hoisting trunks and baggage up to the baggage car, which was connected immediately behind the tender, the Durnfords settled in to the very first of the stage-coach like cars.  Andrew, Marie-Charlotte and Barba sat on the hard bench facing toward the back of the car, while the children were wedged in among other passengers in the first of the three hard benches facing forward.

With the bell clanging loudly, the train left the Baltimore station promptly at eight o'clock in the morning, and four hours later it pulled into the station at Washington City.  The locomotive and tender were transferred to what had been the rear of the train by way of a hand-operated turntable immediately after the passengers got off, and the train left for the return trip to Baltimore.

Richmond, the final destination of the Durnfords, was two days south of Washington City.  The stationmaster at Washington City told Andrew that it was necessary to take another steamboat from Washington, this time on the Potomac to Acquia Creek.  The steamboat would cover the fifty-five miles to Acquia Creek in a little less than six hours, including two stops, he said.  From Acquia Creek, the Durnfords would travel direct by rail to Richmond, a distance of seventy-five miles. The time required for the train trip should be a little less than seven hours, taking into consideration fuel stops, cattle on the track, and other unforseen problems with the roadbed, the stationmaster told the Durnfords.  And since the train did not run at night, it was necessary that all passengers spend the night at Acquia Creek and be ready to board the train to Richmond at dawn.

The station building at Washington City was a small house pressed into service to meet the requirements of the new mode of travel.  And it was to the station that Andrew had gone to inquire into accommodations for the night.

"None of the hotels here about cater to Nigras," the station manager told him. "But if you want a place to put up, you can stay at one of the Nigra houses down the road.  The addresses of them that's in that busi-ness are posted on that board."

"Thank you, sir.  How far is it to this one?"  Andrew pointed to an advertisement for a well-equipped rooming house promising good, clean accommodations.

"That way, about a mile and a bit more. I can rent you here one of these trucks for your baggage at two bits. I'm sure you'll find someone there to accommodate you. No other Nigras have come through here today."

Durnford rented the baggage truck for two days, having allocated one day for observing the works of the Federal Government and Congress.

The streets of Washington City were not paved. Since it had rained hard the day before, they were still covered with mud, and it took all the strength of Andrew and Barba pulling with Marie-Charlotte and the children pushing to struggle the mile and a half to the address advertised. When they got there, the house was, indeed, willing to accommodate them for the night.

It was a pleasant frame house, painted white with green shutters. Attached to it on one side at the rear was a newly built, yet unpainted small wing made of rough-sawn lumber, which the Durnfords later learned was the kitchen and new eating room. The house was owned by free blacks, a large woman with a round face and short hair, and her husband who owned a blacksmith shop which catered to the Washington elite.

"I would like three rooms, one for my wife and I, one for the children, and one for my servant."

"Bless your soul, we've never had a Nigra fambly with servants before. What country you from?"

"We're from New Orleans, madam."

"Well don't that take it all." The fat lady who owned the house and rented it out to boarders leaned back with large hands on her large hips and bellowed with laughter. "N-a-w-l-i-n-s. I knowed there was free people of color there too...but with servants...my soul."

"Please, we're very tired," Marie-Charlotte said.

"Well I don't have three rooms for you. I don't even have beds for you all. All I have is the garret. Two beds up there. Someone must sleep on the floor. And that's the best you'll get. I say that 'cause I know no one hereabouts has any better than what I got."

"Well then, we'll take it," Andrew Durnford said. "How much for the night."

"Only rents by the week."

"We only need it for two nights, madam."

"Rents for $3.00."

"That seems a little much for two nights."

"Only rents for the week."

"All right. All right. We'll take it."

The lunch fare at the boarding house consisted of fried eggs, fried bacon, corn bread, and a large bowl of molasses, into which the entire party at the table dipped a very good wheat bread. For supper, fried potatoes were substituted for fried eggs, and each person was given a larger portion of fried bacon. Breakfast in the morning was again the same fare with eggs taking the place of potatoes again. The meals on the second day were exactly the same. The Durnfords ate with the family of the house, which included the woman, her husband, a large dark man, darker even than Barba, and the couple's two daughters.

And when the Durnfords had finished breakfast on the second day of their stay in Washington, the mistress of the house brought in a large bowl of hominy and served them each generous portions. "You all won't be gettin' much to eat on that train, I hears," she said.

"Perhaps you could pack us a lunch, then?" Marie-Charlotte said.

"Oh, yes, mum. I can do that."

The man of the house, the blacksmith whose name was Ben, leaned across the table and pointed a spoon at Andrew Durnford. "I hear thar is lots of free blacks in Louisiana, sar."

"That's true. There are quite a few."

"*Gens de coulier libre,*" Marie Charlotte said.

"Dey wat?"

"*Gens de doulier libre,* free people of color," Marie-Charlotte said louder.

"Yes, o' course dey is. Some of 'em–a good many of em rich too. Dey born free, I hears, back under Spain, and o' course dey gets rich, ain't got nobody to work for but demselves, and dey gets rich down there. Some of 'em owns slaves–heaps o' slaves. And that are not right."

Marie-Charlotte put down her spoon. "Not right! Why not?"

"Well, you don't think it's right for one nigger to own another nigger, does you?"

The Durnfords never used the word "nigger" and rarely heard it used. Andrew Durnford assumed that the word carried no mean connotation in Washington City. He knew that was the case with many of the Negro population in general, as well as most of the genteel white plantation owners. Marie-Charlotte, however, suspected that the word had been employed by their host for effect. Barba knew that was exactly what the blacksmith had done, and Barba smiled quietly. And when no one answered, Ben continued with a flourish of his spoon, "Bad enough to have to sarve a white man without being paid for it, without having to sarve a black man."

Andrew Durnford coughed and was struggling to think of a way to change the subject when Marie-Charlotte spoke up again, "Some of them treat their slaves very well."

"No sar, they don't," said Ben. Thar ain't no peoples so bad masters to coloreds as dem free blacks, is what I hears, though could be some was very kind. But I wouldn't sarve 'em even if they was—no sar!" The blacksmith leaned back in his chair, folded his thick, muscular arms across his chest and looked around in satisfaction. There followed a complete silence at the table, which the expression on his face indicated he did not comprehend. And since he apparently believed he should play the good host and continue the conversation, he put his hands on the table again and said, "Does you has you office in the old part of the city, Dr. Durnford?"

"Ah...no. We live in the country, on a plantation. Down river from New Orleans."

Ben stirred his hominy absent-mindedly. After a while he looked up and studied, one by one the Durnford entourage around the table. "Sometimes I do talk too much," he said. Then, without another word, he got up from the table and left the house.

It had started raining again by the time the Durnfords boarded the steamboat for the trip down the Potomac. And it was still raining when the steamboat reached Acquia Creek. The passengers were segregated for the overnight stay, with the whites taken off under umbrellas to a clapboard hotel of recent construction, while the blacks were pointed in the direction of a long, low barracks, where they threw blankets upon straw and slept the night.

Durnford noted that discrimination extended to toilet facilities, both outhouses stood side by side between the two buildings, one marked "Whites," and the other marked "Colored."

With Marie-Charlotte scolding and wagging her finger at him for having made a late start, Andrew led the procession to the train waiting below on the tracks. He instructed Barba to climb to the roof of the first car, and he said that he would hand up their trunks and baggage, since there was no separate baggage car.

"No Nigras allowed in this car," said a well-dressed white man seated next to a black man who stared at the Durnfords.

The train to Richmond had three long cars behind the tender. Each coach was about twenty feet long, with benches along the sides. The floors were of rough planks, and overhead was a solid roof supported by wooden posts which held the baggage. The first two cars were painted yellow. The third car was unpainted, gray wood.

The white man who had just spoken to Durnford pointed to the coach at the end of the train. "That one back there is for coloreds," he said. "This here boy rides with me 'cause he's mine."

"Thank you for your instructions," Andrew Durnford said. And with Marie-Charlotte muttering under her breath, they dragged their luggage to the rear of the train, where they loaded their trunks onto the roof and took seats on the wooden bench at one side.

The coach for colored people filled up quickly, leaving the last ten or so black passengers without seats. Andrew Durnford looked around and saw that the yellow cars reserved for whites had ample room for more passengers. The children were learning lessons of the world, he thought. There was no way to keep them from the harsh realities of American life. They had to learn to live as he had learned, bowing gracefully to the whim of the white man. And when they finally went to Paris for their education, they would be treated as free and equal. And again, as he had done, they would return to ease into the narrow slot occupied by free blacks in Louisiana society.

The engine of this train was of an older type, three or four years old with an upright boiler. Thomas said he thought it looked like a giant grasshopper. Power was transmitted to the wheels by a roundabout through overhead rocking beams and a pair of countershafts fitted with meshing gears which doubled the rotating speed transferred to four 36-inch wheels. And once the train started, Andrew agreed with Thomas that indeed its motion was like that of a locust's hind legs.

Durnford smiled at the analogy. He was proud that Thomas took an interest in things mechanical. Although Andrew Durnford's first interest was medicine, he was always fascinated by the engineering marvels which seemed to develop at such a rapid pace during those years. First the steamboat, then the railroad.

The rail bed of the second part of the Baltimore & Norfolk, upon which they now continued their train ride, was one of the first in the country and had been built about five years earlier. Andrew watched the rails disappear behind them as they left Washington and took note of the broken stone ballast, the cross-stringers set eight feet apart, the pine rails topped with oak with a traveling surface for the wheels made of strap iron on top of that. The wood and iron rails of this section of track, he saw with concern, were no longer true and straight, but had warped with time and usage.

Except for an occasional boiler explosion, he had not heard of any accidents on the railroads. All and all, he knew, the rails were far faster and safer than the overland stagecoaches which suffered their share of disasters from broken axles, broken undercarriages, and collisions with trees, as well as frequent falls down embankments.

Andrew Durnford had watched railroad developments through articles in the New Orleans *Picayune*. And the one article that bothered him the most was the one he read shortly before their departure. The English, it seems, were developing their railways to keep pace with the potential speed of the next generation of locomotives. The cash-strapped American companies, on the other hand, were laying down much lighter track and going to the limit of sharp curves to avoid the expense of earthworks. But the roadbeds still held and there were no accidents.

The equipment that ran on them were mechanical marvels. Where bodily needs were concerned, however, both ingestion and excretion had to wait until the next stop. Therefore, most stations had built up a high reputation for their restaurants and luncheon baskets. And rather than suffer the indignity of eating with his family at the back windows of the station restaurants, Andrew Durnford had decided they would make do with luncheon baskets.

The Durnfords had just finished a mid-morning snack of biscuits and peach preserves, washed down with bottles of water, when Rosella started yelling and pointed to a cow sleeping on the tracks around a long curve ahead of the engine. Suddenly there was a tremendous uproar from up front as the fireman fiercely struck the bell, the engineer clanged a shovel against the boiler, and both men shouted in high-pitched voices to awaken the cow.

Not until the train was almost upon it did the cow attempt to raise itself from the tracks. And before it got up on all four legs it was struck by the blunt engine and knocked down and quickly run over. The top-heavy locomotive lurched and swayed as it pounded over the unfortunate animal, and in turn the tender jumped but stayed on the tracks as it ground the unfortunate beast to smaller pieces. And by the time the third passenger car, occupied by the Durnfords, passed over the cow, there was not a piece large enough to offer a jolt to the otherwise jarring ride. The sweet smell of fresh blood wafted up through the loose boards, and Andrew saw shards of torn meat and bone as they passed over the slaughtered cow.

Thomas and the other passengers stared in numb disbelief at the remains of the animal so quickly turned to shredded flesh as it disappeared behind them, while Rosella cried openly and said a quick prayer for the dead cow.

They traveled on through mostly pine forest where not more than a third of the country along the track had been cleared. The land that was worked, Andrew saw, was planted in corn and narrow beds of wheat with carefully tended drainage. Both crops, Andrew thought, looked good. Certainly the corn looked much healthier than what they grew on the plantation.

Then, in those areas where the pine forest gave way to a long coarse grass, he saw many plantations standing far away upon hilltops among trees, usually white oaks. Almost all of them were built of wood, two stories, whitewashed, and with a dozen or so crude log cabins scattered around them to house the slaves. Now and then he saw a red brick mansion or something made from white, heavy stone. A few had large porches and some galleries above porches, but none were of the magnificent style seen along the Mississippi back home.

And there were also the common houses of the white people along the tracks. These were made either of logs or loose boards with a brick chimney running up one end on the outside. These houses were generally lower down in the valley and closer to the tracks, and everything about them was disorderly and dirty. Pigs, dogs of every size and description, and children, both black and white, mixed freely together and lay about in the dirt around the houses. Andrew Durnford knew he was in the South once again, where blacks and whites mingled more closely, and as the train went by he saw both black and white children playing together and black and white faces popping out of the same door to see the new-fangled machinery.

Shortly after noon, the train arrived in Friedericksburg, a busy, but rather poorly built town, where it took on additional wood for fuel, and water was added to the barrels in the tender. There was no train station at this town, and they had simply stopped in the middle of the street. During this time, the white passengers disembarked and went directly to the new restaurant. The black passengers were equally divided between those who ate at wooden shelves below the kitchen windows in the back, and those, like the Durnfords, who took luncheon baskets and walked up the sloping hillside to sit upon the soft needles of a pine grove as they ate their fried chicken and coarse bread.

Once the refueling had been completed, the passengers boarded the train and it lumbered south, toward Richmond. It pumped and belched throughout the long hot and humid day. Andrew Durnford noted a lack of wind in the tree tops. And the smoke from the engine settled upon the cars and came in both sides of the open coaches. With some amusement, Andrew saw that most of the burning embers landed upon the clothing of the white passengers in the first two cars, and he smiled as they swatted at their fine dress, which was quickly holed and sooted by the product of their progress.

The grades and curves grew proportionately as they went south. Still the old engine stuttered and squealed along at ever diminishing speed. Finally, the engine could do no more. A fact which Andrew saw was anticipated, as teams of six horses were hitched to the engine at two different points in the afternoon and hauled the entire ensemble, with locomotive puffing and cracking, up steep and curving inclines.

Later in the afternoon, they began a never-ending descent, with the train picking up speed it had not shown earlier in the day. Rosella slept with her head in her mother's lap. Thomas joined Barba on the rough boards of the carriage floor and quickly fell asleep. Andrew, who had put an arm over his medical bag and wedged himself into a corner began to nod off, when he heard a sharp popping noise and felt a sudden jolt.

Then came screams of terror.

Andrew spun around and looked ahead. The train was in a long, descending curve. And with a noise like thunder, the rear axle of the leading passenger car had snapped into two fragments. As Andrew watched, it tore away from the coach's frame. The first car immediately dropped to the tracks and started plowing ground as it lost its rear axle. The two broken pieces of axle, each still connected to a wheel, ripped up the wooden floors of the second car as that carriage passed over the cart-wheeling sections. And as Andrew jumped to his feet, the first car, which had lost its rear axle, slowly disintegrated, dumping its passengers onto the tracks, where they were run over by the rest of the train.

As the first car disintegrated, passengers were already falling through huge gaps in the floor boards of the second car. Andrew watched in horror as they slipped beneath the iron wheels. Then the second car broke completely in half across the middle, dumping its remaining passengers, baggage and broken floor boards onto the railroad bed.

All was turmoil and screaming and swearing. Bodies, flapping arms and legs, and severed arms and legs, were suddenly passing swiftly under the Durnford car to flop in the roadbed behind them. One of the black men across from Durnford shouted for help, as he pulled on the emergency brake to stop the third coach. Durnford seized the wooden handle of the brake on his side of the coach and pulled with all his strength. The coach, which had broken its coupling to the train, slid to a stop.

The fractured forward coaches continued down the track, bumping and grinding behind the locomotive and spewing bits and pieces of lumber. Unfortunate people, men, women and children were still falling from the cars to be clubbed senseless or severed in parts by the disintegrating coaches. Finally, the remnants of both cars slid down the embankment, leaving the tracks for a quarter mile ahead of the Durnford coach and a half mile behind it covered with bodies, debris, broken rails and the wounded.

The engine stopped far down the track, reversed, and came coughing and chugging back to the scene of disaster.

Andrew Durnford announced loudly that he was a doctor, as he leapt from the colored passenger coach. Half of the white passengers were outright dead. He estimated another fourth were seriously wounded, most with severed limbs, and the remaining were in such a state of shock they were completely helpless. Andrew pushed and shoved and shouted, and by sheer force of his will and his commanding presence, organized the survivors, along with the black passengers, including children, into an emergency medical force. They tore clothing into bandages and tourniquets, as Andrew rushed about the injured, binding stumps and instructing others how to stop the flow of blood.

About a hundred yards back down the track, he found the black slave who had fallen from the lead car, lying across the rail with both legs gone. Dirt, gravel, and clothing were ground into his mangled flesh. And a few feet away was his white master, sitting in a daze and clutching the stem where his forearm had once been. Andrew quickly twisted a tourniquet around each of the black man's leg stumps, knotted them, and was then interrupted by the white owner.

"You'd best tend to the white people first or you'll pay a heavy price," the white man said through clenched teeth. "Besides, that boy's no use to me now. He'll be just a burden, don't you see."

The black man moaned and whispered hoarsely, and Durnford bent close to hear. Then Durnford reached down and loosened the tourniquets at the black man's legs.

"Did you hear me!" the white owner said. "Let 'em be and tend to those that's important. That rascal's no good to me now."

Andrew Durnford left the black man after putting his coat under the slave's head, and hurried to the white owner sitting between the tracks. "Sir, you are in shock," Durnford said. "Quick now, lie down here, sir, and let me get a tourniquet on that arm."

"I don't take kindly to orders from a nigger," the white man said. "Leave me be!"

"Sir, I am doctor. I am a graduate of the Paris Academy of Medicine. And you are a dying man. Now do what the doctor tells you and forget about the color of my skin."

At that the white man broke into tears and lay back on the track. "I'm sorry, doctor. I don't know what I'm saying. I don't know what I'll do without Sam. Will he live? I've owned that boy since he was a baby, and I do love him so."

Andrew wrapped a tourniquet around the white man's arm where it had been severed just below the elbow. Then he looked straight into the white man's face. "It was too late for your man. So I loosened the bandages and let him go. Besides, he told me, sir, that he didn't wish to live without legs, and didn't want a harsher life than he'd already lived serving you. There was no reason for him to suffer any longer. I'm sorry."

Durnford moved methodically among the wounded, calming them, encouraging them. And whenever one of the surviving passengers assisting him faltered, he seized and shook them, black or white, man or woman, and brought them to their senses. There was no time for tears and timidity, he told them, people were dying all around them. Only quick action and careful attention to his instructions would save those who could yet be saved.

He found Marie-Charlotte comforting a white man who kneeled next to where his wife lay a mangled corpse, with their child, about eighteen months old, by her side, covered with the blood of the dead mother. The top of the mother's head was cut off, and fluffy, pink brains covered the ground. The woman's body, feet arms and legs, were broken and twisted.

"Sir, let me reach the child," Marie-Charlotte insisted. But she was unable to make the husband, then in complete shock, understand.

Andrew seized the man by the shoulders and lifted him away from the bodies. The man struggled and screamed, and Andrew put both of his big arms around him and held tight. Then Marie-Charlotte pulled the baby from under a severed leg of its mother. She wiped blood from its face. "The child is alive," she said. "And I find no injuries."

Andrew took the child, examined it, and handed it to its father. "You are fortunate, sir. Your daughter is perfectly well."

The man took the child in his arms and ran around among the crowd, weeping and wailing and imploring assistance to help his poor daughter. Andrew Durnford shook his head. "There is nothing we can do now," he said to Marie-Charlotte.

"The poor soul is in shock, he does not understand that the child is alive."

Durnford was accepted as a doctor without regard to his race, and became the master of the scene. He organized a field hospital by placing the more seriously injured in the remaining car, and others in the shade of a lean-to erected from the canopies taken from the other two broken passenger cars. At his suggestion, the engine and tender were dispatched to Richmond to bring additional help and replacement coaches to carry the wounded and remaining passengers to that town.

As Durnford watched the engine and tender disappear toward Richmond, an official-looking burly man with a gray beard, who seemed to be a businessman of some sort from Richmond, wiped tears from his eyes and stated that he was taking command. At his insistence, the remaining coach reserved for colored was wheeled over the broken track and placed firmly upon the rails leading to Richmond. It made no sense, he said, to spend valuable time waiting for the engine to return when the route before them to Richmond was mostly down hill. They could push the car up the small hills, he said. And they would use its brakes to control the speed of the car downhill. They would save at least two hours by continuing on until they met the returning train.

Then the burly man announced that since none of the surviving blacks were injured and there was only room for the white passengers in the car, the blacks would have to get to Richmond on foot.

"Except for you of course, Durnford. We'll need your medical skills," the burly man said. Then pointing to Barba, he continued, "And we could use your big boy there to help push us up the hills."

"I have a wife and two children with me."

"Your wife and children can come along. The others will have to walk."

"Sir, with all respect, I don't think the wounded should be taken in such a fashion. There is always the danger of too much speed and the car jumping the tracks."

"I have made a judgment, boy. I'm surprised that you would raise such a question."

Andrew Durnford looked around, stroked his chin for a moment, and still examining the wounded passengers in the car, said, "I think the risk is too great. I must decline."

The burly man stepped forward. "You assume to substitute for my judgment that of yours, boy. We will take that up again when you reach Richmond."

And then the injured were loaded and all the white passengers climbed aboard the coach. Two strong men, under the direction of the burly man, put their shoulders to the wheels, setting the carriage in motion, and jumped aboard. Slowly, the coach gathered speed. At last it disappeared around the bend.

The black passengers fell into a column behind the Durnfords and started the trek to Richmond, about thirty miles to the south, according to Andrew's estimate, based upon the time and speed they had traveled.

They walked on into the night, following the shiny rails in the dim light of a half-moon. A little after ten o'clock, Andrew heard low moans ahead of them. He broke into a slow trot, leaving his wife and children and the others behind him. At a sharp bend in the railroad he saw what had happened. Almost half way to Richmond, where the coach had just descended a long hill and was being brought under control by the brakemen, the returning locomotive had come sweeping around and was unable to check its speed. The coach, carrying all the white passengers and injured, collided head-on with the racing engine. The coach disintegrated immediately, killing almost all on board. The engine, tender, and the two empty coaches it was pulling, jumped the track and crashed three hundred feet down a ravine, killing the engineer, firemen, and most of the emergency medical staff it was bringing to the scene.

The survivors had arranged the injured along the tracks.

The black passengers all cried as they came upon the desolate scene. The burly man was dead. Two young men, Durnford was told, had gone to Richmond at a run for help.

Durnford splinted broken limbs, stanched the flow of blood, and did what he could to comfort the injured and dying. Then, finally, Andrew Durnford sat down on the tracks, and he too wept.

# Chapter Five

Only after careful study had Andrew Durnford selected Richmond as the center
of his slave-buying expedition.  It was just seventy-five miles up the James River
from Norfolk.  It was served by both the railroad and steamboats, and it lay in the
heart of the slave-breeding country.

Like others before him, Durnford came to hunt bargains.  But in addition to being
black, Durnford was unlike the average planter in many ways.  Most could barely
read and write.  Only one out of ten had any book at all on the plantation. Durnford
was well educated and intent on imparting a good education to his children as well.
To that end, he had taken his family with him.

The Durnfords had been received in Richmond along with the bodies and
survivors of the train wreck two days earlier.  They were not received as heroes,
but simply as travelling colored folks who had been lucky enough to survive the
disaster.

They spent the next day, Saturday, recovering from the tragedy.  Then still
shaken and thoughtful, Andrew Durnford walked with Marie-Charlotte and the
children through the beautiful city. Barba stayed behind at a farm on the road to
Norfolk, where the Durnford's had rented an old house, a wooden frame structure
in need of paint with a tin roof, for their stay.  It was Barba's job, along with a
free woman hired to cook and clean, to make the house comfortable for the
Durnford's stay in Virginia.

The family walked around the capitol grounds and the park, and then strolled to
the First Methodist Church, where funerals were being held for victims of the train

wreck. The church was reserved for whites only, but they were allowed to stand and look in.

When Andrew's eyes adjusted to the darkness within the church, he froze and a cold chill went up his spine. High up in the corner of the church addressing the congregation from a tall pulpit was the guest speaker, the Reverend Thomas Hollingsworth. Hollingsworth was preaching a sermon based upon Ecclesiastes. Durnford listened quietly to the ringing words of the clergyman: "As they did in Jerusalem, we do many great things. We build mansions. We purchase men slaves... women slaves; and breed slaves on our plantations as well; We gather to ourselves silver and gold, and the treasures of kings. We acquire every luxury, chest on chest of it. Then we do as they did in the days of the Bible. We look on all the works that our hands have wrought, and on all that our labor has brought us? What vanity it all is, and chasing of the wind. And do we then realize there is no real profit in anything we have done and that only in God the Father is there wisdom, and all else is nothing but madness and folly?"

An uncomfortable murmur ran through the assembled mourners as Hollingsworth paused and the parishioners squirmed in their seats.

Just then Durnford realized the reason for the pause in the sermon. Hollingsworth recognized the black slave owner standing in the doorway. And as their eyes met, Durnford stepped quickly back into the sunlight.

Durnford glanced at the children and then looked at Marie-Charlotte. The children had not heard the sermon. They were intently pursuing a butterfly, perhaps one they did not have in their collection. Marie-Charlotte was listening. Her face glowed. "Such a beautiful service, Andrew," she said. "But it doesn't have the grandeur of our mass for the dead."

Nodding quietly, Durnford realized she had not recognized the figure in the pulpit, but he said nothing because he was afraid his voice might betray the emotions boiling within him.

They strolled down to Broad Street and Monumental Church, and read the plaque there which explained that in that large wooden building the Constitution, framed at Philadelphia, had been ratified by Virginia. From Monumental Church they walked the unpaved streets of the city to the Valentine house, where Aaron Burr lived while on trial for treason. Andrew told the children of Burr's famous plot to seize Texas and Louisiana from the United States. And it was while relating that tale of treason Andrew Durnford felt again a tremendous pressure building in his head and became aware of that familiar, faint smell of musk. Over and over he repeated to himself the words he had just heard at the Episcopal Church: "What vanity it all is, and chasing of the wind." Then he remembered the words of his own poem: "I am the fool of time and terror." What was he, Dr. Andrew Durnford, doing here in Virginia on a slave-buying expedition? He was committing treason–treason against those of his own race. He was not really his father's son after all. And now he was in Virginia, hoping to save money on slaves. Hoping that for the price of one good field hand in Louisiana he could return with two. Andrew Durnford took a deep breath and shook his head. Why were these uncomfortable thoughts plaguing him? Slavery was morally wrong, but he was not responsible for it. The "peculiar institution" was something that was "fixed upon the South." The South could not do away with slavery, even if it wished. Half the population of Louisiana was in servitude. What would those people do free? They would all starve. And freeing the slaves would collapse both the sugar and cotton industries. That wouldn't be good for anyone. It was his duty to make the best of a bad thing. He would lessen the evils of slavery as much as he could. And by showing the world that a black man could be just as successful as a white man in the sugar game, he was promoting the interest of the black race in America. So having again reassured himself of his purpose in life, Andrew Durnford raised his head, straightened his shoulders, and walked with his family down the street.

There were other free blacks on the streets of Richmond that Sunday, many of them dressed in the latest style. And in the more fashionable streets Marie-Charlotte pointed out that there were many more well-dressed colored people than whites. They saw the finest French cloths, embroidered vests, patent-leather shoes, silk hats, kid gloves and beautiful brooches worn by people of color. They were out on parade. They walked with style and grace, and there was not the slightest sign of inferiority, except that the blacks, no matter how well dressed, always gave way to the white people they met on the streets, no matter how poor, ignorant and slovenly dressed the whites were. And so did the Durnfords. "Always be quick to give them the ground," Andrew had lectured the children, "but never bow or lower your head because that would be a sign of weakness."

On their way to the livery where they had left a rented buggy, Durnford bought a newspaper. After glancing at the news accounts, mostly part fiction and part truth, and all editorial, as was the case with Southern newspapers, he turned to the section advising of letters waiting for pickup. In the column of letters for men he read his name.

The post office was closed by then, so the next day, the first thing Andrew did was to pick up his letter. The letter was dated May 14, 1835, three days after the Durnfords had left the plantation. It was from his friend, benefactor and mentor, John McDonogh. From the letter, Durnford learned that his English cousins had ambushed him by filing a surprise motion in the court upon his departure. The motion was for a receivership of St. Rosalie Plantation on the grounds that the English heirs were the rightful owners. They had pleaded the necessary elements of waste and irreparable damage and posted bond.

John McDonogh was the richest man in Louisiana. He owned more plantation land, more buildings, and more businesses than anyone in that state, and he owned as many slaves as anyone. His lawyers were the best. Durnford knew that. And he knew he could rely on McDonogh's assessment of the situation when the old man advised in his letter that a full hearing could be delayed until Durnford returned, but not without the testimony of Andrew. For that reason, McDonogh's lawyers had agreed to a deposition of Andrew to be taken in Richmond.

McDonogh further advised that Quincy Smith would assist Durnford at the deposition, and Andrew was to contact that lawyer for further directions.

Durnford carefully folded the letter and stuffed it in his vest pocket. This was bad news he had to share with Marie-Charlotte. She had been in favor of the trip east. She had agreed that buying slaves in Virginia was a sound business judgment. And they both had decided to go ahead with the trip and not wait until after the trial was over. This was the slow time on the plantation, a time when there was little to do but hoe the rows of cane and watch it grow. The court case could drag on, as cases invariably did. And when harvest time came, late in the fall, who would be cutting the cane and running the rolling machinery and looking after the kettles, and cutting wood for the fires? They had no choice. Andrew had put four hundred more acres into production, taken out a huge loan, and they needed slaves for the harvest. If they delayed, all would be lost.

He thought about how he would tell her. McDonogh was a powerful man in Louisiana. But he didn't own the newspapers and he didn't own the courts. And he had lost cases before when the newspapers had turned against him and brought a popular indignation to bear on the judicial system. The newspaper accounts of the case had thus far been favorable. Although he was black, Andrew Durnford was a native son; and the plaintiffs were foreigners.

What Andrew Durnford feared the most was a trend he had seen in Louisiana over the last fifteen years. There was a growing schism between the black and white races. He saw it in the newspapers. He saw it in the cafes, restaurants and theaters as he became less welcome and then barred entirely or set off in a "for colored" section. There were fewer white families that entertained blacks. Some of the private schools no longer accepted colored children. There were more and more reprints of English articles and essays disparaging the Negro race. England, the country which had once knighted blacks, and had accepted blacks into the highest classes of society, was now exporting quasi-scientific studies purporting to prove that no black could ever be a "gentleman."

The Black Code, the *Code Noir* of old Louisiana, originally written in 1724, granted to manumitted slaves the same rights enjoyed by freeborn persons. The only restriction was that blacks and whites were prohibited from marrying each other. And until Louisiana became a state in 1812, free blacks had the right to vote and all the other rights of citizenship. The new State Constitution limited the rights to vote, serve in the legislature, and bear arms to free white males. Free black people were then required to add "free man of color," or "free woman of color" after their names whenever they wrote them. Then whites were restricted in passing on their wealth to their mulatto children. In 1830 a law was passed prohibiting the writing or publishing of anything that might breed discontent among the slaves, as well as the teaching of any slaves. These particular provisions which had often been dismissed by the fun-loving upper class whites, now became more and more the object of scrutiny in the popular papers. A witch-hunt was on for the author of certain pamphlets espousing the education of slaves in religion as well as other matters. No one could uncover the anonymous culprit. But Andrew Durnford knew who the man was, the author was John McDonogh, one of the largest slaveholders and the richest man in the State of Louisiana, the last man the narrow-minded citizens suspected. Durnford shuddered to think what the effect on his case might be if the newspapers ever learned the truth about McDonogh.

The louder the abolitionist rhetoric exploded in the Northern newspapers, the tighter grew the noose upon the civil rights and freedoms of the people of color in Louisiana. There was even talk of secession in the Carolinas, an idea ridiculed in New Orleans, but the voices of ridicule, still by far in the majority, were quieter and softer now.

All of these things were sifting through Andrew's mind as he left the post office and entered upon a narrow dirt street. The first people he encountered were a comfortably dressed Negro man leading three slaves by a rope, two men with a woman between them. The slaves were all handcuffed at the front, and the rope ran through and was knotted at each pair of handcuffs. The woman was wearing a thin calico dress with an old ragged handkerchief over her head. The slave men, one older and one younger, were dressed in equally worn gray cotton. Andrew stopped for a moment and looked at them.

"What are you doing with these people?" Andrew asked sternly.

"Come down in a canal boat heah to be sole. Dat are a likely gal, I reckon."

Durnford fell in step with the leader of the procession and asked for further explanation. The Negro with the rope over his shoulder was a picked man, he explained to Durnford. A slave himself, he worked for the slave traders and met the railroad trains and canal packets that carried slaves consigned to Richmond for sale. He was taking these people to the market.

Durnford stopped and watched as the trio in bondage shuffled past. The younger man, not more than a boy, had a doleful look on his face and mumbled as he went past. The woman turned around with an angry face. "O pshaw! Do shut up!"

Farther down the street, opposite the livery, the group turned the corner into a short street, and Andrew Durnford followed. He had been there earlier that morning, before going to the post office and before anything was open. Lining the street on each side were a number of plain brick small buildings with signs above the doors reading "Slave Dealers," and "Slaves for Sale," or "Slaves for Hire." The well-dressed Negro towing the three slaves entered one of those buildings.

There was, generally, one door in each brick building with a window on either side. Looking inside earlier that morning, Andrew had seen nothing but a large room with a row of benches and an old desk in one corner.

Andrew strolled down the short street. There were three men lounging about smoking cigars, and they nodded as he passed. A red flag stuck out over the door of each office. On each flag was pinned a piece of paper advising of the sales for that day. On the first was the announcement: **"Will be Sold this Morning, at half-past nine o'clock, two Men and a Woman."** This was the building the roped slaves had been led into.

Durnford went past, unwilling even to look in through the window, and entered an office a few doors down. The note pinned to the red flag over that door indicated that a man and a boy were to be sold that day. This auction house, much like the others contained a few rows of benches in the center facing a small raised platform. Wooden chairs were scattered along the walls and around the fireplace. An older gentleman wearing a worn black suit sat at a desk by the window and shuffled papers. Even though it was past the hour for the advertised sale, not another soul was in the office. Durnford looked around awkwardly, and took a seat by the cold fireplace.

"You are from Louisiana," the old gentleman finally said after getting up from his desk, walking over to the fireplace and looking Andrew Durnford steadily in the face. "Are you here to purchase?"

"Sir, I am from Louisiana. But I do not want to purchase."

"I knew you were from Louisiana because none of the free blacks from this area ever come on this street. But I've seen free blacks from your state before—I even seen 'em purchase Nigras."

"I am traveling on pleasure, but I shall feel obliged by your letting me know the prices at which Negroes are sold this year."

"I will do so with much pleasure. Do you mean field hands or house servants?"

"All kinds. I wish to get all the information I can."

The old gentleman nodded politely and shuffled off to his desk and began to write up a sheet of prices. Apparently, this effort required careful consideration, as the old gentleman stroked his chin, scratched at the paper with his pen and then gazed out the window.

A lean man with a wide hat, and chewing tobacco, entered and took a chair near Durnford. He was about to speak to Andrew when the objects of that morning's sale, a man and a boy, finally came through the door, completely without escort. The man and the boy looked around, and quietly walked to a bench in the back and took seats near the corner. Without uttering a sound or showing any emotion, they looked for a moment at the man with the wide hat and then at Andrew Durnford. The white man with the wide hat chewed vigorously and keenly eyed the pair. The two slaves were better dressed than most, each wearing gray wool coats, pants, and vests, with bright red cotton neck cloths, clean shirts, coarse wool stockings and stout black shoes. The older slave wore a black hat, much like the hat of the tobacco-chewing man who eyed him. The slave boy was bareheaded. Under the searching gaze of the white man, the slave pair seemed to grow a little uncomfortable, but said nothing and looked now and then at Durnford with mild curiosity.

Suddenly, as if by impulse, the white man jumped up from his chair, crossed over in front of Durnford without uttering a sound, and strode to the back bench where he grabbed the slave man's arm, and poked it. He than pinched and squeezed the slave's other arm. Next he examined his fingers, told him to open his mouth and show his teeth, which the slave did in a very submissive manner, and having finished his examination, the white man returned to his seat and slumped down without even a glance at the slave boy.

Andrew Durnford leaned toward the pair on the bench and asked the older Negro his age.

"Don't know sactly, suh. Maybe I's thirty."

"And how old is the boy."

"He be seven. I knows dat for sure."

"The boy is your son?"

"Oh, no. He be a cousin."

Just then the old gentleman from the desk shuffled up to Durnford and handed him a sheet of paper. "The market is a little dull this year. I doubt there never could be a more favorable opportunity of buying at a good price."

The old gentleman stood his ground and looked at Durnford expectantly.

"Thank you for your trouble, sir. But I am not here to purchase. The information is for a friend. He asked me to check into the prices this year."

"These two here is mighty fine specimens. You won't see many better."

Durnford thanked the man again. The man turned quietly and walked to his desk. The document he had prepared listed the best men, age 18 to 25 years, at $800 to $900. Those listed as "fair" were from $550 to $650. Young women were $400 to $600, and boys and girls ranged from $350 to $150, depending on size.

No one else came into that office during the next hour and the one white man grew restless, got up and left without saying a word.

"Why are you being sold," Durnford asked the man who had not changed his position or expression at anytime that morning.

"Don't know, suh. Reckon Massa need the money."

"Do you have a wife?"

"Yes suh, I do. And children too."

"Where are they?

"They still on the farm. Last year crops not good. Reckon that why the boy and me be sold." The slave man spoke in an even, calm voice.

This was the first time Durnford had ever seen a slave sold from his home. All other purchases he had made were at the auction in New Orleans, where slaves were brought from all over the South—Virginia, Kentucky—far away homes. The game seemed innocent enough then. Those people were already separated from their families. It wasn't his fault. But now he realized that if he purchased this man it would be to take him away from his wife and children. Perhaps he could take the boy, but then the boy might have a mother, father, even brothers and sisters on that poor farm that had done badly last year. Durnford didn't want to know anymore.  So with a nod to the old gentleman at the desk and purposely ignoring the two forlorn slaves on the back bench, he quickly left the auction house and stepped outside into the warm sunshine.

He retraced his steps to the office advertising the two men and woman he had seen roped together earlier and entered that building.  That trio now sat quietly without ropes or handcuffs among a large group of slaves on wooden benches. Already a small group of well-dressed white men had crowed into the room.  From their appearance, Durnford guessed they were from the cotton-plantations of the South.  Some were seated around a fireplace on the right-hand wall and others huddled in the middle of the room.

Durnford's entrance went almost unnoticed, and he took up a position at the opposite wall, from where he studied the faces of the slaves offered for sale that day.  None showed any signs of passion, neither fear nor anger, nor did any one of them utter a single word.  They sat there, almost as disinterested spectators, in perfect humility and resignation.

One of the planters had come with his dog.  The dog was a mixture of various breeds of hounds, a gray color with short hair and a long, thin tail.  The dog chased its tail in circles, and the slaves seated on the benches chuckled as they watched the dog at play.  Then the dog's owner called it to his side and held up a piece of bread from his pocket.  On command, the dog stood up on its hind legs, and danced a slow circle, once around, then around again, and then still on its rear legs, it stretched out its head and nimbly took the piece of bread from its owners hand. Everyone in the auction house laughed, and the slaves roared and clapped their hands.  This performance was repeated several times, and each time the slaves laughed and clapped until the dog's owner had exhausted his supply of bread.  The dog then lay down at his master's feet and went immediately to sleep.

Then, as if upon some secret signal, the prospective purchasers filed along the benches and began examining the slaves offered up for sale.  They felt the slaves' arms, looked into their mouths and at their teeth, and finally paid particular attention in investigating the quality of the slaves' hands and fingers.  They were quiet and methodical as they worked down the rows of benches.  There was nothing unpleasant in their manner.  There was nothing rude in their examinations.  They were almost polite—and all business.  The slaves, looking almost indifferent to the process, seemed to accept the nature of the transaction.  It was almost as if they were interviewing for jobs as servants.

Durnford felt at ease. There was not to be any agonized emotion, no tears, no sobbing. This was simply business. It was accepted by everyone in the large, dusty room as such, whether purchaser or slave. No one seemed to feel the least distress.

As the examinations proceeded, Durnford walked up to the woman he had seen roped to the two men earlier. They were seated together in the first row. She was a rather beautiful young woman with fine features, features he had noted before in African people from the far northeast of that continent.

"Are you married?"

"Yes, sir. I am."

"And is this man your husband?"

"No, sir. My man is in Madison County."

"I see. How many children do you have?"

"Seven children, sir."

Durnford was dismayed at this news. He had considered a bid for the woman, especially if she were being sold with her husband.

"When did you leave your family?"

"Two days ago, sir. My heart is almost broke." The woman who had shown no emotion that morning now was near tears.

"Well—ah, why is your master selling you?"

"I don't know why he's selling us. He wants money to buy some land, I heard. I suppose he sells us for that."

Now Durnford realized that behind the stoic expressions of the slaves sitting on the benches that morning there was probably a similar tale of sorrow. It was far better not to ask too many questions. These people would be sold. It wasn't his fault. And they would be better off with him than any other planter, he was certain of that. It was time to get his mind back to business. He wanted to play the role of a disinterested traveler satisfying his curiosity as long as possible. Perhaps that way, when the bidding got slow, he could pick up a bargain or two.

"Sale is starting now! This way! This way!" A man at the door cried out to those lounging outside. When all interested parties had crowded into the room, a Negro assistant led a woman and her children to the auction block and helped them up on to it. The woman stood in the center with a baby in her arms and a young daughter at each side.

The auctioneer stepped forward and put one foot on the auction block. He was a striking figure with a flowing black coat and silver hair and mustache. "Well, gentleman," he began with a flourish of his hand, "you see before you this morning the finest products of Virginia, a sound woman and her three children, all in the best of health. Who is going to start the bidding for this fine family. Come, now, make me an offer."

There followed several minutes of silence.

The auctioneer looked carefully around the room until he came to Durnford standing against the wall. "I put the whole lot at five-hundred-fifty dollars. Will no one advance upon that? This is an extraordinary bargain, gentlemen. A fine healthy baby she has. There, hold it up. Good woman, that will do. A fine woman here, gentlemen, and three children, all for five-hundred-fifty dollars. An advance if you please."

A voice from the corner bid $560. "Thank you, sir. Five-hundred-sixty," the auctioneer spoke rapidly and glanced around the room, repeating the bid of $560 several times with one hand raised high in the air and the other pointing at the woman and children on the auction block. Then his voice dropped. "Anyone bids more?"

Andrew Durnford spoke up. "Five-hundred-seventy dollars."

The voice in the corner came back with $580, and Durnford bid $590.

The bidding stopped there, and Durnford waited for the closing of the sale.

The auctioneer stared at Durnford for a long, silent time. Then he glanced to the other bidder in the corner, and then looked down at the floor and shook his head. "Gentlemen, gentlemen, you know that won't do. I cannot take such a low price." He turned to his Negro assistant. "Take her down."

The assistant led the woman and her children down from the block and to their former seats on the benches. The children calmly took their places as if nothing had happened. The woman looked at Durnford. At first Durnford believed she too stoically accepted the proceedings. Then Durnford noticed there was a look of indignation in her eyes—the woman felt deeply insulted that Durnford had tried to buy her and her three children for the paltry sum of $590.

Durnford stepped back into the crowd, which had accepted him as a bidder without a murmur or outward sign of surprise. The woman and her children would have sold for about $700 in New Orleans, and if the auctioneer meant to go that high here in Virginia, Durnford was not likely to find the bargains he had hoped for. He took the list from his vest pocket and looked at the prices the old gentleman had composed for him at the previous auction house. Durnford had assumed the prices were inflated. But clearly that was not the case. Slaves were trading high.

Durnford looked around him. Many of the planters were equally upset. These prices were high, they mumbled. And then he heard someone at his elbow complaining that it was all because of those reckless men from Alabama. They had driven everything up with wild, speculative bidding.

The auctioneer paced back and forth in front of the benches, and then, as if spying a prospect likely to spur interest and set the fiery pace he wanted for the event, he pointed to a solid black man in the third row. His Negro assistant led the slave to a corner where a canvas screen shielded him from view. There the slave was ordered to undress, which he obediently did. A crowd of perhaps a dozen or so moved forward and began a thorough inspection, again including the mouth and teeth, and especially the arm muscles and hands and fingers. Durnford stayed at the outside of the throng and peered in. The slave's skin was dark and clear. There were no signs of sores or disease, and Durnford felt he was well nourished, healthy and strong. A perfect specimen. Then the slave was ordered to put on his clothes, and led from behind the screen to mount the auction block.

The auctioneer opened the bidding at $600. Durnford shuddered. The man would have been started off around $550 in New Orleans, and might have gone for as high as $700. Soon the bids were up to $650. Then silence. The auctioneer begged, he railed, he pleaded. But there were no higher bids, and again the salesman despaired. He could not let such a good man go so low.

Several other men were taken behind the screen, examined, and put on the block. The bids, almost as high as anything offered in New Orleans, were finally rejected. Except for one boy, about 15 years of age, there were no sales. Durnford knew that boy was no bargain. There was a weakness about his legs that the boy had carefully masked. The muscles in the boys thighs were wasted. The boy was suffering a disease of the nerves, and the prognosis was not clear. This was a market, Durnford said to himself, where the buyer had better be cautious.

"There you are my man, jump up there. That's a good boy." The auctioneer himself helped the young man from the roped trio Durnford had followed down the street. Next came the woman and the other man. And to Durnford's surprise, the bidding went higher, and the woman was sold to what Durnford heard from the crowd was one of the Alabama men. The older man went next, again for an exorbitant price. But there were no bids for the younger man.

"Now, now, gentlemen," the auctioneer said, putting his hand on the shoulder of the young man, "here is a very fine boy, fourteen years of age, warranted sound—what do you say for him?" The auctioneer waited a few minutes for a bid from the floor. "I put him up at $300, $300, $300. Any one say more than $300?"

Two hundred dollars was bid.

"What? That's nonsense. You see he is a fine, tall, healthy boy. Look at his hands."

A few men pressed forward and the young man held out his hands and opened and closed them quickly.

A bid was made at $270, then one at $280.

"Gentlemen, that is a very poor price for a boy this size. Go down my boy and show them how you can run.

The boy grinned and jumped down from the block, and ran smartly from wall to wall across the floor several times. Durnford, with the others in the room watched him race back and forth.

"Now that will do. Back up here, boy."

The young man leapt from a distance away and landed expertly on the block with short but stout legs. The exertion, which would have left Durnford gasping, apparently had not affected his breathing in the slightest.

The auctioneer called for bids again, but there was nothing. "All right, gentlemen. I will sell him for the last bid, $280. Do I here more? Last call. $280 going once, twice.... " The auctioneer's hand which had been held high during the bidding process dropped slowly. "Gone."

"This way, gentlemen, this way—down the street, if you please," the auctioneer shouted after having run through the remaining lots of Negroes for sale at that house with minimal success.

Durnford was the last man out on the street, and as he glanced around the dark room before stepping into the sunshine, he saw a clerk fastening tags around the necks of the slaves who had been sold. He followed the tobacco-chewing man with the wide hat he had seen in the first establishment, and that man dropped back a little to the side of Durnford. "I would reckon that you ain't from these parts."

"No."

The man spat a brown stream into the dust. "We has free Nigras here in Virginia, 'round 40,000 tallied by the last census. Almost one gone free for every ten that's a slave. But I don't reckon we has any of 'em that owns other Nigras....
Where did you say you're from?"

"New Orleans."

The white man spat again and then asked, "You own slaves there, do you?"

"I am here on behalf of a friend."

"I see. But you did bid on that woman. What would you be doin' with her, was you to take her back to New Orleans?"

"Yes. That was my intention."

"I suppose your friend is in the cotton. Well, there is a lot of those planters here, and it does make it difficult for us 'cause these prices is gettin' mighty high. Spose those that has 'em for sale thinks that's all right. But a little farmer around here gets unusual flared up when he can't buy any field hand for a good price." The man chewed thoughtfully for a moment and then spat into the dirt as they walked along. The throng of buyers followed the auctioneer into one of the houses farther down the street, and when Durnford stopped outside the building, the tobacco-chewing man stopped with him. The white man leaned against the doorframe, and looked up and down the street. Then he looked at Durnford with a steady gaze. "Our Virginia was a good place to work a farm once. Many years ago this here area had a great deal more wealth and more people than any other state in this Confederacy. But things has changed a good bit. We are losing out to everyone around us. Less than a third of the land is worked now, and good land it is too."

"I would think these prices high for such conditions as you describe, sir."

"Well that be true. They are unusually high. And that is because of outsiders like you."

Durnford, in an attempt to be polite and end the conversation, said, "Yes, it is a sad thing to happen to you farmers."

"Oh, I'm not a farmer. I'm the owner of the *Richmond Enquirer*. Now if you are looking for bargains, and have a little time, your best bet is to look at the advertisements in my paper. Many farmers are in trouble around here, can't buy workers at these prices, so a good few of 'em are selling off."

"But still you are here bidding at auction."

"I'm not looking for field hands." The white man spat in the dirt again. "I'm after a printer helper. And some of these niggers is not as dumb as they look."

Durnford had already come to the conclusion that he would find better bargains dealing directly with the small farmers in the area, and he had seen such advertisements in the white man's newspaper. Nevertheless, he thanked the man for his information and went off down the street, looking for the office of the lawyer, Quincy Smith.

# Chapter Six

Andrew Durnford left the slave auction houses that morning an hour before noon. He planned to locate the law office of Quincy Smith and leave his card, with the object of returning at a latter time. And directly across Main Street, above the office of the *Richmond Enquirer,* he saw painted on the window in large black letters the lawyer's name.

It was the first week in June, but already hot and humid. At the top of the stairs, which led from a plain green door in the street below, Durnford stopped and wiped the sweat from his face with a handkerchief. The landing ended at the lawyer's open door, and looking straight in he saw the man with his feet on his desk and a slouch hat pulled down over his eyes.

"Durnford you look like a worried man," the lawyer said without raising his head or moving his feet from the desk.

"Its the heat," Durnford said, still wiping at the sweat on his forehead. He stepped gingerly through the door, feeling as though his very soul was about to be exposed to scrutiny. "And you already know my name."

"You look like a black plantation owner from New Orleans. Not many people fit that description." The lawyer sat up in his chair and tossed his hat on the desk. "Sit down, Durnford."

The lawyer had the thinnest face and the largest nose of anyone Durnford had ever seen. And his eyes were set wide in his narrow face, giving the impression they belonged on another person altogether.

Durnford sat down in a dusty wooden chair at the edge of the lawyer's desk. "I have not had any experience in matters of depositions."

"Its all quite simple enough."

"Do you have instructions, then, Mr. Smith?" Neither party had taken a move toward shaking hands, and Durnford very purposefully and slowly stretched his hand across the desk.

The lawyer grabbed his hand and pumped it firmly. Then he pulled open a drawer on his desk and took out a large envelope. He leaned back in his chair and turned the envelope absent-mindedly in his hands. "This came in about a week ago. Been expecting you since."

He opened the letter, and fired questions at Durnford. As Durnford answered, the lawyer made notes in the margins of the letter, which consisted of five pages. They covered the Durnford family history and explored the transactions which occurred before and after the death of Thomas Durnford, Andrew's father.

"It's a pretty clear case of circumvention," Quincy Smith said.

"Does it seem so?" Durnford looked across the desk with surprise.

"Appears that way to me. And our job is to answer the questions as simply and innocently as possible..., and in a way that the case isn't all that clear when we're done."

"I guess I don't understand."

"Well now, Durnford, your father died without leaving any will at all. Whatever he owned belongs to his next of kin. That of course excludes you. There never was a binding acknowledgement of your paternity, Durnford. That's the law in Louisiana." The lawyer waited, looking at Durnford with suppressed curiosity. And when Durnford said nothing, the lawyer continued. "But I believe you already knew all of that. I think you also know what your father did was rather clever. Had he executed a will and openly left the plantation to you, it would have fallen at the first attack because it is far more than one-third of the estate, the maximum he could have given you under Louisiana law."

"Mr. Quincy, the plantation lands which make up St. Rosalie amounted to just about one-third of my father's estate. My father could have given those lands to me by will had he acknowledged paternity. But he did not, and he was negligent in that regard—at least I must assume that his omission was not intentional. In any event, Mr. Quincy, there is no subterfuge practiced by me or my father in regard to St. Rosalie. I purchased the land for fair value from John McDonogh, who in turn purchased the same from the estate."

"Yes. From the estate of which he is the administrator and without ever having obtained the necessary approval of the probate court." Here the lawyer paused again. "You say the plaintiff's are your cousins?"

"My father was only fourteen when he sailed for Pensacola to work for his uncle, Colonel Elias Durnford, the Lt. Governor of British West Florida. He left behind his parents at Ringwood, England."

"The plaintiffs are the children of your father's brothers and sisters, then?"

"No. They are the children of Colonel Elias Durnford, my father's uncle."

"I see. Well, I talked with the lawyer here who's going to cover the case for the plaintiffs," Quincy Smith said. "He owes me a favor or two and I think he'll let me take a peek at the questions their side will submit."

"Is that the right thing to do?"

"Oh, sure," the lawyer said carelessly. "It won't get anyone into trouble."

"What do I say if one of the lawyers in court back home asks me if I'd seen the questions before the deposition?"

"Well, that's another matter," Quincy Smith said uncertainly, and then hesitated. "I don't think I'd tell anyone that we had a little preview of the interrogatories."

"But I'd be under oath and bound to tell the truth."

"Well, Durnford would you rather we didn't have an advance look at those questions?"

"I'm not supposed to see the questions before the deposition. I think that is the way we should handle it. And I don't want to know whether you have looked at them or not."

"Well, Durnford, I don't want to take up much of your time today. This deposition happens to be a rather simple thing, as I said. We lawyers will work out a time when we can all go down to the courthouse. There won't be any judge there and it won't be a formal session. We'll sit around the table and their lawyer will ask his questions. You answer them. I will read off our questions and you then answer those. Then each side usually throws in a few more questions to cover anything that needs explaining. All of the questions and answers will be transcribed by the stenographer, who will swear you to the truth before we start."

Quincy Smith stuffed his hands into his pockets, walked over to the window and from that position told Andrew Durnford that he expected the deposition to be scheduled in a few days. Durnford was to check with him every other day or so.

Durnford thanked him for his interest in the case and asked, "Do I pay you something now?"

"What's that?"

"Do you want your fee now or later?"

"My fee is all paid up, Durnford. John McDonogh sent me a handsome bank draft."

As Durnford got up and started for the door, the lawyer returned to his desk, sat down with a sigh, and put up his feet. Then fixing his slouch hat over his eyes once again, said, "You enjoy your stay in Richmond, Durnford."

The heat and the humidity were building as Durnford saddled his horse at the stable and rode back to the farmhouse. But it was nothing compared to Louisiana, where the climate could be unusually dry and cool in the winter, but oppressive in summer. Already the saddle was uncomfortably hot. He was anxious to get home and change from his wool pants, as light as they were, to comfortable, airy cotton.

As he tethered his horse to the porch rail under a lilac tree, the door opened with a bang, and Rosella rushed out and jumped into his arms. "Papa, this is absolutely the best vacation ever."

The excitement in her voice was like a tonic to Andrew.

"Oh, Papa, the pony is pure joy. We ride in the wind and go forever. Papa, I never dreamed of land like this. Mile and mile of solid earth. We ride without fear of swamp or snake." She hugged him and kissed his cheek. "Say you'll ride with me this afternoon, Papa."

"I would surely love to, Dear Rosella..." His voice faded off as he thought of the conversation he must have with Marie-Charlotte. When his wife learned of the depositions and the motion for receivership she would explode. Anything that threatened St. Rosalie aroused a storm and fury unequaled by mother nature. No matter how much Andrew reassured her they would prevail in the end, she refused to believe it. And Andrew was determined to get through the storm as quickly as possible. He put Rosella down on the porch. "Maybe tomorrow."

"Oh, Papa. Don't you know perhaps and maybe never come?"

"Well then, I promise. Tomorrow we'll go riding for certain."

As Durnford expected, Marie-Charlotte sighed, then screamed, then flapped around the house incessantly crying out and slapping her hands together and upon her legs and the furniture when he told her. Her voice was high and piercing. "Mr. Durnford..." That was how she always addressed him when she was unhappy with something. Invariably he heard very little after those words.

For the next few days Andrew Durnford rode with the children and relaxed. Except for his daily trips to the post office and lawyer's office, and his daily review of the classified section of the newspaper, Andrew Durnford left the business side of his life for the first time in many years. The daily affairs of the plantation had always taken too much of his time. He needed help. People he could depend on. He needed intelligent people who learned quickly and worked with little supervision. The plantation was too big and there was simply too much for Andrew Durnford to supervise. But he refused to consider an overseer. The overseer was, without question, the evil of the slave system. Only men with certain qualities ever went into that line of work. And all of those qualities were bad. Slaves on small plantations were generally treated well. The owners themselves worked with them in the fields. But on large plantations, where the business was carried on by an overseer, and everything was discipline, it was entirely different. The future of the overseer depended on production. A successful overseer's skill consisted in knowing exactly how hard to drive the slave without ruining him for the next day's work. The slaves on those plantations spent their lives in constant labor. They worked in all sorts of weather. They worked at all seasons of the year. They worked without any relief except when sickness struck, and in many cases not even sickness brought them escape from the fields. The overseer did not care if they died, so long as they did not die during his tenure. His goal was to make money for the owners, and then move on to a better position. The slaves had nothing to look forward to. When a bad overseer left, another would follow, just as bad, or worse. The slaves had not the smallest hope of any improvement in the rotten food they ate or the coarse clothing they wore. All their long, dreary life, nothing would change. They were rung to bed at nine o'clock, immediately after bolting down food they cooked themselves at the day's end. They were rung out of bed by the plantation bell again at four or five in the morning to start all over again. That was the way an overseer ran a plantation. Andrew Durnford knew it was impossible to find an overseer who possessed any other qualities. Even if he told an overseer to go easy on the slaves, it would not work. No overseer planned to stay longer than five or six years. When he moved on, his new employer wanted to know only one thing: How much sugar per acre did you produce on your last plantation, Mr. Overseer?

This search for slaves with unusual capacity for work and responsibility had brought Durnford to Virginia. Not only did he look for bargains, but the exceptional slave as well. The owner of the Richmond paper was right, some of the slaves were quite trainable. They could be taught to read and write and to set print, even if it was against the law. And Andrew Durnford had found that contrary to popular belief the more intelligent a slave was the less of a problem he was. At least that was his experience.

Keeping slaves was not easy. Keeping them content and working was even harder. If the slave had little intelligence or was easily influenced by others, the problems multiplied. Just two years earlier, Durnford had purchased Lewis, warranted to be a good field hand, at New Orleans for the sum of $620.00. The year before he had bought five other people at bargain prices: Silvie and James for $1,060, Mary for $437.50, and Jane and Catherine for $875.50. Durnford realized he had made a mistake with Lewis. And he knew that he had made a further mistake by not spending more time with these people. But the plantation was very busy then. They worked shorthanded. He did not take the time to get to know his new people, and for them to get to know him. Then in May, a month after he bought Lewis, the entire group of new slaves ran off.

Durnford searched up and down the River Road, stopped at every plantation, and asked everyone he met on the road whether they had seen his people. The runaways had gone north, along the west bank of the Mississippi. An overseer from one of the plantations stopped them, and while he was questioning them, they suddenly bolted and ran off toward the swamp, away from the river. This information was the worst possible news. The slaves were from Kentucky and Tennessee, knew little of survival in the swamps, and would probably get lost and die.

Durnford hired Baptiste, the overseer from one of the neighboring plantations, to recover the missing slaves. Baptiste was a raw Cajun who knew the land well and knew how to live off the swamp. But not until twenty days after they had run away did Baptiste come upon the missing people. They were all sick with fever, half-starved, and severely weakened.

It was a lesson Durnford never forgot. He lost more than a month of work from six slaves. He was up nights nursing them back to health, and he lost almost another month before the runaways recovered sufficiently to carry their weight on the plantation. In addition, Durnford paid a heavy fee to Baptiste for the return of his people.

Durnford did not believe in punishment. The poor people were all homesick for their former plantations, friends and families. But no plantation owner, not even Andrew Durnford, could ignore the fact that the slaves had run away. Without any punishment it was certain to happen again. Lewis, the instigator of the sad event, received five lashes. It was the minimum punishment that could be administered, and Andrew Durnford laid them on with his own hand. Whether Lewis learned anything from the punishment, Durnford could not say. That slave did not seem quite right in his head, Durnford thought. And the punishment only made him more sullen. But what else was there to do?

Everyone worked hard at St. Rosalie, including Durnford. But he knew that if he was to get three and four hundred hogsheads of sugar and molasses from his land, he would have to buy more people.

The night before the deposition Durnford could not sleep. He tried the shiny black leeches to fight the pressure building in his head. The long worms sucked his blood. But nothing helped. He walked the floor throughout the rest of the night. And in the morning he was ready.

Quincy Smith leaned close to him and whispered in Durnford's ear. But Durnford was not listening. He was determined to answer as he chose. Lawyering was for others. Truth was on his side.

The lawyer for the plaintiffs was a large, ruddy-faced man, and Durnford could smell the whiskey across the table. "Are you related in any manner to the late Thomas Durnford?"

"I may be."

"May be? I see. What is that relationship?"

"My answer is that I know nothing."

"You know nothing! What do you mean, you know nothing?"

"The world said there was relationship between the late Thomas Durnford and myself. There may have been for all I know."

"Now look here, Durnford, this is not a game we play today. Was the man your father? Did you call him Daddy or Father, or whatever you call them in New Orleans?"

"I called him Papa."

"And he was your father."

"It requires a wise man to know who is his father."

"All right. All right. I think we may safely assume that the late Thomas Durnford is your father, Andrew. Your son, I believe is named Thomas as well, is he not."

"We named our son Thomas."

"Thomas Durnford."

"Thomas McDonogh Durnford."

Eventually Quincy Smith stopped whispering in Durnford's ear and slid back in his chair. This pleased Durnford.

The questioning continued through the morning, with everyone, including

Andrew Durnford and the court stenographer, a rumpled, ancient man, smoking cigars.

The ruddy-faced lawyer traced the black and white Durnford history. Thomas sailed from England as a boy and clerked for his uncle, the Lt. Governor of Pensacola. Thomas stayed on and looked after his uncle's private business matters in New Orleans and Pensacola even after the Spanish drove the English from West Florida in 1781. In 1799, the year before Andrew was born, Andrew's father left Pensacola for better business opportunities in New Orleans. His uncle, Colonel Elias Durnford, the former Lt. Governor of Pensacola, had died a few years before that on the island of Tobago.

The plaintiffs' position was that Thomas Durnford acquired the Colonel's estate in New Orleans without the benefit of legal proceedings. The plaintiffs' then made claim to all of the estate of Thomas Durnford, including St. Rosalie Plantation, on two grounds. First, they were the heirs of their father, Colonel Elias Durnford and claimed all that Thomas Durnford owned he had acquired directly or indirectly and illegally from the Colonel. Secondly, since Thomas Durnford had died without any legitimate children, his cousins were his only lawful heirs and entitled to his entire estate. The supposed sale of the St. Rosalie land to Andrew Durnford was a sham.

Durnford asserted that he had no knowledge regarding the matter. "Thomas Durnford kept his affairs to himself. I never knew what his holding were exactly, nor did I know of the nature of his business dealings."

"But when he died you must have looked into his estate."

"No, I did not. I had no interest in his estate under the law, and I had no interest as a personal matter. John McDonogh would know about that, perhaps."

"Yes. On the very day your father died, May 3, 1826, John McDonogh petitioned the Orleans Parish Probate Court and was granted the curatorship of the Thomas Durnford estate."

"They were friends. They were partners."

"And the friendship and partnership was extended to you, was it not?"

"The friendship, true. The partnership, no."

The other lawyer shuffled through his papers. Thomas Durnford and Rosaline Mercier were living in New Orleans when you were born?"

"I assume that to be the case."

"Your father died unmarried and without a will."

"I understand that was the case with Thomas Durnford."

"You deny he was your father?"

"I am not my father's son. For a long time I thought I was. Then for a long time I was not certain."

"Someone other than Thomas Durnford was your father, you claim?"

Quincy Smith sat up and said, "Andrew Durnford is the son of the late Thomas Durnford. That is a conceded fact. Now can we move forward?"

"Well let's get into some of these interesting transactions," the plaintiffs' lawyer said, searching through his huge file. "On February 28, 1827 the estate paid your mother, Rosaline Mercier the sum of $1,000 for services rendered to Thomas Durnford during his lifetime."

"I know nothing of that"

"Nothing? Well a few months later you were paid the sum of $1,500 and as your mother's agent you gave a receipt to the estate for that amount."

"Yes. I recall that transaction. I did not know what the sum was for."

"The receipt, Mr. Durnford, says that it is for the second installment ordered paid to Rosaline Mercier for services rendered and that she had then been paid to date the sum of $2,500."

"I see."

"No, you do not see, Mr. Durnford. The sum of $1,000 and $1,500 add up to $2,500. How can you claim no knowledge of the earlier payment."

"I was never a mathematician. That is why Noel keeps the plantation books."

"Now Mr. Durnford on—"

"Dr. Durnford," Quincy Smith interjected.

"All right, then, Dr. Durnford, less than a year later your mother purchased from John McDonogh a parcel of land on the New Orleans side of the river, along with four slaves who worked the fields. The land and slaves had belonged to your father."

Quincy Smith asked, "Is that a question?"

"The price paid by your mother was $1,300."

Quincy Smith leaned forward and slapped the table. "I ask again, is that a question? And then I object because it is not proper form. You need not answer, Dr. Durnford."

"I have no problem with the question. I am aware of what my mother paid for the people. But those people did not belong to Thomas Durnford. Noel and Barba had always been owned by John McDonogh. My father rented them from Mr. McDonogh. My mother did purchase them. She purchased them on my behalf.

And you are also mistaken in regard to the land. The land belonged to my mother, who inherited it from her father. It was never the land of Thomas Durnford."

"What became of the land, Dr. Durnford?"

"It was sold, as the records of Orleans Parish should clearly indicate."

"At a nice profit?"

"Profit? The land belonged to my mother by inheritance. It was sold at a good price."

"What happened to the money?"

"It belongs to my mother."

"And the slaves, what happened to them?"

"They are at St. Rosalie."

"The slaves are carried on the books of St. Rosalie, are they not?"

"Well, certainly they are. If you understood these transactions, you would not have asked the questions."

The big lawyer's face reddened. "When did you become a planter, Dr. Durnford."

"May of 1828. On my 28th birthday."

"Yes. And you were 19 in 1819. Do you remember Elias Walker Durnford?"

"No."

"He was the son of Colonel Elias Durnford. And he came to New Orleans and confronted your father with the fact that he had confiscated his uncle's estate in New Orleans."

"I never saw the man."

"Had your father ever mentioned how he acquired his uncle's property?"

"I know nothing of the business transactions of the deceased. But I am not surprised that he is accused of theft when he can no longer defend himself."

"I am not accusing him of theft! The accusation was made by your cousin, and your father was alive at the time, and you heard them arguing, did you not?"

"My previous answer stands. I will not participate in character assassination. These silly ideas simply reflect the distorted view held by the plaintiffs."

Quincy Smith leaned forward and blew cigar smoke across the table. "This is argumentative, my friends. It gets us nowhere. I ask both of you to cease."

The questioning continued in a calmer tone, and the plaintiff's lawyer established that the 1810 census of Orleans Parish showed Thomas Durnford living on Girod Street with a free woman of color, with one child and two slaves. The 1820 census identified the woman as Rosaline Mercier. The two slaves were Ned and Charlotte.

According to the estate inventory, however, the household furnishings on Girod St. did not even include a bed and were worth only $53.24. Andrew Durnford explained that the family actually lived in a lavish home owned by his mother, Rosaline Mercier on Tivoli Square, and that the slaves, Ned and Charlotte, belonged to her and always had belonged to her. They were not purchased from McDonogh or the Thomas Durnford Estate, as the plaintiffs' lawyer claimed. The Girod house was used as a business office and was mistakenly entered as the family residence at the time of the census.

Then the lawyer for the plaintiffs established that the parcels of land which now constituted St. Rosalie Plantation were purchased by Andrew Durnford from John McDonogh, beginning in 1828. All of that land had belonged to Thomas Durnford.

Andrew Durnford replied that he had paid full value for the properties. The terms were generous, however. Nothing was paid as a down payment, and the interest on the mortgages to John McDonogh were at six percent, while the standard rate was then ten percent.

"I am much indebted to John McDonogh," Andrew Durnford explained, "He has been my mentor and my benefactor. I owe him much gratitude in addition to a considerable amount of money."

"Are you aware, Dr. Durnford, that the land you now claim as St. Rosalie Plantation has never been transferred from the Estate of Thomas Durnford to John McDonogh, or anyone else for that matter? That is, Dr. Durnford, the title to that property still belongs to the estate."

"John McDonogh is the administer of the estate. I have every confidence in him. I understood the land was transferred to him in payment of debts my father owed."

"So, you know for certain of those debts and what they were for?"

"No, sir. As I said, I actually knew nothing of my father's affairs."

"But you did know the St. Rosalie land belonged to him?"

"Yes."

"You knew that your father still owned it at the time of his death?"

"I am not certain. He could have transferred it to Mr. McDonogh in payment of debts before his death."

"But you know nothing of any such debts or any such transfer?"

"No."

"And you know that under Louisiana law the sale of lands from an estate requires notice to the legal heirs, a court proceeding, and an order of approval by the court?"

"I am not a lawyer."

"And you also know that the court records in your father's estate show nothing of a sale to John McDonogh—there is no petition of such a sale, no notice to the heirs, and no court order authorizing such a sale—you are aware of that are you not?"

Andrew Durnford shrugged his shoulders and sank back in his chair. "I have full confidence in John McDonogh. He would do nothing wrong—and I am certain he will set all in order."

"Well let's talk about the Barataria tract of land," the lawyer for the plaintiffs said, pulling another document from his large file. "Do you know for what purpose Thomas Durnford deceased transferred to John McDonogh the Barataria tract of land?"

"I have heard very little about the Barataria land."

"Was not the land transferred to McDonogh for the purpose of preserving it for you."

"That is nothing that I have any knowledge about."

"Do you not expect to receive some benefit from the success of McDonogh establishing his claim to this tract of land?"

Andrew Durnford took a fresh cigar from his vest pouch and carefully examined it. Then as he lit the cigar, he explained, "I know very little of the affairs of the late Thomas Durnford, he kept the knowledge of his affairs in a great measure to himself. He was successful in business. He denied himself nothing. He denied those about him nothing. He sent me to Paris for an expensive education. I know that at the time he sold the Barataria land to McDonogh he was in account with him, and had borrowed money from him, John McDonogh. The Barataria tract was sold to John McDonogh by Thomas Durnford, it was not transferred to McDonogh to be preserved for me or any other person. I have never heard Mr. McDonogh say anything to that effect. I expect to receive no benefit from the success of John McDonogh defending his claim to this tract of land...the Barataria tract."

"Well, you seem to know all about the Barataria tract and very little about the St. Rosalie lands. Do you not find that interesting?'

Quincy Jones sprang to his feet. "Objection! Objection! Do not answer that Durnford. This deposition is over."

It had been a long day, a long hot and humid day, and the ruddy-faced lawyer for the plaintiffs was sweltering. He raised a stubby, fat finger and pointed it at Durnford. "One final question. You say McDonogh is your benefactor. From the testimony that appears to be the case. But what reason can you give the court for such conduct on his part?"

"Let not what I am about to tell you, my dear sir, give your delicacy any uneasiness. John McDonogh is the richest man in Louisiana. He has a very large house, a mansion, two very large wings, all built of brick and with the finest apportionments. It is located across the river from New Orleans, in the town of McDonoghville. In that house are a suite of rooms. Rooms furnished in the best taste and with the finest furniture. Those rooms are reserved solely for the use of my family and me. We go there often, this family of free people of color. We dine with John McDonogh. We spend as much time as is available to us with him. He was the friend and partner of Thomas Durnford. He is my friend. He is the godfather of my son, Thomas McDonogh Durnford. He has no family, no children, and we are much in the nature of his family." Andrew Durnford paused and looked into the eyes of his interrogator. "I think that explains his conduct."

Quincy Jones jumped to his feet. "I object to this last statement. It was not responsive to the question and I insist it be stricken from the record."

"I'm not surprised you do object," the lawyer for the plaintiffs said. "I think this little explanation is the most helpful thing your client said all morning."

Back in the office of Quincy Jones, the lawyer shook his head and slid into his chair. "Now do you see why you should have looked over those questions, Durnford?"

"I thought we did well."

"Durnford, if I were you I would get yourself home as soon as possible and have a long discussion with your good friend John McDonogh."

"Why?"

"Because, my friend, it looks to me like your plantation is still titled in the Estate of Thomas Durnford. The plaintiffs' are the only heirs of the Estate of Thomas Durnford, and your plantation belongs to them."

# Chapter Seven

"It must be the leathers, Miss Remy." Durnford worked the pump handle furiously. "Prime it again."

"Fine, Andrew. But the water we saved is almost gone. What do we do then?"

"Mr. Steinbach will have to fix the pump. It's his pump."

Marie-Charlotte poured water into the top of the pump and Andrew rocked the handle. Again, nothing happened. The pump was a marvelous device. Situated just outside the door to the kitchen it served the house well. But it wasn't working. She'd planned on heating water so the house servant could do the laundry. Now they'd have to wait until the pump was fixed or carry water all the way from the pump at the new house where their landlord lived.

"Don't worry. Wolfgang Steinbach is German. German's can fix anything," Andrew said. "I'll talk to him about the pump."

There was no pump at St. Rosalie Plantation. In fact, Marie-Charlotte had never seen a pump before. Drinking water at the plantation came from a cistern which held rainwater collected from the roof. Water for bathing and laundry came from the river or shallow wells. And that was how things were done in Louisiana. There, the land was flat and just a few feet above the water table. Digging a well for drinking water was useless. Water flowed into it from the ground and the water was always bad. It could be used for watering the livestock, but not for humans. Marie-Charlotte had understood that since she was a small girl. Drinking water from a shallow well gave you the fever. And the fever could kill you.

Andrew Durnford rode off to search for slaves. The children took their ponies and went riding south of the farm. And since there would be no washing to do, Marie-Charlotte sent Barba and the house servant off to Richmond to buy staples. There was nothing left for her to do now but sit down on the kitchen steps and wait for the landlord.

The German came almost at once and disassembled the pump. He spoke very little and what he did say was not understandable. Andrew had worked with Germans before, and he learned enough of the language to make known to them what it was he wanted done at the plantation and to understand what it was that they wanted. The Germans she had watched working on the plantation were a rough lot. Andrew used them for the most disagreeable tasks. They did the heavy labor of digging ditches in the rain and cold. Work that slaves never did because there was too much danger of them coming down with the fever and dying. And if a prime field hand were lost the cost to the plantation would be enormous. A German could be hired for a month of toil at a mere fraction of the value of a good slave.

The Germans had come to Louisiana with the Irish in hordes, searching for a better life. In fact, so many Germans had come and settled into farming up the river from the city that the area became known as the German Coast. The Irish lived closer in, and the section on the outskirts of the city they occupied took the name of the Irish Channel. While the Germans became farmers, the Irish competed with free blacks for the skilled trades of masons and carpenters. But there were far more immigrants than farmland and jobs. So most of them lived lives of hard physical labor, being paid little for the work of brutes.

When the Germans came to the plantation they brought their families with them. The plantation housed and fed them. They slept in a rough lean-to, far inferior to the slave cabins. They ate cheap cuts of pork and inferior barrels of cod and the cheapest cornmeal bread. Marie-Charlotte at first implored Andrew to give them something better to eat. But as she watched them gorge on the putrid fare and saw how they lived in utter filth, she felt less sympathetic.

There was in the nature of the Germans something of a sub-human class, Marie-Charlotte thought. And it was with no surprise that she read in the *Courier* an article pointing out that all the crimes committed in New Orleans were by men with German names. And Germans made up less than 10% of the population. The article raised the question whether a tendency toward the criminal and brutal was a cultural trait of the Germans or whether it was a defect of nature carried in their blood.

As a result of prejudice against the Germans, they began shedding their native language and culture much faster than the Irish. Whenever possible, the Germans traded their names for the French equivalent and eliminated every trace of their native tongue from their speech, so heavy was public opinion against them.

Marie-Charlotte had never learned German, which she thought was a rather barbaric tongue. Andrew understood the language. He told her that the German farm couple had landed at Philadelphia not long ago with seven children. They were very industrious, and soon the family had earned enough as field workers to buy their own farm. That was when they came to Virginia. Farmland in Virginia was only one-third the cost in Pennsylvania. The reason for this, Andrew Durnford told her, was that slave labor in Virginia was only about half as productive as free labor in the adjoining states. Since land had no value at all until it was worked, the natural result was that the land was worth only half when worked by slaves.

In addition, most of the land had been overworked for years by the tobacco planters. So seeking cheaper land to work, the Germans went to Virginia. And in Virginia the German couple prospered on worn out land that others worked in poverty. Soon their farm was paid for and the new house was up. The Germans had proved they could work the land themselves more successfully than their slave-owning neighbors.

Slavery in Louisiana was another matter. Although the use of slaves to harvest tobacco and vegetables was impractical, nothing could compete with a huge slave force moving through a cane field larger than twenty Virginia farms.

Andrew had explained this to Marie-Charlotte before leaving New Orleans. Virginia was not at all suited to slave labor. For that reason, slaves would cost only half as much there. Even after adding on the cost of transportation back to Louisiana, slaves bought in Virginia would still be a bargain.

The argument made sense, she agreed. So they came to Virginia and nothing was working out as they planned. Andrew had not found one slave at a bargain. That ridiculous lawsuit hung over their heads. The deposition was nothing to worry about, Andrew had told her. It had gone very well, very well indeed. He'd laughed when he told her about it and grinned and slapped his thighs. She should have been there, he exclaimed, and seen the disappointed look on the other lawyer's face. But she did not need to see the other lawyer's face. All she needed was to look at her Mr. Durnford's face. No matter what charade he acted out, she knew her Mr. Durnford. She knew it had not gone well. But she did not let Andrew know that. They must hurry, was the only thing she'd said. Get done with buying slaves and get back to the plantation.

Those were the things she thought about that sunny morning while she watched the German fix the pump. The sun was warm and she felt its rays caress her body through her thin cotton dress. Like a little girl, she drew pictures in the dirt with a stick. There was nothing for her to do but wait for the pump to be fixed. It was only at times of such forced inactivity Marie-Charlotte relaxed. Otherwise she rushed about the plantation, seeing after the women who made clothes for the other slaves, supervising the cooking, directing the cleaning, managing the house. Now she was here with nothing to do. Not since before she married Andrew had she enjoyed such leisure.

She kicked off her shoes and twisted her feet into the loose, warm sand. The German noticed this and he smiled and grunted. Then he seemed to be explaining how the pump was made. Except for the rod attached to the cylinder, the machine appeared to be entirely of wood. Even the pipe which went far into the ground was made from small, hollowed-out logs fitted together. She listened and to her surprise found that she could understand much of what the stout man said. He showed her the leather valve fastened to the wooden cylinder. It was worn and torn.

The German carried his tools in a large wooden tray with a wooden handle. In the tray he also carried leather. She watched as he pulled several pieces from the tray for a thorough inspection. Selecting one that met his satisfaction, he cut the leather to shape. And after replacing the torn leather attached to the cylinder, the German indicated that he wanted water. Marie-Charlotte understood that he wanted to prime the pump. She left her shoes and went into the kitchen to retrieve what little water was left. When she turned around, the German stood in the doorway.

"Oh! You startled me. Here's the water."

The German took the water pitcher and set it down just inside the door.

"I'm sorry, I thought you wanted water...for the pump." She quickly put a hand to her mouth to suppress a giggle. What in the world could he have asked for, she wondered? There was nothing to drink in the house but water. They'd brought no wine with them and purchased none. And they never touched beer, which is what she had heard these people loved most.

Then he stepped quickly forward and grabbed her by the wrist and she knew what he wanted. She screamed, she twisted about, she struggled. But there was no one in the house to hear her, and the new house was far away. The German was hard and strong, much stronger that she suspected, and much harder than Andrew. Suddenly she was going down to the floor and he was bearing down on top of her.

She screamed with all the power she could muster, but her strength felt like that of a fly against a lion. And then as he pushed into her she stopped screaming. Terror, cold gray terror enveloped her and her mind went completely blank.

She never told Andrew what had happened that day. But she also made certain she was never left in the house alone again. The Durnfords had no social contacts with the German farm couple and saw them rarely, and there was never an occasion to fear accidentally giving away her dark secret. What had happened, Marie-Charlotte had decided, must have been largely her fault.

So it was that when Andrew came home from his fieldtrip, the children had long been studying mathematics, Barba and the servant woman had returned and worked to put the house in order, and Marie-Charlotte had finally composed herself sufficiently to get through the day.

"I see the pump is fixed," Andrew said as he dismounted his horse. There was below the spout a large basin full of water, and Andrew walked up to it and splashed his face. "These Germans can fix anything. They're cold as stone, and somehow the world's manners passed them by, but they are a hard-working, frugal lot."

Barba stood by with a towel at the ready, Marie-Charlotte at his elbow. The mere mention of the German left her with a hollow, cold feeling of fear and despair. She wanted to say something. She wanted to enter into Andrew's warm embrace. But it was as though her mind was paralyzed. She bit her lip and said nothing.

Later that evening, sitting at the dinner table with Barba and her family, Marie-Charlotte was silent and moody.

"Perhaps," Andrew Durnford said to her, "you do not believe the deposition went well. But I assure you again, it really went quite well." He smiled and waited for a response, but she only looked down at her untouched plate of pig hocks and sour cabbage. "Now, I wouldn't want you to think that we were pressed at all. I said very little to Quincy Smith about it. Nevertheless, untrained as I am in the law, I think we did very well. Yes, very well indeed."

Marie-Charlotte nodded and seemed to brighten a bit. Andrew took this as a sign to leave the subject.

Except for an occasional comment from one of the children, the meal was finished in silence. Everyone at the table sensed that Marie-Charlotte was too upset by the legal proceedings to engage in social chatter.

After the meal, a quiet evening was spent in the parlor in candlelight. The children went to bed.  Barba left for his quarters over the stable.

"I went to see a family of four children, father and mother for $1,800 of yellow complexion.  I acted and played the indifferent saying they were too high.  Another family of a father and mother with two children for $1,200....  I expect to have a better bargain....  At any rate, I will do for the best.  I must act with indifference for a few days.  I tell them all that speaks to me on the subject that I am travelling for my health, being attained with a liver complaint.  And if I should find a few family at a low rate I may purchase them for my own use, otherwise I go without."

She was not listening, he knew.  After the candle sputtered out, he took her by the hand and led her up the dark stairs to bed.  She lay beside him with eyes open. He watched her silent face in the moonlight.  How is it, he wondered, that these women always know the truth?  And then he fell asleep.

Marie-Charlotte wanted to talk.  But if Andrew thought she was worried by the law case, that was all the better.  The law case meant nothing at all to her now.  The only thing that mattered was her family, Andrew, and the children.  She had since the horrible experience of that morning reevaluated everything around her.  Andrew had never been brutal to her.  No one had been brutal to her before.  She knew the children were incapable of brutality, and Andrew was a gentle and kind man.  She thought that she must do something, she must not let the panic and fear and horribleness of that morning control her life.  What she needed was for Andrew to hold her very tight.  But she was unable to tell him that.

In the morning Andrew Durnford awoke to find Marie-Charlotte exactly as he had seen her last, eyes open, staring at the cracked plaster of the ceiling.

Once Andrew had departed that morning, she had a few hours to herself before the children's lesson.  She spent the time at her desk with the shutters closed to the bright sunshine.  Before her on the desk she had her journal, a large book in which she kept a diary of events as well as an accounting of the household budget and any other matter that interested her.  It was her habit to make an entry every week or so of the most important events.  She knew she would never enter into her book what had happened to her the day before, and that was not her purpose at her desk now. Instead, she read slowly, starting with her first entries at age thirteen.  Quietly, slowly, she examined the pages.  There was always on her mind the horrible, brutal attack of the vulgar German.  She saw his face floating before her.  It was a face she hated.  It was a face she would always hate.

Then, without realizing it, she had gone several minutes  without thinking about the German.  A small smile, unnoticed, had crept upon her face when she was reading the entries made at Isle Brevere. It was the time when the charming, shy but confident Andrew Durnford first visited her there.

Could she ever again physically love any man, she wondered? She felt dirty, soiled, despoiled. Even the physical pain of the cruel attack would be with her a long time, she felt. "Violence is nothing new," she said to herself. "I know that. Women have always suffered the indignity of rape. And they have always suffered alone, all alone. There has never been an army to call upon to come rushing in and save us. We suffer alone in a dark world."

Then her suffering and self-pity turned to anger. The anger was cold and cut through her. And suddenly she was determined to have revenge. How could she go on living at this little house knowing that the German slept with his wife up the hill, slept without conscience or regret. Perhaps he even remembered the rape with pleasure.

She sat there at the desk, with teeth clamped tightly together and tears streaming down her face. There was nothing she could do. Andrew could avenge her, probably would whether she wanted it or not. And if he did, he would hang for sure. So she could never tell him what had happened. Then Marie-Charlotte thought of Barba. Barba she was certain was a stronger man than even the barbaric German. She could confide in Barba. He would keep her secret. And Barba was capable of violence when necessary. There was even a rumor he had beaten a white man nearly to death when he was in the North.

Then throwing herself back in her chair she shook her head. No. No. Barba could do nothing. What chance would he have? A black slave attacking a white man in Virginia. No matter what the reason, Barba would hang for sure, just as Andrew would, even if the white man lived. All of this, she realized, was pure fantasy and silliness. There was no possibility of revenge. She shuddered and looked again at her journal. The pages went unread. Nevertheless, she felt comfort from the nearness of her recorded past. And slowly she gained control of her feelings, realizing that she did not want revenge. All she wanted was to leave Virginia and the German. She knew that would happen only when Andrew had accomplished his purpose.

With a resolve unrealized before, Marie-Charlotte closed her journal and stood up, straight and tall. Then she walked to the front door and called the children from where they took turns swinging on an old rope thrown over the limb of an oak tree. It was time for their French lesson. It was time for her to continue her life.

Marie-Charlotte had begun to resolve the turmoil within her. She had survived the destruction of her life of innocence. But she did not know then whether she would ever be intimate with Andrew Durnford again. Her wounded mind was healing, not by understanding, but by a searing, which was like the closing of torn flesh by a hot iron.

# Chapter Eight

"Take that road there down by the creek at the south end of town—you'll see where it's most travelled and it's simple enough to keep to it, at least for about a mile or so, and that's farther than you need go on it."

Andrew had brought his horse in to the livery stable to exchange it for a more durable steed for what was to be a longer journey than he had previously taken. The directions given to him by the livery owner were for the shortest and quickest way to Daniel Wellington's farm. That farmer had advertised for sale a woman with two children for the sum of $750.

The farm was several miles distant and for that reason Durnford sensed a bargain. Apparently the farmer was not willing to sell through one of the auction houses, and Durnford felt none of the planters visiting Richland would take the time and trouble to go such a distance.

"...Then there's a shallow place there and you'll cross the creek and when you get to the other side there is a fork, and you take the right; go on about half an hour or so and pretty soon there's some big trees fallen there." The stable owner paused and scratched his chin. "You may have a little trouble finding where the road is, but you just keep bearing off to the right, there where the trees are the most thin, and then pretty soon you'll see it again. You just keep going along that road, you see, no problem with that road there, well marked where you can see folks have traveled before. And that runs along like that for maybe a mile and you'll find a crossroad. Keep a clear eye for that, because that is a little bit hard to find. As I remember there is a big dead oak tree right there off to the left where that crossroad is, and that's the way you go, to the left, you see, and then you'll just have to watch where the grass is laid down by horses and wagons.  Well, you must take that to the left, and pretty soon you go by two cabins.  One of those cabins is old and all fallen in.  The other cabin, you'll see is a new one.  A white man lives in that cabin.  You can't miss it.  Anyway, you go past that cabin the white man lives in about a hundred yards or so and there's a fork there and you take it to the right.  Watch real careful because it just turns square off all of a sudden.  But it's fenced in for a good bit and you can't miss it.  Keep going along by that fence and you can't get lost there.  Right straight beyond that you come to a schoolhouse, that's the schoolhouse you would see if you went the road to Norfolk way, which is a lot longer by about six miles, and anyway there's a gate opposite it, and off there there's a big house— but I don't reckon you can see the big house from there because for the woods.  Anyway about three hundred yards beyond that schoolhouse you'll find just a little bitty road running off to the left through an old field.  You take that road about a half mile to where a path goes square off to the right.  Get on that path and keep on it until you pass a little cabin in the woods.  Nobody lives in that old cabin now and you'll see that pretty clear the way it's all run down, but right there that path turns to the left a little bit, and you keep following that path along there until you come to a fence and a gate.  Look straight up across the field there and you'll see a house.  That's George Kalhorn's plantation.  Go off to the right there and when you come to the end of the fence turn the corner—don't keep going straight, but turn the corner right there, you can't miss it.  Then it's straight on until you come to another creek.  This creek does have a bridge over it though.  But don't go over the bridge.  Just turn to the left, it's that simple, and keep along the creek there and pretty soon you'll see a meetinghouse off in the woods, you probably can't tell it's a meetinghouse, but that's what it is, and you can't miss it.  Go right up to that meetinghouse and as you get near it you'll see a path bearing off to the right.  Now that path looks like it's going right away from the creek, but it ain't.  Take that path and pretty soon you'll come on a sawmill right on the creek, up higher apiece.  Now right there is where you cross the creek.  You just cross the creek right there and go into the sawmill, it's on the other side right there, you can't miss it, and you'll find some people working there at the sawmill, and they'll put you right straight on the road to Mr. Wellington's farm.  You can't miss it."

"Well, how far is that, sir?"

The stable owner scratched his chin.  "As I recollect it's about four hours to the sawmill.  And Mr. Wellington's gate is only a few miles or so beyond that, and then you've got another mile, maybe a little better, after you get to the gate. But you can't miss it. You'll see some slave quarters right off there, they belong to Mr. Wellington, and if some of 'em are around there, they'll show you the way to the house."

"I'm not so sure I can remember all of those directions. Would you be so kind and write it all down for me?"

"Well, sir, I would most kindly do so, but I reckon I can't write."

Having negotiated a rental of two dollars for a spirited filly, Andrew Durnford set out for Wellington's farm. The horse was frolicsome and playful, and its joyful mood was contagious, creating in Durnford a light-heartedness and happiness, and Andrew cantered along enjoying the coolness of the morning and watching the sunlight filtering down through the trees, and in three hours he was lost.

He was surrounded by pine trees without a trace of a road in the soft needles underfoot. Placing the sun first over his left shoulder and then his right, he tacked back and forth, generally in an easterly direction until he had a distinct road ahead of him again. Following the road, which went over fallen trees and underbrush which was all beaten down and chewed by wagon wheels, he came to a clearing which was just beginning to be grown over by young pine trees. On the other side of the clearing he saw an old cabin. The door was off its hinges and a few logs had fallen out along the side. The entire structure leaned to one side, as if it were intent on escaping into the woods beyond.

The road passed to the side of the cabin. Beyond it about a quarter of a mile he came upon a second cabin in a fresh clearing. There was no white man about, and Durnford wondered whether this was perhaps the second cabin he had been told about, which would mean he was back on track. A large wigwam, made of sticks and animal skins, was on the other side of the cabin along the road. At the entrance to the wigwam, two blacks sat husking corn. Durnford was about to dismount and ask directions when two bony hounds bounded toward him, barking and growling. The half-starved animals stopped short and set up a din of barking and yowling that echoed from the woods around. The two Negroes near the wigwam looked up for a moment and then returned to their conversation and their husking.

Andrew continued along the road at a slower pace, with the dogs barking behind him until they were out of sight. Then he came upon an ancient grove of very large pine trees. Seated in the middle of these trees was a long log cabin with a door in one of the narrow ends and a crumbling chimney made of sticks and mud in the other end. Along the side of the cabin facing the road were four small windows, closed by wooden shutters.

Dismounting and leading his horse by its reins, Durnford went to the cabin door. It was secured by a wooden latch and held in place by leather hinges. The door was unlocked and he opened it and peered into the dark room. He saw several crude tables made of large half-logs supported by rough-sawn cross trees, to which were fastened benches. This must be the schoolhouse, he concluded, but there were no children or teacher anywhere about, and from the amount of cobwebs, dust and accumulated dead leaves and twigs which had blown in through the cracks between the logs and around the loose shutters, it appeared no one had used the building for some time.

Feeling confident that he had found again the way to Wellington's farm, Durnford set out at a brisk pace to make up for lost time. The filly seemed to enjoy the trot and Durnford's spirits rose in tune with the frisky animal. They went on and on for miles. But they never came to a meetinghouse, a creek, or a sawmill. Durnford slowed the horse to a walk and stood up in the stirrups. They were in an area of old fields, land that had been in cultivation years earlier and all used up. The coarse, sandy soil now supported nothing more than a few small pine trees, tall grass, scraggly evergreen bushes and blackberry vines.

Except for wild pigs, there was not a living creature anywhere on the landscape. The pigs, lanky and bony with narrow heads dashed across the path in packs of a dozen or more. They went straight across, almost at a gallop with short, gasping grunts.

Finally Durnford saw far away in the distance across the fields a large house. He dismounted. There was no path leading in the direction of the house, so he continued on, walking the horse in a wagon track. He walked for an hour or so. His rear and thighs were covered with saddle sores and blisters that stung from the sweat. He knew he had done a stupid thing by going at a trot when he was far from broken to the saddle. There was some relief through walking, but at that pace it would soon be dark and there would be no hope of finding the way to Wellington's farm.

At last he came upon a grove of old oak trees. Running through the middle of the oak trees was a very small creek. The creek flowed with water barely sufficient to turn the wheel of a small gristmill on the other side.

Durnford led his horse across the shallow brook. Behind the mill, which was not a sawmill at all, but a mill for grinding corn, he saw two small cabins and several Negroes. One of the Negroes wearing an old sweat-stained hat and a long, black, ragged coat approached him as he stopped under the trees near the mill.

"Yeh, sar," the Negro told him, he knew the way to the Wellington farm, knew it well. It wasn't far, maybe four or five miles.

The Negro led him along a narrow path that eventually turned and ended at the creek. The Negro pointed to where the path continued on the other side of the stream. "You juss keep de straight road, Massar," he said several times, assuring Durnford that the path went directly to the Wellington farm.

At last Durnford was near his goal. Anxious to reach the farm before dark, he remounted the spirited filly, settled slowly into the saddle in spite of the searing pain from his blisters, and set out along the path on the other side of the stream. Each jolt of the saddle sent shivers of pain through his legs and buttocks where the open blisters rubbed and festered. Despite the pain, he went on at a clip in good spirits for about a half mile when he came to a fork in the small road. The Negro's words echoed in his mind. "You keep dat road right straight, and it'll take you dar." But which way now?

The path to the left was the straighter and more traveled one and he was soon satisfied that he had gone the right way. It led him up a slope out of the oak woods and into an evergreen forest where he was cooler in the dense shade. There, protected from the hot afternoon sun, he stopped in the soft pine needles to rest his horse and eat his lunch of dried jerky.

Following the path through the pine woods again, Durnford eventually came out into open country with young trees and fenced fields. He found a gate and another path, which he followed straight to a farmhouse.

Several Negro children took off at a run for the farmhouse as he approached. Passing a stable and cattle-pens and a vegetable garden, Durnford moved on toward the house far up the sloping hill. The path led around small cabins and then a corncrib. When he finally reached the house he was met by an old white woman wearing spectacles. The old woman squinted at him as if she were not clear as to what she was witnessing, a well-dressed, obviously well-to-do black man on an expensive horse.

Durnford sensed immediately that he had not reached his goal. "Madam, I have lost my way to Mr. Wellington's house. Would you kindly tell me how to get there?"

The woman looked at him dumbly and did not answer. As Durnford was about to dismount, a very large black man carrying an axe came around the corner of the house.

"I am a stranger, travelling to Mr. Wellington's house," Durnford said half to the woman and half to the huge black man. "Would you please direct me how to get to Mr. Wellington's place?"

"You want to go to Wellington's?" the old lady asked.

"I do, madam, indeed I do."

"Well it's been many years since I been there, and I reckon I don't remember the way."

The black man fingered the sharp blade of his axe and looked at Durnford curiously. "You need to go to Missy Herbert's. Take dat path runs long by de hog pen right straight dar."

"But I'm looking for the Wellington farm."

"Missy Herbert ken tell you how to get dar."

Durnford thanked the black man, bowed gracefully to the old lady, and rode off in the direction of the hog pen. He had gone twenty minutes or so along that path when he came to a cabin that fronted on a wide, well-traveled road. Over the cabin door hung a wooden sign upon which was painted in white letters the word "Grosery."

The long, low store was crowded with shelves, tables, and barrels. At the far end of the room was a fireplace in front of which sat a man, smoking a pipe. The man rose as Durnford came through the door. Durnford asked him the directions to Wellington's farm.

"Go up the road a spell to the Court House."

Durnford pointed to the east and asked how far it was.

"That is not the right direction to Wellington's. You'd better turn around and keep right straight till you get to the Court House, you can't miss it."

"And how far is that, sir?"

"About a mile."

"How far from there to Mr. Wellington's"

"To Mr. Wellington's? I should think it's about ten miles."

Durnford traveled on throughout the afternoon. He passed the Court House. He passed other small cabins, and now and then a larger house. He came to forks in the road, asked and received directions. Near sunset, he was back again in an area of pine forest and dreaded the thought of traveling the dim path at night among the fierce wild hogs. He approached one small house after another and requested lodgings for the night and was at each summarily turned away.

Finally he came upon a black man walking in the road and wearing the plain clothes of an ordinary laborer. Durnford asked where he might find quarters for the night. The black man directed him to the third house along the road, and said he was certain he would be put up there.

The house recommended was a simple two-story house with a porch at the front door and a small wing at one end, belonging to one of the wealthier citizens of the area. A dog barked as Durnford approached. A stout man with a sullen and suspicious expression came out to see what had excited the dog.

Durnford asked if he could be put up for the night anywhere on the farm. The man stared at him for a while, then examined his horse, and without saying a word, went back into the house and closed the door. Durnford waited, and was about to remount his horse, when the man came out again. "You can stay if you'll take what we give you."

In the kitchen, Durnford was given a supper of cornmeal mush and then led to a room in the back of the house at the top of the stairs. He settled onto a lumpy mattress and pulled a thin blanket over him and fell instantly asleep. Not much later he was awakened by sharp, stabbing pains in his legs and feet. Then he felt movement throughout his bed. Bugs. At first he tried to ignore them and go back to sleep, because he was exhausted and anticipated another long day ahead of him. But it was impossible. Finally he leaped frantically from the bed and slapped at his legs and feet. He shook out his clothes, carefully put them on and went down the stairs to the parlor. Although he was afraid of waking the residents of the house and fearful they would put him out for being so crass as to make himself at home in the living quarters, he knew it was impossible to sleep in the room they had given him.

He arranged the chairs in the parlor in a row and lay down to sleep on them. But the seats were too narrow, and made of deerskin which was certain to be full of fleas and bugs. Rolling his coat into a pillow, Durnford lay down under an open window in the moonlight, feeling that bugs would stay to the dark side of the room. He was saddle-sore, exhausted and stiff, and desperately in need of sleep. But the instant he lay down the fleas were all over him. There was nothing he could do but brush them aside. Finally he dozed off, too tired to respond to the pestering insects. He slept fitfully through the night, slapping and brushing at insects, some of which crawled across his face. Then in the early hours of the morning, he returned to his room and sat in a corner. Bugs were everywhere. But in that position, few reached his face.

In the morning, Durnford thanked his host for his hospitality, paid him $1.50 for lodging and meals, and took the road to Mr. Wellington's farm.

The Wellington farmhouse was an old brick mansion with a large wooden porch. Several old oaks surrounded the house, and under those trees were situated a number of slave cabins. Durnford learned that tobacco was the main crop of the farm. Although tobacco returned the greatest profit for the labor involved, it rapidly wore out the land. The Wellington land was approaching a state of exhaustion, and the owner, once he recovered from the shock of seeing a Negro respond to his advertisement, told Andrew he was selling off some of his slaves to buy more land. Durnford tactfully questioned the wisdom of this approach to the problem, and Mr. Wellington informed him that tobacco was all he knew and all he cared to know. If he were willing to buy more land, and received a good profit from it, he did not know why he should not wear it out.

After much haggling and negotiations which left Durnford worn thin, he managed to purchase the woman and her two children for the sum of $625. This was well below the advertised price of $750, and Durnford knew he had made his first real bargain. These people he were healthy. The woman was both handsome and intelligent. She was tall. She stood straight and strong. She would make not only a good field hand for working the cane, but would be invaluable in the sugarhouse as well. The woman, Phyllis, was 32 years old. Her daughter, Wainy, was eight, and her son, Frank, just seven. Her husband had been sold five years earlier, and neither she nor Mr. Wellington had any knowledge of where he now lived. "Kentucky, probably," Mr. Wellington offered. "But can't be certain he'd still be there because a good many of those traders house them there for a while before shipping 'em down river."

Before his final bid, Durnford had taken the mother and the two children and walked with them for a while under the oak trees. He was anxious to know how the woman would react to being owned by a black man and taken to Louisiana, certainly a long way from here, never to come back. But the woman seemed to have little interest in whether she stayed or was sold to Durnford. All spirit had left her. The children were wary and followed the lead of their mother, expressing neither joy nor sorrow over the prospect of leaving the Wellington tobacco fields.

"We don't play much here," Wainy said when Durnford asked whether she would miss her playmates. Then it suddenly occurred to Durnford that this family spoke none of the broken and confused language used by most of the slaves. He stopped at the base of an oak, and taking a stick, scratched some letters and numbers in the soft dirt under the tree. Neither the mother nor the two children could read the letters. Then he wrote into the ground the word "Wainy," and saw a smile flicker across the girl's face before it was quickly suppressed. A light shone briefly in the mother's eyes and was instantly extinguished to be replaced by a placid, dull submissive look. But it was too late for the mother and children. Durnford knew their secret. This family could read and write. And a slave that could read and write was a dangerous slave. Such a slave would soon have ideas of freedom. The man or woman who could write could also forge a pass, a pass that could lead down the road to freedom.

So Durnford thought Wellington knew the family was literate, and believed the tobacco planter would let them go for less than advertised. But what was considered a dangerous attribute was, for Durnford, a valuable asset. Not only did he seek the better educated and intelligent slave, he even looked for teachers among them to help the others learn to read and write. The more they understood of the world, the more likely they were to be contented with his treatment.

By most standards, Wellington was considered to be a wealthy man. But he lived a simple, rustic life. Most of the time, when other men wore a coat and cravat, he lounged about in a shooting jacket.

Durnford dined with him in a room which made up a small wing at the rear of the house. The kitchen was in another building made of logs with a huge brick fireplace. The finished meals were brought up to the house by Negro servants. The old man's wife had died some time ago, and the obviously lonely man entreated Durnford to stay on for a few days. It was a temptation. The meal served in the dining room consisted of the best hot cornbread he had tasted. Sweet potato, roasted in ashes came with four varieties of pork, wild fowl, fried eggs, cold roast turkey, and a baked piglet. Durnford helped himself. The piglet was prepared in an unusual way and had a distinctive flavor Durnford did not recognize. He was curious as to the recipe.

"Well, sir," Wellington responded, "that is not a sucking pig. It is opossum, cooked in a most delicious way." Durnford choked and Wellington squinted at him. "I do not myself know the recipe."

The door to the dining room was left open all during the meal. Little Negro children came and went freely, hanging around the chairs of Durnford and their master, giggling and eyeing the food. A stout, firm black woman was in charge of the table and she was assisted by two mulatto boys, whom she constantly sent running back to the kitchen for the next course.

The owner of the plantation drank alternatively milk and whiskey, both to a considerable degree, and Durnford joined him, refilling his glass about half as often as Wellington. Finally, when long shadows from the spreading oaks covered the ground, the plantation owner had brought to him a writing quill, ink and parchment. Then in a flourishing handwriting of beautiful loops and scrolls, he wrote out the document of sale, copying a yellowed and stained form he kept at his elbow. As he finished the paper of sale, he handed it to Durnford. It contained the standard language which transferred the ownership of one human being to another:

*"Know all Men by these Presents, that Athol Wellington of the plantation bearing his name, County of New Kent and Commonwealth of Virginia, of the first part, for and in consideration of the sum of Six hundred and twenty-five Dollars to him paid by Andrew Durnford of St. Rosalie Plantation, Parish of Plaquemines, State of Louisiana of the second part, the receipt whereof is hereby acknowledged, has bargained and sold, and by these Presents does grant and convey, unto the said party of the second part, his executors, administrators or assigns, all the right, title, and interest which he holds in and to the Negro woman, Phyllis, the Negro girl, Wainy, being the daughter of the same said Phyllis, and the Negro boy, Frank, being the son of the same said Phyllis, To Have and to Hold the same said Negroes unto the said party of the second part, his executors, administrators and assigns, FOREVER. And the said party of the first part, for himself, his heirs, executors and administrators, does covenant and agree to and with the said party of the second part, his executors, administrators and assigns, to Warrant and Defend the sale of said property, goods and chattels hereby made, unto the said party of the second part, his executors, administrators and assigns, against all and every person or persons whatsoever."*

The document had then been dated and signed by Wellington, his signature containing a great number of exquisitely-crafted scrolls and embellishments.

The signature of a gentlemen upon such a document, Durnford knew, was always a work of art. The Negro traders, business-like in all their endeavors, signed with a simple, scratchy line of humps and slants, most being none too sure of the spelling of their own names.

"Since you are not a trader," Wellington said with a soft smile as he handed over the bill of sale, "I assume one document should do."

Durnford nodded. Slaves bought by traders were for immediate resale. Anyone accepting such goods from them demanded the bill of sale from the original owner as proof of marketable title. Since families were seldom sold together, a separate document was required for each family member. But Durnford never broke up a family. "These people will not see the auction block," he said.

"Perhaps not in your lifetime."

Durnford looked at Wellington for a moment as if to say something, thought better of it, and again studied the bill of sale.

Wellington sat quietly for a moment, then said, "I could have sold to a trader for more."

"Perhaps."

"I think well of these niggers, Durnford. I know you'll give good care."

"It is well known that I care for my people."

Wellington turned and stared at the long shadows under the oaks. "Our days on earth are as a shadow."

"The Book of Job, I believe."

Wellington leaned forward over the table toward Durnford. "Dr. Durnford, Phyllis is a child of the plantation. Bargaining time has passed, I know, but could you see it clear in your heart to make provisions for the freedom of her children at your death."

A child of the plantation was one who's father was not known, or whom had been fathered by the plantation owner. Durnford sat up straight. This was an unusual request and a strange admission. Was Wellington the father, he wondered? Or perhaps Wellington's father? Phyllis' features were distinctly of the white race, and her skin was lighter than Durnford's. The Anglo-Saxon heritage showed even more clearly in her children, Wainy and Frank.

"I am yet young and have no thoughts of death. Circumstances permitting, though, I will do my best to carry out your wishes, sir." And then Durnford realized the truth. There was no husband of Phyllis who had been previously sold by Wellington. It was not Phyllis who was a child of the plantation, although that could also be the case, but her children, Wainy and Frank. And the man sitting across the table was probably the father. Why he chose to sell them, to send them on a long journey with their mother to a distant land, rather than make his own provisions for their emancipation, Durnford could not fathom. But then was this so unusual? Did not Durnford's friend and mentor, McDonogh send his own children to Africa only after they had earned their freedom? And what of those who would still be slaves when McDonogh died? Was there a provision in the old man's will for them?

After an exotic coffee, the two men went outside under the spreading oaks and smoked expensive cigars.

"I may have some difficulty getting the woman and her children back to Richmond," Durnford said.

"Why so?"

"Well I was a day and a half getting here and I don't know how long it would take going back, nor am I certain I could find the way."

"First, my good sir, I would suggest shipping them by rail. There is a watering station at Colonel Gillin's place just a few miles up the road. I can arrange a guide to go with them and he will deliver the family to your agents."

Durnford was dumbfounded. "There is a railroad running from here to Richmond?"

"Oh, yes. If you would like to leave your horse in my care, I can send a man along with you to show you the way. The train customarily picks up passengers at Gillin's watering station."

Durnford explained that the horse was rented from the Richmond livery stable and that he felt obligated to return it as soon as possible. But he thanked Wellington for his assistance, accepted his offer to have the slaves shipped, gave Wellington the name of his agent, and inquired as to the best road to Richmond.

The old man pointed to a gate at the opposite end of the grounds. "It's a dead straight path from here to the Richmond road, Dr. Durnford. You can't miss it. No forks or twists to it. And I can send along a servant if you like."

Durnford thanked him for his hospitality, declined the assistance of a guide, and early the next morning, mounted the filly for the road to Richmond. The path ran straight and true, as promised, but Durnford had gone only a short distance when the way became less and less clear. An hour later, he was off the horse, stumbling along a dark path through the woods and looking for any sign of civilization.

Finally he came across another path which looked considerably more travelled, and he turned in that direction. Almost immediately, he came upon two Negroes riding a mule who were going to the Richmond road, they said. Following them for about an half hour, he came out upon a broad, well-traveled country road.

"There be a short-cut," one of the Negro men on the mule said as he passed them. "Bout a hundred yards up dis road here is a pat, goes off to the right. You goes dat way, until you sees a mill across dat creek. You cain't miss it. Den—"

"Thank you. Thank you. But I think I'll stick to the main road."

And by the middle of the afternoon, Durnford was back at the livery stable in Richmond.

# Chapter Nine

Durnford scoured the countryside, seeking bargains to stock his Louisiana plantation. In the middle of June, he wrote to his friend and mentor, John McDonogh. The deposition had not gone well, Durnford finally admitted, and he was anxious to learn how the plaintiffs would make use of his testimony. He knew he had to return to Louisiana as soon as possible. But his plans for securing slaves had not gone well either.

"This is to say that I knew things could be difficult, but I find much more difficulty regarding my purchases than I thought possible," he wrote. "I bought a fine woman and two children for the sum of $625, and I have two or three other bargains on hand, but so high that I dare not come to a hasty conclusion. A woman of thirty, her daughter of twelve, a boy of seven, a boy of three, all for $1,350. I have made an offer of $1,000 and will stick with it. Another family intrigues me. The mother of thirty-five years, a girl of ten, a boy of eight, a boy of six, a boy of four, a child of four months. All offered to me for $1,900. I have been brought another very good woman at a good price. But I will not buy her without the remainder of the family. The man has gone back to bring me the husband and two children of the same woman eight to ten years old. I expect he will make me pay a high price if I will have them. I will not break up the family, and since I am the only hope of keeping them together now that he is determined to sell her, I feel I must take them."

Ten days later, Durnford wrote again. He desperately wanted to talk to John McDonogh about problems other than business. Marie-Charlotte spent most of the day in a trance. She seemed to respond well to the children, but was cold and indifferent to him. He suspected that she had suffered from a brain fever while he was on one of his excursions. Had he been home at the time, he might have bled her and saved her from much torment. Now the only thing to do was wait and hope for a change with time. But these thoughts he did not pass along to his friend in Louisiana. Instead, he wrote, "This is to advise you that a few days ago I bought a man and woman, stout and able hands, with three children for $1,526. One child is a girl of seven in September next, the second a boy going on five years, the last a girl of near three years old. The woman is pregnant."

He was buying slaves at a quicker pace. But he was not convinced the market made any sense. "I must do for the best," he wrote. "This is not the time to buy. Some Alabamians are going back home with their money, saying that people are higher than they have ever known. I am certain that in October, when these miserable crops are in, there will be three people offered for every one for sale now, and at much better prices."

By the end of June, Andrew Durnford, the black plantation owner from Louisiana, had purchased a total of twenty-five slaves for the sum of $6,876. He had not done well. But if he were careful, they would all be back in New Orleans at less cost than if he had bought them at home. He was pressing hard to accomplish his goal now.

Marie-Charlotte showed a little improvement, and his hopes for recovery were restored. Again, these were thoughts he did not share with his friend in Louisiana. But he had come to the conclusion that the trip had worn her down. What else it could be, he did not know, having finally ruled out a brain fever. He only knew that she was improving, and that whenever he talked of leaving Virginia, her spirits lifted. So they would go home. He'd spent enough time searching the countryside for bargains. "I will keep the balance of the money," he wrote. "My thighs are all blistered riding round or within twenty miles of Richmond. The farmers are aware of the prices now, and will hold on. Only after the harvest will people be cheaper. *Il n'ya pas pourles demandant,* even family they buy. I could have bought some cheaper, but they are what I call rotten people. Good young men and boys and girls are as high here or more than in New Orleans; out of what I bought, there are at least twelve or fourteen that will be able to do good work. I could have purchased more people, as I said, but they are diseased. There are a cunning set of people in this country and gentlemen too, or considered as such. But I know it is much better to have one good healthy person than two diseased ones."

Anxious to draw his campaign to a close and return to the plantation, Durnford began making plans for transporting them home. His original idea was to send them back by sea. With that opportunity no longer likely, he wrote, "Before I left, we discussed the route of returning by the rivers Ohio and Mississippi. Now it appears I must take them through by land from here to Guyandotte on the Ohio, as there is no vessel that will leave here before the first of October. I may find it necessary to hire a wagon or buy one with two horses."

A few days later Durnford wrote again, advising McDonogh of the complications in transporting slaves. "I find I will have much more difficulty than I was aware of in their transportation. The journey to Guyandotte will be at the expense of $350 for wagon, horses, and so forth. And then I would not be nearer New Orleans than I am here. I have been making inquiries respecting the route. It is a job of twenty-five days. If a few of my people get sick on the way, I will have to lay up and expend what few dollars I may have left. I will do better if it can be done, that is, if the steam packets will take me from Norfolk to Charleston. I will go there and ship my people, and come home by land, as the passage will be long, and warm and I think I can travel faster overland. I am anxious to be back at work and have a curiosity toward the situation with Noel on the plantation."

Durnford wrote to the packet agents in Norfolk, setting forth his request to ship his newly-purchased slaves to Charleston. If that plan failed, he saw no alternative but to take his family and leave for New Orleans. "I will have to stay here a little longer," he wrote to McDonogh, "to make a selection of good healthy people, and save the expense of their detention. I can leave them in the hands of Lancaster, Denley & Co., where they are boarded now. I believe that firm to be honest men. I will leave money enough with them to pay the peoples' board at twenty cents a day. There is, as I wrote earlier, a vessel that will leave here for New Orleans on the Ist. of October, and not before. I have seen a Baltimore paper, wherein an offer of heavy freight is made for New Orleans. If it is taken up, I will write to Baltimore to inquire if they will take my people along with Barba to New Orleans. Please write me if there is any vessel put up in New Orleans for Charleston."

Another ten days went by, during which Durnford bought three more slaves at good prices, but his transportation problems were getting more complicated. And he was worried about Marie-Charlotte. She had, he was convinced, a severe disease of the mind, or was overcome with melancholy, although no one else seemed to see anything unusual in her conduct.

He was now desperate to get out of Virginia, and he wrote to John McDonogh, "I had an expectation of getting the schooner *Susan*, just arrived from New Orleans, to go back, but my hopes have vanished. The Captain refuses to carry people. Going by land is now too risky. The cholera is at Wheeling and all along the rivers of the western country. A few weeks ago a farmer of Alabama started by land, and I have been informed since that one half of the slaves he had just purchased in Virginia were taken sick and he had to stop on the way. Many of my lot are children. They can't walk, and if half a dozen big people should get sick on the way, it would fill up my wagon and prevent my traveling.

"I have written to Morton in Baltimore as I had seen an advertisement offering freight to New Orleans. The brig *Ariel* is at Norfolk from New Orleans now, and Morton expects her to continue on to Baltimore. He writes me that it is probable she might return to New Orleans from there. The construction of his letter makes me believe that the brig will take on part of her cargo in Baltimore and still have room for my people. "I also wrote to Charleston to W. Jones, the consignee of the brig *Warsaw*, but I see by the Charleston paper that the *Warsaw* has already cleared for New Orleans without any response to my request.

"My alternatives are growing slim. The price demanded by the agent of the steam packet from Norfolk to Charleston for the passage of black people is immense. $10 a head for big persons, and $5 for those under ten years. Then there is no certainty of getting a vessel from Charleston to New Orleans when I should arrive there. So I am fearful of being detained and at a heavy expense which would absorb a great deal of money. My only hope is to leave my people in trusty hands to be shipped on the Ist. of October, as I wrote earlier. Now I have been advised not to buy any more and leave them in houses of detention on account of diseases of all sorts. I could have bought today a family of eight for $2,500. The father is a likely black man and the mother a mulatto woman, with six children. But I must decline. If I buy any more, it must be a bargain at the lowest market price, until I know how to transport them."

In despair, Andrew Durnford wrote his last letter from Virginia to John McDonogh on July 6, 1835. He had not received any news or advice from his friend since the deposition. "I write to say that I will leave here tomorrow for Guyandotte on the Ohio River with twenty-eight people of all description. I have agreed with the wagoner to take me there for $75, and a man to go with me for fear some of my people may steal away when passing near their home. I can't stay longer. I wrote to Baltimore to get passage on board of the brig *Harriet* cleared for New Orleans, but the Captain would not agree to take slaves. So of two things one must be done, either to leave the people here at a great expense or to run the risk of transportation on the Ohio and Mississippi. I will do for the best in taking care of my people. If I don't buy any more on the other side of the mountain (for on this side there is no change and prices are too high), I will, if I should stop any length of time in Louisville, buy a few mules for the plantation if any are to be found at reasonable prices."

But Durnford did buy one more slave at Richmond. He had dropped the reigns of his horse over the hitching post at the livery stable and gone to the post office to mail his last letter, and was returning to the livery, when a voice cried out, "You there. Are you not Durnford, the slave buyer from New Orleans?"

The voice came from the direction of the jail, which was set back up a side street near the post office. The jailer came rushing up before Durnford answered. "You are him for sure, ain't you?"

"Well, sir, I am from New Orleans, but I've been traveling mainly for my health. I have a liver ailment, you see—"

"Yes, yes, I know that. But I have a man you should see."

The jailer took Durnford by the arm, and without asking whether Andrew wished to accompany him or not, rushed him off to the jail.

Inside, the jailer pointed to a black man behind the bars of a cage. "This is the man I wanted you to see."

The jailer left him standing there, went outside with his pipe and sat on the steps.

The prisoner gripped the bars with both hands and scowled. He spoke clearly and concisely and with an accent Durnford did not recognize. "Are you Dr. Durnford?"

"Yes I am. Might I ask what ails you?"

Dropping his hands from the bars, the black man stepped back a little and glanced at the floor. Then he looked up. "You are my only hope, Dr. Durnford. I am not a sick man. But my condition, which is not of the physical, is not good. You see me here behind these bars, where I do not belong. I am a citizen of England, but no longer a free man."

These were the people Durnford was careful to avoid, free blacks who had, by one cause or another found themselves again enslaved. They were never a bargain at any price. They were sullen, refused to work, and escaped at the first opportunity.

Durnford said, "I do not see how I can help you."

"Buy my freedom," the black man said. "I am for sale cheaply enough. And I promise you upon my word as an English gentleman that I will work hard to repay you. Only when you are satisfied that I have earned the right, will I ask that you undertake my passage back to England."

His first impulse was to dismiss the man's request out of hand, but Durnford was curious. He shook his head. "How did you come by this..." Durnford shook his head again. "This unfortunate incarceration?"

Sighing and wringing his hands, the black man lowered his head and spoke more to the floor than to Durnford. "It is a sad tale, indeed. I come from near Horncastle on the Witham River, where I have three children on a farm. The land was once part of a much larger estate owned by my father, Sir John Spalding."

"Your father was a white man, then?"

"No, sir. He was not. He was a Negro from the area of Kampala, on what is now know as Lake Victoria. My father was a very rich and traveled man and had done considerable commerce with the English. He eventually moved to that country where he adopted the English name of John Spalding and became quite successful and married into the high social class after being knighted. But that was long ago, you must know. And when he died his estate was divided among his children, I being but one of seven. Had my father not willed otherwise, all would have gone to my older brother. But my father was a democratic man, and disposed to treat his children equally." The black man paused and looked rather dolefully at Andrew Durnford. "I, his miserable son, with the name of Henry Spalding, worked the farm successfully for many years. But when my wife died, I despaired, started drinking much too much, and soon was in debt. Hoping to renew my life, I left the operation of the farm to my brothers, kissed my children goodbye, and set out upon a career in his majesty's mercantile fleet. Life as a British sailor, you may know, is not pleasant. I have been in many ports since, but never back to England. On this voyage we sailed from the south of Spain to the islands of the Caribbean, and from there to Norfolk."

"The man ain't got all day," the jailer shouted from the front steps where he puffed impatiently on his pipe. "Make your point Spalding."

"Yes, sir.... Well, I drank heavily in Norfolk, ended up drunk here in Richmond, did a considerable amount of damage to a dram shop, and have been sold off to pay for it all. That is I am to be sold off. And that is the reason I find myself here in Richmond. But no one bids at the auction house, even though my price is rather cheep, $175."

Durnford scratched his head and backed away from the holding cell. "I assume you can read and write, and are quite fluent in expressing yourself in that manner?"

"True. Yes, that's true."

"Well, my friend, at $175 you are no bargain."

"I can be a good worker. When necessary, alcohol and I part company. And I know my horticulture." He stretched out his arms. "These hands know the meaning of hard labor. Look at the calluses."

Durnford spoke slowly and forcefully, "With your knowledge of writing there is nothing to prevent you from walking off at the first opportunity, obtaining pen and paper, and writing out the forgery necessary to establish yourself as a free man. Even if that were not the case, you do not fit into the scheme of slave labor. You would not be accepted by the field hands anymore than would I. In a matter of days there would be resentment and dissension. I have no need for such disrupting influences at St. Rosalie."

Durnford watched as the prisoner's shoulders sagged under the weight of the bad news. Andrew realized then that he was the man's last hope. "I am sorry for you, but you are the engineer of your own disaster. I assume that time does not permit sending to England for a sum sufficient to purchase your freedom."

Shrugging his sagging shoulders, Henry Spalding half turned away, and said, "There is not that amount of money on the farm. Nor can I impose upon my brothers. My fate is in your hands. I can only swear I will give service worthy of your trust in me."

Without answering, Durnford walked outside into the sunshine and sat on the steps with the jailer. "Why did you involve me in this matter?"

The jailer sucked on his pipe, then spat into the dry dirt on the steps between his shoes. "Durnford who else could I turn to. He is not your ordinary Negro slave. And I have compassion, though you may find that somewhat strange." He paused and looked directly at Andrew. "I've fed that man and listened to his story for over two months, now. You want to send him off to field labor? He'll run for sure. When they catch him, he'll be flogged and flogged again. In the end, he'll kill someone or maybe even himself. That what you want?" When Andrew Durnford did not answer, the jailer took from his pocket a printed bill, smoothed out the wrinkles, and laid it on the steps. "You will have good title to the man," he said. "He was advertised according to the law. No one claimed him. He was put up to the highest bidder at public sale and no one bid. If you take the man, the Sheriff will give you a bill of sale that gives title in law against any and all claimants."

Durnford rubbed his face for a moment, then picked up the printed hand bill and read it:

**TAKEN UP AND COMMITTED to the Jail at Richmond, Virginia, on the 14th day of May, 1835, a Negro Man by the name of Henry. Said Negro is about 35 or 40 years old, light complexion, 5 feet 9 inches high, slim built, good teeth; says he is trained in farming. He was taken up to be sold for payment of damages by reason of his negligence and/or insult upon the property of one Jason Artemus Webster in the City of Richmond, and committed as a runaway. His owner is notified to come forward, prove property, pay charges and damages, and take him away, or he will be dealt with as the law directs.**

Edmond D. King, Sheriff

Below the printed notice was a hand-written affidavit of publication in the Richmond *Inquirer* for the time prescribed by Virginia statute, duly signed by the editor of that paper, sworn to before a notary public, with the signature and seal of the notary.

Folding the printed bill in his hands, Durnford said to the jailer, "But the man has no owner. He is a free man, a seaman from England. There is no one who can come forward to claim him."

"I suppose a lot of them say things like that. And if we believed every story the runaways told, there wouldn't be a slave left in Virginia. Anyway, you can have the man for $175. If you leave him here, Durnford, you are leaving him to die. I was hopin' you wouldn't do that to one of your own people."

"You heard his manner of speech. He is obviously an educated gentleman. Certainly you must believe his story."

Dr. Durnford, I work for the law here in Richmond. The law says the man inside my jail is a runaway slave. He is for sale to the first man that wants him for $175. He has been for sale for that meager sum for two months now, with no takers. I think we both know why no one buys. But sooner or later someone will take him. And that's the way things are. So I'm telling you no, I don't believe his story. If you believe him, you'd better take him, Durnford. You're the only hope he has."

The streets of Richmond were filled with immense wagons, drawn by six mules each, and among those huge wagons were men on horseback, a few carriages, and other wagons of all sizes and descriptions pulled by horses or mules.    Andrew Durnford walked along the main street, dodging those horses and wagons, with his latest purchase at his side, Henry Spalding of Horncastle, England, who was now his property.

# Chapter Ten

Eleven days after leaving Richmond, the Durnford caravan plodded on along the banks of the James River, having followed that water course all the way to the Blue Ridge mountains. They were tired and hungry. They had climbed steadily, following the river valley as it cut through the mountains, until they were on a plateau at an elevation of 4,000 feet. Leading the procession were Andrew Durnford, his body servant, Barba, and Henry Spalding of Horncastle, England. The wagon followed behind them. It was filled with supplies, small children, and the sick, including Marie-Charlotte.

Behind the wagon stumbled the slaves, wearing hard, clumsy shoes and coarse cotton garments. A few were bareheaded, but most wore a scarf wrapped around their head or an old slouch hat, male or female. Each one carried their entire earthly belongs over their shoulder, slung in a thin blanket. Bringing up the rear, with a loaded gun, was the hired man of the wagoner.

The children in the wagon bounced along on a cushion of hay, which got thinner as the grazing for the horses grew sparse.

Andrew Durnford walked with two stout sticks, setting the pace. His feet were blistered and raw. His leggings were dirty and torn. The trail they followed had never been steep. It was carved into the earth by wheels and animals that had gone before them. At times it ran close to the water. At other times it wandered higher up the bank among huge rock slabs that lay flat on the ground. The pine trees of the lower regions had been left behind, and now they wove their way among the sparse hardwoods, oak, maple, poplar, walnut, hickory, and the occasional birch.

It was late in the day. Dark clouds rolled over the blue mist shrouding the distant hills. After studying the black clouds advancing upon them, Durnford called a halt. Then he led the wagon off the trail, through a patch of thornless blackberry, and stopped in a clearing, where the wagoner unhitched the team and left the horses to graze on long ropes.

"Tonight will be a wet one," Durnford muttered to Barba and the Englishman. "Get some of those saplings from up there and start a lean-to."

The other slaves gathered firewood, shaved off splinters with an axe, and started a fire with an oil-soaked brand which they ignited with a flint. Except for short-lived cooking fires, it was the first time they had a night fire since leaving Richmond. The air had been much too warm. And nights were spent lying in the open, swatting at mosquitoes. They had left the warmer air and most of the mosquitoes behind, now. This night promised cold wind and rain.

Henry Spalding, the black man from Horncastle, provided them with meat. In the early morning and late evenings, he loaded Durnford's hunting gun with shot and demonstrated his expertise in bringing down raccoons, wild turkeys, a white-tailed deer now and then, and the daily wild pig, which rooted everywhere. The meat was either hung from the wagon to dry or roasted over a fire, and supplemented by cornmeal bread and bacon slabs, fried together in large pans.

The wagon was covered with a white canvas, and on this first cool night, it became the sole dominion of the Durnford family. Barba and Spalding, sensing the coming rain, crawled under the wagon, with the wagoner and as many of the slave families as could wedge themselves in. The remaining Negroes opened their bundles, wrapped themselves in their thin blankets, and slid into the lean-to, where they stretched their legs to the fire.

Thomas and Rosella lay near the back of the wagon. They usually counted shooting stars until they fell asleep. There were no stars that night, just black, ominous, roiling clouds with a full moon peeking through now and then.

Andrew and Marie-Charlotte moved farther up in the wagon, with Andrew's back to the barrels and boxes of supplies. There he spread a wool blanket over the hay to make a comfortable mattress. Slipping an arm under her thin shoulders, Andrew pulled Marie-Charlotte tightly to him. "Miss Remy," he whispered in an almost teasing manner, "are you not happy?"

There was no answer. Marie-Charlotte stared, eyes wide open, at the canvas ceiling.

"Things go well for us now, Miss Remy. We manage almost twenty miles each day." It was, he had been told, impossible to cover more than fifteen miles from dawn to dusk. But he had been pushing hard. They had to do twenty every day to make the Ohio by the first of August. It would take them a good month on the big rivers, if they were lucky, and he wanted to be at St. Rosalie by September. Planting was long finished before they left. Nothing much left to do on the plantation but hoe and gather firewood, and tend to the animals and the vegetable gardens. In late November, December with luck, the hard work started. It was important to leave the cane in the field as long as possible. Otherwise, the sugar yield could be pitiful. But if the frost came before the cane was cut, the sugar could be ruined. It was a guessing game. After a while, when Andrew could wait no longer, the decision would be made. Delay no more. That's when they worked around the clock, grinding and boiling the cane into sugar and molasses.

The last information Andrew had received was the letter mailed by McDonogh in May, and it was now a long time to be out of communication with the plantation. "I can see us now coming down the river," he said to her softly. "We'll come around the bend and there it will be. St. Rosalie, gleaming white in the sunshine. Hammocks hanging on the gallery. Green shades hung in front of them to keep out the sun. Mama will come running with Noel, and all of our people will come out of the fields to meet us when they hear the whistle."

He watched her face for a long, silent time. She was thinner now, thinner even than when they'd left Richmond. Hardly ate a thing. And when did she sleep? He always fell asleep watching her open eyes staring at the sky. And when he awoke in the morning, she was always gone, getting breakfast for the children and him.

Marie-Charlotte seemed to be perfectly normal during the day. But night was another story. He could not recall her having said a single word to him in bed since his first expedition at Richmond. "Miss Remy, you must talk to me," he whispered again. But she did not answer.

The first heavy wind came as a surprise. He had known it was going to storm, knew there would be hard wind and awful rain. But his thoughts were with Marie-Charlotte and what to do for her, when the storm struck. The wagon rocked. The canvass flapped and shuddered and the wind shrieked around them. Hail, heavy and flung upon the wind, came next. It sounded like marbles falling down a staircase as it struck the wooden wagon sides.

Thomas pulled the rear flap tight against the rain which followed.

Andrew climbed around the boxes and barrels at the front of the wagon and eased out onto the drivers board in the howling wind and stinging, cold rain. The fire in front of the lean-to hissed and steamed and was out in a minute. Then it was black and dense, and nothing could be seen, not even the ground below the wagon.

Having slept with his clothes on, as did the others, Durnford felt for a hold on the wagon wheel, and slid to the ground. His coat was wet instantly and whipped around him. He stood there for a moment, already shivering, when a yellow light poked out from under the wagon. Barba had managed to start a storm lantern, and he shoved it before him as he pushed out from under the wagon. The ground was flooding rapidly.

"Damnation," Barba said. "What fools we is, Massa Andrew. Deh's a riber runnin' under dat wagon."

The wagoner stuck his head out from under the wagon into the circle of yellow light cast by the lantern. His haggard face squinted into the slanting rain. The wagoner's hired man crawled out beside him and then they both stood up. "Reckon the onliest dry spot be in the wagon," the hired man said, peering at Durnford though narrow slits of eyes. His hair was thin and black, and showed as dark, wet streaks on his shiny, wet skull.

"There isn't room for all of us in the wagon," Durnford said, "so we must do the right thing, and stay out. If some of the smaller children get cold, I will let their mothers take them into the wagon."

Durnford looked around at the stormy scene. The rain poured in a steady stream and the men were soaked through. "Barba, take the lantern to the lean-to and these men can go in there."

"Huh!" the hired man said. "You wants me to sleep with them. No sir, thank you."

Nevertheless, the hired man followed the light to the lean-to, as did Durnford, Barba, and the wagoner. All in the shelter were awake and sitting up. Babes in arms were crying, barely to be heard above the storm.

The men squeezed in, drawing their legs up under them, and had no sooner settled when the wind picked the canvas from over their heads and sent it flying. Everyone scrambled. Durnford chased after the fleeing canvas and soon lost it in the dark. He returned to the huddled group just as the lantern sputtered out. It was a long, miserable, cold and wet night. All of the children packed into the wagon, and the adults who couldn't find room in the water underneath it, stood sentinel with Durnford. The rain never stopped. It continued into the day, even after they broke camp, found the missing canvas from the lean-to, and started the wagon on its journey toward the Ohio.

Trudging on at the head of the column, the wagon following, Durnford looked over his shoulder. The slaves tramped on, holding the canvas, now torn almost into two pieces, over their heads for protection against the cascading water. Durnford was wet. He was no longer cold, as the morning rain was much warmer and the effort at moving through the slippery mud heated him. Soon, he had Barba and the Englishmen ahead scouting the trail. They stayed off the worn road as much as possible to avoid the mud. And for most of the day, in a steady downpour, they led the wagon along next to the trail, at times on one side and at times on the other, sometimes way far off the trail, so that Durnford questioned those men, and was always reassured that their grassy detour would return to the correct path.

It rained into the second night. They put up the lean-to again, on the side of a hill. And this time it held. All were wet. And as the chill set in, the slaves, Durnford's people, started to cough and sputter.

When it had actually stopped raining, Durnford did not know. He had fallen asleep at the edge of the lean-to with his head between his knees. The warm sun brought him to consciousness.

He moved around. Took stock. Looked at tongues and throats, and learned the worst. Half his people were sick. Some had fever. And they were a long way from the Ohio River.

"Best way to dry your clothes is to walk in them," Durnford told his slaves. It was what he was going to do, and he wished Barba had never suggested building another fire, as the women were in favor of drying out that way and now moaned and groaned and wailed as they wrapped up their wet belongs and slung them over their backs.

Durnford made another inspection and selected those to ride in the wagon. Those with chills and high fevers. All of the children, too, except Thomas and Rosella, they were big enough to walk when required, and they were dry. Marie-Charlotte joined him at the head of the parade without Durnford asking. And so they set out again, still farther behind schedule.

They went on that way for several days and left the river behind them. They struggled up steeper slopes, always following the trail. And most of the sick ones got better, and some of those who hadn't been at all sick came down with the fever. Wainy, the little girl who had been his first purchase, was near death.

They crossed the Great Valley and followed the cut through the Appalachian Mountains, living off the land and staples from the wagon.

One night they slept in the barn of a large farm. They slept among the packed

animals, and the heat from the cows revived them.    Andrew Durnford had
replenished his medical bag at Richmond.   He now poured down the throats of the
suffering syrupy medicines and plenty of hot molasses.   Wainy and her mother,
Phyllis, rode in the wagon with little Frank, who, unlike Wainy, slowly recovered
from his fever.   Marie-Charlotte helped Andrew with the sick, and walked with him
as they traveled.   She walked beside him in a trance.   And Andrew Durnford could
do nothing to bring her out of her depression.

On the other side of the Appalachians, where they had stopped in the afternoon to
rest and eat, it was warm and comfortable again.   Durnford ate little.   He was
falling rapidly behind his schedule and his spirits were in despair.   Wainy was
loosing ground.   She would die for sure, he knew.   Maybe Marie-Charlotte as well.
His wife was suffering from loss of weight and loss of heart.   She was now a
skeleton, quiet, answering to only the basic questions of existence, and taking very
little nourishment.

After the afternoon pause, they again walked on into the night, with only a pale
moon to guide them, and finally stopped when they were too exhausted to take
another step.

Durnford left the fire where Henry Spalding roasted rabbits on a spit.   He walked
aimlessly along the moonlit trail they would resume in the morning.   Then he
climbed a low hill to a small grove of hardwoods at the top.   There he rested
against a boulder and peered down into a valley which lay before him.   In the valley
was a small village.   And in the village was a church with a steeple which shown
bright white in the moonlight.   Durnford walked around the boulder and sat in the
grass, looking down at the church steeple.

The pressure in his head that had troubled him for so many years now built into
an unbearable pain.   Through the pain, he saw a strange, white light in the black
sky. The light took on the shape of a funnel. The top of the funnel was in the stars,
and the bright light narrowed as it went down to meet the church steeple.   The
familiar smell of musk swept over him as he marveled at the brilliant light, which
broke into streamers in the funnel.   And at once he realized the fragrance which
had always come to him with the throbbing pressure was the smell of incense
burned at the mass for the dead in St. Louis cathedral.   It was the incense of his
father's funeral, and of his mother's many relatives.   It would be the incense
burned at his funeral some day. He stood and swayed unsteadily on his feet.   He
closed his eyes and began his prayer. "Our father who art in Heaven..." He prayed
three "Our Father's" and then he made the sign of the cross and prayed in his own

words.  First he prayed for Marie-Charlotte.  He had never really prayed much before, and the words were halting and difficult.  Then he prayed for Wainy, and for all his people.  While he was praying the pounding in his head retreated, as did the uncomfortable fragrance of incense.  And when he finished with his prayers, he knew he must resist the temptation of St. Rosalie.  He should never have come to Virginia.  Slavery was the evil it was named by the North, and it was not for him.  God called for him, Andrew Durnford, a black man, to set his people free.

"There is a village on the trail ahead of us," he said in high spirits to the gathering around the fire when he returned.  "We will rest there tomorrow, providing we find accommodations."

He took Marie-Charlotte and walked with her through the moonlit grass.  "Miss Remy, I have seen the most wonderful apparition.  It was a message from God."

She looked at him uncertainly.  "Andrew, we are all worn and exhausted."

"Oh, it was so beautiful, Miss Remy.  And so bright."  He explained to her the vision and the beautiful church with its white steeple.

She put her hands on her hips and stepped back.  "You saw a church, and a village...?"  She thought Andrew had been talking about a village that was still miles ahead.

Andrew took her hand again and rushed up the slope to the boulder.  "Down there, you can see it through the trees."

Marie-Charlotte squinted into the dark empty valley.  She saw no village, and she saw no church and no white steeple.

They returned to the campfire and Marie-Charlotte, who now seemed to call upon some mysterious reserve of strength, addressed the group lounging about on the grass.  "Well," she said with a short, nervous laugh.  "I'm afraid there is no village.  At first I thought I saw it too...the way the moon strikes the rocks down there, and the shadows...it looked something like a village."

She was lying, Andrew knew.  Lying about the rocks looking like a village.  There was, he realized, nothing at all that looked like a village.  And when he glanced into the eyes of his people, Barba, the slaves, the wagon master and his helper, he thought they knew she was lying too.

Marie-Charlotte took one of the metal plates stacked at the edge of the fire and cut herself a generous portion of rabbit.  She piled on a good helping of corn meal.  Then going to Andrew where he rested under a small tree, she sat down beside him.  "I know I have neglected you, Andrew.  I haven't been well...but I'm better now."  She fed him corn meal with a wooden spoon, and ate from it herself.  Then they shared the rabbit, eating it with their hands.   Andrew had carried them forward, all on his own, she thought to herself.   She must be a comfort to him now.

This small attention was a tonic to Andrew.   He felt renewed strength, and a calmness came over him.   He had not been calm in a long time.   There was, he said to himself, a need for communication with his wife.   Miss Remy was a part of his life he had never bothered to think about before.   And to have her keep herself away from him was like being cut off from part of his own existence.

Then Andrew wondered about the village he had seen.   It was as real as anything he had ever witnessed.   Perhaps they would see it yet on the road in the morning. Perhaps there was something about the night air that made it appear and disappear.

Two days later, they were following the trail along the Guyandotte River, where it had carved out a deep valley in the plateau which slopped steadily toward the Ohio. They passed now and then settlements of lonely cabins set back up the hill from the trail.   Toward evening they came upon a large farm, with fields enclosed by rail fences, well-constructed out buildings and a red barn with a large door, painted white.   The farmhouse was sided in clapboards of fine style, and painted bright white. The shutters were black.   Glass panes were in the windows.   It reminded Andrew of paintings he had seen of New England country estates.

*"Gruss Gott!"*   Those words came from a tall man, dressed all in black and wearing a black hat.   He was leaning against the gate as Andrew came up to it.   "I heered yer horse nicker a way off," the man said, "while you was around the bend. And you are an interesting sight.   A colored man, leading a rag-tag bunch."

"We are travelling this road to the Ohio," Durnford said, "and we would be obliged to stay the night.   Could we take shelter in your barn, sir?"

"Would not turn you away, friend, no matter who you were."   The man dressed all in black opened the gate.   "You may have the barn for the night."

He walked with Durnford as the column proceeded up a small hill to the large barn.   He had several hundred acres of land in cultivation, the man told Andrew. And cattle and milk cows.   His was a large family and all worked hard.

Inside the barn, Durnford thanked the man for his kindness, opened his map and asked where they were.   The man pointed to a spot in the valley.   "Five days from the Ohio," the man said, "And long ones, too."

There was room in the loft for all of his people, the man told Durnford.   And then taking Andrew by the arm, he walked him to the door and pointed to a cabin behind the white house.   "You are welcome to the use of our kitchen as well."

"We are thirty people and my family of four," Durnford said.   "At one cent each

I can pay you thirty-four cents for the night. Would that be satisfactory?"

The tall man rubbed his chin and smiled. "I don't see that it would cost me anything." He shook his head. "Payment is not expected, friend."

"But we will use your kitchen, your wood, sir?"

"No. I expect you will cut your own wood." He smiled briefly, then asked, "Where are you to, friend?"

"We shall go on the Ohio, then down on the Mississippi to past New Orleans, where I have a sugar planting."

"Well, workers never went well with us. I hired a fellow once, wanted help with some corn. The man was a wanderer. Wanted $6.00 a month, all in advance for six months. I paid it to him, $36.00. Gave it to him in silver. Said he wouldn't work unless I paid it to him right then. Was a man of God, though, as we are. He worked well enough for about a month. Then he just left, and I ain't seen a sight of 'em since. Said he was sick. Didn't look sick."

Now Durnford smiled. Had that hired man been a slave, the farmer could have brought him back with hounds. "And so you have no idea where he is?"

"Yes. Yes. He's around here abouts. Lot's of folks told me they seen 'em. He got well mighty easy after he left this farm. Reckon I'll never see my money." The farmer looked around at the slaves huddled in the barn. "You come all this way for workers?"

"Yes, to Virginia here. Came with a load of sugar and molasses from my plantation. Sold it in Philadelphia."

"Then your workers here must be slaves, I think?"

"Oh, yes. All slaves. Taking them down the rivers now." Durnford felt uneasy. They were still in Virginia, a slave state. "Thought I might buy some more on this side of the mountain, if I could find me a bargain or two."

"Well, sir, we are mostly Germans here. Very few people own slaves on this side of the mountain. None of us Germans do. We know slavery is wrong, and God will bring it to an end. When that time comes, friend, there will be woe in the land. You must prepare for it. Make it as light as possible. Do nothing to make it worse."

"Perhaps a hundred years from mow," Durnford said, "it will come to an end. That is what I believe. For now, though, I can see nothing better for these people." He swept a hand toward his flock. "They could not take care of themselves."

"And you are of the same color," the farmer said with a pleasant smile. "It is interesting to hear you talk so. Ah, self-interest warps men's minds wonderfully, don't you know."

The farmer spoke in such a direct, friendly and non-accusatory manner that Durnford was not offended. He responded to educate, rather than argue. "I do not believe my people could live free. They need a strong hand to obtain from them systematic labor. A strong hand, but a fair hand to guide them along life's path. A firm hand to restrain them from a senseless waste of life and property." The farmer listened politely, and Durnford warmed to his task. The man had no experience with the system and needed enlightening. "I know hosts of Negroes who possess extraordinary talent. A good many of them can read and write, something few white men in Louisiana can boast of. I talk about free people of color. They were born to it. But the slave, the slave is another matter. Perhaps some day they can be freed. But I see it a long way off. Then there must be some system of training them...Lord knows I don't have the time now. The plantation is a heavy burden. I have over fifty people working the land. And a happier, more contented lot you've never seen." Andrew Durnford turned to address his slaves as well as the farmer. "My people are not driven hard. We stop three times a day for meals. Plenty to eat. Best food. Good clothes. Some of them are learning to read and write. Saturday work stops at noon. Sundays off too...except in the grinding season. I work with them, right alongside them. Then when the sugar's done, when we are done rolling, we have a party. Let the good times roll. Nothing to be ashamed of, quite a simple party."

The farmer shrugged his shoulders and attempted another smile. "Well, we do not judge. We are Mennonites around here. Come down from Pennsylvania country. They call us 'Dutch.' Don't understand, don't you know, that we are 'Deutch,' all related in one way or another, come first from Germany a hundred years ago."

The farmer left Durnford and his people to make themselves comfortable in the barn. And when they had done so, and gone to the kitchen, which was the little cabin behind the house, the Mennonite family, husband, wife, four sons and two daughters, came out and mingled and talked with them, Durnford, Marie-Charlotte, the children and the slaves.

At first Marie-Charlotte found it difficult to speak to the family. They were Germans, and that thought brought back painful memories. She could not, would not, she decided, bear hostile feelings against an entire people for the acts of one depraved man. And once she had made that determination, her mind relaxed. It was only a small chink in the masonry shield she had thrown around herself after the horrible experience. But it was a beginning. And where there is a beginning there can be hope, she said to herself.

Henry Spalding traded freshly killed rabbits and venison for chicken pot pie, schnitz and knepp, fassnachts (raised doughnuts), and shoofly pie. The farm family said a prayer in a strange language Durnford did not recognize as German. They spoke a dialect as different from German as English, the Mennonite father explained to Durnford. Then the Mennonite family joined them in their meal. Little by little, the Durnfords, Barba, the black Englishman, even the slaves, forgot their sore and blistered feet, their hurting backs and swollen joints. They sat and ate in the tall grass behind the white house under the light of lanterns hung from tree branches. It was a feast.

A little later Durnford and his people went to the barn, all in good spirits. They had eaten well. They had listened to the German farm family explain their religion: simple lives they led, stressing the direct influence of the Holy Spirit upon the believer's heart. And the slaves told of their beliefs, Baptists all.

When the last lantern had been turned down, some woman off in a dark corner started a low and mournful hymn, and was joined by others. Andrew Durnford lay with Marie-Charlotte by his side in the loft, the children somewhere beyond their feet in the hay. He listened to the mellow voices. A second spiritual followed. Then another, always sung lowly, almost sadly, and the words were indistinct. Being a Catholic, Durnford knew none of the religious songs. And hearing them for the first time, he was not yet certain whether he approved. Apparently the Mennonites believed in such songs less than the Catholics, Durnford said to himself. But for the slaves, maybe this was best.

Then he sat up with a start. He had forgotten to take a count. Had one of his charges slipped off, struggling through the night to return to friends and family, only to get lost and die in the wilderness. "Are you all here!"

"Yes, Massa, we's all heah." The voice came softly from the dark.

"Do yersef no harm, cause we's all heah." This from a second voice far away, followed by a snicker and chuckles around the loft.

# Chapter Eleven

The *Martha* was neither a large nor a small steamboat. Her twin steam engines and coal fuel were packed well toward the front of the lower deck, leaving room behind for cargo and deck passengers.

Just aft of the side wheels was a midships gangway. Those stairs led up to the first deck. It was divided by a narrow passageway, onto which small cabins opened.

The saloon was at the rounded stern. It contained a long skylight, and was decorated with red satin draperies, gilt-edged mirrors, walnut paneling and thickly padded carpeting. It was in this saloon that the passengers ate their meals. The evening meal on the steamboat was a serious affair. The extended dinner took up more than three hours.

The Captain's table was next to the stern windows. There, the first class passengers chatted with the Captain, the first mate, and the off-duty pilot, while they watched the dark shore drift by.

The white families dined at tables under the skylight. Andrew Durnford and his family were assigned a table in the corner.

The waiter announced that fricassee pork and breast of chicken in Madeira sauce were offered that evening. Before the trip was over, he promised, they would have an opportunity to sample calf feet in mush-room sauce, calf feet in Madeira sauce, bear sausages, hurricane tripe, stewed mutton, beef's heart fricasseed, beef kidney in pickle sauce, and calf head in wine sauce. And they could also choose from roasted entrees of veal, pig, Muscovy ducks, mutton, barbecued shoat, and bear meat. There would be boiled entrees of ham, corned beef, bacon and turnips, codfish egg sauce, leg of mutton in caper sauce, barbecued rabbits, and boiled tongue.

The vegetables that first night were boiled cabbage, cold slaugh, hot slaugh, and pickled beets. Before the steamboat reached New Orleans, the waiter promised, the passengers could savor much more: creole hominy, crout cabbage, oyster plant fried, parsnips gravied, stewed parsnips, sweet potatoes spiced and sweet potatoes baked, Irish potatoes creamed and mashed and Irish potatoes browned, boiled shallots, scalloped carrots, boiled turnips in drawn butter, and white beans.

For dessert the passengers could choose from rice pudding, Irish pudding, and pound cake. The thin waiter looked down his nose. Before the final docking there would again be more: currant pies, coconut pie, sliced potato pie, cheese cake, orange custard, green peach puff paste, huckleberry pie, rhubarb tarts, plum tarts, calves feet jelly and orange jelly.

But there was just one soup to be had on the entire voyage, oyster. "Why?" a well-dressed businessman asked loudly. The waiter responded, "Because that is what we serve!"

And saying that, the waiter disappeared into the starboard kitchen, built into the aft housing of the paddle wheel. On the other side of the boat, built into the housing of the port paddle wheel, was the kitchen that served the Captain's table. While Marie-Charlotte selected a menu for the entire family, a ritual in which the children had no say, and which Andrew never contested, Andrew watched and noted that the fare served those at the Captain's table did indeed include many of the tempting items his waiter had promised before the end of the river trip.

Cantilevered out over the water, and built into the forward housing of the paddle wheels on each side, one for men and one for women, were the "washrooms." It was important that the children "visit" the washrooms before retiring for bed, because Marie-Charlotte could not speak for their safety if they endeavored to do so during the night. And so it was that the children were chaperoned into the washrooms after dinner that evening, and then forward to the cabin.

The cheaper staterooms, one of which Andrew Durnford and his family occupied, were forward of the paddle wheels, just behind the smokestacks, and over the noisy engines. The cabin floor was hardwood, tobacco-stained and scarred. The ceiling was plain tongue and groove. The walls were covered with rough-hewn lumber.

The crew's quarters were on the next deck. Above the crews quarters was the pilothouse, with windows all around. The open deck behind the crew's quarters was covered by canvas stretched over wooden bows supported by wooden posts.

This open area was for upper deck passengers. At night, the occupants of the upper deck slung hammocks from posts, or made beds from their knapsacks and blankets and slept on the flooring. They were not provided with meals. They cooked what they carried with them on an open fire, and looked with envy down through the skylight at the more fortunate passengers in the luxurious main saloon.

Durnford paid $72.00 for cabin passage, including meals for himself, his wife, and their two children. He paid another $55.00 for transportation of his twenty-eight slaves, Barba, and the Englishman, Henry Spaulding. The fare for the slaves was reduced by $5.00 in return for loading and stacking of firewood during the passage. The slaves did not receive meals, cabins, or beds. Durnford purchased a camp stove for their use below on the boiler deck, and thought he had provided for them generously.

He sat at a desk which also served as a washstand under an open window. In the light from a small oil lamp hung on the wall, he wrote down the provisions he had purchased for the slaves:

| | |
|---|---|
| 1 barrel biscuits, 2 barrel potatoes | $1.20 |
| 1 keg lard, 4 boxes codfish, 1 barrel mackerel | $1.75 |
| 1 barrel flour & 1 box of apples | $.75 |
| 6 half-barrel rice, 1 barrel pork jowls, 1 turkey, | |
| 1 doz. chickens, 1 box soap, half bag onions | $3.10 |

He leaned back on his stool and ran a hand through his heavy locks. This business was expensive, indeed. But he had the best people from around Richmond. He smiled. Good people. He had chosen wisely. Then he bent forward, dipped his pen in ink, and continued with his travel journal. He would transcribe all of these entries into the plantation journal when he got to St. Rosalie. Nevertheless, he made his entries carefully with a beautiful, sweeping penmanship. He mumbled to himself as he wrote. "Three pair brogans at $1.00 each, 1 large frying pan, $.75...."

Andrew's desk was built into the outside wall of the cabin. To his left were bunk beds for he and Marie-Charlotte. To his right were the smaller bunk beds for the children. The door to the cabin was at his back.

Marie-Charlotte wedged herself into a lower bunk with Harper's *Gazetteer of the World* balanced on her knees. Light came from the moon shining through the open window and the lamp swinging over Andrew's desk. Marie-Charlotte traced the route to New Orleans from Guyandotte on the Ohio, where they had boarded that morning. Already they'd steamed a hundred miles. The current added to the boat's speed, and even though they stopped at many landings, or whenever someone on shore waved a white flag on a stick, they made better progress than could be dreamed on foot.

The children slept soundly in narrow bunk beds against the opposite bulkhead.

The scratching of Andrew's pen was barely audible over the thump and hissing noises from the engine room below and the rhythmic pounding and splashing of the paddle wheel. The songs of birds settling in for the night came in through the open window.

The cabin floor was warm from the hot boilers, and even though Andrew had left the door open for cross ventilation, the air was heavy with the smell of lamp oil and the aroma of chewing tobacco soaked into the wood floor.

Someone was snoring loudly on the other side of the bulkhead next to Marie-Charlotte's bunk. In the cabin across the hall, she saw six men gathered in a circle on the floor. They drank from the same whiskey bottle and rolled dice.

"Andrew, we'll be home to St. Rosalie in a little more than days."

Durnford turned around on his stool. Resting one elbow on his travel journal, he smiled at her. Ten days, even twenty days, would be a blessing. Less chance of one of his people getting sick. Less provisions consumed by his idle work force. But he knew the trip would be longer.

"The Captain says we can make Louisville in three or four days, but it will take another twenty days from Louisville to New Orleans."

"Why Andrew, it's less than a thousand miles down the rivers to New Orleans from Louisville." She closed the *Gazetteer* and swung her feet to the floor. "And you said we're traveling more than ten miles to the hour. You're such a pessimist, dear." She rose and went to him, placed her hands on his shoulders and started a soft massage. "You worry and fret so, Andrew. And nothing comes of it."

"Perhaps so, Miss Remy. But the moon won't last. The Captain told me we can't run on dark nights. Too many snags, especially in the Mississippi."

Marie-Charlotte had been in a state of high excitement since they boarded the boat. The long, dreary march over the mountains to the Ohio was over. They were going home by steamboat. Traveling in comfort. Andrew, always the cautious one, always the last one to relax and enjoy himself, could not dampen her spirits. "Then I will suggest to the Captain that we light torches. And we can steam right through the night."

"Miss Remy I already made that request, even offered to pay the cost of the torches. Then the Captain told me there were two things I did not understand. I did not understand what a snag was. Nor did I understand what a Captain was."

"And did the Captain enlighten you, Andrew?"

"He did, Miss Remy. A snag is a tree. They fall from the banks or are washed into the rivers by floods. They break off. And they end up with their heavy roots deep in mud. The broken end angles up like a lance just below the surface. A good pilot will spot them by eddies in the current. When an unfortunate boat comes upon a snag, it pierces the hull, then rips out the entire bottom."

Andrew pulled her onto his lap. "The Captain has no say when it comes to navigation. He owns the boat with partners and manages the business of the steamboat. He has nothing to do with getting it down the river. That is the job of the pilot, the man in the wheelhouse. The pilot will not run at night, torches or not, it would be foolhardy."

She leaned forward and kissed Andrew on the forehead. "You frown so, Andrew. Can it make much difference whether we are home in ten days or thirty days?"

"That is a question I can not answer. We are out of communication with the plantation. Perhaps by the time we get home our land will belong to my English cousins." He sighed. "The thought of losing St. Rosalie is a constant dagger at my heart." And it was true, he had not been at peace since the deposition. Now on the steamboat there was another source of irritation. Hollingsworth, the New Bedford Methodist minister was on board. Durnford spotted him at a corner of the Captain's table near the stern windows at dinner that evening. The man did not seem to recognize me, Andrew thought, or perhaps he chose to ignore me. What uncomfortable remarks could be forthcoming when the abolitionist realizes I have a cargo for St. Rosalie of which he approves not one whit.

Below on the boiler deck, the twenty-eight slaves purchased by Andrew Durnford in Virginia were spread among the cargo. Some wedged themselves in between wooden crates and slept on the hard floor, using their bundles of meager "belongs" as a pillow. Others slept on bales of cloth and packages of dry goods bound for river ports on the Mississippi. Still others slept sitting up, their backs against huge coils of rope and cordage. Those who could not find places in the cargo, sprawled along the outside decks, legs and arms dangerously close to the edge, where the flat deck ended over the water without benefit of a guardrail.

At the very stern, Barba sat on the deck facing down the river, with his back against barrels of grain destined for New Orleans. Sitting on the deck next to him was the Englishman, Henry Spaulding.

Holingsworth sat on a cask of nails, and spoke to Spaulding. "I saw you below me as I gazed upon the river from the saloon. And I heard you speak. Such a refined voice. A black man. I could not place the accent. My curiosity compelled me to seek you out, sir. And now I am most distressed to learn that you, a citizen of England, are slave to Durnford, as are the other unfortunate souls here." Hollingsworth waved a hand to indicate the boiler deck. "And you...ah...."

"Barba."

"Yes, Barba, I remember you from the ocean voyage to Philadelphia. You are the overseer?"

"No, suh. I are the personal servant ob Massa Andrew."

"But he has placed great trust in you, Barba. Are you not in charge of your brethren down here?"

"I are, suh. Fo de trib home."

"It is a sign from God, you understand, that I find myself here. No, it is not a coincidence that I traveled with your Andrew Durnford on the ship from New Orleans to Philadelphia. And now, on my way to St. Louis, I come upon him again with the fruits of his endeavors in Virginia. Certainly it is a sign to be recognized."

Up forward a Negro slave started to sing. His voice was strong and rose above the splashing, slapping sound of the paddle wheels and the thumping and hissing of the steam engines. Soon he was joined by a few women. Then other slaves awoke and joined in. They sang softly but strongly, and with deep emotion:

> "We raise de wheat,
> Dey gib us de corn;
> We bake de bread,
> Dey gib us de cruss;
> We sif de meal,
> Dey gib us de huss;"

Hollingsworth spoke a little louder, "Yes it is a sign from God. We are engaged in a grand movement, and I speak most directly to you Mr. Spaulding. To stand by while men enslave others cannot be justified for any purpose, moral or political. And those who stand aloof from it, even though they oppose it, and do nothing to end it, are equally at fault. The abolition movement is a glorious and holy one. Being much involved in that movement, and being directed by the Lord in all my endeavors, I am compelled to say to you, Mr. Spalding, that time is upon you--you must act now." Hollingsworth paused to listen to the mellow voices of the slaves:

"We peal de meat,
Dey gib us de skin,
And dat's de way
Dey takes us in.
We skim de pot,
Dey gib us de liquor,
And say dat's good enough for nigger.
　　Walk over!  walk over!
　　Tom butter and de fat;
　　Poor nigger you can't get over dat;
　　　Walk over!"

Now Henry Spaulding spoke. "Mr. Hollingsworth, I am not certain I understand you, or perhaps I prefer not to understand you. I am a slave, that is true. And Andrew Durnford is my master. But he will not be my master forever. I will again be free. In the meantime, I have given him my word. And I am a man of honor, above all else."

"But your contract is not of an honorable nature, Mr. Spalding. Certainly God does not recognize it. There is no higher authority."

"You suggest I do what?"

"Take these people North. That is what God has brought me here to talk to you about. It is no coincidence that I am here, as I said. It is no coincidence that you also are here."

"And fo me, Reverend? What God goin' say fo dis here brack man? Dat I goes up de North. Dat I lives in yo house. Dat I maybe goes to yo church da. Kneels wid yo white peoples at de alter?"

"Barba, you need not insult a messenger of the Lord." And deliberately turning a shoulder to Barba, Hollingsworth spoke to Spalding. "I believe you have been selected to lead your people. Just as Moses led the Israelites from Egypt."

"I am committed to Durnford for at least a year. I wish him no harm."

"Harm? It is not to harm him that you and I are here, Mr. Spalding. You are an educated man are you not?"

"Ah, but a wasted education it was. After Oxford, I rose to the noble cause of farming."

"What I mean is that you read and write?"

"In English, as well as Greek and Latin, my good sir. But to no useful purpose."

"The purpose shall now be the will of God. I shall bring you tomorrow evening a map. The map is the route to freedom for you and your people."

"You are saying, Mr. Hollingsworth, that I should flee to the North?"

"To Canada. And take your people with you."

"I can not do that."

"But Mr. Spalding, what I am telling you is the word from the voice of the Almighty, you can not refuse. You can not refuse because Durnford is an evil man. And it is the evil in the situation that vitiates your pledge to him. Because he is also of the fallen race descended from Ham, his actions are all the more evil in the eyes of God."

Barba leaned forward. "Yo say Massa Andrew more evil den white massa, 'cause he a brack man?"

"Precisely."

"Den no brack man de equal ob de white man, is yo meaning?"

"You don't understand, Barba. We are all equal in the eyes of God."

"Den why Massa Andrew more evil jus 'cause he a brack man? Are my massa not equal in yo eyes?"

"Certainly not!"

"'Cause he a brack man?"

"No. Because he is a black slave owner!"

"Ceptin he a white man, owns dem slaves dah, he be bad den, ceptin he a brack man and owns dem, he be most evil man."

"Now that is what I am telling you, Barba. I think you understand now."

"I understan de brack man do bad, he evil. White man do bad, he jus bad. Brack man not equal to de white man."

"Barba, I'm afraid you will never understand the simple logic in the situation. For a black man to own another black is a most evil thing. The black man already bears the mark of our fallen brother Ham. You can not understand the logic of that. You never will."

"Because I be a brack man?"

"Because, Barba, you are ignorant. You do not have the training in logic that I and Mr. Spalding have. Logic is beyond the ability of your poor brain. Please do not take offense, I say that not in anger or to belittle you. It is just a fact. And you will never understand that."

Reverend Hollingsworth stood up, dusted his coat, and said to Spalding, "I shall return at this time tomorrow evening with a map which we shall study together.

We must act quickly. Cairo is your last chance to get your people off the steamboat. That is where I leave to go north to St. Louis, and that is where the Mississippi goes south to New Orleans."

"I beg of you, sir, do nothing so rash, as I can not deceive my master. I have given him my pledge."

"The Lord shall be your guide. Seek Him in your prayers tonight. And remember, you must go before Cairo. Cairo is free territory, the last chance at freedom you will have. The last chance to go North."

Barba spoke up very quietly. "I been der already, suh. Neber was happy. Gwan back to Louisiana."

"Mr. Spalding, I caution you on one thing…you can not do this without me. There are many traps. If you swam the river and stood up on the other side, thinking you were free, you would be a fool. For one, the Kentucky border is on the north side of the Ohio, it runs up to the high water line. You might reflect on the reason for that. Then there are those who will make you a prisoner at once, and collect a ransom for your return. You can only do this with my help. The map will show you the way, just as the Lord shows me the way to help you."

In the early afternoon of the next day, Andrew Durnford, along with several passengers, crowded against the rail just forward of the pilothouse, as the steamboat nudged its bow into the public landing at Cincinnati. The river shoaled at that point and the boat ground to a halt with its bow three or four feet short of land. Then the engineers reversed the starboard paddle wheel, while the port wheel churned forward. The boat pivoted and angled a little farther into the bank. Planks were quickly run out by roustabouts, who then shouldered boxes, kegs, and barrels destined for that port. The freight was unloaded at a run, and then casually loaded into waiting wagons, while passengers rushed forward and teetered carefully along a plank with stanchions and rope lines for their safety. The pilot had put the steamboat in among a dozen other riverboats at a place which Durnford assumed must have been reserved for the *Martha*, because that was where the boat's new cargo destined for downriver ports waited on shore. Just as quickly as freight was taken off, the new cargo was loaded.

There was no wharf at Cincinnati. From the river's edge a gently sloping area of paving stones of a hundred yards or so ran up to the street which was at a level about sixty feet above the water. The first buildings of the city, each three and four stories high, contained warehouses, mercantile offices, and a few stores and businesses, and were on the other side of the street, leaving a wide, sweeping area along the river, where shipments were stored for pick-up by the steamboats.

The city was smaller than New Orleans, perhaps a third its size, Durnford noted. Nevertheless, it was a surprise to Andrew that a settlement this large and so busy and industrious had developed along the river. From his readings, Durnford remembered the settlement as being nothing more than Fort Washington and a few log houses among the trees. Now the only trees to be seen were those in the high hills behind the city. The city itself rose in terraces from the river. High above the mercantile center were the big houses and mansions of the wealthy.

At last, Durnford went down the springing plank, with Marie-Charlotte and his two children ahead of him, all stepping carefully with both hands guiding along the safety ropes. Barba came behind, bringing clothing and toiletries carefully packed into two carpet bags by Marie-Charlotte. They would be staying overnight, and join the *Martha* after it negotiated the locks at Louisville.

Barba shook his master's hand and scrambled aboard the steamer, where he stood proudly in the bow. He was the trusted servant left in charge of the slaves. Durnford knew they were as safe with Barba as with him.

Suddenly, the planks were run in, and the steamboat backed into the current. The entire Cincinnati procedure took less than fifteen minutes. Andrew Durnford wiped his brow. It was a great relief to him to see the amount of river between the boat and shore grow bigger and bigger. This was the first landing the boat had made on the Ohio side. What would he do if some of his people escaped? He had thought of taking some protective action, but couldn't think of any reasonable way to prevent anyone from leaving the boat. Thank God he'd bought only families. No mother or father was likely to run without taking the family with them. And that would be difficult.

Other slaves were on the *Martha* in addition to Durnford's people, perhaps thirty or forty, he estimated. All were being shipped down to New Orleans for sale at market. They were there when he came aboard. None of those Negroes were the quality of his people. They belonged to slave traders, rough, uneducated and foul-smelling men who could barely read and write. Nevertheless, they made good money at what they did. And none of them seemed concerned that a slave might escape. Perhaps he did worry too much, just as Marie-Charlotte had said. For a slave to take the first step to freedom, to venture away from the confines of the familiar and into the unknown would require great courage. Slaves knew that those who escaped were almost always brought back. Then they were severely flogged. Andrew Durnford hated flogging. But it had to be done. He had flogged Lewis, the instigator, when his poor, misinformed and unfortunate people had run away. Without punishment, there would be no guarantee they would not go again. Then for each slave returned a reward had to be paid. You could not run a plantation that way.

Most plantation owners left the flogging to overseers. That Durnford would never do. He had no overseer, and never would. He preferred to work alongside his people, to be close to them. If a flogging was necessary for some infraction, he did that too. An overseer often flogged in rage, bruising and breaking skin and muscle. Durnford was compassionate, a doctor as well, and he never went beyond what was required. When he laid on lashes, he did so with compassion.

Rarely did Durnford lay on lashes. It was, he knew, the certainty of the whip which operated as a deterrent, not the severity of the flogging. And so on his plantation, he would go two or three years, sometimes even longer, without resorting to the raw-hide. Those who failed to make punishment swift and certain were no friend to their slaves. Sooner or later things got out of hand. Then only the most severe and cruel punishment would bring the slaves under control.

The steamboat turned down river as Durnford watched it from the landing. The Ohio was heavy with traffic. Two steamboats were ahead of the *Martha*, going for the bend. Another came up the other side of the river. Keel boats and flat boats were everywhere.

It was hot on the landing and flies buzzed around. Durnford stood in the heat with Marie-Charlotte holding his arm, and he watched the steamboat until it disappeared around the bend. He wanted to talk to Miss Remy. That morning she had at first seemed so warm and receptive. But she froze and left his bed. What was happening to the marriage? What had he done?

As these thoughts were running through his mind, he remembered seeing the Methodist Preacher, Hollingsworth, watching him from the upper deck with a curious intensity as the *Martha* left the Cincinnati landing. For a moment, Durnford had considered raising his hand to Hollingsworth in a sign of acknowledgement. But just then Hollingsworth backed into the crowd at the rail of the steamboat and the crowd pressed around him and bore him off. They were anxious to return to the cabin deck, the men to the card games in the saloon, and the women to the quiet of the staterooms. The excitement of the Cincinnati landing was over for them.

After the *Martha* went into the bend, Durnford looked across the Ohio to the undulating hills of Kentucky, a land of slaves and tobacco. Behind him, the city of a free state climbed a semi-circle of terraced hills. Cincinnati, he knew, was the headquarters of the newly formed Underground Railroad, the route to Canada for runaways. Abolitionists were in every street, always willing to hide the escaped slave. Had his people broken and run down the plank while the *Martha* was at the landing, some of them would have won their freedom. It was with a great feeling of relief that he watched the steamboat carrying his acquisitions disappear down the river.

Cincinnati, he had learned from McDonogh, was also a city of contrasts. The great majority of the inhabitants were pro-slavery. They made their living from that peculiar institution. The city was the focal point of slave commerce. Through Cincinnati passed goods to the South and products of slavery to the North, traveling along the Ohio River, and out to the cities along the Great Lakes by way of the newly constructed Miami canal and Lake Erie. In many ways, most of the citizens of the progressive city depended on slavery for their living. There were advertisements in the papers for recovery of escaped slaves. And the same section of the newspaper carried advertisements for the services of those who would recover the runaways, wherever the desperate slave might venture. For the right price, they would go into Canada. But the thought of the expense of it all caused a shudder to pass down Durnford's spine in spite of the heat. He very easily could have lost a lot of money, had but one slave the courage to break and urge the others to run with him.

Durnford wore a cream suit with vest and the newly stylish panama, a large lightweight hat whose basic structure was natural straw, hand-plaited with narrow strips from jipijapa leaves. Marie-Charlotte was dressed all in white and held a white parasol over her head. Her dress skimmed the ground and was buttoned to her chin, with lace at the collar and sleeves. The children were dressed in a brave imitation of their parents.

As they approached a covered carriage, the driver raised his hand, signaling to Andrew the conveyance would accept no further passengers. This was, Durnford concluded, because of the steepness of the road up the hill to the inner city. Horses could pull only so much, even though the carriage was but half full. The next driver made his point more clearly. "Don't take coloreds," he said.

The Gibson Hotel was in the business section, on a terrace about fifty feet above the area containing the wholesale and manufacturing buildings. The Gibson advertised deluxe accommodations and reasonable rates. Durnford thought the hotel was a little too expensive, but it was the only hotel in downtown Cincinnati.

The Athens of the West, as Cincinnati was called, was paved with stone. Durnford noted however that one great error had been made in its construction. There were no drains. It was more than two days since it last rained, but all of the water in the entire city had flowed down the semi-circle of hills and collected in the streets. Planks were laid to provide a crossing through the water, deep with collections of garbage, pig droppings and horse droppings, mixed with human waste which washed out from the privys, all of which bubbled in the intense heat. The horrible, putrid smell was overwhelming.

So without benefit of carriage, the Durnford family picked its way carefully over the streets. Walking close to the buildings, Andrew led his family up the hill, found the street leading to the four-story Gibson, and finally entered the hotel. His suit was soaked. Marie-Charlotte's white dress was sweat and stained. The children were miniature reflections of their parents' state.

Andrew walked through the deserted lobby and slapped a hand on the bell at the receptionist's desk. No one answered. The family sat down on the upholstered furniture of the small lobby and waited, while Andrew intermittently rang the bell.

"We don't house niggas heah." The low voice came from a small slit of a window below the boxes holding room keys. The thin white lips were barely visible.

# Chapter Twelve

"There has been a great misunderstanding, Durnford. Unless you know one of the colored families down there, I'm afraid you'll find no accommodations in Cincinnati."

"Mr. McMicken, sir, it may be that I am entirely in error. I had hoped to make arrangements for the education of my son, Thomas. Can it be this is not the city of enlightenment I believed."

"You have a brash manner about you, Durnford. You may be aware that I have large holdings in your State of Louisiana and I am indebted to John McDonogh for looking after them. Were it not for your letter of introduction from him, I would be compelled to treat you with less than kindness."

Cecil McMicken was a philanthropist in the process of establishing a university at Cincinnati. He had come out upon the porch at the circular drive of his mansion over-looking the city after reading the letter from John McDonogh Durnford had given to the McMicken house servant. He looked down upon the Durnford family, dirty, dusty and sweating. "You may wait in the stable. I will have water and towels brought around so that you may refresh yourself. Then I shall introduce you to people of a more liberal bend and consider my duty done."

Yet that morning the Durnford family were led by a black bondsman, the McMicken house servant, three streets to the west at the same level on the hill above the city. The servant carried with him the letter of introduction from John McDonogh and a second letter from Cecil McMicken.

Samuel Foote, a well-dressed man with a beard, roared with laughter as he read the letters. And then dismissing the McMicken servant, he brought the Durnfords into his parlor. "I fear nothing more in life than a good Presbyterian getting up from his knees to do the will of God," Samuel Foote said.

The neighbor children were summoned to entertain the Durnford children. Rosella went hastily and brightly to examine a girl's doll collection and Thomas went in pursuit of two boys chasing metal hoops propelled by sticks.

Morning tea was served. Samuel and his wife, Elizabeth were members of the Cincinnati cultured elite. They told the Durnfords that the Semi-Colon Club would meet at the Foote house that very evening, and the Durnfords were invited. "We are," said Elizabeth Foote, "an unusual lot. Transplanted New Englanders with a bent toward literature and stiff religion."

Samuel Foote had been to sea for many years, and finally returned to New England where he married Elizabeth. The newlyweds followed Samuel's brother, John, to Cincinnati where the brothers invested in real estate, started a water works, and were immensely successful. Samuel Foote was a Presbyterian vestryman and a trustee of the newly founded Lane Theological Seminary. But his character had been formed at sea and in his travels to exotic places such as Morocco, Turkey and Europe. He had Muslims in Constantinople as friends, and in Cincinnati Roman Catholics and Jews were his close acquaintances. "He sees virtues in all of them," Elizabeth said with a wink, "and believes it to be his duty to defend them against attacks by our beloved Calvinists."

"My wife refers to my good friend, the Reverend Lyman Beecher," Samuel said. He set his teacup and saucer on the low table with a clatter and leaned forward. "Lyman means well. I would introduce you to him, but that would be a cruel joke. He is the president of our Lane Theological, a most liberal institution by New England standards. And he promotes the interests of the downtrodden, although those citizens of the non-Anglo-Saxon race would not be welcomed as students. Your son, Thomas could never entered those hallowed halls."

"It seems I have blundered," Andrew Durnford said frankly. "In speaking with John McDonogh before I left New Orleans, we discussed the possibility of returning to New Orleans by river, and he advised me to investigate the availability of studies here for Thomas. However the doors to the University are closed to the Negro."

"As is Lane, Dr. Durnford. But Oberlin College has recently passed a resolution admitting Colored. I can recommend the school most highly, and it is but a few miles from here."

"Well we shall visit Oberlin, then, and see if it suits our purpose," Durnford said to his wife.

"Perhaps you were wiser, my friend, to attend our Semi-Colon meeting tonight and learn a little of our society before venturing further in that regard. The Reverend Lyman Beecher will not be here. But you can talk to his daughter, Harriet Beecher, who is my niece, and her fiancee, Professor Calvin Stowe."

A mischievous expression came over Samuel Foote and there was a strange light in his eyes. "My niece is the author of fiction, a most sinful occupation, and she has published short stories under her own name, producing a shock under which we suffer yet. I am afraid I have led her further astray by taking her to the theater, which is a yet stronger taboo."

"We do not wish to be an embarrassment to you," Marie-Charlotte said. She paused with her teacup at her lips. "Nor do we wish to be an embarrassment to ourselves. Perhaps we would not be well received in your house tonight."

"I think it might take some courage on your part," Elizabeth Foote said in reply. "But the question of slavery is seldom, if ever discussed in Cincinnati. The presence of black slave-owners at the Semi-Colon could be a most refreshing influence."

"We are not insensitive to censure," Marie-Charlotte said, "nor to asperity."

"You will hear no sharp-toothed unkindness from our group," Samuel Foote said. "And in all sincerity, I believe it would be a productive session. We are taught that all people are equal before God, and above all we are a religious people. But we are weak in the knees. We are afraid to treat blacks as equals. We are cowed before those who insist blacks are clearly inferior. Many honest Presbyterians see no wrong in slavery. Most of us are, at best, ambivalent. Some of us are abolitionists. Some see abolition as an evil. The Reverend Lyman Beecher himself, said, 'Abolitionists are made up of vinegar, aqua fortis and oil of vitriol, with brimstone, saltpeter and charcoal to explode and scatter the corrosive matter.' He feels, as many of us do, that the violence advocated by the abolitionists will cause the South to stiffen and retard freedom for the slaves. And although I hope for freedom for the black people some day in the future, it is clear to me that many thousands of slaves are backward. They are simple, unable to look after themselves in an advanced civilization." Samuel Foote paused in his discourse, and turned abruptly to Andrew Durnford. "How do you see the question, Dr. Durnford?"

"The first thing I must say is that I do not see slavery as an issue of race. Look only at history. Look only at Russia. The serfs live under much worse conditions than my people. Nevertheless, I do know that some day they must be free. At this time, though, they would be unable to provide for themselves. It will take, I believe, at least three generations before the slave is ready for freedom." Durnford looked at his hosts for a reaction.

But there was no reaction. It was as if they were discussing the price of tea. It appeared as if nothing he said on the controversial issue touched the social conscience of his hosts. But then again, he knew, his attitude on the subject was also rather blase.

"Young Samuel P. Chase will be here tonight," Samuel Foote said casually. "He has recently established himself in law practice in Cincinnati and defends escaped slaves. He's known as the 'attorney-general for runaway Negroes.' It could be an interesting evening."

"Well good," Marie-Charlotte answered. "Perhaps he can explain then why the State of Ohio does not permit the Negro to vote, or to hold office, or to testify in court against a white man."

The Foote mansion was one of the largest homes in Cincinnati. It stood at the corner of Vine and Third Street, overlooking the city, the Ohio River, and the wooded hills of Kentucky. That evening, sixteen members of the Semi-Colon club assembled in the right wing of the mansion. Harriet Beecher came with her fiancé, Professor Stowe.

The daughter of Lyman Beecher was about five feet tall, average for a woman, and an inch or so shorter than Marie-Charlotte. She had a weak chin, and a large, irregular-shaped nose. But altogether, Andrew Durnford thought she was a handsome woman. She seemed to possess some sort of sly wisdom. Her forehead was high, her mouth firm but gentle, and her high cheekbones gave her face an oval shape. But the most striking thing about her was that she had the expression of an absolutely confident woman.

Marie-Charlotte noticed that Harriet Beecher was dressed in the current style, clothing cut full which tended to disguise her slender and graceful figure. Her dark dress buttoned to the neck with a lace collar. She wore a jacket of the same smooth material, and a full skirt. There were no shoulders to the jacket, and the style made it appear that she had no shoulders at all, just a long body running to her neck. Harriet Beecher's dark hair was parted in the middle and dropped rather becomingly in ringlets at the sides. She wore a thin band around her head just above the ringlets, Indian style, and her ringlets hung down to touch her shoulders.

The meeting of the Semi-Colon club commenced promptly at 7:30. The Durnfords were introduced as house guests of the Footes, and then Daniel Drake, a well-known medical educator and physician to most present, read an essay by an anonymous member of the club. The author of the piece, it was whispered about, was Harriet Beecher. The essay was a witty and sarcastic portrayal of Cincinnati Society as represented at the Semi-Colon Club.

Having finished his reading, Dr. Drake sat down grandly next to Andrew Durnford, and sitting stiff and straight, said, "I understand you are a medical man, Durnford."

"Yes. A medical doctor."

"They have then such schools for colored in New Orleans?"

"Unfortunately, they do not."

"You feel, though, qualified I presume, to treat your brethren?"

"Quite so, sir. And before my St. Rosalie adventure the majority of my patients were of the fair race."

"That is indeed unusual."

"Not as unusual as the situation I find in this enlightened city."

"I fear I do not understand."

"I find your sanitation methods lacking."

"Well then, just what is it that you do not approve?"

"It is no coincidence that this city has serious events of the cholera, the last, I believe occurring just this past year, when several hundred were carried off with the disease. It remains a mystery to me why this new city is built without a thought to drainage. Below, vapors rise from a vast accumulation of garbage and waste, human and animal. Those vapors, you must know, carry with them elements of consumption, cholera and sundry diseases. A most unhealthful situation."

"Rubbish. Cholera results from a weakness of the constitution, as does consumption." Dr. Drake sat stiff and rectangular, his body a perfect perpendicular. "This is the most healthy city in the world."

"I must respectfully take issue with that statement, sir. The mortality rate is alarming, especially among the old and very young."

"I will grant you a command of the English language that deserves respect, Durnford–"

"If you please, sir, I must insist upon being addressed as Dr. Durnford. It is my proper title."

The physician drew back, frowning. "Very well, Dr. Durnford, certainly. But I must claim the superior knowledge in these things. You see, I have formal training and the certificate of Medical Doctor from the Medical College at Hartford. Therefore—"

"I would not challenge your credentials, sir. But you should know that my degree is from the Medical Academy at Paris. I believe the French are advanced in that department."

Just then Harriet Beecher leaned into the conversation, and standing before the seated gentlemen, said, "Oh, you two must not talk shop here. This is a literary society."

Both men jumped to their feet. Dr. Drake turned a chair, and as Miss Beecher took her seat, they sat down again, forming a small circle with Harriet between the two physicians and Marie-Charlotte to one side. "Now what rough comments have you made about our Porkopolis?" she asked Durnford.

"I confess to lack of understanding."

"Porkopolis? That is the bantered about name for our fair city. Have you not seen the pigs? The country lanes are thronged with swine driven in from the surrounding farms. The smell of the slaughterhouse fills the air. We love these animals. We pile our garbage in the middle of the street for them to eat. And finally, we eat them."

"Dr. Durnford entertains the fanciful theory that fumes from the flooded debris of our streets contribute to cholera," Dr. Drake said sternly."

"Not a very complimentary statement, Dr. Durnford. Nor is it one with which I would take issue. But then what could I know about medicine?"

"If you will excuse me, Miss Beecher," Dr. Drake said, rising still stiff as a poker. "I see Dr. Stowe alone in the corner and feel compelled to join him." He turned and bowed to Durnford and Marie-Charlotte. "Dr. and Mrs. Durnford, I respectfully yield the field."

"Well," Harriet Beecher said, "you have brought a flush to Dr. Drake's cheeks. I dare say the excitement has been beneficial. Now what did you think of the reading?"

Marie-Charlotte smiled and touched Miss Beecher's arm. "It was whispered about you were the author."

The reaction of Harriet Beecher might have gone unnoticed by most people of the North. It was a very slight, involuntary shifting back in her seat as Marie-Charlotte touched her arm. But Marie-Charlotte recognized it as the invisible shield she had seen erected between her and white people in the North.

"We do love to make fun of ourselves. We New Englanders here in the West are much like fish out of water."

"And what do you make of us?" Marie-Charlotte asked Harriet Beecher.

"A refreshing approach! Well, you are a curiosity. Black slave owners with a plantation near New Orleans. I don't know. I suppose I am indignant. I have never been to Louisiana. Connecticut, New York, and this meager section of Ohio are the extent of my travels. But I have studied much, even written a Geography which is the standard text in our schools. So I know well that the free blacks of your country possess an unusual status. You are at liberty to sue in the courts, free to own property—slaves are your property. So it should be no surprise that you are engaged in the peculiar commerce."

"I never thought of slavery as a commerce," Marie-Charlotte said, "but I suppose it is a true description. And what do you think of slavery?"

"Oh, I don't know. I visited a large plantation in Kentucky once. Uncle Samuel, our host, took me there to see for myself. It was a very large tobacco farm. The owner is a friend of Uncle Samuel. The workers were well treated and lived in neat log cabins, all grown over and covered with vines. Very picturesque. Each family had their own small house, with a garden for their personal use. The plantation family were fair and honest Christians who loved and cared for their slaves. But nevertheless, it was all very sad. Especially sad was the situation of the house servants. One in particular, a bright young girl, was very fair with flowing, raven hair and smoldering eyes. I wondered what would happen to those poor souls when the owner died, or worse yet, if the crop failed and they all went on the auction block." She paused and a far away look came into her eyes, as if she were having a vision. "Perhaps I shall write a novel on the question some day," Harriet Beecher continued. "Then, perhaps I will understand what my feelings are."

At that moment, a short man, roughly dressed, with ink stains on his hands, stopped before the small group. "I could not help overhearing what you just said, Miss Beecher, and I believe it means you are truly a writer."

"Now Mr. Birney, are you finally admitting I am a writer?"

"Certainly. Not only are you modest, but you confess to not knowing what you are writing about until you start."

"Oh, no. I said I might better understand my feelings by writing a fiction piece on slavery."

"How easily you escape, dear woman."

Harriet Beecher introduced her adversary.  James G. Birney, she explained to the Durnfords, was from Kentucky, a southerner who had just recently converted to abolition and freed his slaves.  Run out of one town after another, he brought his printing press to Cincinnati where he published the *Philanthropist*, an anti-slavery paper.  "This unassuming man is the object of much popular hatred and contempt here," she said.

Birney stretched out an ink-stained hand and shook the hand of both Durnfords.  "Unassuming I am not," he said to them.  "You will find that Cincinnati is, in many ways a Southern town.  It can be quite violently pro-slavery.  There has already been one attack on my printing office.  Then just last week a citizen's committee of very respectable citizens, with the mayor presiding, raised the question whether they would permit the publication of abolition papers in Cincinnati."

"Surely you are joking," said Marie-Charlotte.  "Even in Louisiana we have heard of the First Amendment right to free speech."

"I am not joking."  Birney stood before them with his short, powerful arms folded across his chest, hands balled into fists.  "The issue as to whether or not I may publish remains to be decided.  Even my fellow members of the Semi-Colon club are divided."

Just then Harriet Beecher motioned to her fiancé, who ambled over.  Calvin Ellis Stowe was a professor of biblical literature at Lane Theological Seminary, the institution where Harriet's father, Lyman Beecher served as president.  Stowe was a tall man with a commanding presence.  He looked every bit the part of a lion, with a large head, a full beard, and a deep, resonant voice which filled the room.

James Birney surrendered his chair to Harriet's fiancé, saying as he rose, "Professor Stowe is obsessed with Ohio history.  Don't ask him how this city got its name, because he will never stop talking."

"We named this great city after the Society of Cincinnati," Stowe boomed proudly.

"Well, I apologize for my ignorance, Dr. Stowe, but I've never heard mention of that organization," Andrew said.

Stowe, as if lecturing a student at the seminary, responded, "The Society of Cincinnati was organized by officers of the Revolutionary Army.  Its purpose is to promote the memory of those brave individuals who breathed the fire of freedom."

"A restricted society, I presume?" asked Marie-Charlotte.

"Indeed.  Membership is limited to the descendants of those who served their country in honor of their fathers who, like Cincinnatus, left the plow to serve their country."

Marie-Charlotte smiled. "I have heard of Cincinnatus."

"An appropriate name for our city, I think," said Stowe.

"How true," said Marie-Charlotte. "Cincinnatus, as I recall, was an unyielding patrician who violently opposed any attempts at the equalization of the Roman plebeian."

Harriet Beecher laughed. "You have met your equal, Professor Stowe. A woman more outspoken than I."

"If such is possible, my dear Harriet."

"Attention everyone." Harriet Beecher rose and clapped her hands. "We have with us, as you know, two natives of Louisiana, blacks who own a plantation and slaves. I respectfully submit that we change our topic of tonight's discussion to the ownership of slaves by people of the Negro race."

Everyone turned their attentions to the Durnfords. Andrew immediately felt as if he were the focus of some judicial inquiry, the way a defendant in the dock must feel in the criminal courts, and from the look on her face, he thought his startled wife felt the same.

But the new subject of discussion was bantered about as if the members of the Semi-Colon Club were exploring concepts in agriculture. It was, thought Marie-Charlotte, a group of rather shallow intellectuals, people Andrew normally held in low esteem since they did not seem to ever have put a hand to any physical labor. However, Andrew, the central topic, seemed to warm to the attention and soon appeared to enjoy the conversation immensely. And in a short while, Marie-Charlotte also saw more substance to the conversations then she expected. To her surprise she noted that Professor Stowe was actually a shy, reserved man, embarrassed by the topic, who took refuge in flights of idealistic fancy, and never seemed to come to grips with the issue. He was, Marie-Charlotte thought, much like Andrew who could never enter the mind of the slave and experience that life. Harriet Beecher, on the other hand, handled the question with grace and subtle charm. She got to the core of the matter without offending, as if she were peeling an onion under water, and for the first time, Marie-Charlotte felt uncomfortable in her role as mistress of a slave plantation. She and Andrew were aristocrats in the free black society of Louisiana, *gens de colour libre,* whether it was right or wrong to own slaves had never before been discussed. The Durnfords were good masters. They provided their people with homes and clothing and food. It had never occurred to Marie-Charlotte that anything should be different. But when Harriet

Beecher said, "Pity the poor slave woman, a Christian, who watches her young daughter, trained in our father's religion and raised in virtue and Christian principles, sold off to a lecherous white man who has but one intention. The poor Christian woman, the mother of the fair maiden, can do nothing to protect her daughter, who must submit to the most atrocious indecencies. But for the grace of God, that poor slave woman could be Harriet Beecher." And Marie-Charlotte knew at once Harriet meant the slave woman could easily be Marie-Charlotte and the daughter her own sweet Rosella.

Marie-Charlotte was lost in thought now, and suddenly realized the conversation had turned to other matters. Harriet Beecher told the assembled intellectuals that her father was continually at war with alcohol and the "Godless" faculty of Harvard college, who were scarcely aware of his existence.

And with the laughter that followed that statement, the discussion ended.

Dancing, sandwiches, and coffee came after the discussion. Then champagne, wine and a fine brand of Madeira. The evening finished with a merry Virginia reel, led by Harriet Beecher, and her fiancé, Professor Stowe.

Andrew Durnford, his wife, and their children slept that night as guests in the house of Samuel Foote. But Andrew did not sleep well. The windows were open to the humid and warm air, which carried cries and shouts from unruly citizens of the enlightened city. Andrew lay awake most of the night, wondering why there was so little enforcement of ordinances against such conduct, while Marie-Charlotte tossed and turned, struggling with thoughts of slave mothers weeping over the plight of their daughters.

Before the light of dawn came to the open windows, there was a loud and urgent banging on the bedroom door.

"Dress at once prepared to travel," Samuel Foote shouted through the sturdy oak. And when Andrew opened the door, Foote explained that there had been race riots during the night. James Birney had been killed and his printing office destroyed. His press was smashed with sledgehammers and tossed into the river. Abolitionists' houses and homes of colored families were in flames. The good citizens of Cincinnati had formed a vigilante committee to establish control, but the outcome was in doubt. Samuel Foote had made arrangements for passage to Louisville on a riverboat, which waited at the landing with boilers charged.

And so the Durnford family left Cincinnati, the enlightened city, in haste before the light of day. They were rushed by carriage to the landing, the plank was drawn as soon as they were aboard, and as the boat's paddle wheels churned the dark water, Andrew and Marie-Charlotte, with their children between them, stood at the rail. They looked up at the city, where sparks and flames shot up from fires in the colored section and small houses farther up the hill. They saw tiny figures in the streets, rushing about with torches held high, and did not know whether the men were part of the mob or the citizens' committee. Soon the steamboat was around the bend, and the only evidence of civilization was a faint glow in the sky beyond the wooded hills.

Late that same afternoon, Andrew Durnford stood on the hurricane deck watching the approach to Louisville. He looked at his watch, noted that the hour was approaching five o'clock, and returned the watch to his vest pocket. From inside the wheelhouse, he heard the pilot discussing the situation with his apprentice. They were fast overtaking another boat that refused to yield. It was a race to see which boat would first enter the locks at Louisville. There the Ohio river dropped nearly twenty-six feet in the course of two miles.

Before the locks were built, it had been a treacherous run through rocks and between islands. Keel boats and flat boats had gone down the falls there on a regular basis, always losing a large percentage of boats, passengers, and cargo to the river. Even an occasional steamboat rode the turbulent, white water. But no boat ever came back up the Ohio. Just five years earlier a canal was dredged along the Louisville side of the river. In the two-mile long canal were three locks. Locks had been around for a few hundred years, but Durnford still thought they were an engineering marvel. Boats went up and down the river in those locks. Each lock had a set of doors that swung shut against the current at each end. For boats coming up the river, the lock was drained through a valve until the water level was equal to the lower portion of the river. Boats were pulled in by lines, the down river gates closed, valves opened, and as the lock filled with water, the boats rose slowly to the level of the upper part of the river. When that level was reached, the upper gates opened and the boats moved out and continued their journey. And all of this was accomplished by using only the water itself, no pumps or human or animal labor was required.

Shortly before the opening to the first lock, the pilot spun the boat's wheel sharply to starboard and cut into the offending steamboat which had clearly lost the race. Durnford grabbed the rail as the two steamboats collided, and the deck under his feet lurched and pitched from the blow. But the pilot had judged well, and the slower boat was pushed wide aside. Durnford himself chuckled as the loser's pilot struggled with the wheel. The paddles of the offender churned in reverse. Then with a loud crunch the other steamboat struck a large bundle of wooden pilings designed to retain vessels waiting for their turn to lock through.

The other boat struck with such force that Durnford knew grave structural damage must have been the result. But he was glad his boat had won the race. It would take hours to pass through the two-mile canal and three locks to where the *Martha* waited at the wharf in Shippingport, a commercial subdivision of Louisville. The captain of the *Martha* had told Durnford that he would lie at Shippingport two days undergoing maintenance to the boilers. Nevertheless, Durnford was anxious to rejoin his slaves. He had full confidence in Barba, but this long delay must be a temptation to his twenty-eight charges, torn from homes in Virginia and looking at freedom just across the river. Had they not won the race for the lock, it would have been very late in the night before he would have rejoined his people.

As they locked through, Marie-Charlotte was below in the saloon with the children who labored at their studies. She was the disciplinarian. For Andrew, the locks offered the more important lesson. But he had long ago realized that interference with the children's education was not to be. So neither the children nor Marie-Charlotte witnessed the snappy way the lines were tossed to men on shore who fastened them to cleats and bollards in a whirl. In minutes, they were secure inside the lock and the upriver gates were swinging shut behind the steamboat.

The gates were closed by a man on each side near the hinges, who turned a large metal wheel. Each wheel was connected by gears to larger, wooden gears, which operated upon a toothed half-moon attached to the gate itself. There was, Durnford noted, a certain rhythm and synchronization of the movements of the two men at the gate wheels. One gate was closed ahead of the other, and the second gate swung slowly behind it, with its large leathers overlapping to form a seal against the water.

"Ease off! Ease off! What manner of snag be that?"

"Snag? Well I reckon that be the best dressed snag I ever'd saw."

Durnford looked down to where the men were pointing. Among the sticks and dead grasses jamming the heavy gates to the lock he saw a long coat. And in the long coat was a body wedged between the leather seal and the inside gate.

From his position high on the deck overlooking the stern, Durnford thought he could smell the musty scent of death. The gates swung slowly open, creaking as they moved, and the flotsam eddied and swirled silently in behind the boat. A roustabout edged out along the steel frame supporting the riverboat's stern wheel, and with a quick and rapid thrust, speared the long coat with a pole and hook. And as the roustabout steered the body back along the framework, the sullen mass turned slowly in the water to reveal a cold face and stark, open eyes. It was a familiar face, someone Durnford couldn't quite place. The body had been in the water a long time, perhaps a day or so. Durnford had seen bodies like that before, floating down the river from New Orleans. Those were the luckless ones who'd wandered the city too late at night. A gambler here. A fool with a little too much money there. Rarely was it ever an accident that they ended up in the Mississippi. It was a convenient dumping ground. And the bodies looked like the one Durnford saw now. There was a pasty whiteness to the face, but a nose like that was one that didn't change much even in death. "I know that man," Durnford finally said.

The captain below and several passengers leaned out over the rail and looked up at Durnford. "That is the Reverend Thomas Hollingsworth, a Methodist Minister from New Bedford," Andrew said.

# Chapter Thirteen

"Not a suicide," the coroner said dryly. "Took a hard blow to his right temple. Could have slipped and fell against a post, then simply slid overboard. Dead before he hit the water."

The coroner, a very fat man dressed in heavy, dark clothing sweated profusely in the small room at the courthouse used for the inquest. He stared at Durnford across his scotch. Then he wiped his thick lips and leaned forward across the table. "Lucky for you, Durnford, you weren't on the *Martha* when this happened. Reverend Hollingsworth was alive and well in Cincinnati. Time of death appears to be ten or twelve hours after the boat. I'd say he fell overboard during the night."

Durnford did not respond to the challenge. He had heard the testimony. Passengers recalled recognizing the voice of Hollingsworth the night before. He was down below, practicing abolition on some unsuspecting slaves. The fool got only what was coming to him, was the general opinion. "And whose slaves were those?" the coroner had asked. "Why that nigger right there." And each of the three witnesses had pointed to Andrew Durnford.

Now the coroner sat and looked at Durnford. His dull grey eyes were quiet, waiting patiently for some statement from the black slave owner. Sweat rolled down his face. He took another sip of scotch. Looked up. Finally grinned. But the eyes never changed. "Didn't know niggers owned slaves." The coroner tapped his fingers quietly on the table. "Now I know you did this, boy. How you did I don't know yet. And I sure would like to see the hot breath of the law on your neck. But we are governed by principles here. Those principles, unfortunately, I've got to apply to this case. Death by accident. That's it."

"I am innocent of any wrongdoing, I assure you, sir."

"Well, I'm glad you're so brave, boy. But a murder conspiracy stretching down the Ohio all the way to Louisville here is something I just can't tackle right now. I have other fish to fry. Go now, before I change my mind."

As Durnford reached the door the coroner called out, "You, Durnford. Mind what I say. Go out of here. Go on down to your home, boy. Cause I have ways of getting at the truth. It scares the daylights out of me to think what your overseer might say about all this. And you would be mighty surprised what we can get out of a nigger like that once we start on 'em."

When Durnford returned to the *Martha* boiler repairs were completed and the waiting captain had steam up. Durnford had hardly stepped off the gangplank when the boat backed from the wharf, and by the time he joined Marie-Charlotte in the saloon, the steamboat had entered the river. Andrew pawed absently at his lunch and watched MarieCharlotte and the children finish their bread pudding.

Marie-Charlotte looked at her husband for a long time. She could not recall having seen Andrew drawn quite so taut. The look in his eyes was almost that of a haunted man, or was it a hunted man, she wondered? "Andrew, are you certain everything went all right at the hearing."

"I beg your pardon."

"The hearing, Andrew. Did it go well?"

"Oh, yes. Of course. Quite well. It was pretty clear to me, a medical man, what happened. The poor soul slipped over the side at night and drowned. No rail on the lower deck, you may have noticed. That could happen to anyone. I suppose now they may consider some alterations."

"But Andrew, why would Reverend Hollingsworth be on the lower deck at night?"

Andrew paused for a moment, thinking of the coroner's clear threat. But he had no answer to give her. Hollingsworth was on the lower deck, stirring up the slaves, Andrew was certain of that. And so instead of answering the question, he said, "Hollingsworth was quite well known. His name has been in the papers in Louisville and in northern cities. Wasn't much liked this side of the Ohio, though."

She gave him a tolerant smile. "You're impossible, Andrew. You seem quite affected by this man's death, and I suppose it is because he turns out to be rather well known. But I don't think the world's a lessor place because of his loss." She folded her arms across her chest and gave him a harder look. "Let's forget about that man. We have the rest of our trip to look forward to. A journey to enjoy." Then her face softened with a pleasant, determined thought. "The children will be quite safe by themselves here in the salon, Andrew. Let's go along to our cabin for a little rest. You look completely exhausted."

Clouds covered the moon and stars that week, and although the journey from Cincinnati to Louisville took just a little more than a day, they were now in the slower currents and confronted by frequent snags. The pilot went along at half speed.

The evening after leaving Louisville, they spent the night at Yellow Bank on the Ohio. The following night the steamboat put in at Henderson, and the day after that, the boat slid slowly past Cave-in-Rock Island, rounded up, and stopped for the night in the shelter of the island.

One of the passengers at a table near the Durnfords that evening, an old dentist, a huge, muscular man with arms as thick as tree limbs, announced that Cave-in-Rock was a cavern one hundred and twenty feet deep. It had been a hiding place for river pirates who struck out at unsuspecting flatboats for years. The pirates usually massacred the crew, including entire families, so there would be no witnesses. And then, the old man explained to his enthralled audience, that the population of Louisville, all eligible males, came down en masse and shot all the pirates in their sleep. Since then, there had been no problems at Cave-in-Rock.

"How is it that a dentist from Detroit knows the history of this island," a middle-aged woman asked suspiciously. She was a teacher returning to New Orleans from Vermont, where she had spent the summer.

"I was not always a dentist in Detroit," the giant old man said. "I worked the flat boats down the rivers for many years. That's how I got to be a dentist. The biggest and strongest man on the boat always got the job of pulling rotten teeth. Well I could yank a tooth quicker than anyone on the entire river. So pretty soon I was making more money pulling teeth than boating, and so I married a pretty little thing and settled down in Detroit. Been pulling teeth ever since."

As the light softened into dusk the next day, the pilot eased the steamboat into shore across the river from the town of Cairo, Illinois. The *Martha* swung around in the current with her bow facing north and her stern facing south toward the point where the Ohio met the Mississippi River two miles downstream. Durnford sent his slaves ashore on the Kentucky side of the river for firewood, with Barba and four roustabouts from the steamboat to guard against any of his people slipping away.

Dinner was served before the light of day completely left the river and now in the twilight of early evening, the Durnfords again dined in luxury. The sun set on the Illinois side of the river and the trees at Cairo cast shadows across the water. Looking past the captain's table out the stern windows, Andrew surveyed the small town of Cairo, the last hope for any slave with thoughts of fleeing North. Down near the shore was a magnificent, two-story home, round, white and brilliant, with columns on all sides. A wedding cake. Farther up the hill was another large mansion with several outbuildings. Smaller homes and farm animals made up the remainder of the small town. Andrew thought the entire population could be not much over one hundred. There were no stores, no businesses, no merchant enterprise of any nature to be seen.

At last they had come to that section of the country where there was little chance of a slave escaping. Durnford felt safe and secure. It had been a start to see Hollingsworth at the rail when the boat left Cincinnati. And the entire trip down the Ohio River, so close to the free states, had taken a toll on his nerves. But he was peaceful now. In the morning, the boat would fire up boilers. The *Martha* would swing out into the current, leave the free state of Illinois behind them, and start down the Mississippi. If things went well, if none of his slaves became sick, or died, his venture to Virginia would yet turn out to be profitable.

The next morning they were out in the wide Mississippi. The river was high and the current strong. Pacing the hurricane deck, Durnford made out snags, quite close at hand. The water gurgled and boiled around those deadly obstructions. On each side of the boat, the giant paddle wheels turned lazily, giving just enough momentum to maintain steerage in the strong current. And even though the paddle wheels turned in slow motion, the dark banks still rushed past, so fast were they driven south by the current.

Along the banks as the day lightened to a new sun, Durnford saw keelboats hugging the slower water close to shore. Those boats were poled northward in an endless battle against the water. Strong men leaned to poles set into the river bottom and shuffled, stooped over, along the deck boards of the keelers, pushing the heavy boats forward as they walked to the stern.

Out in the river were other keel boats going south. There were flat boats too. None of the flat boats ever came back up the Mississippi. It was impossible to push them against the current. Only the keel boats, and not many of those, ventured north against the strong river. It was far more profitable to break up the boats at New Orleans, where there was a demand for their hardwood planks. Some of the planks were used for sidewalks, especially in the new American section upriver from Canal Street.  Other wood from the boats went into new homes, mansions, stores, factories, and restaurants.  Even the interior of St. Rosalie was built with good hardwood from Ohio, Kentucky, Illinois and Tennessee.  Wood that had first seen service in the river trade.

A good many of the river craft were family boats, piled with men, women, children, cows, horses, chickens and pigs, and all manner of furniture and furnishings.  Those boats stopped at new settlements in Kentucky or Tennessee.  The biggest part of the river traffic, though, were heavily laden, commercial freight boats.  Most were simply floating with the current.  Some of the more enterprising were rowing, some with as many as eight or ten oars in the water, to make a faster pace to the Crescent City and settlements along the way.

They left civilization behind.  The banks of the great river were barren of any signs of life.  Trees and thick bushes and wild vines and grasses came to the water's edge.  Now and then, Durnford spotted a lone spiral of thin smoke, and knew a lonely cabin was hidden from view.

Back in Shippingport, the commercial section of Louisville, the waterfront had bustled.  Piled high on the wharves were kegs and barrels with **WHISKEY** and **FLOUR** stamped in black letters.  Other barrels held iron castings and millstones and glass.

While Marie-Charlotte waited for Andrew to return from the inquest, she and the children had watched huge tobacco casks rolled to the wharves by horses hitched to shafts fastened to axles run through the casks.  The axles were pulled out, and then the casks were taken by strong men and stacked on top of one another.

Wooden cages rose in tiers on the wharf.  In the cages were chickens and turkeys for shipment south.

All morning long while she waited at Shippingport, Marie-Charlotte watched boats up from New Orleans unload exotic cargos from Europe and the West Indies.  Pleasant smells filled the air.  She saw barrels of molasses and spices, and tea.  There were crates and kegs and casks of chinaware, and fabrics, and coffee, and mackerel, and wine, all brought ashore by slaves contracted out for wharf work.

Merchants in elegant frock coats and beaver hats rushed about, overseeing the loading and unloading of boats, and sweating in the heat.


On the wall of the *Martha's* saloon was a magazine rack.  There Marie-Charlotte found the New Orleans *Picayune*, New York Papers, Philadelphia papers, all months old. She also found old and worn copies of *Harper's Weekly*.

Now that they were on the Mississippi, with an endless sameness to the scenery, Marie-Charlotte settled into her newspapers and magazines in the saloon, while Rosella took advantage of the space at the writing desk in the cabin to polish her French.

Andrew took Thomas up to the pilothouse for a better view of the river. Startled by the warm greeting from the old man at the wheel, Durnford simply nodded. Since the inquest at Louisville, he had not expected much from white people. But the pilot was from the Natchitoches settlement on the Red River, near the Cane River Colony where free people of color and whites lived harmoniously. The thin man with a full beard, wearing a magnificent frock coat and a tall hat welcomed Andrew and Thomas into the pilothouse.

The spoked steering wheel was immense, filling the wide pilothouse. It was taller than the apprentice, a boy not much older than Thomas, who gripped it tightly.

The pilot pointed out the window with a long thin arm, and spoke as much to Thomas as he did to the apprentice at the wheel. "At the head of that island there is a bar putting out towards the right shore. Now you must go around that bar and still keep about one-third of the river to your right because there is a breaker there you must watch out for. There, see that ripple?" The apprentice nodded. "Well remember what you learned last time. Just keep that breaker, that rock where the ripple is, off to your right. Keep it close in now."

The steamboat slid along with its starboard paddle wheel clearing the ripple by about twenty feet. "Good. Good," the pilot said. Now bear in towards the island. That's good. Now what are you going to do?"

"Well, sir," the boy said, affecting a husky voice which just squeaked, "I reckon I'll take along close in a little bit to the island, and when we come down on another ripple, which means about half way down the island, I am to leave a bar to the right and some breakers to the left."

"Well said. Now what is the name of this island?"

"Hog Island, sir."

The pilot smiled at Thomas. "This island forms a considerable impediment to this part of the river. The channel is uncommonly crooked, narrow, and difficult to spot. Great care is required here. Now look...we take the chute there, which runs directly across to the island, then we run close under the foot of the island, leaving a broad, flat bar to the right up there, on the head of which there is a danger of grounding. After we get through the Hog island chute, we float in near the left shore a short distance. The channel bears to the right considerably then, and at the distance of half or three quarters of a mile below Hog island, keeping about two-thirds of the river to our left then, we pass a third ripple. This is at the head of a very small island, which you can't see just yet. It is a very small island, and in floods, like this, nothing is to be seen of it but the willows growing on it. The channel is difficult and snakes in very low stages, but we will have no problem now. A bar extends upwards from the head of that island, which forms the ripple I mentioned. To avoid that bar, we must pull for the right shore as soon as we get near it, leaving the head of the bar and the island to the left. After that chute to the right, we bear again towards the island, to stay in the channel." The pilot paused, stretched, and looked around him. "And that's the way it goes all down this river."

Durnford stood in the doorway to the pilothouse. He felt at ease now. He was pleased the pilot showed an interest in his son, Thomas. And he felt again like a man. The harsh statements made by the coroner at Louisville were behind him. Life was as it should be. Then the pilot came over to the door, and Andrew stepped aside to let him pass. Outside, the pilot beckoned to Andrew. And as Durnford walked to the rail where the pilot stationed himself, the thin man said, "You see why we cannot run at night, do you not?"

"Oh, yes, sir. That channel would be invisible in the dark, I would suspect."

"Quite true. Invisible to all but the eye of God. And life is like the river, I find, Dr. Durnford. There are times of darkness when one should not venture out. And even in good light, we must watch for signs to keep in the channel. The channel for you, Durnford, can be a little dangerous."

Durnford said cautiously. "I guess it can be."

"You were very lucky at Louisville."

Durnford opened his mouth. Closed it again. He should say something to keep the conversation going, he thought. But where was the pilot leading. Durnford did not want to think about Louisville. His anger was gone. He did not want to dwell on what happened to Hollingsworth or why the coroner had accused him.

"The preacher who drowned.... No, not drowned. He was dead before he went over the side.... The loss of that man is an embarrassment to me, Durnford. You see the captain is an owner of this boat. Business is his business. It's what he does and cares about. Me, though, well, I serve the function you might expect of a captain on a sea-going vessel. I am the one responsible for getting the boat up and down this river, with its cargo, and its passengers."

Watching, careful to maintain a demeanor of respect and submissive-ness, Durnford waited for the pilot to continue. And all the time he wished for an escape. He longed for the comfort of the saloon. He'd had enough of an inquisition at Louisville. No more, he thought.

"Along about midnight back there on the Ohio, when there was a good moon and good light for night running, when everyone on the boat was asleep, I was up here. My apprentice was at the wheel. I stood right here, along the rail. Of course I didn't hear a splash. Too much noise from the engines and the paddle wheels for that. But right down there where I happened to be looking, I saw two of your slaves slide that body over the side."

The pilot paused and looked at Durnford. Andrew stood up a little straighter.

"It was a good moon." The pilot paused for a long moment. "And I saw the man they let slip over the side, too. It was Hollingsworth. I knew him from the captain's table. Quite a fire-eater. An abolitionist."

The pilot turned his gaze down the river, then barked out a steering command to his apprentice. "You may wonder why I did not stop the boat. Well, I knew there was no life in that man when they dumped him over the side. My hope was the body never would be found."

Then with his eyes intent on the river again, the pilot spoke out, "Pull for the right shore now, Davy." Then to Durnford, he said, "It was a night with a good moon, as I told you. For sure your number one man was there, the one in charge of the group that goes after firewood. The other Negro I've seen talking to him at times. I'm sure you know who they both are, Durnford. What I don't know is whether you were planning to do anything about it."

"Well, until now I had not thought my people were involved," Durnford muttered. "I don't know what I will do."

"Do nothing, Durnford. Not on my boat. And don't have a sudden fit of conscience and think about going to the authorities. That's my point. I have a job to do. My job, as I said, is to get this boat down the river. Now neither one of us, Durnford, will be going anywhere if there is a further inquiry. Even though we could expect a pretty swift trial and quick hanging, why, I'd be tied up at least a week. And without me, this steamboat isn't going anywhere." The pilot looked a little anxious and a little remote. "There were two things bothering me. First, I thought there might be a chance you were an overly religious person and believe it was your duty to bring those boys to justice. But the more likely prospect, the one that worried me the most, was that you might think things over, get a little nervous, and then go to the sheriff and point out the villains to save your own neck. If you ever had such thoughts, Durnford, put them aside. You would swing right along next to your boys."

The pilot walked away down the hurricane deck and Durnford did not follow him. He stood there at the black iron railing under gray clouds and a freshening wind that suddenly felt very cold. The pilot's attentions, he realized, had been motivated by a desire of expediency. The pilot did not want his world turned upside down, even for a week, by the death of one lone Methodist minister. As Durnford was standing at the rail, Thomas came up to him. "Papa, Papa, what's the matter? I've been talking and you don't answer."

"I didn't hear you, Thomas. I was just enjoying the river."

"Davy said I'd never get to pilot a steamboat. Do you think that's true, Papa, because were colored people?"

"Well, Thomas that's not true. There are men of color on the river now, piloting boats just like this one." But what Andrew did not tell his son was that he knew those days were coming to an end. As it was in all areas of society, the black man's options were fewer and fewer. Soon, there would be no more black pilots on the river either. But he did not say what he thought. Instead, he smiled at Thomas and said, "But Thomas I'm not raising you to be a river pilot. You are going to be a medical man. One of the finest doctors in New Orleans."

As Durnford led the way toward the gangway to the saloon deck, the port paddle wheel ran over a log, making a terrible clatter and bumping, like a stagecoach running over a rough log road. The pilot who had been lounging at the rail, rushed into the pilot house and seized the boat's wheel. A collection of curses Durnford had not heard in years filled the air as Andrew hurried his son down the gangway.

Durnford delivered Thomas to Marie-Charlotte in the saloon. His mind was on Barba. Was it true? Had his trusted servant, the playmate of his boyhood, killed a man? And for what reason? Could it be possible Barba was a slave gone bad? The pilot was certain in his description. Hollingsworth had been struck and hit hard enough to kill him before the minister went over the side. Durnford knew that a fall against a post was unlikely to inflict that severe a trauma. So Hollingsworth was murdered. Killed by Barba. The Methodist minister would have been carrying a large amount of cash, enough to finance his travels and return to New Bedford. That was more money than Barba would accumulate in a lifetime. Barba had never been one to pinch a penny. Any sums he received for his personal use was spent the first opportunity. Sometimes he thought he didn't know Barba. He certainly never expected him to run away from the plantation. But he had. And now a thief?

When did it start? Durnford found the gangway to the boiler deck and started down in a trance. Perhaps Barba was planning to run again. Freedom tasted once could be a cancer eating away at his old friend. It couldn't be done without money. Barba had made it all the way to New England the last time. And Barba nearly starved. He was sorry he had left, Barba wrote through the services of a scribe. True to his word, Barba returned when the money for his return passage was sent to him. Now almost seven years had gone by and Barba showed no inclination to run again. But seven years is a long time.

Barba was surprised and a little dismayed to find that he had been sold to the friend of his boyhood. There had been only a flash on Barba's face, soon gone, but Durnford had seen it. Owned by McDonogh since birth, Barba's working life started at age ten. He started the fires in the morning, laid out his master's clothes. Brushed his suits and shined his shoes. Ironed his collars and cuffs. Sharpened his razor and kept a watchful eye on the old man's inventory of toilet articles. Then during the free times, after lunch and before the end of the master's working day, the two boys did what most boys did. They played marbles in the sand. Hunted with imaginary guns. Ran in the woods.

The good servant was not a man of letters. He never learned to read and write, though he had the opportunity, which was prohibited to most slaves. Barba was lazy in that respect. Or at least he had a lack of ambition, which was a good quality in a body servant. No need to fear a lot of unhappiness or moodiness. Barba had no goals, and thus had no disappointments.

When the senior Thomas Durnford died Barba was out of a job. He returned to his master, John McDonogh. Just why Andrew's father had rented the slave all those years, instead of buying him, Andrew did not know. And Andrew thought of buying Barba for a servant immediately. At that time, Andrew had been back from his studies in Paris for two years. He was modestly successful in his medical practice but it was still a question of the funds necessary for the purchase. Whether he actually needed a body servant was less of the question. Andrew thought he would be doing Barba a service. But when Andrew casually mentioned this to Barba on one of his many visits to the McDonogh mansion, he sensed a reluctance on Barba's part. It was something subtle only a friend of many years could detect. There was always that agreeable submissiveness of Barba the slave, his instant acceptance of the subservient position, practiced and honed through the years. It was an attitude to which Barba had been trained, much the way a dog is taught to heel, and he knew no other life. It was the role of the black servant. Even the rare black slave who learned from the Bible that he was equal to the white man knew the white man was more than equal. So what now with Andrew? Andrew was a black man too, not any different than Barba. They were almost the same age, about the same height and build. They were best friends. How could a friend own his friend? No. It was a bad idea, Durnford thought at the time.

But when McDonogh suggested a way to buy St. Rosalie, offered funds to purchase slaves and equipment, Durnford knew he had to have his body servant. Not long after the purchase, Barba ran away. After Barba ran away, had been gone then several months and wanted so desperately to return, the matter had to be examined. Few owners would take a runaway back. Most refused to consider it. It was either untold numbers of lashes or the auction block in New Orleans. Durnford chose neither. He simply sent the money for Barba's return and never said a word.

But this time he could not be silent. Andrew knew he must confront the friend of his youth, his trusted body servant, Barba. And what would he say to him? Durnford did not know. He knew only that Barba was a dangerous man. He'd killed for money. He could not be trusted. The anger and resentment festering in the humble servant for seven years had surfaced in the outrageous act of taking another man's life. And now Barba must be taken to the agent in New Orleans, put on the auction block and sold for the best price the agent could get. No one must know the reason for parting with the long-term slave. That would do Barba no good because he would be a marked man, sold at a cheap price for heavy labor, watched and lashed constantly, until he finally ran away or died.

"Barba, we have matters to discuss." Durnford had found his old friend sitting on a small cask in the middle of the lower deck. He was surrounded by Phyllis, her children Wainy and Frank, and several of the other slaves purchased in Virginia. Barba was describing to the newcomers the plantation life at St. Rosalie. He was animated, in a joyful mood, and enjoying his position of respect among the slaves. Barba gave a slight start as Durnford put a hand on his shoulder.

"Massar Andrew I didn't heared you come up." Barba jumped to his feet. His smile faded when he saw the serious look on his owner's face.

Durnford nodded. "Yes, Barba, we have some business to discuss." Then Durnford led the way to the back of the steamboat, where there was an open space between the lower deck cargo and the spoon-shaped stern. Durnford rolled a keg out and sat down on it, motioning to Barba, and the slave dropped to the deck and sat cross-legged before his master. Slowly, Durnford filled his pipe with tobacco, tamped it down, and lit a match. He puffed a cloud of blue smoke, almost absently turned the pipe in his hand, and finally said to Barba, "Do you remember the Methodist minister who traveled with us from New Orleans?"

"Oh, yassar, massar. I members that ones."

"He was on this boat too. I saw him when we got off at Cincinnati."

"Well I sawed him too, massar. Right on this old steamboat. Just big as life there he was again."

"Do you remember the body they pulled from the lock at Louisville?"

"Oh, yassar, massar. That war him again. I heared 'em say were the minister, that Hollinsword."

"Well, Barba, that was indeed Hollingsworth, the same Methodist minister we saw often on the ship out of New Orleans. And how do you suppose he came to be in the river, Barba?"

"Well I reckon he falled in and got drowned, massar."

"Barba, you know there was an inquest at Louisville?"

"I sorry, massar."

"Why are you sorry, Barba?"

"I not know what a quest be, massar."

"An inquest, Barba, is an investigation into the cause of death. It is a hearing conducted by the coroner, who has the power to subpoena witness and put questions to them."

Barba nodded, his face a somber and blank expression.

"I was compelled to go to that inquest, Barba, because I was the one who identified the body."

"Yassar, massar. I heared you call out it was Hollinsword."

"Do you know how Hollingsworth died, Barba?"

"Well he falled in de riber an drownded, massar. Just like you said."

"Well why do you say he drowned, Barba?"

"Cause he found in de riber, massar. And I heared you tell to Missy Remy and de chillins dat de man done drownded, massar."

Durnford paused and studied his servant's face. There was on his face a peaceful and composed look, a total lack of concern. "Barba, the coroner made a finding that Hollingsworth did not drown, he was dead before he went into the river."

Now Barba frowned. "How he knows dat, massar."

"They cut open his chest, remove the lungs and squeeze the tissue. If the tissue is dry, the lungs not full of water, the man did not drown. He was not breathing, and was dead before the body went into the river, Barba."

"So they did dat, massar? Cut open dat Hollinsword like dat. What they do dat for, massar?"

"Barba, that is a standard medical procedure in drowning cases, to determine the manner of death. Did the man die by drowning in the river, or was he dead before that? Was he thrown into the river to hide the body? It happens many times. And what few people know is that dead men do not sink to the bottom. When a man drowns, of course, his lungs fill with water, and likely he will then sink to the bottom. But if a man is already dead, his lungs are full of air, the body floats."

"Well dat be some interesten facts, massar."

"Do you know anything about how Hollingsworth died, Barba."

"No, suh, massar! How I know dat? I not be seein' nothin' bout it."

"The coroner made a finding of accidental death, Barba. He surmised that Hollingsworth slipped on the boat, struck his head on a post, which blow killed him, and then fell over the side."

"Oh, dat can be so, massar. Dat can be what happen, fo sure."

"Is that what you saw, Barba?"

"No suh, massar. I seed nothin'. How I see dat man fall off de boat up der, massar?"

"Well, Barba, he did not fall off one of the upper decks. That would be impossible. The upper decks all have high rails along the sides. Only down here, on the cargo deck, are there no rails. So I thought perhaps he had struck his head down here and fallen over and that you might have seen him do that."

"Why, massar I seed no such thing. And dat man Hollinsword, why he come down here, massar? That white man have no business down here."

Durnford twisted his pipe in his hands. It had gone out and felt cold. He tapped out the tobacco on the floor, watched as the wind blew the ashes and unburned fragments over the stern, then looked at Barba. "Witnesses said Hollingsworth had been down here, Barba. He had been down here a few nights before. Sitting about where I am now. They heard his voice. He was talking to some of the slaves. Talking about abolition and such."

"Well, I declare, massar. Right down here and I never did seed him. Spect I sleep at de time."

"You know nothing of how Hollingsworth met his death then, Barba."

"Neber seen him down heah, massar. Can't say what happen to de man."

"Very good, then, Barba. Very good. You can go back now. And, Barba, send Henry Spalding to me. He was sleeping near the boilers when I came down."

Durnford repeated the same line of questioning with Henry Spalding, and received much the same answer. He was surprised and disappointed to learn that Hollingsworth had been down on the cargo deck and never seen by him. It was, he said to Durnford, an embarrassment, as he prided himself on his alertness. Did Durnford want anything else?

"Barba has told me much the same thing. He never saw Hollingsworth on this deck, and has no information on his death."

"That, I would think, is not unusual, sir. And I rather suspect someone is mistaken when they claim to have heard the minister's voice from below."

"Spalding, I can talk to you in confidence, can I not?"

"You can, sir."

"There is a man who claims to have seen what happened." Durnford spoke slowly, watching for the slightest clue in Spalding's face. But there was nothing in his expression. "The man says he saw two men slide the body into the water from the deck down here. And he identified one of the men as my servant, Barba."

Spalding drew a deep breath and leaned back on the cask upon which he sat opposite Durnford. "I could act surprised and continue with this charade. But the truth is that I was the other man. Barba and I disposed of the body."

The truth went through Durnford like an electric shock. He had heard what he sought to learn. But now he wished he'd never started his quest for the truth. What could he do now but dispose of Barba as quickly as possible. And what role did Henry Spalding play in this? Did they divide the money between them? Spalding certainly had his motive. The sooner he raised the money to purchase his freedom, the sooner he would be with his wife and children in England. "What do you know of his death?" It was too late now. The question rolled out automatically. There was no turning back. It was too late.

"He came down here to instruct us on an escape plan. It is true. He had been here before. He pleaded with me to lead the slaves to freedom in the North. Barba was not involved. Had not the slightest idea what Hollingsworth was up to. And the man was bringing me a map that night. I told him it was useless, I had no intention of carrying out his plan. But he was insistent. Came down here with that map he made. Here it is." Spalding pulled from his pocket a crude drawing. "I suppose it was a little stupid on my part to keep this. Rather incriminating. But I did keep it. I like to believe I would never use it. But in a way it was some guarantee of my freedom some day.  That is if something happened to you and I was sold out, or if you changed your mind.  Anyway, he came down here, Hollingsworth, and I watched him making his way along the edge of the deck.  A very dangerous place.  Suddenly he lurched forward.  I swear I believe one of the people down there tripped him.  Could not be sure.  And he tried to save himself.  Grabbed at a post.  Missed.  And fell and struck his head on the corner of a crate.  When I got back to him, he was dead.  That was when I took the map from his pocket.  Well, there is no such thing as a fair hearing for what happened.  How could we hope to explain it all.  A white man down here and dead.  Looked more like someone had done him in.  No one would believe us.  Barba agreed with me.  So we just shoved the body over the side."

Durnford took the map from Spalding's hand, unfolded it, and stared at the wrinkled paper.  Five places for a safe landing along the Ohio were marked, and from each of those the trail led to Cincinnati.  Along the route were houses where the slaves could expect to be hidden by sympathetic abolitionists.  And the final destination in Cincinnati was high up the hill, in the stables behind the mansion of one of the most influential citizens of that city.  Durnford looked more closely at the map. All routes led to the house of Cecil McMicken, the man to whom John McDonogh had sent Durnford with a letter of introduction.

# Chapter Fourteen

"Sell Barba! You might as well kill Barba, Andrew. Why on Earth would you ever want to sell Barba?" Marie-Charlotte spun around on her stool at the writing desk. She had been entering details of the river passage in her private journal.

"Because of San Domingo, Miss Remy."

"How could San Domingo possibly give any meaning to selling Barba?"

Andrew stood just inside the open door of the hot cabin. Looking past his wife, his gaze fixed on the gray-green vegetation that rushed past the window of the *Martha* as the steamboat pushed down the Mississippi. Below his feet, the rough cabin floor boards vibrated and pounded in rhythm with the steam engines. "I believe Barba killed Hollingsworth."

"The methodist minister? Now whatever brings you to such a ridiculous notion, Andrew?"

Durnford explained that Hollingsworth's death was not an accident. The facial bones at the temple were soft, meaning they had been crushed by a heavy instrument. And when the coroner confirmed death occurred prior to the body falling into the water, Andrew knew someone on the *Martha* had killed the man

"But, Andrew, at Louisville you told me he'd drowned."

"That's what I said because I thought he'd been killed by Henry Spalding. My plan is to free the Englishman next year, and his leaving would have solved the problem."

"And now you put the blame on our faithful Barba?"

Durnford told her what the pilot of the *Martha* had seen that night, and then he repeated the story given to him by Henry Spalding. "Barba claimed he'd seen nothing at all. Barba lied." Walking slowly across the cabin and placing a hand on his wife's shoulder, Andrew said softly, "Spalding gave me the map." Andrew unfolded the sketch Hollingsworth had made of his escape route and laid it on the writing desk.

Marie-Charlotte traced the escape routes to the house of McMicken. "We touched a raw nerve with that man," she said. She looked up at Durnford. "You're wrong, you know. Barba could never have killed Hollingsworth. Barba is as gentle as a lamb. He could do nothing like that."

"We can never know what money will do to a man, Miss Remy. I think Barba wanted to go North again."

"But that's just the point, Andrew. Barba didn't go North. If he killed this man, took his money, why wouldn't he have just left the boat at Louisville?"

"I think Barba did plan to leave the steamboat before we reached the Mississippi, Miss Remy. But when the body turned up, Barba realized that flight would have done nothing but point suspicion at him. It was too late." Durnford shook his head and looked out the window at the passing world a long time before continuing. "And it's very fortunate Barba didn't run before the body was discovered. Had he gone earlier, he would now be hung for certain."

"Oh, Andrew, are you quite willing to believe our Barba did this horrible thing? Could not the story Spalding gave you be true?"

"No. That story is made up to protect Barba. The blow to Hollingsworth's head was struck with great force by a very heavy object. A fall could not have made that injury."

Andrew Durnford sighed. "I will withhold my judgment and think this through. But if what I think is true, we must sell Barba. A slave who kills once will kill again. We know that from history. We saw that at San Domingo." Andrew had been speaking almost absent-mindedly out the window. Now he turned around suddenly and his voice was louder. "The slaves down below know what happened. They know Barba killed this man. And they are watching us—that I do realize. They are watching to see if Barba is caught, to see whether he is punished, hung for his crime. If not, he becomes even more clever in their eyes. He is already a leader. And now he's a leader who can no longer be trusted. Too many people trusted the slaves at San Domingo."

Marie-Charlotte looked at Andrew, perplexed. "I know our Barba, Andrew, he would not harm a fly."

"If Barba killed this man, Miss Remy, would he hesitate to kill you, or me, or the children? No. That is the lesson of slave management. We can not keep the rotten apple".

"Is Barba the bad apple? Perhaps Spalding killed for the money. Maybe one of the other slaves did it. We must reason this out, Andrew. We can not make a mistake."

"The pilot clearly saw Barba that night. There is but little chance the pilot is mistaken. Nevertheless, it is far better to make a mistake in selling Barba than to fall prey to wishful thinking, Miss Remy. We can not accept the risk. Not for us, not for our children. Barba must be removed from all influence at St. Rosalie. And even if someone else killed Hollingsworth, Barba should have disclosed that to me. Barba lied. Barba must for that reason alone no longer be trusted."

"Well, Andrew we have time to make up our mind. When we reach New Orleans maybe we'll know what to do."

"Miss Remy, it is a question of facing up to our responsibilities." Andrew Durnford felt cold and sick to his stomach. He had wanted to let Hollingsworth's death go unquestioned. But he'd known he could not do that. He could not have lived with himself. It was not a question of what he wanted to do. He was facing up to what a plantation owner had to do. He looked at life as it was, not as it might be. Not as it was so often portrayed in romantic novels. The unpleasant situation was not his making. It was what he was confronted with. The choice was no choice at all. He would do what the master must do. If he did not make these hard decisions, who would?

The steamboat snaked down the Mississippi along the Kentucky shoreline. At dusk the *Martha* rounded up at the foot of an island. There the boat would be protected from river traffic and trees swept down by the current. The twin boilers had exhausted the supply of wood taken on board the night before. The pilot told Durnford slaves were needed to stock up from the fueling station on the island. Once again Durnford sent his people ashore under the care of Barba and Henry Spalding. Durnford watched while the slaves worked. Silhouettes against the dark sky came up the long gangplank carrying heavy loads of short logs wrapped in canvas hods slung on their backs. Then sliding along again down the wooden bridge they returned to the island to heft another load, until the floor behind the boilers was stacked to the roof with fuel for another day's run. It always amazed Durnford that boilers could consume so much of nature's product. It was the same at harvest time at St. Rosalie. What looked like a small mountain of wood burned so quickly to keep the kettles boiling.

It was hot tucked in behind the island that night. Andrew slept fitfully. Dreams stormed through his mind. And again there was that terrible pressure in his head. Off in the distance was the faint smell of musk. He dreamed of Barba and the hard life at St. Rosalie. Then he dreamed he was at sea, and that the ship rolled and plunged. And it was hot. Much hotter than earlier.

Suddenly he was awake. It seemed his very skin burned, so hot was it in the cabin. Durnford sat up. He put his feet on the warm boards. Marie-Charlotte breathed softly in the bunk above him. Across the room, the two children slept quietly in their bunk beds. Andrew pulled on pants and a shirt and slipped into his boots and went out of the cabin.

The hallway on the saloon deck was dark and he felt his way along to the gangway and then up those creaking planks to the hurricane deck. It was dark everywhere. Not a light on the boat. Bright stars poked holes in the clouds and a thin silver moon penetrated the haze, yielding a light which barely illuminated the horizon. Durnford stopped at the rail. It seemed to him the steamboat was alive. The rail vibrated. But no engines ran. The deck trembled. The air was full of the incense of musk. His head throbbed. Then there was something stronger about the musk. No. It was not musk any longer. It was the smell of sulfur, unmistakable. This Andrew had never experienced. Was the pain in his head stronger? No it was not. It was receding. Now he was to be tormented by sulfur? Was there never to be an end to it?

He listened to the loud snooring of deck passengers at the stern. From far below came now and then the hollow cough of one of the slaves disturbed in his sleep. Not another human was awake on the boat. Not even a watch was posted. And it was silent. Silent on the boat. Silent on shore. With a start Andrew realized that the sounds of the night birds were absent. Not a cricket stirred in the distance. Not a frog croaked. There was no wind. Where were the mosquitoes, the plague of any warm night?

Durnford clipped a cigar, struck a match and was himself startled by the sudden glow and the strong smell of sulfur from the match. When he had the cigar going well and the match was long out, he could barely taste or smell the tobacco, so strong was that terrible incense that now pursued him, the overwhelming burden of sulfur in the air all around him. Could it be this new aroma, this disgusting sulfhur had nothing to do with the incense that had plagued him for so many years? There was a physical precense about the sulfhur he had never experienced with the smell of musk which always accompanied the pounding in his head.  This time, he realized, the incense was real.  It was in the air.  But where did it come from?

Andrew walked around the pilothouse to the rail overlooking the bow of the steamboat.  Ahead he could barely discern the outlines of the island.  Then in the heart of that land mass, he saw a strange glow, an orange light.  Was this the embers of a campfire, he wondered?  No.  The light seemed to dance, to grow and even boil.  Strange.  Andrew looked east.  On the shore among the trees he saw similar fires.  All had that strange orange glow.  The fires seemed to ripple with yellow and red and orange hues.  As he watched, one fire spouted a bright red stream, a geyser, which broke and fell back to earth like a spent rocket.

Then the clouds parted and the thin moon cast light upon the landscape like a weak morning dawn.  Suddenly, with a huge crash, and a cracking, roaring thunder, the island split in two.  Water rushed in, and burst into instant steam, hissing and foaming.  The trees on the island swayed in a circle and crashed to the ground.  The land heaved and buckled.  Andrew dropped to one knee in a reflex of protection and covered his forehead with one hand, the other hand gripped the rail.  He watched as one half of the island, the half nearest shore, rose high and then turned slowly onto its side, collapsed, and disappeared into the muddy, boiling water.  The remaining half seemed to stand on its end, and then slip slowly and determined below the water, like a ship sinking at sea.  The island was gone.  Not a tree was to be seen.  It had all sunk below the muddy Mississippi water.

The shock wave struck a few seconds later, sending the steamboat bucking and plunging.  Durnford struggled to his feet. Ahead he could see the hawser stretched taut, quivering against the raging current.  The anchor held.  The steamboat sailed back and forth in the current, like a horse straining at its tether.  The boat rocked dangerously.  Huge tree trunks came down the river and struck the hull with an agonizing thud. The boat shuddered, groaned, and rolled first to one side, then the other. Screams from the upper deck passengers filled the air.  People came out of their cabins, rushing around like blind mice in the dark.  Shouts of horror and pleas to the Lord for salvation came from down on the cargo deck, where slaves struggled to escape the slipping cargo and rolling kegs.

Andrew stumbled along to the gangway. Passengers, men, women and children, were rushing up, and he made little progress against the human tide.  Panic had seized the *Martha*.  He knew he must reach his cabin, find his family and lead them to safety.  But where to safety? There were no lifeboats.  No way to reach shore.

Pushing and straining against the flow of desperate people, Andrew reached the saloon deck. There, a flickering candle in a wall holder lighted the way. Durnford rushed to his cabin door opened it, and slipped inside.

Marie-Charlotte had lit the cabin lamp and it swung in its gimbals. The children huddled around her in the middle of the floor.

Andrew explained what he had seen. He did this in a strangely calm manner. His panic had left when he saw the frightened faces of his family. No, he did not know what was happening, he told them. But the land was convulsing. The island had completely disappeared. They had nothing to fear on the water. The anchor held. As long as the hull remained intact, they would ride out the storm, whatever it was. And the boat had a sturdy, solid oak hull. The safest place for them was in the cabin. If the steamboat should commence dangerous rolls, they would go to the bow, where they stood the best chance of surviving a capsize. And they would take with them all the thick mattresses from their bunks to float them to shore.

The thought of drowning was a terrible feeling of anguish Durnford felt was shared by his family. Except for Thomas, who had always ignored his father's reprimands and swam in the alligator-infested bayous with the slaves, no one could swim.

They waited throughout the humid, sulfur-soaked night. Marie-Charlotte sat on her bunk, her Rosary in her nimble fingers and the children at each side. Andrew turned down the lamp and stared out the window toward shore. He heard the rumble of thunder deep in the earth and the cracking and snapping of trees. The cabin rolled and swayed. Explosions rocked the night, and earth and flames spewed and hissed and soared higher than the treetops. In between were moments of silence and then from the shore came the screams and cries of birds and wild animals in panic.

Suddenly the cabin door burst open and Barba rushed in, followed by Henry Spalding. Barba dropped to his knees on the wooden floor, his wide eyes rolled white in the dim lamp light. "Oh, Massar, I been a bad brack man," Barba wailed. "And de Debil is come fo me fo sure!"

"I'm sorry, sir," Henry Spalding said. "I can not restrain or reason with him. He just babbles on and has gone crazy."

"I de poor sinner what de Debil wants," Barba went on with tears rolling down his cheeks."

Durnford grabbed his slave by the shoulders and pulled him to his feet. Then pushing and shoving, he took him out into the hall with Spalding and closed the door behind them. "Barba, make sense!" Durnford insisted.

Wailing and gnashing his teeth, Barba explained that he was the cause of it all. He had killed the man Hollingsworth. And now the Devil had come to take him down to the bowels of the earth. Barba was sorry for the misery he had caused. But he was scared. He was a coward. He had to go, that he knew. Had to just go over the side and let the Devil take him and leave his poor master and all the good people alone. But he was so scared. He pleaded with Durnford to intercede with the Lord. To save him from his fiery death in Hell.

The boat rolled and rocked. "This is not the work of the Devil! Barba, get a hold on yourself. This is an earthquake. It is nature," Durnford said. "Barba, listen to me. I have enough problems without you behaving like a hysterical old woman."

Barba stopped babbling. "I sorry, Massar."

"He did it for you, sir," Henry Spalding said.

"Did what?"

"Barba heard Hollingsworth pleading with me to lead the slaves to freedom. He heard the minister say he would come back the next night with a map. The map I was to follow once I got the slaves to shore in Ohio. And Barba laid in wait for him." Spalding paused and looked sternly into Durnford's face. "Barba struck him down to serve his master."

"I a bad brack man," Barba said. "I be strong now. No hysterical old woman. De Debil come for Barba now. And Barba know he go to him."

"Barba you are not going anywhere. This is not the work of the Devil. It is a simple earthquake. It happened before. Remember when we were children? I was just eleven then. There was a terrible quake in these parts. Killed many, many people. Do you remember that, Barba?"

"Yassar, Massar."

"This is nothing. Just a few convulsions of the soil. Escaping gas and fires from the earth. Nothing new."

"Yassar, Massar."

"So you understand it is not the Devil?"

"Not de Debil what come fo Barba, Massar?"

"No. It is not the Devil's work you see here." He shook Barba by the shoulders. His servant's eyes were wide and rolled about, and Durnford realized what he'd said made no impression on the terrified man.

Then turning to Spalding, Durnford said, "I am placing him in your charge, Henry. Calm him down as best you can. Then lash his wrist to yours. I will hold you responsible if anything happens to Barba, understand?

"Oh, yes, sir. I certainly understand that."

Durnford watched as Henry Spalding led a stumbling and mumbling Barba down the hall. And as Spalding turned, and started down the gangway to the lower deck, Durnford was certain he saw the man shake his head.

Dawn came with a purple and yellow haze smelling of strong sulfur. During the night, the steamboat had swung completely around on its anchor. The river had reversed and flowed backwards for about an hour. Now, in the morning, all was calm again. Marie-Charlotte and the children slept huddled in a lower bunk. Andrew leaned against the desk and gazed out the window. Tall trees swayed on the shore, but there was no wind. Frightened birds and wild ducks and geese flew aimlessly about, piercing the air with their sharp cries. Smoke and ashes filtered up from fissures in the black earth.

Andrew left his family sleeping and went up on deck. Dazed passengers milled about in groups of two and three, mumbling to each other reassurances and faith in the Lord. The river was a glowing reddish color, and it churned and boiled with thick mud and foam. Out in the stream, Andrew saw a broken and crushed flatboat floating swiftly in the current. Behind it came an overturned canoe and then two overturned rowboats. Now and then he spotted a dead cow or horse and sometimes a deer floating with legs stuck straight out. Later, a dead woman floated by.

A few minutes after seven o'clock, the engineer had steam up in the boilers, the anchor was hoisted aboard and they pulled away. As the steamboat came about, there was another deep rumble, and a shock, almost as violent as those during the night, and the bank and trees on shore near where they had anchored, lurched, heaved, and collapsed into the swollen river.

The passengers slowly revived. Breakfast was served. The steamboat returned to normal. All that day the old pilot steered the boat around hundreds of trees and floating debris which filled the river. The sky was overcast. Sulfur hung heavily in the hot, humid air. At night they anchored again behind the safety of another island. And when they continued the journey the next day, the sun was bright, the air was fresh and clear, it was cool and dry. Everyone on the boat was again in good spirits. The nightmare was over, if not forgotten. They were on their way to Memphis, with stories to tell.

Memphis was a new town, sitting on the lower Chickasaw Bluff on the east bank of the Mississippi. "It was laid out in 1819 by that other Andrew, General Andrew Jackson," Durnford said to his children, Rosella and Thomas, as the steamboat approached the settlement. "The year before, that site was still under Indian control. The steamboat has changed all that. Look at the size of that town. In just fifteen years it has grown to over ten thousand."

Marie-Charlotte taught the children English, the Catholic Catechism, and refined their native tongue, French. But when it came to philosophy, history and politics, Andrew Durnford was the instructor. "Jackson named the city Memphis because it reminded him of that ancient Egyptian city, situated on a similar river."

It was a strained discourse. The children had wanted to know all about Barba and why he was raving so. Durnford was determined they would never know. His mind was closed when it came to Barba. The decision made, no longer tormented him. Barba would be sold at New Orleans. Life would go on. In final answer to the children's persistent pleading, he told them that. The slave had done something he would not discuss with them. Barba would be sold and he would not hear any further discussion. Nor were they to bother their mother with questions.

The steamboat stopped at Memphis only long enough to take on wood and provisions. Barba, his old self and knowing nothing of his fate, was still in charge of the slaves. He supervised the loading of the steamboat, just as he had before. To change anything at that point, Durnford had decided, would achieve nothing. Barba was loyal, a bit demented, perhaps, but for the time being, still trustworthy enough to carry out his duties. If the slave decided to escape, flee North, Durnford had determined to let him go. And Durnford secretly wished Barba would do just that.

The river was broad and smooth now, and by the light of torches hung far out on poles at the bow, and a pale moon, the steamboat ran at night again. The next day they passed Vicksburg at the mouth of the Yazoo River in Mississippi Territory. Two days later they were at Natchez. Natchez was one of the oldest cities in the South. A French garrison had established an outpost there in 1716, Durnford told the children. The French antagonized the Natchez, and the garrison was massacred in 1729. In retaliation, the French massacred the Indians. Now all that was left of that tribe was the name given to the town.

Marie-Charlotte refused to allow the children to go ashore. The town, which lay along the soggy bank, had a reputation of vice and crime. The Durnford family watched from the rail as the other passengers went merrily down the gangplank for a two-hour respite from the river. The boilers were clogged with mud and weeds, the pilot had advised. They would pump water over them, and when cool, clean and restore the pipes to working condition. At the end of the expected layover, the pilot would sound the whistle, anyone not aboard within ten minutes would be left behind.

Even from the safety of the hurricane deck, the children were exposed to filthy language and obscenities. But rather than make an issue of it, Marie-Charlotte chose to ignore the raucous life ashore. She pointed to the high bank above the lower town. There, on the bluff, were the magnificent mansions and churches of the wealthy, those who prospered in the commercial trade from the river.

Natchez was at the lower end of the Natchez trace. That trail ran all the way to Northern Kentucky through Mississippi and Tennessee, connecting the hinterland with the flourishing river trade. It was also the trail home taken by flatboat men who broke up their craft and sold the lumber in New Orleans. They came this far by steamer, then struck out along the trail for home, pockets loaded with gold and silver. Many of them never made it. Thieves and pirates lay in waiting, and those who were foolish enough to travel alone ended up robbed and dead.

As they headed south from Natchez, the Durnfords began to feel at home again. Plantations lined the banks, and slave children and a few white children rushed to the levy to watch the steamboat sail majestically by. Ivory mansions sat back from the river in the shadows of majestic live oaks. Those trees had huge, gnarled lower branches which stretched far out and rested their elbows on the ground. Spanish moss, silver and gray, hung heavy in the trees. Cotton fields surrounded the mansions, and in the fields Negro slaves scratched at the earth with wooden hoes.

Late that evening, the boat put in at Bayou Sara on the west bank, opposite Saint Francisville, for more wood to fuel the boilers. The children were in the cabin, reading by the lamplight. Andrew and Marie-Charlotte strolled the deck over the saloon. They knew what each was thinking. "Yes," Andrew said, "it is a shame to be so close and no time to visit your mama and papa."

"Can we go home soon, Andrew? We have not been there now for three years."

"This is not an easy life, Miss Remy. I make the best of it. I struggle and just break even. It will be a harder time now with all those new people below to feed. I will be in the fields day and night, cultivating the land. I had to expand, you know. More people. More fields. I had to do it. All the plantations around us are growing, and we must grow with them. The price of sugar goes down. Only with a larger crop can we make it a success. That is why we made this trip. And we have good people. None of them sick. You wait and see what I do with the new sugarhouse. When the crop goes up to New Orleans next fall, we will be rich again. The money from the molasses alone will see us clear."

Andrew slept little that night. Several times he left the cabin and walked the upper deck as the steamboat surged south toward New Orleans, located on a crescent in the Mississippi about a hundred miles from the Gulf of Mexico. The town had been the capital of the French colonial empire of Louisiana and a social center of high culture, approaching that of Versailles. Destroyed by a great fire, it was rebuilt during the period of Spanish control and assumed a Spanish character in its buildings, although the heart and language of the town always remained French. Then it was given back to Napoleon, who promptly sold all the Louisiana Territory to the Americans and it became a part of the United States in 1803. With the Americans came an entirely new city upriver from Canal Street.

While the Creoles, those descendants of the French and Spanish, lived in beautiful houses looking inward to courtyards and gardens, walled away from the busy street, the Americans built huge mansions with massive lawns and gardens for all to see. The plantation houses along the river were also in the American style, as was St. Rosalie.

In the morning they passed Baton Rouge on the last of the high land fronting the river. Three hours later, the *Martha* nosed in at New Orleans, just above the old square, where a hundred steamboats rested their bows on the flat shore. Downriver from the steamboats was a forest of masts marking the location of the sea-going sailing vessels that brought in the riches of the world. And upriver from the mangle of steamboats were the keelboats and the flatboats. Everything was organized to take on and off cargo as quickly and efficiently as possible.

The long batture, over a hundred yards wide, bustled with activity. Drays and wagons darted among the piles of cotton bales and kegs of cargo. People of all colors and languages swarmed everywhere. Steamboats, square-rigged ships and flatboats crowded the Mississippi for miles. The giant river was a nervous highway of vessels and ships and steamboats of every description, loaded with cotton and sugar and flour, meat, lard, grain, and manufactured goods, going up and down to ports on the Mississippi and connecting rivers, and to and from Europe and South America. The city was a boomtown of river commerce. The population had tripled in the first seven years it belonged to the United States, it tripled again in the next ten years, then tripled again, and kept on growing. Huge buildings, four and five stories tall crowded the levee for miles and extended back as far as anyone could see.

It was a city of progress. The first railroad west of the Allegheny Mountains ran from the lower end of the French Market on the river all the way to Milneburg on Lake Ponchartrain. And the New Orleans and Carrollton Railroad, which opened just before Durnford left for Virginia, now connected the town of Carrollton, upriver, to New Orleans.

With the coming of the Americans, New Orleans had grown into two cities. The original settlement, the Vieux Carre, retained its Spanish architecture and French language and culture. On the other side of the broad avenue named Canal Street, the Americans built in the grand Greek Revival style and refused to learn French. There was little mixing of the two cultures. Each city within the city had its own public square; the Place d'Armes which became Jackson Square in the Vieux Carre, and Lafayette Square in the American Sector. Each had its own opulent avenue of residential mansions; there was the Esplanade in the old French Quarter and St. Charles Avenue in the American Sector.

The Creoles refused to speak English, although they were forced to understand it because it was the official language, and the Americans never bothered with French. Durnford knew English because his father was one of the wealthy English-speaking businessmen of the city. But at home, the family of Andrew's childhood spoke French; and at St. Rosalie French was spoken inside the mansion and English in the fields.

The Americans brought their prejudices with them, so after he left home and married, it was in the French Quarter that Andrew found acceptance. Although he was restricted to the Negro section of the opera house, most restaurants and public places had been open to him and his family. Things were different in the American sector, though. And watching from the steamboat's deck, Durnford knew that now things were changing in the old French Quarter too.

As soon as the *Martha* ran out her planks, passengers and cargo streamed ashore. The Durnfords watched this activity from the upper deck, where they had a good view down into the city. The river was still high, and the town streets were lower than the water. Only the levee kept the river at bay.

In less than half an hour, the only passengers remaining on the steamboat were the Durnfords and their slaves on the lower deck. The only cargo remaining was the provisions and hard goods purchased for use at St. Rosalie, thirty-five miles down the river. With a blast of steam and screaming whistle, the *Martha* backed into the current. A few hours later, the steamboat rounded up at St. Rosalie.

# Chapter Fifteen

Like the Creole planters who were his distant neighbors, Andrew Durnford wanted a house that reflected his status. He would not be satisfied with a cheap imitation. Through shrewd buying, contracting with craftsman who were willing to teach his people the trade, working with his own hands, and manufacturing brick on the premises, Durnford created a structure which would have cost a leisure planter three or four times as much. It was to that grand house that the Durnfords now returned with the human cargo Andrew had purchased on the East Coast.

The Virginia slaves had kept up a constant babble since the steamboat left New Orleans. But a hush fell over the boat as the slaves realized the rounding about meant they were landing at a new home.

The climate was oppressive. Hot. Humid beyond all expectation.

Lying on the west side of the river, the plantation house was a beautiful, gleaming white. The home, encircled by huge columns supporting a gallery and overhanging roof, sat back behind the levee, facing the river. The house was perfectly square, and two stories high. Along the southern gallery which bore the brunt of the hot afternoon sun hung a dark green curtain in bulky folds. Hammocks drooped in the shade of the lower veranda. Manicured bushes, manicured lawn and pampered flowers surrounded the mansion. Huge oak trees stood off to each side of the house.

Durnford knew that his beautiful home would not last forever. He had defied nature. The house was made entirely of brick. First, Durnford had laid in a brick foundation five feet wide. Then the walls constructed on the foundation were made of double brick three feet wide at the base and tapering to a foot at the top. But the soft, spongy ground formed by river mud centuries earlier was not meant to support such a weight of brick. The elegant mansion already showed signs of stress. The heavy walls had cracked along the north side. These cracks Durnford filled with stucco, cleverly grooved to match the brick joints and hide the fissures. Some day, he knew, the entire structure would come down.

The house was designed for the climate. The walls were thick and cool, and the breeze came in through all the open windows and doors and down the long halls. When the hot and humid summer gave way to the cold and wet winter, fires crackled everywhere. The parlor, drawing room and dining room each contained a massive fireplace with a huge, carved mahogany mantle. The music room, library, and servant's parlor also boasted large fireplaces, but with simple, brick mantles. Even the family bedrooms were heated by a combination tile stove and fireplace Durnford had imported from Paris.

A few feet behind the main house stood the low kitchen, an unpainted brick and frame building with a brick floor. Far off to one side was a carriage house. And between the carriage house and the kitchen stood the hospital, a long, narrow wooden building.

Closer to the river and about a hundred yards to the north was the red brick sugarhouse with its two towering chimneys. A few yards back from the sugarhouse was the dirt street dividing the slave cabins, now eighteen in all, since Noel had competently seen to the construction of additional cabins to house the Virginia people.

The slave cabins stood about two feet off the ground on cedar pilings. Each building was painted with whitewash and contained two cabins. In each cabin were beds made with wooden frames through which ropes were woven and stretched to form the platform for a mattress filled with Spanish moss. Cooking was done on pots hung in the fireplaces or over open fires outside when the weather was warm. Oak chips and bark made good hot coals and clean ashes. Cornbread was baked in the ashes. The slaves mixed a little water with cornmeal and patted it into shape with their hands. The cakes were put into the hot ashes, and scraped clean after they were baked and raked out from the coals.

And all around the plantation, as far as anyone could see, upriver and downriver, stretched the fields of tall cane. Everywhere, ditches and connecting trenches drained the land, with everything flowing with the land which sloped gently to the rear toward the swamps and cedar forest

There were three wells on the Durnford property, all brick lined, but used only for washing and the livestock. All of the drinking water for the mansion came from a huge cistern on stilts at the rear of the house. Rainwater from the cedar roof was collected by a series of wooden gutters running to the cistern. In times of severe drought, the wells went dry and the cistern soon emptied. Like the other planters up and down the Mississippi, the Durnfords were forced to obtain water for themselves and for the cattle directly from the muddy river. The river water was collected in barrels and allowed to settle. Only the clear water at the top of the barrel was used for drinking, and then only sparingly.

In the summertime, life in the big house was comfortable. Ice had already become available on the river. It came down from the frozen North in keelboats and flatboats, packed in sawdust. The ice was used for making drinks and for making ice cream, and the ice was kept packed in Spanish moss and sawdust in chambers beneath the floors of the main house, where it was damp and cool. Perishables were also stored in those chambers, including meat when it was not salted or dried.

No plantation was devoted solely to its cash crop. St. Rosalie followed the pattern, and was self-sufficient. The plantation boasted horses, mules and milk cows and fruits and fresh meat from wild deer and wild pigs. There were small garden plots at the sides of the slave cabins, a large vegetable garden for the mansion, a chicken yard with coop, and two small cornfields. Additional corn, as well as peas, was planted in with the sugar cane.

This was the estate that Andrew Durnford surveyed from the hurricane deck as the *Martha* rounded up on the Mississippi to come alongside the landing at the sugarhouse. In the stateroom below, Marie-Charlotte dabbed Pozzoni's complexion powder on her face. Down on the cargo deck, the children, dressed in their best clothes, clung to posts and leaned out over the water, eager to see and be seen by slave playmates left behind.

The slaves in the cane fields had only glanced up at the *Martha* as it passed, not suspecting their master had come home. Then the pilot blasted the boat's whistle and the plantation came alive. There was Noel suddenly on the veranda, dressed in a white tailored suit which fit his slender frame well. Andrew's mother rushed out upon the gallery above. She was dressed all in lavender with a full skirt and carried a fringed parasol with her for protection from the sun. Durnford could not remember when she had dressed differently, or a time when she ever left the house without her parasol. The house servants came running around the corner of the mansion from the kitchen.   There were shouts of joy and screams of ecstasy everywhere.   Thomas and Rosella waved and shouted.   But all the Virginia slaves, the people Durnford had so carefully handpicked and selected, were silent.

Durnford waved to his mother, and then to Noel and was silent too.  The first business he must tend to was the unpleasant task of taking Barba to New Orleans. He had resolved to inform his faithful servant of his fate in the morning.   Then there was the lawsuit brought by his English cousins.   Was he still the owner of this beautiful mansion, the work of his own hands?   He had left St. Rosalie in the middle of May.  Now it was early September.   Since the deposition at Richmond, he'd received no word on the vexatious lawsuit brought by the English Durnfords.

At first he was tempted to stop at the McDonogh mansion across the river from New Orleans.   But he was in no mood to talk to John McDonogh just yet.   It would be difficult to tell the old man his plan's to sell Barba.   And it would be even more difficult to pretend nothing had happened.   Once the slaves were settled into their new quarters he would have time enough to take a horse north along the River Road and learn what his English cousins had accomplished.

McDonogh's lawyers were confident. They always were confident. McDonogh had used the same firm for years in his many legal battles.  But they did not always win.

The gangplank went ashore and the children rushed into the arms of their grandmother, Rosaline.   The Virginia slaves watched quietly from the cargo deck. They did not speak.  They did not even whisper among themselves.   All were on their feet, attentive, curious, wondering what life would be like working for this pleasant family of colored people. They dare not call them black people.  They had learned that much from Marie-Charlotte, their new mistress.   Black now meant backward and ugly and uneducated.   Slaves were black people.   To call someone black was almost as bad as calling them an animal.   And just a few years ago, to call a Negro a black man meant nothing.   It was just like calling a Caucasian a white man. But this was Louisiana, a society of free people of color.   The Durnfords were free people of color, *Gens de couleur*.   But the Virginia slaves were not familiar with French.   "Gents ob de colored," was how most of them pronounced it.   And Marie-Charlotte quietly suggested they use the English term, "people of color."

Andrew Durnford left the hurricane deck and went ashore to hug his mother. Then the Virginia slaves, silent and sullen, came down the gangplank in single file. Several of the men came first: Noah, Ambrose, William, there were three by that name, and John and Austin and Edmond. There was Lydia, forty-three years old, followed by Sam, thirty-three, and his wife with her daughter of four years, Mary, and the twins Horace and Nely, three years old. They were followed by Phyllis, who would be thirty-two in October, and her children, Wainy, eight years old and Frank, now seven. Next came Crissy Ann, thirty-two carrying her baby, the other Sam, called Samy, and her three-year-old son George Washington, alias Boulgers. And that was about the extent of Andrew's memory.

"Why Andrew, what have you done with your time? You can not recite the names and ages of these people?" Rosaline Mercier Durnford believed in knowing everything to be known about the slaves. That was her legacy from San Domingo. Because her family knew their slaves well and respected them, they escaped massacre.

Marie-Charlotte had not bothered with the slaves since they boarded the steamer at Guyandotte on the Ohio. But before that, during the arduous overland trip, she had spent days in the wagon with the slave children, feeding them, nursing them, and comforting them while their parents trudged along behind. She remembered each one and now whispered their names. "Louisa, six, I think. John about three. That baby there is Cera, about seven months old now. And that woman is Rosana and she I believe is thirty-six. The boy now stepping off is Henry and behind him is his older brother, the other Sam, and he's about eight. And there comes Louisa and her birthday I know is in October and she'll be six then, but I can't think of her parent's names now. The last slave down the plank was the Englishman, Henry Spalding. Andrew called him over and Spalding walked slowly and respectfully up to the Durnford group. Andrew introduced Spalding to his mother and then to Noel.

"Henry Spalding will sleep with you tonight, Noel. And then we will make up a bunk for him in the sugarhouse. Maybe we can save the cost of a sugar maker this year."

The cooks killed the fattest chickens, which were deep fried in oil and served with sweet potatoes, peas, and turnips and a good French wine. In the past, Noel and Barba often ate meals with the family. But this evening was for the family alone, Durnford explained. He had spent too many evenings away from the old matron of the house, his mother Rosaline, he said. Andrew told no one the truth. He could not sit down to the same table with Barba. And this was an evening he wanted to enjoy, without being reminded of his duty.

After dinner, Andrew opened his correspondence in the library. His desk faced the silent fireplace. It was hot. The room dripped with humidity. The letters and correspondence collected for him since May were heavy with moisture. A light breeze, full of heat and dampness and mosquitoes and carrying no relief, came in the windows, open from floor to ceiling. Before beginning his task, Andrew Durnford looked around the familiar room. Shelves crowded with books ran from the floor to the ceiling on each side of the fireplace and along the walls. Most of the books had been purchased in large bundles in New Orleans. Many were in English, most were in French. And a great many of the volumes came directly from France or England by special order. There were classical works and geographies and volumes of philosophy and encyclopedias in both languages. There were books on mathematics and science. It was a complete library. One from which the children could obtain a good education.

Durnford got up from his desk and walked slowly to the books over the fireplace. There were two volumes by John Locke and also *Dicks Philosophy*. He had meant to send them up to McDonogh before he left for Virginia on his slave-buying excursion. Durnford thoughtfully turned over in his hand the second volume of Locke. "How well he knows the frailty of poor humanity," Andrew said to himself quietly.

Next, he picked up the back copies of the magazines the plantation subscribed to on a regular basis. Although business must come first, he yearned to open them and spend the evening deeply engrossed in them. There was *Little's Living Age, Revue des Deux Mondes, Price Current,* and *Delta*. Durnford also noticed that the first volume supplement to *Cy Americana,* and *Buhring's Geography* had arrived by steamboat during his absence.

Finally returning to his desk, he sat down heavily. He was very tired, exhausted, and had not realized the extent of his weariness until the relaxation of old and familiar surroundings. Home. He swatted at the mosquitoes. Business could not be put off.

There were letters from creditors, and letters from debtors and statements of accounts with the steamboats that ran up and down the river, delivering supplies and purchasing firewood. He glanced at memorandums and accounting summaries made by Noel. These were all of little interest. What he opened first were the several letters from John McDonogh. He started with the last letter. Only once did NcDonogh mention the lawsuit. The hearing had been adjourned to October. "Do not concern yourself unduly," McDonogh had written, "the plaintiffs have little chance of success."

All were in bed when Durnford finished with the business matters of the plantation. Nothing required urgent action. Noel had done his job well. Bed beckoned.

Andrew went up the dark stairs and stopped before the canopied four-poster in which his wife, breathing quietly, lay asleep. He looked around the room. In the corner was a cherry and walnut armoire she had purchased in Chartres Street. In the center of the room was a walnut table, surrounded by slat-back armchairs. At the foot of the bed was a chestnut chest. And on the plain wooden floor was an expensive carpet Marie-Charlotte had added to the room just before leaving on the Virginia trip. At first he had opposed the lavish furnishings which now crept into all corners of the house. But she had made shrewd buys, he finally admitted to himself. Their house was going to be just as elegant on the inside as on the outside.

Durnford adjusted the mosquito netting around his wife's bed, then turned around and walked to the open window. The heavy window curtain was tied back to let in the breeze. He stepped out upon the gallery. The moon shone through the trees with an uncommonly brilliant light, turning the Spanish moss silver. Small bats skidded about in the night, chirping to guide their flight. Bright stars blinked in the black sky canopy. The Mississippi sparkled as it churned south. In the distance he heard laughter and voices from the slave cabins. Well, he thought, candles burn in the new cabins and everyone seems to be crowded into them and spilling out onto the street. My Virginia people are happier than they would like me to think.

1856

February 16. Received in a bag on board Steamer
Ophelia, from Boimare, the following
works.

    Fontenelle Oeuvres complètes 11 vol 5 ½c.

    Le duc voyages aux Iles 2 vol cartes    2 „

    Beckford voyage en Espagne &c. 1 vol   1 „

    Billiard voyage a Bourbon 1 vol cartes   1 „

    Choix de causes célèbres 1 vol. portraits   1.25

  „   „ Reliure des ouvrages suivants.

    Théâtre contemporain 2 gros vol grd.   3 „

    Harpers gazetteer of the World    1.50

    Fournier traité de Navigation, 1 vol   1 „

    Rohlf's Russia, Austria, Scotland &
    Fremont's California    1 „

    Lafayette's History by R. Warin 1 vol 1 „

**Journal entries of books received at the plantation from
onboard the steamer *Ophelia*.**

Select Powdered Drugs prepared by

Jarvis & Woodman.

And put up in bottles containing 1 to 1/2 and 1/4
ounces, each bottle enclosed in a paper bag to exclude
the light. Most these powders can be had in bulk.

Liste of Select powders.

Acacia (Turkey) currents.
Assafœtidas.  Dracontium Skunk cabbage
Althæas.  Digitalis
Anisum  Diosmas (Buchu)
Arnicæ (fol)  Dulcamaras.
"  (Radix)  Ext coloeynth comp
Aconitum (fol)  "  Glycirrh.
"  (Rad).  "  Krameriæ
Aloe Soct.  "  Jalapæ.
"  Cape  Ergot
Ammoniac Nanics  Eupatorium (Boneset)
Alumen Exsiccatum  Gallas (Galls).
Angusturæs  Gambogiæs
Arum Dragonroot  Gentianas
Aurantii cort.  Geranium cranesbill
Belladonnas.  Glycyirrh
Calamus.  Helonias dioica
Canella Alba.  Hydrastis canadensis
Cantharis.  Hyoscyami fol.
Capsicum Baccatum  Ipecacuanha
Carbo Ligni  Iris flor.
Cariophyllus cloves  Inulas

Nux vomica
Opium
containing 10 p.ct.
Morphiæ
Podophyllum
Potassæ Nitro
Potassæ Sulphas.
Pulvis Aromaticu
Pulv. Ipecac. et opii
(over powder)
Prunus virg.
cherry Bark
Rheum indicum
"  Russicum
turkey.
Sabinæ
Salep.
Scamonium Lacry
unicorn root. virg.
Scammony.
Sanguinarias
Stramonii fol.
Salsaparilla Honduras

**Durnford's journal entries of powdered drugs available from
Jarvis Woodman in New Orleans.**

# Chapter Sixteen

The plantation bell rang at five o'clock in the morning, calling the slaves from their beds. The regular hands went to the fields before it was fully light. The house servants arose even earlier to open everything up to the new day and put all in order while the cooks tended to the Durnfords' breakfast.

That morning Andrew took Henry Spalding to the sugarhouse, a maze of tanks, tubs, vats, filters, pumps, pipes, steam engines, boilers and machinery. Many plantations still depended on horses or mules to grind the cane between rollers, which squeezed out the cane juice. Durnford began that way. But already St. Rosalie operated with two steam-powered sugar mills, among the first in Louisiana.

"To make sugar is one of the most difficult things in the world," Durnford said to Spalding as they entered the brick sugarhouse. "And to make it right is nearly impossible. A good sugar man, a man with intelligence, one who can sense when the product has boiled enough and is about to granulate, makes the difference between success and failure. Last year was not good. I lost about two thousand dollars. This year I have planted new fields, and we have the Virginia people for a good harvest."

Durnford paused and looked proudly around him. Noel would never become an expert at the tricky game, he knew. Noel was good at books and numbers, but he was too much the dreamer and no scientist at all. He was responsible for last year's losses. Noel hired an inexperienced sugar maker when Durnford was downriver on a medical emergency. But now Durnford was confident. "This year, Henry, we will make it all back, and more."

They stopped next to the first set of heavy rollers. "Did you see the fields?"

"Oh, yes. I saw them. They remind me of bamboo."

"Bamboo? You have seen bamboo?"

"Yes. I have been to China. The cane looks very much like the fields of bamboo. It was difficult to tell them apart. They both have those same long thin leaves and jointed stalks."

Durnford knew that the sugar plant was transported to Spain from China. Columbus brought it to San Domingo on his second voyage. From there, it made its way to Louisiana.

Growing sugar cane in Louisiana had always been more difficult than in the tropical islands. In the islands, cane fields were planted only once in seven years. When cut down, the sugar cane grew back from the same roots. In Louisiana only three crops could be grown from the same roots. Therefore, one-third of the crop each year had to be set aside and saved for seed.

Harvesting of the sugar cane was accomplished with a wide knife about two feet long with a wooden handle, Durnford explained to Spaulding. The blade was razor sharp and had a hook on one side. First, the field hand grabbed the tall stalk and bent it over. Quickly he slashed off the top three feet of dense leaves, then deftly slid the small hook down each side of the stalk to remove the remaining leaves. The leaves were sharp, and the field hand wore long sleeves and gloves for protection.

Once the stalk was cut into six-foot sections and stripped of leaves, it was thrown down sideways between the rows. And after the entire field was cut, it was set on fire where it laid in rows to burn off any remaining leaves. After the controlled burn, the cane stalks were collected in carts and taken to the sugarhouse. There, the stalks were slashed diagonally into smaller pieces to help release the juice, and fed into heavy iron rollers, driven by steam engines. The bagasse, the residue of crushed cane after the juice had been extracted, was dried and burned as fuel in the boilers which provided steam for boiling the cane and running the roller engines.

Durnford had been watching Spaulding carefully as he spoke and suddenly he stopped and stared at the Englishman. "Henry, you mock me. You know already about sugar. And I must demand an explanation."

"I have been here before, sir. I lived in New Orleans. I worked with Norbert Rillieux."

"You were here? In New Orleans? Working with Rillieux? When?"

"Two years ago. I was out of ship then, and answered his advertisement in the *Picayune*. Rillieux wanted men with technical experience. I am a graduate of

Oxford. He thought highly of my European education."

Andrew Durnford knew Rillieux well. He was six years younger than Andrew, the son of a wealthy engineer and planter. His mother was a slave on his father's plantation. And when his father noticed the superior intelligence of the boy, he sent him to be educated in France.

"Henry, why have you deceived me?"

"Would you have saved me from that Richmond jail if you thought I knew this area well?"

"So, Henry, do you plan to escape? To leave me without repaying your debt, then?"

"No, sir. I do not. I am a man of honor. On that you may depend."

"Well then, Henry, you tell me what you know about making sugar."

Going through the steps and pointing out the machinery used, Spalding explained in detail just how it was done. The entire crop had to be cut in a period of about sixty days, usually starting in October. The sugar mill ran at a furious pace to keep up with the cane cutters. First the crop was run through a series of rollers to squeeze out the juice while hot water was pumped over it to extract every bit of the sweet syrup. The dirty brown liquid ran through screens to filter out the trash and mud and then the juice flowed into large pans beneath the rollers.

Less efficient plantations processed the cane juice through six pots, or kettles, each sitting over a separate fire. The juice ran into the first kettle as it came through the screen at the end of the rollers. When the juice reached a boil, slaves added lime to force impurities into a scum at the surface. The scum was skimmed off, and the hot liquid ladled into the next kettle, where the process was repeated. At each step the juice was ladled from larger to smaller kettles. The final kettle was called the battery, and that was under the direct control of the sugar maker. At exactly the right moment, the sugar maker made the decision to "strike." That was when the sugar was quickly ladled out into large wooden coolers to crystallize. But if the strike were called too early, the juice would not crystallize and had to be returned to the final kettle for boiling again. If the sugar maker delayed too long, it could be worse. The juice at the bottom of the kettle would scorch and discolor before it could be ladled into the wooden coolers. The scorched sugar was worth much less at market. In this open kettle method, where the fire was difficult to control, the skill of a sugar maker in calling for a strike to prevent burning, yet allow for crystallization, was absolutely critical.

"After only four years of operation, though, St. Rosalie was a success, and you progressed to advanced methods. You brought in steam engines to power the crushing rollers, and boilers to make steam for the engine as well as the kettles. The kettles you converted to are double-bottomed. Steam from the boiler runs through the kettles, eliminating the need for but one fire. And the steam is easier to control than open fires. Scorching is less of a problem. Finally, you installed one of Rillieux's vacuum pans so that the syrup will boil at a lower temperature and there is much less chance of scorching." Henry Spaulding paused and waited for a reaction from his master.

Durnford was determined to remain calm. Spaulding had made a fool of him, deceived him from the start. He knew all about the St. Rosalie operations.

"So Henry, with all these improvements, what use have I for a sugar maker?"

"The work of the sugar master has not been eliminated. He still extracts a bit of the boiling liquid, pours it onto a six-inch square glass, and holds it up to a strong light. The size and shape of the crystals are visible to his naked eye. A good man sees when the formation of the crystals is at exactly the right stage to form sugar. He calls for the strike, the liquid drops into the cooling trays, and after crystallization, the oozing mass is poured into wooden barrels where the molasses slowly drains into cisterns below, leaving a high-grade, brown sugar. And with all its growing disadvantages," Spaulding concluded with a smile, "Louisiana has one distinct advantage. Your sugar is of a lighter color and better quality than anywhere else in the world."

Durnford's voice was cold and hard. "You knew all of this about me in Richmond."

"I did, yes. The jailer told me about the Negro plantation owner from Louisiana buying slaves. I guessed who it was. I sent him after you. I knew you could not refuse my plea."

"And what am I to do with you now? How can I trust one who has deceived me so?"

"The deception is to your advantage, sir. For the price of a broken seaman, you have gained the services of an experienced sugar maker."

"But a sugar maker I can not trust, and who will desert me at the first opportunity."

"Had I wanted to deceive you, sir, I could have told you nothing. My honesty speaks for me."

"Norbert Rillieux came to see me," Durnford said. "He offered me fifty thousand dollars for the use of St. Rosalie for five years. He wanted to test his new system. Was I a fool to reject his offer?"

"Now I think you are toying with me," Spalding said. "Quite possibly your annual expenses easily exceed that amount."

"I am putting you in charge of the sugarhouse, Henry. I am quite confident you have mastered the procedure."

"And if I demonstrate the secrets of making sugar, what is to be my compensation?"

"We'll talk about that once you have the sugar in hand."

Then Durnford and Henry Spaulding, his slave, sat down on casks in the sugarhouse and talked. At first, Durnford said little. Then he felt a strange friendship with the other man of color. Durnford's mentor, John McDonogh, was white and always a bit distant. Even Durnford's own father was a white man. Now for the first time in his life, Andrew found himself talking to someone he felt understood him. He told him how it all began. Durnford was not a complete stranger to sugar. He had helped his mother on her small plantation and knew a little of the business, he told Spalding. The St. Rosalie land had belonged to Durnford's father. Andrew bought it from John McDonogh, the administrator of his father's estate. There were no improvements on the land. Crude cabins were hastily built to house the slaves and Noel, the overseer.

Andrew Durnford continued his medical practice and lived in the city, visiting the emerging plantation as often as possible. No crops were grown the first year, and Andrew expanded his work force to nineteen slaves, all engaged in clearing the land. The following year, Andrew purchased another 800 feet of St. Rosalie frontage directly north of his property. At the end of the year, Durnford was operating with twenty-two slaves. And even though there was a small house on the property, he preferred to live with his wife and two small children in his mother's house on Tivoli Square.

By the end of the year 1831, Andrew Durnford was finally shipping sugar to New Orleans. He was then the owner of twenty-seven slaves, not including Noel and Barba, and making plans to build a new house to grace St. Rosalie Plantation.

It was during the year of 1832 that the stately brick mansion was completed. Durnford closed his medical practice to build the house, and finally his family moved to St. Rosalie. Next, Durnford bought additional land to the south, and more land to the north, and the old sugarhouse was torn down and replaced. To make it operational, Durnford purchased a steam engine of twenty horsepower. He also bought Lewis, bringing his field hands to twenty-eight slaves. And in May he experienced his first real problem. Lewis, Mac, James, Mary, and Jane, Mac's wife, ran away. He had to lay on lashes, five at a minimum, otherwise they would run again, and it must be done soundly as a lesson to others—

Suddenly, Spaulding interrupted his master. "I am sorry, sir, but I can not agree with you."

"You think five lashes are not enough?"

"No. I think one lash is too many."

"You do not understand, Spalding. Certainly there must be lashes. And not only must the St. Rosalie slaves hear about it, even witness the lashing, but slaves on other plantations must know they cannot dodge their work and take an unauthorized absence without paying the penalty."

The lashes were something Durnford abhorred, he explained. It was horrible. But what could he do? After all, he had treated them well. They brought this upon themselves.

"I have seen the lash and I have felt the lash," Spaulding said slowly. "Not as a slave, but as a seaman. I have never known it to be anything but cruel and unnecessary. When you say they brought it upon themselves you can not be sincere. They sought only what is right and natural, their own personal freedom. You, sir, the owner of their life and limb, are both their complete obstacle to freedom and their only hope for freedom. Surely you will find it in your heart to free them some day, to tell them of your plan to do so, to give them hope?"

Suddenly Andrew Durnford, free man of color, slave and plantation owner, realized he had made a mistake. He had no business talking to his slave about such intimate matters as plantation management. Perhaps if the Englishman himself became a planter, found himself relying on the labor of people he owned, then he might not be so easy with his words of disparagement. But Andrew Durnford said nothing about what he thought. Instead he got up and quietly left.

That evening he sat down in his mansion at his fine desk in his well-stocked library and wrote about it to his friend and mentor, John McDonogh: "As to that part of my disposition respecting the class to whom I belong, I hope a day will come that I will be able to do better for them. But in the meantime, He who sees the remotest part of a man's heart knows that I mean well."

# Chapter Seventeen

"What?"

"I'll give you the harpsichord."

"Give me the harpsichord! Whatever for?"

"You can take it to your house on Tivoli Square."

"Miss Remy, you want me to leave, go into the city in this terrible heat. You talk to Andrew about that. No one goes to the city in the time of cholera."

"Well perhaps you could stay another week. Cooler weather is coming."

"You baffle me, Miss Remy."

"I thought perhaps we'd reached an understanding—"

"And now you're at it again."

"Now, Mama Rosaline, you know we love you so, Andrew and I, but you work too hard here. You need a rest. See your friends." Marie-Charlotte knew she must stay calm. The old woman came to live with them every summer. The city, lying below the level of the Mississippi, was humid, hot, and sickly. Those with resources escaped. For the citizens of the town left to tend to business, or without the means to acquire a country estate, the death rate was alarmingly high. So Andrew's mother came to the plantation in May every year. And each fall it was a monumental task to get her to leave again.

"So now you have your fine clavier, and old Mama Rosaline takes the cast-offs."

"Now, now, you know you love that instrument. And who can play better than you. It's my heart's dearest wish that you be happy. You know your instrument is warped, impossible to tune. And such an ugly thing. Think of how this one will look in your parlor. Up and down the street, everyone will hear its sweet chords flowing from your house. And the way you play, people will throng to your door, and beg for more and more."

"I'm not the simple fool you think, Miss Remy. You need not talk to me like a child. Of course I can play better than most. And I do the new music too. You know that. Who better than Rosaline Mercier can bring alive Mozart and Bach."

Marie-Charlotte knew Andrew's mother was an intelligent woman. When Andrew was a boy, Mama Rosaline ran the household. Andrew's father never interfered with the servants or questioned the domestic accounts. Now Rosaline's mind was growing old, even though she still looked much younger than her age and was remarkably agile. Andrew saw none of the problem. Mama Rosaline interfered too much. She longed to be the plantation mistress. There were times when she completely forgot and took charge. She gave orders to the servants. She rearranged the furniture.

The music room was a mess. Everything shoved about. The clavier, the Americans called it a piano, was back in the far corner now, where it was much too dark and too damp. The harpsichord, which the old woman played so well, had taken center stage near the windows.

"Mama Rosaline, where are the brocade chairs?" Marie-Charlotte looked at the plain, straight-back chairs which she knew came from the old woman's bedroom at the plantation.

Rosaline stood at the harpsichord, her hand caressing its smooth wood. "Well no one was using them down here, child. And the dampness gets to them so. Spect you want them back now that you're finally home. Just the cast-offs for old Rosaline."

"Your furnishings are not cast-offs, Mama. You know your armoire is the very latest style, and it was very expensive."

"These old chairs here are not cast-offs?"

"Yes, Mama, they are cast-offs. And you know I have the matching pair in our bedroom."

She studied the old woman's mischievous face for a moment. "Now Mama I want to talk to you about the servants."

"Well? What about the servants?"

There was a constant problem with the servants. Marie-Charlotte would set them at one task, carefully instructing them on how to arrange the flowers, when to make the beds, when to take up the carpets and replace them with the lighter cloth floor coverings when the weather turned hot. The old woman corrected the servants constantly. Sent them off on some other errand. Changed everything.

"We have brought with us two very bright children from Virginia, Wainy and her brother, Frank—"

"I remember those children. Wainy is eight. Frank is seven. You think this old woman is losing her mind. But I pick up on things. You know I do."

"Those children can read and write. Andrew can take their mother to work in the fields—"

"Phyllis."

"—But those children are to be house servants. The training of a house servant is a delicate task, Mama. We must keep our distance, while instructing with a gentle hand. You are a dear, kind, and warm-hearted person, but you never understood discipline."

"I've never heard Andrew complain of the way I've treated servants."

"The point is, Mama, you would spoil those children. You can't imagine the difficulty I had with your Ned and Charlotte those first few years."

Rosaline Mercier sighed. "Those two are my dear friends, and I miss them so when I'm away."

"That is exactly what I mean. We can not treat servants as friends. They are slaves. They are not our equals."

"They are people. We are people. We are all God's children. That's the way it is and shall always be."

"No, Mama Rosaline. It is not the way it will always be. I want it stopped."

"I'm suddenly very tired, Miss Remy. I must rest. Send Noel up for the brocades. The plain chairs will do me just fine."

Andrew Durnford told Henry Spalding to sling a hammock in the sugarhouse, and went to his medical office in back of the main house. Noel had reported that four of the slaves were sick and kept to their beds there by the plantation nurse.

The long, lanky, and sheepish-looking Lewis, the slave who had led the runaways, was sitting on the bench when Durnford came in. Durnford's nurse was at the medical desk, making entries in her fine hand. She jumped to her feet. "Welcome home, Doctor. I couldn't leave my sick ones to meet you on the levee yesterday."

"You did wisely, Silvie. Are these people as sick as Noel tells me?" Silvie, who had run away with Lewis a month after Durnford bought her, soon stood out as an exceptional woman, and Andrew Durnford chose wisely when he decided to train her as his nurse.

"Yes, they is. All with high fevers. I don't have no idea what it be. At lest it not be the cholera, thank God."

"And what ails our spirited friend, Lewis? I see his mouth is standing open. Is that another one of his practical jokes to keep him from work?"

"No joke this time, Doctor Andrew. Lewis, he gaped about two weeks ago and hasn't closed his mouth since. Comes in here everyday, I excuses him from the fields, but can't do nothin about that mouth."

Durnford bent over Lewis where he sat on a bench in the medical office and took Lewis's large head in his hands and explored the jaw area with his fingers. "Well Lewis isn't faking this one. How has he been eating?"

"Nothing but cornmeal mush, and chokes almost to death on that. Can't seem to swallow much good."

During this conversation Durnford moved his hands about delicately, but firmly, looking for the just the right position on the slave's jaw. "The condilous joint is out of place." Then with a sharp but forceful twist, Durnford forced the jaw into place.

Lewis screamed, jumped up from the bench, and put both hands to his jaw. "Massar, you hurt me most terrible bad!"

"Yes, Lewis, that's true. But it was necessary. You see you can talk now. And you can eat and chew. Now I'll give you the rest of the day off, but tomorrow you're going back to the fields. And remember, Lewis, the next time you yawn that hard, try to hold your jaw in place."

With Lewis treated and on his way to his cabin, Durnford sat down with Silvie and went over the medical history of the four slaves, three women and one man, all down with the fever. Then he examined each of the patients.

All four had high fevers. One woman had a large abscess on her neck as well. "This is felons," he said to Silvie, "has nothing to do with her fever. Make up a plaster from lime and soft soap and that should take care of it."

The next slave, a man, had in his eyes the same vacant look as the three women. In addition to his fever, he had contracted a severe case of ringworm. "Treat this with yellow dock root," Durnford said to his nurse. "Steep in vinegar until the decoction is as strong as you can make it, and rinse the ringworm with it three or four times a day."

Durnford chatted with each of the stricken slaves, patted them on the head, called each by name, and assured them nothing much was wrong with them.

"Well I don't know what it is either," he admitted to Silvie when they returned from the dormitory room. "Just keep them in isolation. Could turn into most anything. All we can do is wait." And having said that, Durnford left the medical office.

Wainy was on his mind. The girl was only eight, but very bright. She would make an excellent nurse-in-training, he thought. But when Andrew got to the house he heard Marie-Charlotte in a dispute with his mother in the music room. It appeared they were arguing about chairs. Not wishing to become embroiled with the two of them on that topic, he quickly slipped into the library, where Noel was at work at his corner desk. Durnford had only glanced over the books, and now he sat down at his desk and scrutinized the plantation inventory. "Noel, I have brought with me twenty-eight people from Virginia, and we seem to be short on provisions. We'll be in a state of starvation in two weeks here if we don't have more corn."

"Well, sir, the weather and want of a proper opportunity has prevented me receiving any. And in addition, the market is not right. After all, to pay nine bits for the article—"

"Nine bits! That's outrageous. We can't afford that. How is our crop coming?"

"In June we had strong winds and heavy rains. Corn turned over. We planted more and straightened what we could that had been blow down by the wind. But we're way behind and won't have nearly what we got out of those fields last year. That storm took fields all around here. That's why the price is up so."

"Well, do the best you can. We still have some Mackerel left from our trip, but it will last only a day or two. What's to be had for meat for our people?"

"The cheapest that can be got is jowls. After the inquiries I made at Boran, jowls in bulk is to be had at Stetson and Avery in Garrison Street at six or six-fifty a barrel."

"Good. I'll give you a draft for McDonogh, sixty-five or seventy dollars. Get ten or twelve barrels. Use your own judgment. Then go on over to Carpenter's Auction Store and see what provisions you can pick up there. There's always bargains to be had, I'm sure. But watch the pork. Some of the last batch we got there was a little rusty and of a profitable nature, which wasn't too bad, but no fat to it and we ended up spending a lot more that we should for lard. Can't seem to cook anything without it. But get what you can, and if it isn't all that good go on over to Davys and buy a barrel of good pork mess, as it will be cheaper to buy than lard, which will cost seven or eight cents."

Durnford kept very little cash on hand at St. Rosalie. The cane, once reduced to sugar and molasses, was taken up to New Orleans.  In New Orleans, the hogsheads of sugar and molasses were stored on the levee if an immediate sale was likely, and if not, the hogsheads were transported by wagon to the warehouse of John McDonogh on Julia Street.  The actual sale of the sugar and molasses was handled by agents on a commission basis.  The sale was usually to sugar dealers, who purchased the product from agents serving several plantations.  The sugar dealers then arranged for shipments throughout the world.  The agent deducted his commission from the sale and deposited the net proceeds to the plantation bank accounts in New Orleans.  The bank deposit slips and copies of receipts and sales documents were sent to the plantations by way of the next steamboat.

During the first two years of operations, sale of sugar and molasses took place at the St. Rosalie landing.  Durnford received the sugar dealer's draft at that time, and made periodic deposits to his bank account in New Orleans.  Then the sugar dealers announced that all future purchases would be on the levee at New Orleans, and all plantations placed their trust in agents.

Although it took only about three hours to descend the 35 miles down river with the current, going upriver to New Orleans was another matter.  It took an entire day, either by road and then ferry across from Algiers, or by steamboat struggling against the swift river.  Therefore, Durnford rarely went to the city.  He had reached an agreement with John McDonogh for the daily business transactions of the plantation.  McDonogh had an office in New Orleans, but usually ran his own empire from his mansion across the river from the Crescent City.  The old Scotsman kept a large amount of cash on hand for his own extensive business operations as a wholesale merchant, real estate developer, building contractor, land speculator, and plantation owner.  When Durnford needed something from the city, he wrote a check against the St. Rosalie Plantation bank account to the name of John McDonogh for the estimated amount of the purchase.  The check was taken to McDonogh by a trusted slave, usually Noel, along with verbal or written instructions.  McDonogh gave the slave the amount of cash requested, and deposited Durnford's check to his own account.

When the sale of the plantation product shifted from the St. Rosalie landing to the levee at New Orleans, Durnford again sought the services of his deceased father's partner, John McDonogh.  All shipments were directed to the McDonogh office and received by McDonogh's men directly from the steamboat.  On each such occasion, Durnford transmitted his instructions in regard to the agent to be used and the sales price he sought.

Although McDonogh always followed the instructions of his protege, he was in a position to advise of a better deal, if available, or another source. In addition, he knew every detail of the St. Rosalie operations, which was a comfort to him, considering the large mortgages he held on the property. Working with McDonogh was somewhat of an annoyance to Durnford, as McDonogh rarely hesitated to criticize. There was between the two men a father-son relationship, and as in all such relationships, problems arose. McDonogh was quick to point out errors, and Durnford was always the over-sensitive son. But both men possessed a keen intellect and mutual admiration and respect.

When he went to Virginia, Durnford left the plantation operations in the hands of Noel, and it was understandable that problems would arise. But the lack of adequate provisions was serious and certain to be noticed by McDonogh. It was just another one of those situations McDonogh would seize upon to lecture Durnford on his "poor business sense." Being a man of supreme confidence, however, Durnford knew when to accept criticism from his old friend and when to ignore it, when to accept advice, and when to go his own way. This time McDonogh would pound into Noel's head the importance of arranging sufficient provisions in advance. And Durnford knew McDonogh would be right. His people were hungry, and he was at the mercy of the market.

"We also had the bad luck to break the horn on our anvil while you were gone," Noel said, "and I don't think we will be able to borrow one from one of our neighbors."

"Then you must get one when you go to town for provisions, Noel. You should be able to find one of about two hundred pounds or two hundred and twenty-five. That old one was a little light. Don't worry about the expense. It is of all necessity for the plantation." And well it was, Durnford knew. Something was always breaking on the plantation and the blacksmith was a busy man. Things of iron held much together and parts must be hammered out for endless things. Nothing was a certainty. The axle always broke on the carts just when they were needed to haul wood or cane to the sugar house, or bagasse to be burned in the fields, or hogsheads filled with sugar or molasses down to the landing. Ploughs broke during planting season. Horses and mules died from no apparent cause when they were needed the most. And slaves took sick and died too, just like the cattle.

Slaves were the most precious commodities on the plantation. Andrew's investment in his work force, sixty slaves now, was equal to half his investment in everything else necessary for a successful sugar plantation: land, the mansion house, the sugarhouse, cattle, equipment, wagons, implements and seed cane. Thank God for the Irish, he thought many times, and the Germans too. Durnford never put his slaves to work digging ditches in hot or wet weather. There was too much danger of the fever. It was better to pay the Irish and Germans $10 or $12 per month for that work. If one of them came down with the fever and died, and they frequently did, he was out nothing. If one of his slaves died he lost a small fortune, for a good field hand was now worth over $700.

The expanded operations at St. Rosalie demanded more work than the slaves could do. Durnford thumbed through the plantation journal. Last year he paid $318.62 to Irishmen for cutting cane; to Louis Fanlan for Negro hire $162.75; to Pierre Pitalien for Negro hire $37.12; to Noel Fredericks hire of a boy to drive bagasse cart $12; and to Jean Girod, a free man of color, as fireman to engine $26.25.

Durnford got up from his desk and walked out of the library and onto the veranda. Yes, it had still cost less than $500 per slave to buy and bring people home from Virginia. He had indeed saved an average of $200 on each of his new people, for a total savings of over $5,000 on the lot. A handsome sum. Durnford looked down at the orange trees lining his drive. Five thousand dollars. Each one of those trees had cost him six and one-quarter cents at Veret's. And his third addition to St. Rosalie, another 1,800 feet of river frontage adjoining his plantation to the north at a price of $25,000 had cost him just five times the amount he had saved through bringing slaves home from Virginia. McDonogh had said it would never work. McDonogh was wrong.

Depression. Durnford was too active for the moods of blue, too busy with the external world of sugar, land and slaves. But that evening of the second day at St. Rosalie, Andrew Durnford, free man of color, intellectual, philosopher of the pragmatic, succumbed to unpleasant feelings. He stood alone on the gallery overlooking the Mississippi. The night was hot but clear. The moon a silver plate coming up the sky with bright Venus close behind. Stars twinkled everywhere in the black-indigo. He pulled his watch from his vest pocket. Almost eleven o'clock. All were asleep, as it should be. Tomorrow was a workday. Early to rise meant just that at St. Rosalie. The bell tolled for all at 5:00 a.m.

The sugarhouse, the trees along the river, all were black silhouettes against the silver expanse of river. Was it not a scene of beauty? But then Andrew Durnford seldom reflected upon beauty. He did not need distractions, which was what things beautiful were all about. The plantation, a blessing and a burden, was always on his mind.

Andrew Durnford said a short prayer now and then when no one was listening, but mostly he talked to God in his mind. And now he asked the same question again: Why Barba? His lifelong companion had crossed the line, done the unforgivable. Barba must be dealt with quickly. No delay. Duty called.

Barba had no knack for pen and paper. His intelligence was for the practical and pragmatic. And if others around him could already read and write, Barba saw no reason why he should waste time trying to learn the game. After all, he had said, to whom would he send letters?

Now Durnford decided to send Barba to the city in the morning, just as he had many times before. The man who looked so much like his master, about the same age, wore his master's old clothes, had his master's build, walked in his master's old shoes, would take to Durnford's agents a letter. What Barba would not know was that the letter would be instructions to put the loyal friend upon the auction block. Irons and shackles would be upon Barba before he realized what was what.

Andrew lit his pipe, walked back and forth on the gallery. The wind was from the southeast, blowing the tobacco smoke from the house, not a whiff went to the open windows of his mother's room at the far end of the gallery. She did not tolerate smoking in her presence. But she was fast asleep now. No worry from that quarter. The worry was all about the selling of Barba. To sell the slave was not the question. Barba had acted. It wasn't Durnford's fault, he knew. He must do his duty. But was this an honorable method? Was it not tricky, something akin to the horse at Troy?

"Well it is done," Durnford mumbled to himself. "Done and finished." But of course it wasn't done at all. What Durnford meant was that he had closed his mind after the decision. Now he would go to his desk in the library and scratch out the letter which his trusted servant would take to his trusted agent. The decision made, the metal of his mind no longer glowing hot could not form another plan.

# Chapter Eighteen

By the steam-powered sloop *Creole,* Captain Gentry master, Andrew Durnford went up the Mississippi to the city ten days later. Durnford had spent those ten days in frenzied activity, instructing the new slaves in the work, and arguing with his mother. The arguments with his mother over Barba had been unpleasant. She knew not the burdens of a plantation master. Her own operation had been small and negligent. Discipline non-existent, and dripping kindness sucking out all profitability. Durnford's nights had been nothing more than closing of eyes and seeing that nightmare of Barba on the auction block and so much for sleep, and guilty thoughts as to whether the sales price of $500 had been got for that rascal.

As the sloop moved upward on the river in the evening light, Andrew finally saw a thousand masts with all their network of rigging penciled upon the moonlit sky. The *Creole* slipped in among them and tied up alongside a Salem ship, which lay to a tier of ships six deep. Durnford crossed the dark decks of the other ships and reached the levee, nearly opposite Rue Marigny, about a quarter of a mile below the Cathedral of St. Louis. And just as he stepped out on the levee the explosion of the evening gun in front of the cathedral broke over the waterfront, rattling and vibrating through the streets, calling the city's slaves to their quarters.

On a firm graveled walk atop the levee, elevated about four feet and lined by Pride of China trees, Andrew pushed his way upriver toward his goal on Chartres Street, the Broadway of New Orleans. The path he walked was lighted by lamps slung on posts and the moon which stood silently over St. Louis Cathedral. Thousands of people of all mixtures were on the levee. Frenchmen passed him, laughing and joking.    An old Spaniard, with his features hidden beneath his sombrero, marched by.  Three old French ladies led a flock of fair girls.

As he continued along the levee the crowd of promenaders grew more dense, with fewer and fewer women among them.  Nearly every man he met, gentlemen all, was enveloped in a cloud of tobacco smoke from cigar or pipe, which added a pungent smell to the decay of the atmosphere.  And all of the scented dandies carried sword canes, and occasionally the bright hilt of dirk or dagger gleamed for an instant in the moonlight.

Another class of men littered the levee too.  Mumbly men, shabbily dressed, unshaven and unwashed, smelling of disease and decay, lounged and slept upon the bench seats and in the grass along the levee.  Durnford passed several hundred of those worn-out types on his way to The Parade, the public square in front of the cathedral.

He passed the market, a massive colonnade, two hundred-fifty feet long.  At the corner of that building he turned and crossed Levee Street. Levee Street was a broad esplanade, wider than five streets of normal size, running along the front of the city. From this spacious thoroughfare narrow streets ran at right angles until they terminated in the cypress swamp less than a mile back from the river.

New Orleans had already been christened The Crescent City because it was built along a graceful curve in the river.  Levee Street angled to follow the river.  The intersecting streets remained perpendicular to Levee Street, so that the city spread out much like the tail of a peacock.  The Parade Ground, a square in front of the cathedral, was a large open green, surrounded by intricate iron railing.  The front of the extensive square faced the river and Levee Street.  On each side of the square stood blocks of brick buildings of Spanish architecture with projecting balconies, heavy cornices, and barricaded windows at the upper levels. The lower stories of the buildings housed retailers of fancy wares, vintners, cigar manufacturers, dried fruit sellers, and many taverns, cafes and pubs.  These shops were all well lighted and within many were merry songs and lively dances.  They might enjoy what time they had left, Durnford thought, because there were rumors that the buildings lining each side of the square were to be replaced by apartment buildings, the first in the city.

Out of seventeen shops on the Rue St. Pierre side of the square, along which Durnford sauntered that evening, he counted ten cabarets.  Upon their shelves were myriads of claret and Madeira bottles, tier upon tier to the ceiling, and in one he heard the shrill tone of feminine anger in a foreign tongue, one of the Scandinavian countries he believed, and the fierce voices of men in French and Spanish mingling in dispute.

At the back of the square, facing the river loomed the cathedral, its dark Moorish towers casting vast shadows over the Parade Ground. Walking with the cathedral to his right, Durnford continued down Rue St. Pierre a block to Chartres Street, where he turned left. Chartres Street ran parallel with the levee. It was the most fashionable street in the city. On each side were cafes, confectioners, milliners, *perfumeurs* and stores with the latest fashions in dress and furnishings. Endless rows of lamps were suspended in the middle of the streets by chains stretching from building to building. All were lit, and the streets throughout the city bathed in brilliance.

At the corner of Chartres and Rue St. Louis, Durnford passed the French Exchange. The lower floor of that large building was lighted by gas lamps, among the first in America, with a glare brighter than day. About three-hundred noisy men, all dressed in the fashion of gentlemen, talked and shoved and swirled in all directions through the spacious room. In the back was a bar with a dazzling array of glasses and decanters.

It was getting late, and Durnford hurried along Chartres Street, stepping quickly across Rue Toulouse to avoid a carriage driven furiously by a black slave. After Toulouse, the buildings were loftier and more modern. More and more English names appeared on signs over the doors as he walked in the direction of Canal Street, and now the shops were almost exclusively occupied by dry goods dealers, jewelers, booksellers, and others with a complete absence of lively cafes and taverns.

Durnford's goal that evening was a boarding house near the head of Chartres Street. Approaching Bienville, he was blocked by a large party of drunken men in a violent argument. French and English voices were mingled in loud confrontation. Durnford crossed to the other side of the street, but the swirling mob blocked that sidewalk as well. The clamor grew louder and louder, and just as Durnford had decided to retrace his steps he heard steel striking steel. He spun around to see several drawn sword canes flashing in the brilliant street light. Then the sharp report of a pistol rang out and a figure slumped to the dirt street. Cries for the *gems d'armes* rang out, and instantly half a dozen officers in plain blue uniforms rushed up with drawn swords.

"Let me through, I'm a medical man," Durnford insisted.

"Yes, yes. It's true." One of the policemen recognized the free man of color whose medical practice had been but a few blocks away.

Durnford opened the fallen man's coat. He saw a huge hole which pumped crimson liquid in unending streams. Already the man had turned pasty white. "It is a mortal wound," the dying man whispered. "I too am a physician. You can not deceive me. Where is William? William!"

A young man bent down. His arm was bleeding through a sword cut in his sleeve. "Yes uncle. I'm here."

"Leave the city in the morning, William. Do you hear?"

"I hear, Uncle."

"Go back to New York. Your mother will never forgive me. Do not wait for my burial. It is nothing..."

The young man looked up as his uncle died in his arms. "This demands satisfaction. Which one of you miserable frogs will die first?" Three drunken dandies stepped forward. Later in that week, Durnford read in the newspaper that the young nephew from New York had fallen with a bullet through his forehead under the oaks in an affair of honor.

The next morning, Durnford got up with the sun, washed his face and hands in a basin near his bed, shaved, and strode out into the crisp morning air. Up and down the street, shutters banged open and servants looked lazily down upon him. Negro women with huge baskets on their heads roamed the streets crying out in shrill French for the sale of rusks, rolls, and bread.

It was a short distance to Canal Street, an enormously wide boulevard with four and five story buildings all along it, and a double row of trees down the middle, which Durnford followed to the river. At the river, he turned left on bustling Levee Street. Horse-drawn drays rumbled dangerously close, sometimes four abreast on the wide street, racing to different parts of the levee to pick up loads.

The stores on Levee Street were all open and nearly every one contained a clothing store or hat shop. All were run by Americans. As he progressed toward the market, into the old part of the city, the stores became French again, and the clipped New Orleans accent of the mother tongue replaced English in the streets. The market, which he had passed the previous evening, now stood out in the sun with its cream-colored stucco walls and columns. Andrew strode into the broad passage running the length of the building and inhaled the fragrance of produce from around the world. In the hot, humid summers, the smell was rank with decay and rancid fruit, and the all-prevailing odor of human urine and excrement from the privys overwhelmed the visitor to the city. But now, in September, the temperature and the humidity had already dropped dramatically. Later in the fall, the climate would become even drier and cooler. In many years the air was too dry. The grass turned brown for lack of moisture. It was a healthy city then, in the fall, with little threat of disease, and air the envy of many Northern cities.

Durnford stopped inside the market and looked around him. Each side of the building was lined with stalls opening both to the central passage and the outside. A dense mass of Negro women shoved about, all balancing baskets on their heads, snapping up vegetables and fruits and beef and fish displayed in bountiful profusion in the stalls.

The stalls were all run by Negro women who rocked back on kegs or three-legged stools and hawked their wares in piercing tones. The entire commerce was handled by black slave-servants, those selling and those buying for the household.

For his breakfast that bright, clear morning Durnford purchased a half loaf of bread, a thick slice of ham, and an orange. On the levee, he sat down on a wooden bench under a Palm of India tree, and took out his sheath knife. On the adjacent bench, a sour-smelling wretch stirred from his sleep, and Durnford tossed him the bread, the ham, and then the orange. Andrew could not eat. His stomach was knotted and tight. He could think of nothing but the man he had sent to auction ten days earlier, Barba, his lifelong friend and body servant. Where could the stout man be now? Probably in the cane fields, or perhaps sold to one of the cotton planters farther up the river. In any event, Barba was gone, and there was a hollow feeling in the breast of his past master. Durnford shook his head and swatted at the flies which swarmed from the derelict he had provisioned. Without a word of thanks, the wasted soul tore into the bread and meat like a starved animal, and then ripped the orange in half and sucked it from its shell.

Durnford got up quickly and walked to the edge of the levee. On the river in front of him were a double line of market boats carrying fish and vegetables. Normally, when Durnford came to the city, he took pleasure in noting the various craft, which were the life commerce of New Orleans. But not this morning. He merely glanced to his left, far down the river to the lower part of town, where ocean ships waited their turn to be towed to sea from their berths in front of elegant residences surrounded by oaks and green foliage. Closer to the market, was the *Creole* in an area reserved for arriving ships, which docked as many as six deep. It seemed to Durnford the boat traffic had grown beyond all reasonable limits. Shipping choked the levee everywhere. Upriver, coastal schooners jammed the shore. Beyond that was a huge collection of steamboats. And farther upriver from the steamboats was the area where rougher craft wedged in, the big flatboats and keelboats which came down the Ohio and Mississippi from the interior carrying corn and whiskey and produce and goods of all descriptions.

The main reason Durnford had come to the city that day was to visit the keelboats. A load of corn could be had most reasonably. By selling off part of an entire boat to plantations on the river, Durnford knew he could secure provisions for his people cheaper than buying from the steamboats. The men from the north country shipped south everything they had when they first heard of the crop destruction in Louisiana. But too many came, and now finding themselves in New Orleans with a load of corn and a saturated market, they would sell at a loss and return home as quickly as possible.

One of Durnford's passions was for the coffeehouses of New Orleans, and much of his time away from the rigors of the plantation was spent in idle enjoyment. However, this was not a day for such enjoyments. He faced a scolding. There was only one man from whom he would take a scolding, John McDonogh, his friend, mentor, and creditor. When visiting the city, Andrew usually stayed with his friend in those rooms furnished specifically for his family. But this time Andrew had spent the night in the city. Morning would be soon enough to explain why he had sold Barba.

The ferry to Algiers, where McDonogh resided on a country plantation, crossed the river at the foot of Canal Street. On his way to the landing, Durnford wandered aimlessly through the old French section of the city. He enjoyed the warmth, which finally crept into the streets with the sun that morning. He inhaled the aroma of the cafes as he approached the slave market near the Parade Ground. A rather large and unruly crowd was assembled at the market, which was unusual as most proceedings were conducted in a dignified manner. Not wishing to mingle with the crowd, Durnford paused across the street, leaned against an iron post, and lit a cigar. There were among the slaves for sale that morning a large number of black men dressed in well-made blue suits and white shirts. They were from the same auction house to which Durnford had committed that fool Barba. The small investment in cloth paid good returns on the auction block, a tradition for which the auction house was well known.

Durnford had never before sold a slave. In buying people, he knew that he provided a better life for his chattel than any slave had known before. But now he had sold Barba, sold him into the unknown. And just as those bothersome thoughts tugged at his conscience, Durnford saw the very man who had depended upon him for life itself, Barba.

Durnford stepped back and grabbed the iron post for support. There, among the well-dressed slaves was Barba, his faithful companion. Suddenly Durnford was very angry. The man should have been sold days ago. What nonsense was this? His agent was guilty of the worst negligence. Certainly Barba, a man in his prime, should have brought a good price, and immediately too.

Then Barba, now on the auction block, looked dispassionately over the crowd surrounding him, and saw his old master standing across the street. The eyes of the two men met and locked. Durnford watched as recognition flashed across Barba's face in a fierce scowl. Then, Barba's faced turned into an expression of stone, while all the time staring directly into his master's eyes. Neither master nor servant heard the clatter of the auctioneer as he rattled off in French and English the bids that were made. "What? *Sacre diable!* I am offered only five hundred and twenty for this fine specimen? Surely there must be more. *Marie, mon Dieu!*" Then the bids came in rapid fire, French and English, and suddenly the hammer came down and Barba was sold.

Durnford watched in silent horror as Barba was pulled down off the auction block by his new master, a giant of a man with stooped shoulders, roughly dressed with flowing unruly blond hair, tall and lanky, with huge, strong hands, obviously not of the planter class. An American. Durnford realized he could have stopped it, called off the bidding, or bid for Barba himself, and he had done nothing. He had stood there, paralyzed in mind and body, stunned by the event, and already Barba had disappeared into the crowd with his new master.

# Chapter Nineteen

Andrew Durnford, free man of color, the owner of St. Rosalie Plantation marched down Rue Royale, where the rich and poor of the city met. He passed under the locksmith's swinging key next to the bank, glanced over at the small shop of the mender of broken combs, and then looked down the street. Delicate wrought-iron balconies overhung the rows of shops. Pretty Latin faces glanced over the pronged railings. Lace curtains fluttered in the windows behind them. Men, young and old, stood leaning on canes around the entrances to the many cafes.

Durnford left the bright street behind him and entered a dark coffeehouse, pushing aside the large Venetian screen at the door. While his eyes adjusted to the dim light, he looked around the room. It was a large room. On the white walls were engravings and splendid paintings of nude women. Beneath the paintings were small tables at which were seated finely-dressed men, enveloped in clouds of cigar smoke. The men sipped negus, a beverage of wine, hot water, sugar, nutmeg, and lemon juice. A few read newspapers, but most were deeply engaged in playing that most intricate of games, dominoes.

Jules Toussaint, the man Durnford sought, was one of the domino players at a table of three near the bar. He sat with his back to the wall. On his left sat a well-dressed businessman of light complexion, and to his right at the small table sat another pale man, equally well dressed.

"Ah, Dr. André, you honor us with your presence." Toussaint glanced up from the oblong ivory pieces arranged on the damp table before him, smiled, and shrugged toward the open chair behind which Durnford had paused.

Durnford sat down uneasily. Toussaint introduced his fellow players, Americans, businessmen new to the city, and Durnford shook hands with them. Andrew did not take notice of the names of the Americans, and when Durnford, speaking in French, declined joining the game, Toussaint replied without looking up from the dominos, "My dear friend, we must be speaking English now, impolite among our friends to do otherwise."

"Barba was sold at auction this morning."

"Jez so," said Jules Toussaint. "And sold well, too. Did fedge the moze high price for a man his age. Five hundred sixty-five dollars, *Americain*."

"Well I want him back."

In a sudden flurry the two Americans attempted to excuse themselves from the table, stating that they had errands to attend and did not want to burden a private discussion. But Jules Toussaint would not have it. "Is nothing," he said, "Our custom to play the dominoes and talk our business. Do not worry, we will not embarrass you, *n'est-ce pas*, André?"

Durnford nodded. He did not agree with the Frenchman, his agent, and he wasn't sure he even liked Toussaint. He had never socialized with the small man with greased hair and a greased moustache, and the two remained only business acquaintances, but neither did he wish to create a disturbance, so he agreed the Americans should stay. "Jules, I have changed my mind. I want to keep Barba. I will take him back at a handsome profit, if necessary."

One of the Americans moved his chair back and declared that he could not touch his coffee, it was wretchedly too bad. Perhaps if they could be excused, he suggested, he and his friend would go to the Market where they would procure some noble coffee.

"Ah!" said Toussaint, "*c'est* very true, *mon Ami*. The coffee is moze terrible here. But we have the dominoes, no? And you muz learn our custom, no seriousness can be got from your expression of distaste. You are no comfortable we discuss so open heah our disagreements. But so is life in Naw Orleanz, my friends. Stay now. We moze finish." Toussaint smiled at the Americans, and moved a piece on the board with a knowing flourish of his hand.

Then Toussaint leaned back, puffed on his cigar and squinted at Andrew through the smoke. "I thing you is juz upset now, André. I been told you seen at the auction. Can be moze distressful. You thing a mistake, sell Barba. Strong in the improvidence, yez. But my papa he own an indigo plantation in them old times.

One day he say to me, 'Jules, me son,' he says, 'I goin to sell that Baptiste what been your friend all your years.' Well I told my Papa no, never should that happen. Din do no good. Baptiste was sold and he did fedge a most good prize which I swore I earn and buy him back. 'Baptiste, he a sassy,' my Papa say, 'Thad why I sell him.' Well my Papa was a wise man, and he right. Baptiste was a sassy. Were no more than a month Baptiste did strike down his new massah most brutal and run away." Toussaint paused and played another piece. Then, with his eyes on the table he sipped his negus, puffed on his cigar, and continued. "You thing it is wrong, a mistake to sell your Barba. Well, I thing it is right—well, then, it is right—you sold Barba for a good reason. You André, am not a man what does act rashly. Your reputation so well known."

"But you see, Jules, every man has his conscience to guide him, which it does so in—"

"Yes, yes! Consien' thad is the bez, Andre. You thing it is wrong to sell Barba— well, then it is wrong. I thing it was right—well, then it is right? Only you, André, know the answer to thad. I older than you, André. I knew you papa well. I know you better than you thing, André. You had moze good reason to sell Barba." At this point, Toussaint looked up from his game and directly into the eyes of Andrew Durnford. "You is the moze juz man I has ever knowed. Good with you people. Tell me now, André, the reason you sell Barba."

"I had good reason." Durnford spoke low and forcefully. He was angry now, angry with himself, and angry with Jules Toussaint who had drawn him into this intimate discussion in front of total strangers.

"Yass!" Replied Toussaint. "I am sure-sure you had good reason. And you thing I be a fool, old Jules who knew you Papa so well, and knows you better than you thing. I thing you will not put light to your thoughts, André. You will not tell the reason for selling Barba in front of our friends here. It would not be from embarrassmen' that you do so decline, but from the truth."

Durnford realized Toussaint was correct, and a wiser man than he had suspected. It was true. Andrew had been taken by the passion of the moment. Barba was sold for more than enough good reason.

"And truth be further thad a great wrong would be to buy back your man Barba. Whatever the reason you sells him before, now you must pay for him much more. And who is the massah after that?" asked Toussaint.

Durnford nodded and agreed. He would wait, maybe a month or so, he decided. And if he felt the same, he would hunt down Barba and buy him back, no matter what anyone thought or said.  And while those thoughts ran through his mind, a glass of negus appeared at his elbow.  He picked it up, sipped it slowly.  Then lit up a cigar, smiled at Jules Toussaint, smiled at the Americans, and joined them in their game of dominoes.


Upriver on the levee at New Orleans was the place where the flatboats and keelboats were hauled high upon the soft mud to discharge their cargos from the northlands.  They came from everywhere.  From the Missouri.  From the Ohio.  Even from far north in Minnesota.  They were stuffed with grain and corn and cattle and all descriptions of agricultural products of the plains areas.  The ugly boats were mostly guided by a long sweep, or oar at the stern, and came swiftly down with the current.  Thousands of head of cattle came to market here.  Kentucky, Indiana, Illinois, Missouri, Arkansas and Texas sent by boat to New Orleans more than ten thousand horned beasts and the volume was growing every year.  A wise man, like Andrew Durnford, bought in bulk here whenever possible.  Many plantations formed clubs and bought by the boatload.  In addition to cattle, there were boatloads of horses, mules, and sheep.  And corn in sacks, and on the cob, the cob being preferred by Durnford because there was less chance of loss by rot during shipment.

The afternoon sun was hot now, and Andrew Durnford could smell the contents of the crude structures he surveyed.  He smelled a boat of apples.  There was the aroma of cheese, and potatoes.  Chickens, pungent in the heat.  Durnford walked along the soft batture past them.  And then there were thirty or more boats, lying side by side, reeking with grease and smelling of pork.  Pork everywhere.  Pork alive.  Pork in bulk in barrels, fresh, salted, and smoked.  And beyond those boats were crude rafts with small cabins hauling down flour from Virginia and Ohio, whiskey from Missouri and Kentucky, lumber from Tennessee, and also from Kentucky, tobacco.

The pork Durnford would never buy here.  He was not interested in live hogs.  Fresh pork could be had at home by sending out Washington into the cypress swamp.  Wild hogs lived there in plenty.  And the article in barrels was not to be trusted.  Durnford preferred buying from wholesalers who inspected the meat and protected their reputations.  He had made that mistake when he started the St. Rosalie plantation.  He bought barrels of fresh and salted pork right off the boat, only to have his labor force sick for months eating it. And there was no alternative. The bad pork could not be wasted. He had not the funds to provision his people with anything else in those early days. It was a costly mistake. The days and hours lost had nearly been his financial ruin.

"Good afternoon, sir," Durnford said, having retraced his steps to the boats farther downstream in front of the American settlements.

"Good afternoon, good afternoon," the boatman replied, rubbing the sleep from his eyes with one hand and mechanically extending the other. The boatman was typical of the rough and hardy men of the Mississippi. He stood over six feet tall, a good half a head taller than Durnford. He was broad-shouldered, broad-chested, large-boned and lean. His hands were massive and bony. His gray and shaggy hair fell uncombed about his ears from under a large felt hat with a huge brim. His wool jacket was much too small and the sleeves stopped about half way between his elbows and wrists. His trousers, rough cotton jeans, barely reached below his knees. No socks were to be seen around his bony shins which disappeared into huge, sloppy, leather boots which had no recognizable shape. The boatman took Durnford's hand without hesitation, not in a token of friendship or equality, but because the black man was seen by every seller upon the levee as a prospective purchaser. The boatmen were seasoned, many having made the trip over periods exceeding twenty or thirty years. They knew there were many free blacks in Louisiana, many of whom owned large estates and several slaves.

"Warming up a bit this afternoon, sir," Durnford said.

"Getting damned warm," the coarse boatman replied, stepping back toward his boat and swiping at his brow with a broad hand.

"What may be the price of corn?"

"Well," the boatman said cautiously, "closed at seven bits yesterday. Running at eight today. Shouldn't be surprised if it ran on up to twelve before it stops. Lots of mildew, rot, a cold summer played the devil with the crops. And I larned that ten boatloads was sunk in the squall up near Island No. 23. But I have a right smart sprinkle of the article thar in my boat."

"I assure you I have some knowledge—"

"Half in sacks, and—"

"—of the market conditions."

"—Half on the cob—"

"I merely inquired—"

"Five thousand bushels in the heap—"

"Out of curiosity, you see, sir."

"Growed on the best rib in old Kentuck—"

"I am very sorry, sir, but—"

"Right from Little Bear Creek. Do you wish to buy?" the boatman asked, drawing a long breath.

Durnford utilized the same approach he had taken in all his dealings, including the purchase of slaves in Virginia. He adopted a position of disinterest, stating that he had no immediate thought in making a purchase, but was only inquiring as to the state of the market.

"But if the price is right, you will buy." The boatman looked at him for a long time waiting for an answer. "Come," he said, "let us conclude our business out of this hot sun. This is my home."

Durnford stepped aboard the crude craft. It was long and narrow, about fifty feet from end to end, with a beam Durnford estimated at about twelve feet.

"I've lived thirty years on the rivers, and this is my last trip. I'm old, as you can see, and the rheumatics is what has got me at last."

The boat was stuffed with corn, fore and aft. The floor and sides were built of thick planks, caulked with tar in the seams. A small, raised cabin stood near the bow, and into this abode the huge man ducked and beckoned Durnford to follow.

Inside, he cabin walls were hung with strings of braided onions, bunches of beets, red peppers, and nets of fruits and vegetables. A small old woman rose from the only chair in the cabin.

"Give us two cups and a flask of the real," the boatman said to his wife.

The boatman pulled two rough stools to the table and draped his bony frame over one. His wife fumbled amid a jumble of pots, pans and cracked dishes in an open locker, producing two mugs and a brown jug.

"A snug home, you have here, sir," Durnford said uneasily. He had been invited in to do talk business, but nevertheless felt like an intruding stranger. The old wife did not seem quite so hospitable as her lonely husband.

"Large enough for us," the old boatman said. "Lived like this for more than thirty years, now, us two. We is used to it. From way back in ought three never lived in anything else. Wouldn't hear of it. Saw the first steamboat that ever came down the Mississippi. Way back in eighteen twelve, I believe that was, in January. Thought then and there it was an end of me, but steam never touched us, though. But the rheumatics is what finally got me, and the little woman too. Now we aims to sell out. Break up the old boat for the wood yard here. Take our money and walk on back home over the old Natchez."

The old woman retreated to her chair in the corner and was silent, never having uttered a word.

The boatman poured and the black man and the old man of the river drank from cracked mugs, while Durnford listened to his story. The old boatman had built a hundred or more boats like this. He knew and mastered every bend and islet from the mouth of the Ohio to the Gulf. Even knew of St. Rosalie plantation. Remembered passing it on his way to the settlements below New Orleans. Year after year, he had sold the boats to the lumber yard, it being always impossible to pole them back up the river against the current, and then he plodded home over hundreds of miles of rough roads and Indian trails, to start all over again, making three, sometimes four trips a year. In his younger days, he'd many times lost everything he had at the gaming tables and saloons in New Orleans. But then the little woman went with him and kept him straight.

He wasn't rich, for sure, the old boatman said. But he had a nice spread near the Ohio in Kentucky. Good soil to farm. A warm cabin for the cold winters. A daughter married well and lived near them with eight grandchildren. And they had enough money for seed and implements. Good mules and other stock.

He had, though, the old man said, suffered early misfortune. His only son was taken by Indians more than thirty years ago. That was why he gave up farming then and took to the river—to forget. But now his son may have been seen up in Michigan. The boy had grown up with the wild men, and no longer spoke much of the English language. The old boatman paused and gazed absently over his mug. "My brother was up there at Mackinac and saw the boy with them Indians. Trading beaver pelts, they were. Could be a mistake, though, I suppose. But the man has the right name. Looks a lot like me when I was younger, my brother says. Won't come home. Wants to live with his people, the Indians, my brother said. I guess that's happened before. My boy would be forty-two now. Imagine that. Lived with them Indians all that time. He was about eleven, you see, when they caught him down by the bank of the river."

The old boatman's eyes were moist, and he was breathing heavily. "My brother said he was dressed just like an Indian. Acted like one too. Had a squaw and three or four little ones. Now how many men have blond hair and gray eyes and the same name as me and remember living near the Ohio in Kentuck and was taken by Indians? I put it to you, sir, ain't that my boy?"

"Perhaps you could get a message to him, tell him his mother and father are alive and want to see him."

"Yes. I would like to do that, yes. But you see he just got in his canoe with them other heathen and they paddle off and were never seen again. And we ain't heard nothin' about him again."

At this point the old woman in the corner sighed and a single tear ran down her cheek.

"What are you asking for your corn?" Durnford said after a long period of silence. If there ever was a man deserving of trade, Andrew decided, this was the man.

"Well, as I said, it closed at seven bits yesterday, goin' at eight today, and on its way to twelve, for sure."

"I can take all the cob corn you have, sir. No use for the sacks, though. What do you say to five bits for the boatload."

"This is the best corn there is in all of Kentuck. Right from Little Bear Creek. Couldn't consider less than eight bits."

"Five and a half. Delivered at St. Rosalie Plantation within two days."

"Sold."


There stood the mansion at the end of a dusty road. All around it were plotted lots on cleared land, some sold, most unsold, and all vacant. The McDonoghville settlement, a monument to its developer, was a singular failure. His mansion at the end of the road was a failure of another kind. It was a monument to failed love. Each time Durnford came to the end of this road the McDonogh mansion never failed to impress its incongruity upon him. Durnford was a young man, just eighteen, when he first saw it. It stood then as it stood now, two halves of an unfinished dream.

John McDonogh's plantation house, had it ever been finished, would have been one of the most beautiful and largest mansions in the South. Construction began almost twenty years earlier and ceased within six months. Unrequited love was the motivation for the beginning and the cause of the ending. Nearing forty years of age, John McDonogh, merchant, planter, and philanthropist, the richest man in Louisiana and the largest landowner on the continent, had crossed the river and bought his first plantation at Algiers. The existing plantation house was all gray with brick pillars below, wood columns above, and galleries all around. He bought the plantation house for Susan, the beautiful daughter of Lane Johnston, a lawyer from Baltimore with ill-fitting false teeth. But the house did not please Susan. It was too close to the river, she said, and would fall in some day. What she wanted was something farther back, and bigger, and all brick. So McDonogh hired an architect, and set his construction crew to work on a magnificent mansion. The new house was to have large wings on each side surrounding a courtyard. The main house in the center was to connect the two wings. And there was to be a double stairway at the front, all in marble, with a carriageway underneath. The wings of the new mansion were built. But before work started on the main part to connect the wings, Susan who had recently converted to Catholicism, called off the marriage and joined a convent of Ursaline nuns.

Now the two wings stood alone and separate. Each had a simple stairway, which ran to the ground at the rear. Shunned by his true love, McDonogh lost interest in ever completing the big mansion. The old man occupied the right wing along with his valet and personal servants. His office was in a room on the second floor at the back. The second floor of the left wing contained rooms reserved for Durnford and his family, as well as rooms for the black overseer and other guests. The floor of Andrew's room was polished hardwood and the furniture was old and weathered, as the windows were frequently left open and the weather swept through.

Andrew peeled off his shirt, washed in a basin provided by one of the servants, and slipped on a fresh collar from the bag he had sent on ahead of him the day before. John McDonogh waited for him in his office in the other wing. When he heard Andrew's soft step in the hall, the old man tossed aside the mosquito net he always draped over himself and his desk when he worked, and sat straight and expectantly in his chair.

McDonogh raised his eyebrows and wrinkled his forehead as Durnford tapped lightly on the open door and stepped into the old man's office. McDonogh looked tired and drawn, Durnford thought. His long hair, swept back and tied in a knot at the back of his head, was grayer than Durnford remembered last Christmas.

The lean man sank back into his cracked leather chair behind his desk and stroked his craggy chin. "Well, you finally come to see me. What was so interesting in the city that kept you there last night?"

Durnford was surprised, but knew he should not have been. The note he sent along with his bags stated he would be up the next day. But McDonogh knew everything that happened in the city. "I did not wish to bother you at the late hour of our landing, so I stayed the night at a rooming house."

"And you wandered the city idly the next day."

"Not so. I made good use of the time. I purchased a boatload of corn, which I will share with my neighbor, Erskine."

"And the price?"

"Five and half bits."

The old man, dressed in a frock coat of the style of fifty years earlier, nodded his approval.

Durnford said, "You asked to speak to me about selling Barba. And you were not sparse in your letter criticizing me on that account. You know you are the only man from whom I would take such a scolding. It is a sign of our friendship. But you will permit me to stand on defensive grounds?"

"Defend yourself if you can, Andrew. But I can think of nothing which would justify selling that good man. He was purchased from me. The least I expected would be a chance to take him back. Now sit down and explain why you did not do that."

Durnford sat down in a worn chair before the mahogany desk of his old friend and mentor. For a moment, he rested his head in his hand. He felt defeated and unsure of himself before he started. Gathering his thoughts, he studied the painting of Susan that hung on the wall. The frail woman, only a few years older than Andrew at the time of her engagement to McDonogh, had been captured in all of her sensitivity by the artist. She had been painted in a pale blue cotton dress, sitting on an iron bench in the courtyard of her father's house in the old part of the city. Now she lived under the high roof of the Ursaline Convent, a weathered white building, where she taught white and Negro and Indian children, safe from the overbearing righteousness of the lean Scotsman who controlled everything within his grasp. Andrew had been visiting the McDonogh plantation at the time of the argument. Andrew, his father and mother, as well as Susan and her father, were at the other mansion near the river, the one torn down later. And the shrill voice of Susan who stood her ground on the one issue where she felt safe, echoed down the hallway. The children would be raised Catholic, Susan had insisted. But McDonogh would not relent. It was a bitter fight. Susan and her father, McDonogh's business lawyer, left that night.

"I think you were a little foolhardy, Andrew, and now you find it difficult to face me."

"No. Not at all, John. Not at all." Then Durnford told the old man what happened on the Ohio at Louisville. Had he never discovered Barba's involvement in the death of the Methodist minister, his faithful servant would still be at his side. "And I do dearly wish I had never learned of it," Andrew said. "Nor could I return Barba to you and ask that you assume the burden of his future."

McDonogh gave a long sigh, leaned forward, and dropped his hands on his desk. "Barba, a murderer. It is so difficult to accept. If only you had taken greater interest in the introduction of religion to your slave force, Andrew, perhaps this could have been avoided. And it was wrong to sell Barba, Andrew. Men, as you should know, can never be converted from errors by harsh measures."

"John, it was not a question of converting Barba from error. You know I would go to the Eskimo country to serve you, but in matters of St. Rosalie Plantation, I must stand upon my own judgment. I too am a man of religion. But religion plays no part in this."

"You profess to be a man of religion, Andrew, but your religion rests too lightly with you."

"I think we have discussed this question of religion enough, John. You have a low opinion of the Catholic Church. Soon you will say something that will bring me to anger. You know enough of my temper. Nothing will prevent me to express myself in strong terms when my feelings are hurt. Now you have too much good sense not to know that you are in the wrong here. As fools have wise intervals, so wise men have foolish ones. You reproach me for selling Barba. Well I am equally unhappy with you on another account. I speak now of the ten acres owned by my father to the north of me."

McDonogh winced and drew back in his chair. The ten-acre tract to which Durnford referred was on the northern boundary of St. Rosalie, fronting the Mississippi. John McDonogh had purchased the land from Thomas Durnford, Andrew's father. And Andrew's father had just purchased it from Jean Baptiste Degruy shortly before that. Then Thomas Durnford died, and Degruy was forced into bankruptcy. Degruy's creditors filed suit against McDonogh on the grounds that the land had been sold for insufficient consideration and belonged to the bankruptcy estate. McDonogh lost the suit. But at the auction sale by the Degruy creditors, the land was bid off to John McDonogh. Since McDonogh was also the curator for the estate of the deceased Thomas Durnford, he simply debited the account of the Thomas Durnford estate for the purchase price at auction and did not lose a penny.

"This is not the time to discuss those ten acres, Andrew. You know I bought them fairly at auction."

"I also know you charged your loss back to my father's estate."

"As I was entitled to do, Andrew."

"John, you offered that land to me with the latitude of paying what I pleased for it."

"I can't say as I remember saying exactly those words, Andrew."

"Then you wrote me afterwards and said for me to do with the tract as comforts best with my own interest in every way. Now years have gone by, and still you refuse to put me in possession, and why?"

"Andrew, this is not a subject we—"

"For the sake of a few dollars that you wanted more than I was able to give. All is not profit in the culture of cane, John. Even you have given up that business. Your cane is all plowed under and planted with vegetables. Your sugarhouse is converted to a warehouse for your brick business. But I still manage to make a go of it, even in these hard times."

McDonogh leaned forward and pointed with one of his long, bony hands. "Now listen to me, Andrew. Your temper is getting the best of you and you have said many things I would not tolerate from anyone I did not consider a son. You do not have the market on wisdom in this world. And, yes, I certainly concede you are the better man when it comes to running a sugar plantation. Otherwise I would not have backed you."

"I'm sorry to speak so sharply, John. But in all the transactions of my life, none ever fretted me more, although it is but a trifling matter to many incidents of my existence. John, I worked hard for fifteen days and fifty-two hands clearing and ditching that land. That labor might have been bestowed on my own land. Then I planted five and half acres of cane. Is this generosity? I who bought ten acres of the same tract to get you to sell the other part. I did it to promote your interest. I did not need that other ten acres. And I hope you will be generous enough to take it back. If it were any one else than John McDonogh I would have made use of my father's land in conformity to the intent and meaning of your letter and let you make the most of the case in court!"

Andrew Durnford gripped the sides of his chair. He was breathing heavily and flushed. A huge scowl covered his face.

"If you have quite finished, Andrew, I will ask you whether you might someday feel obligated to repeat this conversation under oath?"

"What do you mean?"

"I think you have forgotten, Andrew, that the English Durnford heirs are suing me and you. You may expect to be sitting in court before the year is out. The first question to be put to you will be whether there has been any understanding in regard to transferring to you the land owned by your father. I need not remind you that all of St. Rosalie Plantation was once owned by your father. The less we discuss this topic, the better off we both shall be, Andrew."

Andrew Durnford nodded. He had completely forgotten about the lawsuit. What a fool he was. "I see. Yes. Then I shall grind your cane upon the same arrangement we had last year."

"I was down looking at the fields while you were gone, Andrew. It looks like an exceptional crop for me. I think that if you took one-third of the crop in this high market you will receive more than the one-half you got last year."

"That may be true, John. But one-half is what the grinder typically receives. And according to your argument, giving you one-half of this crop would be too much, and you should receive only one-third because that would be more than the one-half I gave you last year.

# Chapter Twenty

The following year was a period of contentment Andrew Durnford had not known for many years. The slaves purchased in Virginia acclimated well and were productive. The corn crop promised to be immense. The sugar crop promised even more---it would be a good year.

Durnford, for the first time since embarking upon his St. Rosalie adventure, took up an old hobby, oil painting. He set his easel under an oak near the river and turned his attention to the slave quarters. If he still had a good hand, he would do the mansion next. Andrew spread light pigment across his canvas as background for the sky. Below that, using his palette knife he buttered a moss green as the general undertone of the land itself. Using a short, flat brush, Andrew outlined the square enclosure, where the slave huts squatted, and then blotted in the trees.

And while he painted, he thought about the good life his slaves lived in those cabins. There were no windows---a wooden slide let in the air they needed. Each building contained two separate cabins and within each cabin itself was a partition dividing the hut into two parts. One part was used for sleeping quarters. From the sleeping quarters, one entered the other room through an open doorway. A wooden sideboard stood against one wall. On it were always sitting a few articles of crockery and kitchen utensils. In the middle of the room stood usually a simple table with a few plain wooden chairs.

Outside the huts were gardens and all was neatness and order. This was in sharp contrast to other plantations Andrew visited on his medical calls. Just this spring he was again dismayed to see the way people lived on the Erskine plantation. The ground around the Erskine slave huts was covered with litter and debris, heaps of old shoes, discarded clothing and chicken bones and feathers. And in all of that mess, pigs and poultry rooted and scrounged and defecated. Not far from the worn cabins, belly deep in a pool of stagnant, muddy water, several mules dozed in the sun. Bony dogs lay in the dirt around the cabins, soaking up the sun. Those rotten conditions bread disease, he had politely warned Erskine many times, all to no avail.

Inside the Erskine cabins, swarms of flies buzzed over tin cooking utensils, attracted by remnants of molasses. Crockery, broken and old, lay scattered about the worn tables, going unwashed from meal to meal. The old clothes hanging on the wall smelled badly of sweat. At St. Rosalie, Andrew Durnford insisted on cleanliness, and made weekly inspections to insure that his people met his standards.

The St. Rosalie slaves, field worker and house servant alike, were respectful to their master. On Sunday mornings when he visited them, they dressed in their best, curtseyed and came up to shake his hand as he approached.

It was Sunday afternoon. Marie-Charlotte, immersed in a recent novel, lounged in a hammock on the gallery facing the river, shaded from the hot sun by the overhanging roof. The low voices of Thomas and Noel, intent on their weekly chess game, came from the parlor.

Rosella and Mama Rosaline were both feeling a bit better now. They each had a slight fever and headache the evening before. Braced by cool lemonade freshened with ice, both the old woman and young girl lay in reclining chairs on the lower veranda facing the river. Rosella read silently from Balzac's *Le Colonel Chabert*, while Mama Rosaline, chuckling all the time, raced through a popular American comedy.

Most of the field hands sought the shade or retreated to the lingering coolness of the damp cabins. Many were off fishing, or visiting other plantations where they had lovers or spouses.

Andrew stabbed at the canvas with his brush, putting into the scene the older men and women who lounged on the ground and cabin steps, the two fiddlers from Virginia who sawed away with energy in front of one of the huts, and a group of little children listening to the music. The children were all dressed the same, boy or girl, in a little sack of coarse calico, which served well the purpose of an all around garment, winter and summer. The women wore the one good dress they possessed. And even though it was summer and progressively hotter through the day, most of the men wore coats, well-made by their women, and hats and good shoes they had purchased from selling their eggs and poultry to the steamers on the river.

When his painting of the slave quarters was finally complete, Andrew turned his attention to the sugarhouse, standing with its doors open. He thought of starting a painting of the large brick building with its two big chimneys which looked like they belonged to a factory. In mid-summer there was no work to be done in the sugarhouse. Not until October would the two steam boilers be fired. Then, when the rolling started, the labor was intense. The sugar hands worked in gangs, day and night, stripped to the waist in the intense heat.

Now in the open space on the dirt floor unoccupied by machinery a small crowd of slaves, ten or twelve, danced a jig to the scrapping of two fiddles. Sweating bodies moved in unison in a double shuffle with limber elbows, pendulous arms and legs, erect heads, arched backs and intense eyes.

Andrew's smile faded when he saw Henry Spaulding staring out at him from a dark corner of the sugarhouse. The Black Englishmen had done his work well that winter. The sugar was St. Rosalie's best. Spaulding though, had soured. His good nature faded. And the new sugar maker spoke only reluctantly to his master since the very day Barba was shipped to New Orleans to be sold on the auction block. At first Andrew thought of talking to Spaulding about Barba. It was, after all, a serious burden running a sugar plantation in Louisiana. Durnford once thought he'd found an understanding friend in Henry Spaulding. Surely the Englishman could see how much more difficult it was to run a plantation than Spalding's simple farm in England. Durnford thought that Spaulding might yet share his pride of accomplishment, a black man successful in a speculative venture that had conquered even a white man like John McDonogh. Was it a yearning for freedom that bore down on Spaulding, Durnford wondered? Andrew had promised him freedom and Andrew was good to his word. Surely Spaulding knew that. At times Durnford thought he should make his position clear again to the man with the tortured expression. Then again, was it necessary to explain? As with all men, Durnford said to himself, if Spaulding does not understand without an explanation, it is unlikely he will see the light simply because I have a little talk with him. He would see my approach as a sign of weakness, perhaps even as a sign that I was wavering and might not be true to my promise. No, no. Let things go and my actions will be sufficient.

That evening, Andrew sat with Marie-Charlotte on the veranda and watched the fireflies skim the grass. A profound silence hung in the heavy, still air. From the distance came a low, rushing sound, like that of the wind blowing through the cane. Only this night there was no wind. The sound came from the powerful river in front of them.

A steamer had passed only thirty minutes earlier, brilliantly lit at each corner by huge torches hung far out over the black water on poles to light the way along the surging current. Then after the steamer had passed, there was not an audible sound except the washing of the river, the distant bark of a dog, and now and then a high-pitched laugh from the slave quarters.

Marie-Charlotte paused in her rocking for a moment. "Your Mama seems stronger today, Andrew, and in good spirits too."

"Yes. I thought so as well. But she is advancing in age, a prospect we must all face."

"But now I am concerned that Mama may be inflicted with something serious, Andrew. She vomited this evening and her fever and headache are returned."

"No need for concern, Miss Remy. A slight indigestion, perhaps. The pork I suspect. I felt a little unstable myself earlier."

"The fever is in the city, I hear, Andrew."

"Yes, dear. Fever is in the city every year. But it never comes this far down the river." Andrew Durnford knew all about Bronze John, yellow fever. It had confronted him during his first year of practice in the city. The disease was insidious, developing so gradually that the poor victim was marked for death before his symptoms were well established. First the victim felt a little indisposed, a slight headache, a touch of chill. Then his temperature rose, but not enough to worry about. He went out, went about his normal activities, ate regular meals. Suddenly his knees gave way and he collapsed into bed. By that time it was too late. The fever had him. His temperature shot up, he thrashed about, his eyes bloodshot, his mouth dry, and he screemed for water. Delirium took over and the sick man struck at those who tried to help him. Sometimes there would be a false recovery, but soon it was clear the situation was getting worse. The victim struggled, his face darkened, the veins distending as if about to break. Blood oozed from his lips, gums, and nose. And he retched up a dark substance, the feared "black vomit of death."

Bodies lay everywhere about the streets of New Orleans during that terrible year. There were forty-five corpses from one boarding house alone. Everyone who could fled the city. Workmen at the cemetery went on strike. They wanted more than the twenty cents per body they were paid or they, too, would leave. The city agreed to pay them a few pennies more. Before it was over in October, the death toll climbed to 1,500 per week.

"I suppose I worry too much, Andrew. But it seemed to me that Lewis came back rather dissipated, don't you think?"

"That rascal. Again he takes a pleasure excursion and visits all our city improvements. If he does that one more time I will fix him so the dogs will not bark at him."

After a long silence, in which both stared off at the mighty river, Marie-Charlotte stopped rocking, and quietly said, "Perhaps you were too severe with Lewis, Andrew."

"He is a wicked fellow. Was he not a relic I would get clear of him."

"But five rounds again, Andrew. Was he deserving of that?"

"Yes, for cutting my cane and corn. For too long I have been overly indulgent of his behavior. I have never been so overcome with anger." Durnford slapped his thigh and jumped to his feet. "I choked to see the unspeakable behavior of that brigand who armed himself with a knife to dare everybody. Had not Noel hidden my gun I do not know what would have resulted from it. His behavior was aggressive, insulting and audacious."

Now Marie-Charlotte was also on her feet and seized Andrew by the shoulders. Looking him squarely in the face, she said, "Andrew, calm yourself. You know it has been long my opinion that Lewis is not quite right in the head."

Durnford stepped back, took his wife's hands in his, and looked at her. Andrew himself suspected that Lewis was unstable. But he had to maintain discipline. He said to her softly. "You do not understand the responsibilities of running a plantation, dearest. Lewis is afflicted with over indulgence in tobacco, true. He is a great hand for smoking and of a weak constitution. But I can not tolerate his insubordination. We must keep a tight rein on our people. Lewis must be made an example. Unless I do that, I will have nothing but disorder to confront me."

Then not wishing to undergo further interrogation on the subject, Andrew excused himself.

Upstairs, Andrew lifted aside the netting of his daughter's bed and carefully observed his precious treasure in the light of his candle.

"Oh, Papa, we must let them go."

"Let them go, my sweetest? Let who go?"

She had been sleeping, and her breathing was light and easy. She'd suddenly opened her eyes and spoke so earnestly it startled Andrew.

"Our people, Papa. We must let them go. I have had the most beautiful vision, Papa. The Holy Mother came to me in her most radiant person. And she told me, Papa, that I would be with her in the morning and that before I left I must make you understand."

Durnford dropped to his knees and placed his candle on a chair near the bed. "Oh, my sweet child," he said, putting his hands on each side of her face. "You have had a dream, a wonderful dream, true...." And then he paused. Rosella's cheeks were burning under his hands. He felt her forehead. It was hotter than her face. Too hot. "Nothing but a dream, my sweetest," he said, struggling to maintain a reassuring tone to his voice. "And you have a fever, which explains it all you see."

"No, Papa. It was not a dream. The Holy Mother came to me. And she told me it was wrong for us to hold our own people as slaves. You have said so yourself—said that we must do something for our people."

Durnford laughed nervously. "True, my dearest, in the end, we must do something magnificent for our people. And that I do intend to do. But slavery is quite a natural state, you see, and it is not limited to the Negro. I have told you before that the Romans in their day had blond Englishmen for slaves. And so it has been throughout history. The Greeks, the ancients—"

"Papa, there is so little time. And now I disappoint Her Most Holy Person, I have failed to make you understand—and in the morning I must go to her." A small tear started down Rosella's cheek.

"Nonsense, my dearest. Of course I understand. What you say is also my earnest desire. But you are not leaving me, not leaving your father and your mother in the morning. You must realize I am a medical man and know these things well. You need fresh air. We will move you to the parlor."

Durnford rose and pulled back the netting, and as he bent over to lift his daughter from her bed, she said softly, "Promise me you will do as Her Lady asks, Papa."

Andrew hesitated. "Rosella, if I made such a promise to you it would be a promise I am bound to keep. This is a delicate subject. And we must talk more about it in the morning. But now you need to rest."

He scooped her from her bed and rushed downstairs to the parlor, calling to Marie-Charlotte, as he went to make the sofa ready. And all the time he carried his daughter down the stairs and through the dark house she pleaded with him for his promise. And each time he assured her, "You have a fever, my child. It is the fever talking. In the morning, when you are better, I will explain it to you. Now, hush,

hush. You must rest. "

At five o'clock the following morning Andrew Durnford was awakened by a chorus of mockingbirds. He'd fallen asleep on the floor next to the couch where Rosella lie in the parlor. Andrew had stood watch over Rosella until three o'clock in the morning, when her fever broke and he felt sufficiently confident of her condition to turn the nursing over to Marie-Charlotte. And when Andrew awoke, he was pleased to see that his wife had also slipped into a quiet slumber in an upholstered chair near the window. Rosella lay peacefully on the couch, an almost holy look of contentment upon her face. As Andrew stood up, he suddenly realized that the peaceful expression upon his daughter's face was evidence of something more than a deep sleep.

Andrew dutifully entered into the plantation journal under July 17, 1836 a debit entry of $10.00 for two coffins, scratching into the record the fact that his beloved mother, Rosaline, and his sweet daughter, Rosella, had gone to God during the preceding night, both without a whisper.

In recording the necessary information, Andrew entered the cause of Rosella's death as murrey fever. It could not have been Bronze John, the dreaded yellow fever, he insisted, and he berated himself for not making a closer examination. A strawberry red tongue would have told him the story---would have confirmed murrey fever.

But when he recorded the death of his mother, his hand paused and the pen shook. She had not died from yellow fever either, and neither was the cause of death murrey fever. He could not ignore the clear facts of her case. Then in short, swift strokes, he wrote down one word, "Cholera."

The funeral took place the following day. Beyond Rampart Street in New Orleans stood a white-stuccoed building. A squat tower capped the building and over the tower was a huge wooden cross, painted glossy white. Inside, at the center of the Catholic Chapel, elevated upon a high altar and covered with black velvet palls were the caskets of Rosaline Mercier Durnford and her granddaughter Rosella. A dozen wax candles, huge and almost stretching to the ceiling, stood in candlesticks five feet high around the caskets. Spread throughout the chapel were other tall candles sparkling in the gloom.

The mourners formed a lane from the altar to the door, each holding a long, un-lighted taper, tipped at the larger end with red, and decorated with ornamental paper cuttings. An old, bent priest and four singing boys, one of them a Negro, all dressed in the black and white robes of their order, chanted the service for the dead. Heavy incense wafted through the hot and humid room. Slowly, the long line of mourners, Marie-Charlotte and the many members of her family, the Remys from the Cane River country and Andrew Durnford with Thomas, and many of the slaves from the plantation, moved forward and lit their tapers from the candle at the head of the two coffins. Then the silent throng fell back while the priest circled the coffins swinging a container of burning spices and gums, filling the little church with the sweet odor of death. The priest chanted in Latin, *"Memento etiam....*Remember O Lord, Thy servants, Rosaline and Rosella, who are gone hence before us with the sign of faith, and sleep of peace. *Ipsis, Domine, et omnibus in in Christo...*To these, O Lord, and to all who sleep in Christ, we pray Thee grant a place of refreshment, light and peace. *Per eundem Christum Dominum nosturm....*Through the same Christ our Lord. Amen."

Three Remy men, cousins of Marie-Charlotte, dressed in black mourning cloth with white sashes extending from one shoulder to the other across the breast and nearly to the feet, stepped forward, followed by a fourth man, similarly dressed. The fourth man was not a free man of color. He was the slave, Barba. Mama Rosaline, knowing that Barba had been sold, nevertheless appended to her will a codicil providing that the former resident of St. Rosalie Plantation should be one of the men to carry her to her final resting place. When Andrew asked Noel to locate his former body servant, the shrewd plantation manager dispatched a messenger by horseback the very morning of death, never revealing that he knew already exactly where Barba worked in a lumber mill. And having provided for Barba's rental for the period and a sufficient sum in addition, Noel soon had the slave outfitted and at the chapel.

The four pallbearers lifted Mama Rosaline's coffin from its station, and followed by four St. Rosalie slaves dressed in the same fashion carrying the coffin of Rosella, proceeded through the line of mourners to the horse-drawn hearse which stood outside. Silently, the mourners followed and lined up behind the hearse to follow it to the graveyard.

Andrew lingered in the chapel, reluctant to bare his soul to the bright sunshine. He was overcome by emotion, guilt, and fear. The incense had brought back in all its fury his migraine. He could not think. He could hardly stand. This thing with Barba, selling him to work the fields, the burden of the entire plantation, St. Rosalie, cholera, Mama Rosaline gone—all this was too much. Had it been just Mama, that he could survive. Mama had already lived longer than most people. Andrew knew her days were limited. But Rosella...his only daughter. Most families lost children, several of them, shortly after they were born or within a very few years. Andrew and Marie-Charlotte had lost a baby girl. But once his child reached five or six, Andrew felt safe. Rosella was someone who would look after him when he was old. He knew he could never depend on Thomas. Boys grew into men and went off on their own adventure. But now Rosella was gone.

Then a monk, followed by two little girls, entered from the back of the chapel. The monk carried a funnel-shaped extinguisher, and reached up and put out the tall candles, while the two girls snuffed the smaller flames between their thumbs and forefingers. Before the light from the last candle went out, the old priest took Andrew Durnford by the shoulder and moved him out into the sunlight to take his station next to Marie-Charlotte behind the two coffins.

The hearse lurched forward. The parade of mourners followed, with Marie-Charlotte taking Andrew's hand, not for comfort, but to steady him, as he stumbled along.

Proceeding at right angles to Rampart Street, the procession plodded onward toward the outskirts of the city. It passed the old Catholic cemetery, now full and closed and sealed, and finally arrived at the new burial place which was surrounded by a high brick wall with a spacious gateway in the center. The wall was about twelve feet tall and ten feet thick. The priest and the four boys, bare-headed and solemn, were the last to enter the cemetery.

Inside were oven-like tombs three stories tall built into the thick wall and extending on every side of the graveyard. The hearse stopped before a section of the wall over which, imbedded in the brick, was a granite plaque engraved in large letters with the word "MERCIER." Each tomb was designed to fit one coffin, and halfway up the wall, side by side, were two gaping spaces to receive the remains of the latest Mercier descendants, Mama Rosaline and Rosella. Once the coffins were slid in place upon wooden rollers, the mourners gathered around. The steady, calm and monotonous voice of the priest chanted the last service for the dead. His words were repeated in dull and subdued tones by the mourners.

Then when the priest and all had left, Andrew Durnford and Marie-Charlotte lingered. They stayed until it was almost dark, when the silence of the still evening was broken only by the cling of tools as the mason proceeded to wall up the gaping apertures to the two tombs. Not wanting to see the final brick take its place, Marie-Charlotte took Andrew's hand and the quiet couple shuffled slowly through the cemetery, never glancing at the various tombs in styles representing cathedrals with towers, temples, chapels, palaces, and structures of all kinds and descriptions which stood upon intersecting street after intersecting street in the city of the dead.

But as they approached the gate again, a scent, powerful and repugnant, came to them from an area along the wall off to the right. Andrew saw across a muddy surface countless mounds of hastily dug graves marked only by makeshift wooden crosses. Newly-dug graves, half-filled with water awaited their unknown occupants as far as the eye could see. It was the temporary resting place of the victims of the cholera plague which now infested the city. The dead were dropped off at the cemetery at such a rapid rate, there was no time to build above-ground monuments. Indeed, for some, no such monument would ever be built, for they were picked up in the street in the morning, never to be identified or claimed. Many were the final survivors of entire families whose bodies lay yet undiscovered in shuttered houses throughout the city.

The bony hand of death had now travelled down the river to visit St. Rosalie Plantation at last. Andrew Durnford, physician and plantation owner, knew that his mother, Rosaline, and yes, Rosella too, were only the first. Now that he admitted cholera had come, Andrew Durnford fought back. Everyone with any symptoms was isolated in the plantation hospital. He washed out their stomachs with warm salt water. His nurse dropped a small dose of calomel on the victim's tongue every other hour. The patients were encouraged to drink as much as possible and fed thin rice water and beef juice and pork broth as much as could be got down them. And thinking he must return to the plantation hospital as soon as possible, Andrew straightened a little and walked a little faster as he and Marie-Charlotte left the cemetery. Far ahead of them on the road the mourners, the slaves, the Remy family and Mama Rosaline's friends from Tivoli Square were walking and would continue walking to the lower end of the city where the steamboat rested with its blunt bow in the batture. Everyone would be there to say goodbye. Everyone except Barba, who must be returned to a sawmill near Madisonville.

Andrew lengthened his stride until he pulled Marie-Charlotte along, protesting. Suddenly, his devastating headache left him. He had decided what he must do.

When they reached the river, Andrew seized Noel by the arm. "Buy back Barba," he instructed. "I don't care what the cost."

"Yes, sir."

"Well, go, Noel."

"Well, sir, Barba has not left. I bought him a week of freedom...it was a small expense...I negotiated well...and—"

"I understand, Noel. Have him sent down to St. Rosalie when his holiday is up."

*Le malade de St. Rosalie,* as Andrew described it in a letter to his friend, John McDonogh, descended upon the Durnford sugar plantation. Gwinne, a house slave who sometimes acted as a nurse assistant and helped in the crowded plantation hospital, fell sick and died within sixteen hours.  He lost one slave child after another, while the sick adult workers struggled through.  Then Reuben, one of his crew leaders died.

Durnford hired Baptiste, the overseer from Erskine's plantation, for temporary help with the slaves.  Erskine's operations were a shambles.  Cholera took most of his neighbor's work force, and Erskine was quite willing to be relived of Baptiste's wages.

In spite of death and sickness, Andrew Durnford expanded the St. Rosalie's operations.  The new and larger slave force augmented by Durnford's Virginia purchases, cleared and plowed new fields even as the field hands, weakened by cholera recovered under Durnford's medical treatment.

More and more, Andrew Durnford was called away from St. Rosalie to tend the sick and dying, white and slave alike, throughout Plaquemines Parish, where he was the only physician.  He served without pay or other compensation.  At times he was gone for most of the week. Administration of the plantation fell upon Noel. Barba, along with the Englishman, Henry Spaulding went to the fields as crew leaders under the watchful eye of Baptiste.

After a long drought, during which time the fields dried out and water in the wells dropped steadily, the disease which had plagued the countryside disappeared.

Then in early September the weather cooled and the rains came.  It rained a deluge for eight days without break.  The fields and yards churned to mud. Andrew could not haul a single cord of wood.  No hay was made. The rain stopped for a few days, then came back in greater vengeance. It rained throughout the remainder of September.  It rained throughout the month of October and into November.  The cane in the fields was fine beyond hope.  But it could not be harvested.  And having expanded to twice its former capacity, St. Rosalie was short of cash.  Andrew needed more shoes, more harnesses and carts and horses and mules to pull them. He had a big crop–the biggest ever.  Finally, Durnford sold the plantation steamboat.  With the proceeds he bought iron to repair the boilers and wood for hogsheads and barrels to hold the sugar and molasses, and mules, carts, and horses, clothing and shoes for the workers, corn and pork to feed them.

Ten days into November the rain stopped.  Two days later Durnford had his field hands out in force, digging ditches to drain the water, building roads through the mud so the wood carts could run from the forest to the sugarhouse. On November 16th he began to cut cane. It looked heavy and full of juice. Andrew danced through the fields. He would be a rich man this year for sure. All of his hunches had paid off. While others drew back, he expanded. All up and down the river, planters were lamenting the sparseness of their crops. Why it happened, Andrew knew not. But hot weather, then cold weather, then rain, had all struck St. Rosalie at just the right times to produce an abundance of luxurious cane. God had smiled upon him. The next day, Andrew shouted out the order to start the sugar mill.

Shortly after noon, Durnford left St. Rosalie, heading south along the River Road with his medical bags slung over his horses' rump. He paused for a moment, and turned his horse to go upon the levee, from where he could survey his plantation. Smoke poured from the sugarhouse. Lines of carts extended from the forest and back, bringing in wood which had been cut and dried to feed the hungry boilers. Other carts rushed to and from the fields, hauling in loads of cane dripping over the sides of the two-wheeled vehicles. Peace and prosperity had come to St. Rosalie. Death and sickness were behind them. As Andrew pointed his horse down the levee to return to the River Road, he waved to Marie-Charlotte who stood on the gallery overlooking the river. She had overcome the grief of her lost daughter, Rosella. Now beside her stood her mother, who came down from the Cane River country to live with them in the room formerly occupied by Mama Rosaline. Andrew Durnford had suggested that arrangement and was pleased to see Marie-Charlotte so happy again. It was not only the presence of her mother that brought a glow to the face of Marie-Charlotte. It was something even more thrilling, Marie-Charlotte, Andrew's wife of twelve years, was pregnant.

# Chapter Twenty One

Henry Spaulding turned and stomped away into the darkness of the silent sugarhouse.

"Spaulding it won't do for you to walk so abruptly from me. We must bring this to a conclusion."

Andrew had been gone a week, giving final care and instructions to those patients still recovering from cholera along Bayou Teche. As Durnford returned along the river road, he strained to see smoke rising from his sugarhouse. There was no smoke. He went straight to Henry Spaulding and lashed out at him before the sugar expert could utter a greeting. There was no excuse for the sugar plant to be sitting idle, Durnford told him, and he demanded an explanation. Now he followed the angered man into the sugarhouse.

Durnford halted a few feet from the Englishman, who turned suddenly to face him.

"Why did I stop? The cane you thought was so rich and full of juice is not. It is mean cane. And it is loaded with aqueous and mucilaginous matter. It would make but bad sugar or tar!"

Durnford slammed his fist into his hand. "Spaulding that is a decision for me to make! I want to be in this market quickly. You do not understand the slightest about running a plantation. Where is the cash to come from if we don't sell sugar?"

"Barba is dying," Spaulding said softly. "He is sweated badly. I am fearful that he will not get over it. He lies now in hospital."

There were only six patients in the hospital. Barba lay by himself along the rear wall of the long, narrow building.

"How long?" Durnford asked his nurse, Silvie, as she led him to Barba's bunk.

"Three days. First the chills, then the fever, then the sweating. It all stop for a while and he appear most normal. Then it start again, chills, fever, more sweating. He rest well now, Dr. Andrew. But he no longer in a conscious."

They stopped before the quiet figure. Barba lay on his back, staring at the ceiling with sunken eyes. His skin was yellow. His face was thin and wasted.

"He be in coma fourteen hours," Silvie said. "And he go bad real quick."

"Not good," Durnford muttered and bent down to put his ear on Barba's chest. "Weak and irregular heart." Durnford straightened up. "First too little water, and now too much. He needs digitalis and something to build his strength. But nothing can be done in this state. All I can do now is bleed him."

"Barba always a vigorous man," the nurse said. "I don't know how this sudden attack come so quick upon him."

"It's not as sudden as it appears. Barba shows all the symptoms of recovery from cholera, an illness he must have regarded as inconsequential. In any event, he had let his cholera go too long untreated. Now he suffers from a general collapse affecting both his heart and kidneys. His weakened condition left him liable to the fever. So now it is difficult to say whether it is the dropsy that will take Barba or the ague." Durnford sighed and put his hand to his chin. "Bring me the best of our leeches. I will spare nothing on our old friend here."

When Silvie returned with a glass jar, Durnford removed the top and emptied the contents on Barba's chest. Sixteen long, shiny black worms crawled from between the wet leaves and placed their large suction mouths on Barba's mahogany skin. The sharp teeth of the hungry leeches sawed through his flesh. Soon all sixteen black worms were busily pumping and swelling with fresh blood from the dying man.

"Could they but suck all the poison out quickly enough," Andrew murmured. "But it is too late I think...too late." He placed his hand on Barba's head. "Good-by old friend. I owe you an apology I fear you will never hear. Now I must go. You know not the burdens of a plantation owner. Neither death nor disease may stay me from my toil. Adieu, Barba."

Andrew Durnford went into the house quickly, where he greeted his wife, Marie-Charlotte, with a sad shake of his head and explained how and why Barba would die. "Not likely will he last the night," Andrew said. "But I must now talk further with Spaulding." He stepped through the large window of the parlor, which served as well as a doorway to the veranda, paused, and shook his head again. "Rather would I tend to Barba this day, but all is not well with our sugar production. Spaulding has completely stopped the rolling, a decision not within his domain, and I must have harsh words with him." Durnford ran a big hand through his heavy locks. "Ah, Miss Remy, you know not the burdens of running this plantation, and I pray God that you never do."

In the dark sugarhouse, he found Henry Spaulding sitting on a barrel, staring at a small piece of glass held out in front of his eyes, upon which was a dirty, thick, brown liquid. Spaulding looked up as Durnford approached. "Observe," Spaulding said, and handed the sample over to Durnford. "Out of thirty-eight acres, we made less than twenty thousand weight. Therefore I have stopped since Thursday in the night. As you may see, the color is not good."

Durnford turned the glass to catch the light coming from the wide door. He knew immediately Spaulding was right. But to stop production without orders. How could he tolerate such insubordination. Durnford muttered, "Nevertheless, to stop the rolling...to let the boilers cool down...when we are so short of cash." Durnford sighed and looked around in frustration. His money was gone, gone for machinery, animals and tools and slaves to expand the fields. Bad sugar to market quickly would be better than no sugar at all.

Spaulding spoke as he reached out and took the sample from Durnford's hand. "Not even old Lebeauche would take such sugar to market." Spaulding stood up. "And you told me we must have not less than a thousand weight per acre. So that is why I stopping the rolling."

Perhaps it was a lie, Durnford thought. But then again he may have said that very thing to Spaulding. A thousand weight from each acre. That was what he always meant to have.

Henry Spaulding walked to the doorway, a dark silhouette in the strong light. "If money is the problem, then think on the Rattan."

Yes, of course, the Rattan, the juicy cane they planned to use as seed. The thick planting cane, saved from last year and yet untouched, had never suffered a frost because of the mild winter. It would yield far more juice. Why had he not thought of that? And he could hold the field crop and let it mature until a hard frost came. By that time the field cane would be thicker and make a better color too, and he could use the very last of it to replace his seed Rattan. Seed Rattan did not have to be good cane. All it had to do was grow new cane. So why waste that juicy Rattan? But he was not ready to thank the Englishman for his insight. "Barba will not be with us long," he said.

The Englishman nodded.

"I'm afraid his dropsy will soon cause mortification."

"Barba was always the faithful servant," Spaulding said. "But I believe you already know that."

Andrew Durnford did not want to be reminded of his folly and the pain he had caused Barba. "Henry, your tone...your entire attitude of late, has not been conducive to retaining my good will. I must put it to you forthright, how have I offended you?"

Spaulding returned again into the shadows of the sugarhouse. "I had hoped my good service would bring the fruit of what had been promised."

So that was it. "Your freedom will come in its time," Durnford said. "But as of the moment I have not the ready funds to purchase your passage to England. Nor can I do without your services in the sugarhouse."

"I do not ask for my freedom now. I speak only of the time after the rolling. I will then have served you faithfully as sugar maker for two seasons. The wages you have saved in one season alone would pay my passage home. And by the end of my second season, you will have recovered your investment in me and made a handsome profit."

"Well, Henry, you speak rather sharply with me, and another master might not take so kindly to it. But we are men of a like nature and I can understand your urgency in wishing to return to your homeland. Nevertheless, St. Rosalie cannot be run entirely according to your schedule. In that department you disappoint me, Spaulding, because I had hoped you understood the demands of such a venture as this plantation. Now, I must tell you it has always been my desire to see you off to your family as soon as possible, and in that regard I fully intend to keep my promise."

Andrew Durnford could not see the expression on Spaulding's dark face against the bright light of the door, so he walked around the Englishman so as to place Spaulding's face in the light. As he did so, he breathed deeply and evenly to stem the anger rising in his neck. After all he had done...saved Spaulding from a Virginia jail and a rough life in the fields, to be spoken to like this!

"I beseech you then, sir, may not the first of the monies from this crop be used to restore me to happiness," Spaulding said as he watched his master circle him.

Durnford was touched by the sudden earnestness in Spaulding's voice and the distressed look in his eyes. But business was business. He could not recall giving

Spaulding an exact timetable. "Do not ask me to promise what I can not give."

Spaulding shrugged his shoulders. "I see."

Andrew Durnford was not at all certain that Spaulding did understand the problems St. Rosalie faced. But Durnford considered the matter closed. There were more important things to talk about then Spaulding's eventual freedom. "In regard to the sugar this year, Spaulding, since we can not get to market early, it may be the wisest plan to keep it awhile and let it be well drained. I have no doubt that the merchants keep it down, expecting a large crop, which will not be the case in this parish, and not with any of the other plantations on this river."

"You plan then to play the market?"

Durnford shook his head. "That is not the term I would use."

Spaulding's eyes narrowed and his face went hard. "I do not think it wise to play the market, sir."

Speaking as evenly as his anger would permit, Durnford replied, "Except for St. Rosalie, the crops have been less on every plantation than what was expected. But the price is no better than last year. Sound business judgment dictates that I sell only enough for current needs, for which purpose, thanks to your suggestion, I shall use the Rattan. Concerning the rest, we shall wait and see.""

Spaulding stepped back, his head dropped, and his face quivered in the pale light of the sugarhouse. "And if the sugar does not sell...."

"I am a man of honor, Spaulding. I do not quarrel with your accounting of your worth. You shall see. I will have you well on your way to England as soon as finances permit. And you shall not return empty-handed either."

Without a word, Spaulding walked past his master and out the door.

Several days later, when the sun had finally done its work on the cane, Andrew Durnford saddled a fresh horse and rode through the fields at a canter. He passed a cart containing a large cask, a bucket full of molasses, a pail of hominy and a number of tin cups. The cask held water for the slaves. The hominy and molasses was for their lunch, to be supplemented with a dried fish for each from a wooden box at the back of the cart. Harry, a big, broad-shouldered man Durnford had purchased in Virginia, was the driver. Durnford reigned his horse up alongside the cart. Harry saluted.

"So, Harry, what do you think of our crop now?"

Harry grinned. "Sir, it be a good crop."

"And Harry, how do you come to that conclusion."

"Chew the cane, master, as you taught. It sweet and flow with juice."

Durnford nodded. "You learn well, Harry. It is a good crop."

Baptiste had gone back to the Erskine plantation for the day, and with a wave of his hand, Durnford wheeled his horse around and galloped off toward his neighbor to the north. Under the bargain Durnford had struck with Erskine, the forces of the two plantations worked together under the supervision of Baptiste, Erskine's key man. It was a practical matter of efficiency and the only way Baptiste could divide his time between the two enterprises. Durnford calculated that each field hand yielded seven hogsheads of sugar a year. In good times a slave would pay for himself in three or four years, and after that, his labor was all profit.

Everything depended upon when the frost set in. In an average season, a planta-tion sent cane to the mill by October. But if a frost did not come until November, or December, or maybe even as late as January, or not at all, the cane grew taller and thicker and swelled with juice, sometimes doubling the sugar production per acre.

As Durnford rode through the fields, he observed the joint slave force steadily at work hacking the soil in a machine-like, plodding manner. None of them looked up, not even the St. Rosalie workers lifted an eye from the ground. A tall and powerful slave, one of Baptiste's men, strutted back and forth at the rear of the hoe-gang, cracking his whip and calling out, "Shove your hoe there! Shove your hoe! Slow down on me, I have you flogged. Now recollect what I tells you."

When the tall Negro slavedriver spotted Durnford on his horse, he pulled his floppy hat from his head, and clutching it to his chest, bowed low. "Welcome home, massah. Welcome home."

Durnford lifted his hat in reply. Driving the slave force down those tall rows of cane accomplished nothing at this time of year, he knew. Hoeing was necessary when the green shoots were young and needed protection from encroaching weeds and grasses. But now that the cane overshadowed everything, stealing both moisture and sunlight, there was nothing to be gained from hacking at the soil where a few starving weeds survived. Baptiste, like most overseers, preferred to see his slave force busily at work, even though it might be unproductive work, while Durnford felt the wear and tear on the workers was not worth the candle.

On the Erskine plantation, the whip was constantly in use. Durnford had no rules on the subject for the St. Rosalie workers, his drivers punished the slaves whenever they deemed it necessary, and the manner and severity of the punishment Durnford left up to them. Durnford never knew exactly what took place when he was out of the fields, but no one had complained of undeserved treatment and his workers were generally happy and productive. Baptiste, on the other hand, was a little more severe than Durnford found agreeable. Durnford once saw one of Erskine's slaves, whom Baptiste was about to whip in the field, strike at the overseer with his hoe. Baptiste parried the blow with his whip, spun his horse around, drew his pistol, aimed point blank at the slave's head, and pulled the trigger. The pistol misfired. Baptiste leapt from his horse, rushed the slave, and knocked him unconscious with his pistol butt. When the slave came to, Baptiste ordered one of the drivers to give him five lashes. But Durnford could endure no more. "Your man has sustained a severe head injury," he told Baptiste. "You will take his life if you do not yield."

"Very well," Baptiste had replied. "You tell me when he has recovered, and I will then have him put to five and an additional five because of the delay."

It would have done no good to take the matter to Erskine. No plantation owner ever called into question the conduct of his overseer when it came to controlling the work force. Good overseers were rare. And Baptiste was, Durnford knew, a good overseer. Many of them were totally unfit and lacked a dispassionate approach to punishment, often injuring and destroying the health of a slave. Others were just too easy and slack with the slaves, and that always brought a lot of trouble. After that happened, the next overseer had hard work of it for a time to break the slaves back in to regular work habits.

Durnford did not carry a gun. He had a short temper and knew it. Too easily permanent damage or death resulted from the ready use of a gun at hand. Durnford did, however, always carry a Bowie knife. And he always kept a pair of pistols ready and loaded over the mantel in his bedroom and a loaded shotgun in the corner of the library. One of the first slaves he bought, a mistreated man from the Kentucky tobacco fields, insulted and threatened him. Durnford ran to the house for his shotgun, and when he returned, the slave, thinking Andrew would be afraid to ruin such a valuable piece of property as he, a solid field worker, insulted his master again, then turned and sauntered away. Andrew ordered the slave to stop. The field hand laughed over his shoulder and broke into a jog. Durnford dropped to his knee, aimed carefully, and put six buck shot into the recalcitrant man's hip. After nursing him back to health, Andrew put the slave on the auction block.

But Andrew had not had any problems with his work force in a long time. They had been happy and content. But not so anymore, and now as Durnford rode back and forth through the fields, checking out the slaves on his way north to Erskine's place, he became quite aware of a smoldering resentment. Perhaps it was a mistake to give Baptiste so much power over his people. But it would not last long. And next year he would make do with the two drivers he had and the big man from Virginia he was training as a field leader. Who was to say, Durnford thought as he urged his horse along, what was the right amount of discipline to impose. It was just like what he had read, again and again, about Northern shipmasters and officers with regard to seamen. Force had to be met yet with greater force, and a showing of compassion was often interpreted as weakness, which lead to open mutiny. No, it wouldn't do to be too soft, the slaves must be made to work, it was not something they took to naturally. And it was far better to err on the side of severity than to suffer the consequences of laxity. In fact, it was much more necessary to maintain proper discipline on a plantation than on board a ship, because the plantation offered much more opportunity to hide away and shirk labor. While the sailor's labor was given in response to a voluntary contract of hire, no slave felt morally or legally bound to work. Too often the slave felt justified in stealing away a few moments of idle pleasure, just as he thought nothing of stealing his master's chicken to sell for tobacco.

Durnford crossed a deep gully and entered a field of cane at the very edge of the forest, where he met Baptiste coming from the opposite direction.

"Well," Baptiste asked as he reigned in his horse, "what do you think? Have we not made good use of your people this last week."

"I must acknowledge you have. The fields have not looked better."

"I stopped cutting and put everyone to work hoeing when your man Henry shut down the sugarhouse." Baptiste paused and chewed on a wad of tobacco. "Pretty poor cane then, I understand."

"Not the best. But now far from poor. And Spaulding read it correctly. It is what I instructed. Give the cane time to make more and better juice if the product looks a little thin. Valuable man, Spaulding. Accepts responsibility and wears it well."

"I see," Baptiste said, and Durnford knew well from the tone of his voice that his borrowed overseer doubted that Durnford had given Spaulding authority to shut down sugar production.

The two men, black plantation owner and white overseer, were again crossing the deep gully, the bottom of which was covered with thick underbrush, when the overseer suddenly stopped his horse. "Who are you there?"

Durnford followed Baptiste's horse into the underbrush where a young girl was hiding in the bushes.

"You are Sam's Sally, I believe," Baptiste said. "Come out of there."

"Yes, sir."

"What are you sulking there for?"

The girl half collapsed to the ground, but did not answer.

"Have you been here all day?"

"No, sir."

"How did you get here?"

No reply.

"Where have you been all day?"

The girl mumbled something unintelligible and glanced up at Durnford. Durnford remembered where he had seen the girl before. She was Washington's wife, not a legal wife, of course, as slaves were not allowed to marry. She lived on the Erskine plantation, while Washington lived at St. Rosalie. She did not have her own cabin and lived with her father. The couple saw each other on Sunday afternoons, or at times Washington would go off at night to visit her and return before the five o'clock plantation bell.

"Don't gawk around when I talk to you. Now why are you down here in this place?"

"I got locked in, sir."

"Locked in? How locked in?"

"The door is broken, sir. And it just jammed up on me awful and I couldn't get out."

"Couldn't get out could you? Well, you are out. How did you get out?"

"Pushed a plank off, sir, and crawled out."

Baptiste was silent for a long time, and chewed steadily on his tobacco while he surveyed the girl on the ground in front of his horse. "That won't do. Get down."

The girl knelt on the ground. Baptiste dismounted, and holding his horse's reins in his left hand, struck the girl several times across the shoulders with the handle of his rawhide whip.

Durnford studied the overseer as he laid on the blows. They were well laid on, and at arm's length. The overseer's eyes were flat and businesslike, and totally without excitement or passion. Durnford counted to himself quietly. He could not interfere, she was not his worker, and even had she been a St. Rosalie slave, Durnford would have been reluctant to stop the beating. To do so would have destroyed the effectiveness of the overseer.

"Now tell me the truth," Baptiste said quietly when he paused with his whip handle.

"I got trapped in the cabin, swear to God I did." It was the same story all over again.

"You have not got enough yet," Baptiste said, even more quietly than he had previously spoken. "Lie down there--pull up your clothes."

Without the slightest hesitation, she drew her dress up under her shoulders and lay down on the ground.

Now Baptiste unfurled the whip and laid upon her bare thighs and buttocks the full length of its leather. At every stroke the girl winced. "Oh, sir!" or "Please, sir!" But she did not groan---she did not scream.

Baptiste paused again. "Now will you tell me what you do here?" And again it was the same story.

His face void of all passion, Baptiste now increased his efforts and with much more strength went about the business of the Erskine plantation. He flogged the rawhide across her naked loins and thighs.    Sally, Sam's daughter and Washington's wife, withered on the ground. She grovelled and screamed, "Oh, don't, sir! Please stop, master! Oh, God, master, do stop! Oh, God, master! Oh, God, master!"

Durnford glanced at the business-like and passionless face of the overseer. Things were going too far. Finally, Andrew could stand no more. He spurred his horse and charged up the steep hill out of the gully. When he reached the top of the bank, he reigned in his horse and listened. Choking, sobbing, and groans came from the gully. The whistling, stinging whip had gone silent.

Baptiste came jouncing up the hill and stopped alongside Durnford. He laughed. "She meant to cheat me out of a day's work, and she has done it too!"

Durnford swallowed his anger. He was upset with himself for having done nothing, more upset with himself than with Baptiste for carrying the punishment on too long. "Did she change her story?"

"No. Stuck right to it."

"Perhaps it was true." Durnford felt almost a religious relief in having conquered his temerity.

"Oh no. Not at all. She slipped out of the gang when they were going to work this morning. And she's been dodging about all day, going from one place to another as she saw me coming. I spotted her in the morning along the edge of the swamp back there. Just a glimpse. But I knew I'd catch her before the day was out. She came along the ridge over there just as you went down into the gully, and she thought we'd join up and go off to the quarters, but we came back this way before she knew it, and she could do nothing but hide in the bushes."

"Well, I know that problem. They do slip off so now and then. I have this man, Lewis, you see he just—"

"Never had one like her. They often run away to the woods, and are gone some time, but I never had a dodge-off like this before."

Durnford took a deep breath. "Was it necessary to whip her that severely?"

"If I hadn't, she would have done the same thing again tomorrow, and half the people on the plantation would have followed her example. Oh, you know how lazy these people are, Durnford. They'd never do any work at all if they were not afraid of being whipped."

Durnford believed that was true. Without the whip, there was no plantation. Slaves did not work in the hot sweaty sun simply because they loved their master. But nevertheless, maybe ten strokes of the whip would have been enough. He'd ordered only five for Lewis, who'd threatened him with a knife. That poor girl, she'd felt the sting of leather forty or fifty times that day.

Perhaps Baptiste's way was right for some plantations. And at first, it was Baptiste who went after any of the St. Rosalie slaves when they escaped. After Baptiste caught up with them, they didn't run away again for a long time. Finally, though, Durnford had found a better way. When slaves ran away he just let them go. If they stayed away very long, he'd make everyone else work on Sunday to make up for the labor shortage and deprive them of their privileges until the runaways returned. The slaves on the plantation could always bring in the runaways if they chose. The runaways depended on them for their food. And if nothing else worked, all Durnford had to do was stop furnishing his slaves with supplies, and in came the runaways.

Durnford did not want to think about runaways and lashes. The frost Durnford had prayed for had finally come to the lower Mississippi valley. The St. Rosalie cane, most of it twice the height of a man, was caught in perfect maturity, full of juice at its sweetest level.

The sun felt warm and comfortable on Durnford's back as he rode through the fields a few days later, weaving in and out of cane rows. The sugarhouse smoked in the distance. All around him cane knives swarmed in precision as the tall stalks were cut and laid in rows, to be forked up into carts and transported to the sugarhouse. Good times, peace and prosperity had come to St. Rosalie again. Barba, contrary to all predictions, was making a good recovery from his fever.

Durnford turned on to the swamp road full of excitement. No one, not even

Erskine, had such a crop. Why he had been so favored with the precise amount of moisture, sunshine and delicate frost, he did not know. But he had looked at the cane to the north and south, and nothing compared to what St. Rosalie had. And as Durnford rode along, passing now and then one of his carts rushing to the sugar-house with a load of wood for the boilers, or piled high with cut cane, Washington waited quietly in the cypress forest, watching his master's progress up the swamp road.

A loaded gun, heavy with shot, rested lightly in the crook of Washington's arm. His breathing was measured, and he remained perfectly still, careful not to spook Durnford's horse. The trusted slave, the plantation hunter, had abandoned the fields that afternoon to seek another prey. Every since he'd heard that Durnford looked idly on while his dear sweet wife was beaten and whipped beyond all reason, had Washington planed his revenge. And when he learned that Durnford was going alone to the fields that afternoon, Washington went to the woods on the other side of the swamp road. His passion and hatred soared as Durnford cantered by. When his master was at a safe distance, Washington crossed the road from the wooded swamp and began his swift, silent run threw the dense cane to catch him. At last, he gained ground, passed his master, and when just a few rods ahead of Durnford, Washington dropped to his knee, brought the shotgun to his shoulder, sighted through the heavy growth of cane which hid him, and pulled the trigger.

The hammer holding the flint snapped forward and struck off a spark, igniting black powder. The black powder hissed and fizzed, and Washington held steady, the true mark of a successful hunter who could hold his target while the small flame flowed down the hole and ignited the main charge inside the barrel to send lethal missiles screaming. Here is where most hunters failed. The smoke and hiss of the prime charge, the one second delay between pulling the trigger and the roaring blast from the barrel, enabled many a prey to escape. But not with Washington. He was one of the few who held steady. But this time the blast never came. The gun misfired.

Washington froze, held his breath as Durnford came up and passed by without seeing him. Washington was, he knew, adequately hidden from view. But would Durnford's horse catch his scent, spook, or turn and betray him? And had his master heard the gun misfire? Would he smell the scent of black powder which hung in the still air about the plantation hunter?

As Durnford cantered off down the swamp road, watching for animal life in the forest and completely unaware of his near death, Washington dropped to the ground and sobbed. "Deah Lord," he cried softly, "I nevered do it again." It was, he was certain, a sign from God that his gun had failed. He was an evil man, he knew. His master, who loved and trusted him so, would have gone to his death at the hand of this poor sinner, had God not taken pity and saved them both. And he would tell no one what had happened, not even Sally. Especially would he not tell Sally. If she suspected that Washington was capable of such an act, killing another human, she would never have talked to him again. And slowly as he sat in the dirt between the tall rows of cane, which came together over his head, his mind cleared, and he could no longer believe he had come this far down such a dark path. He shook his head. Ever since Sally had suffered that terrible beating his mind had been in raging turmoil. He was a crazed and delirious man---with all reason gone. Crazed.... Then he saw in his mind again the bloody welts across Sally's thighs and legs. Heard her crying in the night from the terrible pain and now the infection, which she would not take to Durnford who had done nothing to protect her from such brutality. And as Washington lived again the agony of his wife's terrible suffering and fought back the certain knowledge that she would be dead in a day or two, the rage came upon him once more, and he knew he would act again.

Carefully, he emptied the charge from his gun. Packed it a second time with powder, wad, and shot and rammed it all home. Now the gun would not fail, could not fail. Tears streamed down his face. He poured black powder into the train. Pulled back and cocked the hammer. Then, still sitting in the dirt, swiveled the gun, stuck the barrel in his mouth, reached out with his bare toe and pushed the trigger. The hammer struck, the black powder hissed, and Washington held steady for the last second of his life. This time his gun did not misfire.

# Chapter Twenty Two

The shot that ended Washington's life rang out loud and echoed from the woods. Durnford reigned in his horse, stood up in his stirrups, and called over his shoulder, "Washington! Is that you, Washington?"

He called again, and a third time, and when he received no reply, Durnford dismounted and walked slowly back along the swamp road in the direction of the shot he had heard. He was nervous now. Someone was poaching. Probably after a wild pig. And Durnford had no gun to defend himself.

Suddenly his horse reared, and Durnford caught the scent that had spooked his mare. It was a sweet, sickly smell that Andrew recognized at once. Blood. Behind the second row of cane, he found the body. Washington lay in the dirt, his gun beside him, and the back of his head blown completely off. Fluffy pink brains and bright red blood were spattered down the row of cane, standing out brilliantly against the green leaves.

Andrew buried Washington the day he died. And after Washington died and was buried, his dogs broke down the wooden fence enclosing their kennel and got out and barked and trailed, just like trailing a rabbit. The fence was made stronger and taller, but the dogs still got out. When they could no longer knock loose a board, they dug under the fence or went over the top. The trail always led to the graveyard. There they sat by Washington's grave and howlled with their heads up in the air.

Two days after Washington shot himself, his wife died at Erskine's plantation. When Andrew heard the news he was doubly disappointed. "I don't understand it," he said to Marie-Charlotte. "Why did not Sally come to me for treatment? Why did not Washington insist on that. And as for Washington, I could have consoled him, prepared him for what might happen." Andrew shook his head, laid down beside his wife in their comfortable bed, and stared at the ceiling. "We owe all of this to that rascal, Baptiste. He must have known of Sally's condition. He should have know of her condition. But he was too concerned with his own position to tell Erskine what he had done."

Marie-Charlotte put down her book, snuffed out her candle, and closed her eyes. "I will miss Washington," she said. "He was one of the sweetest slaves I have ever known. A bit intense at times though, don't you think, Andrew?" And not waiting for a reply, she continued. "Perhaps more intense than we realized." She reached for Andrew's hand and pulled it to her cheek. "But there is nothing you could have done, Andrew. Nothing at all. When people sorrow so, and are of such an intense spirit, there is not much that can be done to help them. But I will miss Washington."

"A faithful servant. The only field hand on the plantation I would trust with a gun. I would even trust him with my own life." Then Durnford sat up. "I must truly say I have never known a finer slave than our Washington."

The next day, November 20, 1836, Barba died during the night in his cabin, and that same night Lewis ran away, with all the irons Durnford had put on him. They buried Barba in the rain in the plantation cemetery on the other side of the sugar-house, next to the fresh grave of the plantation hunter, Washington. And then Durnford sent Noel to New Orleans to find Lewis and have him arrested.

Noel came back from New Orleans with an unrepentant Lewis in tow. Andrew Durnford, distraught over the loss of his good slaves, Washington the hunter and his body servant, the old reliable Barba, ordered no punishment for Lewis. It did no good, he realized. As Miss Remy had pointed out, Lewis was not right in the head.

"Lewis, you wear me thin. But this time you will get no lashes, though you surely deserve the whip. Instead, I am giving you a warning Lewis. Run away again, and I will not send for you. You may wander the earth, and I will not care. But you will be hungry, homeless, and nothing but a low, runaway slave. Now, Lewis, so you understand me, I cannot say I would take you back again if you choose to run. Now do you understand your position with me?"

Lewis stood wide-eyed and uncomprehending while Andrew Durnford knocked loose his chains. "I say again, Lewis. Run away and I will let you starve. And if you are of that mind, you can go now. No more punishment, Lewis. Nothing to keep you here but the knowledge you are treated well, have a good bed, and a full stomach. What do you say to that, Lewis."

Lewis stammered. "Massah, ah say I is right sorry I done wrong and won't done it no more. No, sar."

"Did you enjoy your sight-seeing in the city, Lewis?"

"No, massah."

"Good. Then get some hot food into you and see about your work in the fields."

It rained for the next eight days. A deluge. The plantation roads turned to soupy mud. Not a cart moved. Not a single cord of wood was cut for the boilers. No hay was made. The cane in the fields was full of juice, beyond Durford's greatest hope, but not a stalk was cut.

Thomas, the sole surviving child of Andrew and Marie-Charlotte, slipped while running through the mud, fell and cut himself severely on the arm with a sickle. And as in all such cases, it was not the wound itself that presented the danger, but the infection that followed. The accident made Andrew even more aware of his responsibility as a father. He had delayed the boy's education long enough. When Thomas recovered from his deep wound, the Durnfords took him to New Orleans and enrolled him in a private boarding school in a four-year program.

It took three days for the plantation roads and fields to dry out after the rain stopped, and then Andrew put the sugarhouse on twenty-four hour production. He shipped seventeen hogsheads to the McDonogh warehouse by the *Creole,* with instructions to sell immediately. The remainder of the crop he put up into hogsheads and shipped to McDonogh with instructions to obtain insurance and hold until a better price could be obtained. "It is the wisest plan to keep it awhile and let it be well drained," he wrote McDonogh.

Five days before Christmas, Durnford wrote McDonogh again. "Got through my rolling last night, and made ninety-eight hogsheads of sugar. My hogsheads are larger than last year, while the crops have been less on every plantation than what was expected. The price will go high soon, when the merchants learn how poor the crop has become, and I will be paying off my mortgage to you with a good profit to spare."

Christmas was not celebrated as a holiday at St. Rosalie. It was a day of quiet religious observance and no presents were exchanged. Gifts were given the following week, to celebrate the new year, as had long been the custom. Andrew Durnford provided his Negro slaves with basic clothing, two outfits of pants and shirts a year, a pair of shoes, and now and then a coat. On New Year's Day he gathered all of the slaves around the kitchen, a one-room building at the rear of the mansion, and distributed his presents to them. For the men, Andrew handed out one of their rations of suits of clothing, and for the women, a calico dress, head handkerchiefs, and gingham aprons. Throughout the year, Durnford collected simple presents for the slave children as he travelled about, marbles, leather pouches, carved horses and farm animals, and he handed these out with bits of candy, penny figs and vanilla squares, to happy, smiling, dancing children. And there was also some kind of simple present for every man, usually a bit of tobacco and a drink all around, and something for the women as well. For each family, Durnford passed out a little flour, cornmeal, sugar, and coffee along with some simple cuts of beef and pork, and molasses cakes.

When Lewis shuffled up to the kitchen door, Durnford said, "I am sorry Lewis. You have disappointed me again this year." He handed over to Lewis the customary rough-sewn shirt and pants wrapped around coarse brogans, but none of the usual presents. Andrew Durnford, plantation master, studied the face of his problem slave. Then, when Lewis bowed and thanked his master, as was the ritual, Durnford said, "Just a moment, Lewis." And reaching behind the wooden door, Andrew brought out a new double-barrel muzzle loader. He held the gun in front of him, across his chest. The weapon was beautiful, with an oiled walnut stock, checkered grip, and genuine twist barrels, 11 gauge. "This is your's Lewis. So long as you never again run from me. You are taking the place of my trusted Washington, whose gun this was. And you will not dishonor the memory of the man you replace. Am I correct in thinking that, Lewis?"

Tears streamed down the stunned slave's face. "Yassar, massah. Yassar." And Lewis stumbled away, unable to speak more.

The New Year celebration at St. Rosalie lasted three days. Thomas came home from school for the event and received as his sole present a gold pen mounted in a pearl holder with a felt-lined carrying case. It cost Andrew Durnford almost as much as the imported Swiss music box he gave to Marie-Charlotte. When she made the usual protests of extravagance, he rubbed a hand over the polished mahogany box. "It has been a good year," he said with a self-satisfied smile.

Noel, Henry Spaulding, and the house servants celebrated the holiday with the Durnford family, and received presents more appropriate to their stations of responsibility. A cheaper version of the pen given Thomas went to Noel and a white cotton vest for Spaulding.

The holiday season passed and St. Rosalie plantation entered upon the new year with its master, Andrew Durnford, looking forward to riches and prosperity.

Henry Spaulding marketed the molasses with ease. He sold it all to John Sou for the sum of $628.44. "A smart sum indeed," he told Durnford as he handed over the bank draft. "More than enough to pay my passage and provision the plantation for spring. Noel gave me the figures. Here, I have listed them." He held out a paper for Durnford to inspect. "You will see I have covered everything: two mules, iron for the boilers, a new anvil, harness leather, four new plow blades, my passage to England, and still you have left eighty dollars!"

"You assume too much, Henry. I have other expenses. School tuition for Thomas is due---"

"But you have the money from the first seventeen hogsheads...and certainly you can sell more---"

"Henry, I am certain as well we could manage somehow. But the Vachery is for sale. You know, the plantation of old Pierre Jean Pierre. And a bargain it is because there is not a good title to the property, only the undisturbed title of possession enjoyed by Pierre Jean Pierre since thirty years. Well I am willing to risk that title. The tract must be bought. And I can have it for twelve hundred dollars. Then I need three Creole horses, and a Natchez to replace my poor old Toby, and I can get them all for seventy-six dollars off the Vachery, horses that are worth eighty apiece, Henry. And the cattle of the Vachery are to be given away for nothing: fourteen dollars a head for cows with calf, ten dollars a head for cows without calves. I can buy all the Vachery stock for $680.00, more or less. Now if I had a person such as you that I could depend on to take care of them I would venture to buy them and leave them there. Henry I certainly had intended the pleasure of seeing you off to your homeland. But we must be realistic. Now is not the time for an ocean voyage. Not in this winter weather, Henry. You, of all men, know the condition of the Atlantic. But by summer, Henry, I will have sold my sugar at a handsome profit and you will be on your way."

They were in the parlor before a comfortable fire which crackled in the huge fireplace, enjoying a glass of brandy. Snow covered the ground outside and the temperature had not gone above twenty-five degrees in three days. Snow had not come to Plaquemines Parish in the previous twenty years. In New Orleans, farther north up the river, it was much worse. Poor people throughout the city were still dying from the cold and exposure, as few homes were equipped with fireplaces.

"Now what do you say, Henry?"

"I say nothing, sir." Spaulding stood up, placed his half-full glass on the small table next to his chair. "My mind tells me to say nothing. I believe that is the wisest course. Good night. Thank you for the brandy." And Henry Spaulding left.

Durnford glanced down at the accounting Spaulding had prepared. It was not just the money. Not really. This was simply not the time of year to start out on such an adventure. Not this year, at any rate. Good God, the Northeast, even Washington City, was in the grip of snow storms that had raged for weeks, all with no sign of relief.

He watched out the window as Spaulding trudged through the light snow on his way to his bed in the sugarhouse. Then Durnford circled the entry on Spaulding's paper marked passage to London, $300.00. Next to the entry he wrote a note to Noel. "To be paid from sale of Tivoli house." The house on Tivoli Square (later know as Lee Circle) had been owned by Durnford's mother as her separate property, and was the home in which Andrew was raised and the Durnford's lived as a family. It was his now, after his mother's death, and it was worth a considerable sum of money. At first he had put it on the market for $25,000. But when Marie-Charlotte's brother, an agent, found a buyer for that amount, Durnford raised the price to $30,000. Then he raised it to $35,000, and finally to $40,000. It would sell for that sum any day now. Valcour Remy had assured him of that, just as he had assured Valcour that he would never again raise the price. So certainly, Henry Spaulding would be returning to his farm in England that summer. Nothing could prevent that from happening. There was of course, the trial with the Durnford heirs next month. But his English cousins would never win. McDonogh was positive of that. Durnford was equally positive. And based upon the assurances of McDonogh's lawyers, who also acted for Durnford in the case, Andrew Durnford had not even planned for such a contingency.

Durnford slept well that night, and awoke about five o'clock to a chattering of birds in the tree outside his window. He opened the window and was greeted by a warm breeze. The snow was gone. A soft, moist wind from the south had moved in during the night and broken the cold grip of winter on the land.

Durnford dressed, had breakfast with Marie-Charlotte and her mother, and went to the sugarhouse. He must talk again with Spaulding, he had decided. The man needed assurances, and Durnford had decided he would do just that. He would instruct Noel to go to New Orleans that very day and book a summer passage for Spaulding.

The morning light from the open door of the sugarhouse barely illuminated a passage through the machinery to the wooden stairs leading to Spaulding's bed in the loft. Durnford paused next to the cold, silent rollers, and called out. There was no answer. Nor was there any candlelight from the loft reflecting upon the stairs. Andrew paused while his eyes adjusted to the blackness. "Spaulding, I apologize for this intrusion, but I fully expected you to be up at this hour."

Still all was silent and dark within the sugarhouse. Durnford felt his way along the familiar machinery and reached the railing leading up to the loft. A faint light from the small window in the loft shone upon the landing at the top of the stairs. Spaulding had not answered his call, and now Durnford hurried, groping his way up the creaking wooden stairs. Was he to be the victim of another loss on the plantation, Durnford wondered? Surely he would have noticed any serious illness with the Englishman. And it was true, Spalding did not seem full of energy lately. Perhaps Durnford had overlooked the early signs of a fever. Disease struck frequently and swiftly at St. Rosalie.

When Andrew reached the top of the stairs and glanced around the loft, he was at first relived to see that Spaulding was not sick in his bed. Spaulding was not there. He was gone. His bedroll, the leather-covered wooden case which held all of his belongings, a gift from Durnford, was gone too. Durnford was stunned. Spaulding had deserted him.

The fair weather played out after three days and the wind and rain came down cold from the North again. And all this time there was no word from Spaulding, who had not even left a farewell note.

Late in the afternoon of the following week, the trading steamer *Creole* docked at St. Rosalie and unloaded lamp oil, two barrels of mackerel, and a box of shoes, which went against the plantation account, crediting in return the plantation account for eight cords of wood for the ship's boilers. When the transaction was complete and Noel had signed the account, Gentry, the captain of the vessel told Noel that he had a letter for personal delivery to Andrew Durnford, the plantation owner.

Andrew Durnford, with the help of two slaves, made his own hogsheads and barrels, and he was busy in the sugarhouse making up barrels when Noel told him of the message.

The message handed him by Captain Gentry was in a brown envelope, sealed with red wax, and addressed to him at St. Rosalie. "Sir," the message read in printed words. "Have this day at your disposal your property in the man of one Henry Spaulding, slave. Same to be claimed by you upon payment of lodge and board." The note was dated three days earlier and signed, "Will Steuerman, Sheriff, Escambia County, Pensacola."

# Chapter Twenty Three

It was not Noel who went to Pensacola, but Andrew Durnford himself. The trip was important to Durnford. He must show Henry Spaulding his concern, and what better way than for the busy plantation owner to come himself and set his errant property free. He carried in his pocket the very certificate that would make Henry Spaulding a free man again, all duly notarized and recorded in the office of the registry of properties for Plaquemines Parish, Louisiana.

"How come you here, boy?" The young man in the Sheriff's office spoke in a high, piping voice.

"Well, I came by ship, sir. By coastal schooner." The young man to whom Durnford spoke could hardly be eighteen, Durnford thought. "And I have urgent business with the Sheriff. Is he here?"

The young man propped his long legs upon his desk and leaned back in his chair.

"I meant, how did you get in here. Well, anyway, if you want to see the Sheriff you're talking to the right man. I am the Sheriff here. Now who let you in and why?"

"Sir, my name is Andrew Durnford. I am the owner of St. Rosalie Plantation and I've come for a runaway, Henry Spaulding."

Durnford handed over the letter he had received from the Sheriff. The young man took the notice, turned it over in his hands thoughtfully, pulled his legs from his desk and stood up, handing Durnford back his memorandum. Then he lifted a cracked and stained cup from the corner of his desk, stirred the muddy contents with a dirty spoon, sipped, and put the coffee cup down on his desk. "Well, I guess

I've heard of some of you people—free colored—"

"Free people of color."

"Yeah. Free, own land and some of your own people as slaves, too." The young Sheriff rubbed his chin. "Now that's a strange circumstance, don't you think?"

"Yes, I suppose it is. Just as strange as finding but a young boy as Sheriff here in Pensacola."

The Sheriff laughed. "Hell, I'm twenty-seven years old. And it's always the same thing. No one ever takes me seriously. That's why I end up killing a man now and then."

"Forgive me. I meant no disrespect."

"And you've come to claim your property, boy?"

"Yes, sir. I have."

The Sheriff was thin, pale and blond, and stood several inches taller than Durnford. The young man shook his head. "Well, boy, you've made the trip for nothing. Your slave died two days ago. He's buried out there." The Sheriff waved a hand to the back of the building.

Durnford stepped back and grasped the doorframe. "How did he die?"

"Came in one morning, and there he was, dead and stiff."

"Spaulding was such a hard and healthy man. I am a physician, sir. I noticed nothing peculiar." Durnford hesitated, as if afraid of learning the truth. "Did he kill himself?"

"No, nothing like that. He just died, that's all. Now I have work to do." The Sheriff motioned for Durnford to leave. "And, boy, I am sorry you came all this way for nothing." Then the Sheriff closed his office door behind Durnford as the black slave-owner stumbled out into the outer room.

Durnford shuffled slowly across the wooden floor, feeling the gaze of the two Sheriff's deputies on him as he walked out the open door and into the sandy street.

He wandered aimlessly around to the back of the building in search of Spaulding's grave. The yard behind the building was covered with brown and yellow sand with a few pine trees and nowhere was there a gravestone or marker and the shifting sand had erased any sign of a fresh grave. Andrew walked through the yard and out onto the street on the other block. He had gone directly to the Sheriff's office after the coastal schooner docked, and now that his quest for Spaulding had ended in total surprise, he wanted to do nothing but find a quiet place to collect his thoughts. He went to a tavern by the waterfront and took a table where he ordered a glass of port and watched the boat traffic out on the bay. Although he had missed the noon meal that day, Durnford was not feeling hungry and could not entertain the thought of food. He sat by himself, the only man at that end of the tavern, and listened to the idle chatter of several men at a long table at the other end of the room.

Durnford rubbed his face with a trembling hand. So Spaulding lay buried in the sand at Pensacola. It would take a search to find the address of his family in England. But how could he explain it all? Apparently the man's brothers knew he had been sold into slavery. According to Spaulding, his brothers felt the fault lie with Spaulding as well as anyone for the misconduct that had led to his predicament. Durnford wondered whether he should not ship to England Spaulding's belongings. The Englishman had a pipe, a few articles of clothing, miscellaneous odds and ends that any slave in a good position would collect. Those items might mean something to Spaulding's children. Durnford remembered that Spaulding had an impressive collection of books on husbandry and agriculture he intended to take home. But Durnford had completely forgotten to request them from the Sheriff. Well, just now he would rather not face the impudent young man. Andrew decided that first he would visit his brother, Joseph.

Joseph was Andrew's half brother. Before he transferred his business activities to New Orleans, Andrew's father, the white Englishman, Thomas Durnford, had a common-law wife in Pensacola, a free Negro woman.

Pensacola had long been an English possession. But in 1781 the Spanish attacked from New Orleans and drove the British out of Pensacola. Colonel Elias Durnford of the Royal Engineers, Thomas Durnford's uncle, and for whom Thomas Durford worked, fled with the British, but Thomas, who was then twenty years of age, stayed on.

Thomas had no desire to return to English society. He was one of those Englishmen who considered himself a citizen of the world. If Spain had conquered Pensacola, it meant simply that Thomas would now be a Spanish subject. And it was Thomas's cavalier attitude toward his English heritage that endeared him to the corruptible Spanish officials who came to administer the former British colony.

Officially, Spain had declared that any trade between the Spanish colonies and the British was illegal. However, the law was not realistic. The Spanish desperately needed the trade to survive. Thomas Durnford had contacts with the British in the West Indies and was the only Englishman left in the area with any talent for trade. So over a period of almost twenty years, his business interests grew to include Spanish occupied New Orleans, and it was during one of those trips to that city with his common-law wife that she contracted yellow fever. She died and was buried there.

Joseph, their only child, was then nineteen years of age and married to a Negro woman of Pensacola. After his wife's funeral, Thomas transferred his office to New Orleans, leaving Joseph behind in Pensacola.

Within a year after transferring his business to New Orleans, Thomas Durnford had greatly expanded his business relations and real estate holdings in that city. Then he met Rosaline Mercier, who gave birth to his second son, Andrew Durnford.

Thus, when Andrew knocked on the door of his half brother's house that day, he himself was thirty-seven years old and Joseph was a gray-haired man, twenty years older.

Joseph's house was a cottage near the bay with a sand-swept yard and sand on the wide porch.

"Andy, I knew you'd come." Andrew's brother clasped his arms around him in a smothering bear hug. They had seen each other now and then, and more frequently once Andrew started the plantation which Joseph frequently visited, and the passage was always paid for by Andrew who looked after his less fortunate older brother.

Joseph had failed in life. Although he was happily married and the father of one son, Benite, a blacksmith and wheelwright, Joseph lacked in common sense. Joseph was, though, a learned man. He had studied and become a lawyer. When he was young he carried on a lucrative practice, taking on as clients both white and black citizens of the then largest city in Florida. However, Joseph spent all of the fees which he collected on a brick factory he purchased, although he could not sell any more bricks once the massive fort at the entrance to the bay was completed. There was simply no longer a market. Even though his bricks were superior to the bricks of Louisiana, the cost of shipping made it impossible to sell them there. Soon, his clients left him, reasoning that Joseph was a fool to continue making bricks that had no market and they did not want a fool for a lawyer.

When their father died, Andrew assumed the burden of financial aid to Joseph. An accurate account was kept of all the money given Joseph, and it was to be repaid at some indefinite time, with interest, although everyone knew it never would come to that.

That evening, Andrew dined with Joseph and his wife, Martina, a petit woman who's ancestors were free blacks from the islands. Joseph was a big, loveable bear of a man with a heavy beard and a child-like grin on his face, and it was impossible for Andrew to think of coming to Pensacola without seeing him.

"It's a terrible thing, though, Andy, the way your boy died."

"You mean Henry Spaulding?"

"Yes, Spaulding." Joseph shook his head. "Andy, you don't know what happened?"

"No, I don't, Joseph. I don't understand it at all. What exactly did happen to Spaulding?"

"You gentlemen must excuse me," Joseph's wife, Martina, said, "these are things I do not wish to hear." She got up abruptly and left the table. The door slammed behind her as she went out upon the sand overlooking Pensacola Bay.

Joseph offered a cigar to Andrew, and then they both lit up from a lamp on the table.

"Now, what happened to my man, Joseph?"

"Well, what I have been able to piece together, Andy, is that your runaway smuggled himself aboard a schooner out of New Orleans. The ship carried a deck cargo of lumber, all hardwood, from what I understand, from those flatboats those Kentucky fellows break up when they come down the Mississippi to the city. Spaulding got aboard somehow and made him a little hidey-hole in the deck lumber. No one on that schooner had any idea he was there. So I would say he came on sometime during the night. Probably had with him provisions for the journey, too."

"Spaulding was always a resourceful man. It would not surprise me that he managed to conceal enough to make a comfortable trip of it."

"The schooner laid up in New Orleans for some time, and then finally sailed. The lumber, I think, was for the East Coast. As you may recall, Andy, the weather was pretty bad this winter, but we had a few good days, and that's when the schooner decided to make a run for it. Winter along the Gulf here never can be trusted, as you well know, Andy, and soon it was blowing hard and cold out of the east again with a freezing rain. The schooner was running offshore, on a direct line for the tip of Florida when the waves built up and she started rolling. After about two days of heavy weather and very little headway, the deck lumber shifted. Everyone surmises that is when Spaulding was trapped by it and broke his leg.

"The schooner started taking on water and was in danger of floundering, the pumps couldn't keep up. The captain turned the ship around to make his best tack for Pensacola, when the crew spotted Spaulding hobbling around the deck far forward. That was just before dark came on. He managed to elude them that night by hiding in the shifting cargo of lumber, until they were close to land. They had come in early in the morning to where the swells were running a little lighter, when they spotted him again.  By then, he was crawling along.  Well, when they rushed to take him, Spaulding tried to stand up, broken leg and all, lost his balance and fell overboard.

"The captain refused to stop the ship or to put a boat out after Spaulding, and the schooner continued on into Pensacola and reported everything to the Sheriff.  Well Spaulding had made it to shore, more than a mile, although the tide was against him, I am told, and landed on Santa Rosa Island, about two miles down from the fort.  He wasn't picked up until later that day, and he was just lying there in the sand, barely out of the water, and unconscious.

"The Captain of that schooner refused all responsibility for Spaulding, and since he was a runaway, he was turned over to the Sheriff by the fishermen who found him, and clapped into irons.  Now what I hear is that he was unconcious until about the time the fishermen landed him over, here on this side, and when he came to he had enough sense to tell the Sheriff who he was and where he'd come from."

Joseph stopped and puffed on his cigar.  "I am a man of the law, Andy, you know that, and I think I know my field as well as you know medicine.  But let me tell you this," and leaning forward across the table and punctuating each word with his cigar, Joseph continued, "it is settled law that the captain of that ship had a duty to rescue that stowaway and provide him with proper medical attention and food.  Failure of that duty results in civil liability to the owner of the slave, even though the slave is a runaway.  Now, Andy, from what I hear, that slave of yours was worth at least eight hundred dollars and not a penny less.  And here is what I propose, Andy: I will take your case, absolutely no cost to you and I will get for you at least eight hundred dollars for your property.  Andy, if I lose, which will not happen, you will have no fee at all to pay, not a cent. But in winning I think I should get twenty-five percent for that. Now what do you say to that, Andy?  Wasn't that slave worth at least eight hundred dollars?"

"Joseph, are you telling me that no one did anything for his broken leg?"

"That's the point of the whole thing, Andy.  No one did anything for him.  The captain was responsible for the care of your runaway even while he was in jail.  Your property was neglected.  Worse, it was gross-negligence, and more.  Wilful and intentional neglect and dereliction of duty.  The captain just let that boy lay there in irons, broken leg, mighty fever, gave him nothing, no food, no blankets, and it was damned cold, Andy.  Naturally Spaulding died in a few days.  Who could hold out longer than that?"

Andrew Durnford stood up and stumbled backward. His black face was ashen, almost as white as his white ancestor's face. His cigar fell to the floor. His brother's voice came out of the fog before him.

"Andy, are you all right? What's the matter with you?"

He turned and crashed against the wall, then stumbled out the door and stood, swaying, on the porch.

"Andy, aren't you staying the night? What's wrong? Is it your heart, Andy. Now look, brother, you need to sit down right now. Where are you going?"

It seemed to Andrew Durnford that all of his blood had fallen to his feet with a crash. His strength was gone. His head exploded in pain, and he gasped for breath. An acrid stench of musty incense fouled the air around him and seared his nostrils and stung his lungs. The immensity of his crime crushed down on him. What had he done with his life? Who was he, this master of the plantation named St. Rosalie, stocked with slaves of his own race. Now Henry Spaulding was dead, and it was this peculiar system of slavery that killed him. Andrew Durnford, slave owner was responsible for that. It had been so easy to rationalize the system. Hadn't Andrew always said it was nothing more than an economic institution, supported by history. Whites had whites as slaves, whites had blacks as slaves, serfs were slaves to their Russian masters. And in Africa and San Domingo and Louisiana, free Negroes had slaves.

He grabbed the rail and sat down on his brother's steps. Cold sweat ran in rivulets down his face and soaked his dark hair, which dropped in heavy curls about his head. A sorrow, more immense than any human could bear, swept over him. But he did not cry. Nor could he think beyond the raw, miserable fact that Andrew Durnford, free man of color, was in the end, finally and totally responsible for the death of another human being, a man as well educated as he, a man with brothers and children, a man as black as he.

"Well, you gave me a start there, Andy. But you look better now. For a minute I thought you had an infraction...no, that isn't the word."

"Infarction, Joseph," Andrew gasped. "Heart attack. But not me, not now at least. There is nothing wrong with my heart. Nothing physically, Joseph. I'm sorry to have frightened you."

"Did I make my point clear, Andy? I'll take your case, no fee unless we win. The law covering runaway slaves is the same as for runaway cattle. Anyone taking possession of that property has to take care of it. Of course they'll argue that there was no guarantee the captain would ever collect what he should have spent on your slave. But that won't wash, Andy. Not with a jury here in Pensacola. And not with your reputation and wealth. Besides, it's the law, Andy. Whether the Captain can count on recouping what he must pay for food and medicine is not an issue. The law gives him a lien on the property for his expenditures, just the same as if he were a runaway cow, and that is the captain's guarantee of repayment."

"Joseph, dear brother, Joseph. The man's name was Henry Spaulding. He was a citizen of England, where he owned a farm and had brothers and children. He should never have been sold as a slave."

Joseph's face brightened in the moonlight. "Is that what bothers you, Andy? Why, don't worry about that. You acquired him legally and he was your property under the law of every state in this great country of ours." Joseph slammed his fist on the porch rail. "Just let them make that kind of argument, and I might even push for smart money."

"Joseph I can not accept your kind offer of assistance. I could not accept any amount for the death of Henry Spaulding. And why that is so, I can not explain to you, not just now. But that is the way of it, and at this moment, I can not understand how I came to the position of being a human being who should collect money for the death of a noble soul upon the grounds that the particular human being had become his property."

"I see." Joseph paused and scratched his head. "Well, perhaps when you think it over—"

"Goodnight, dear brother. I can not stay." And with that, Andrew stumbled down the porch steps and walked away. He passed Joseph's wife who stood with her back to the road, facing the moonlit bay, and when she heard Andrew on the road behind her, she turned and said quietly, "Adieu, Andrew Durnford, good master of St. Rosalie Plantation."

There was no ship returning to New Orleans by way of the Mississippi River at that time, nor was the quicker and safer inland route taken by the coastal schooners open to Andrew. A northwest wind had blown the water out of Lake Ponchartrain at the back door to New Orleans, trapping the Pensacola coastal schooners in the shallow water at the mouth of Bayou St. John.

The fierce wind out of the north continued to blow for a week, and Andrew Durnford huddled in his dingy room on the second floor of a hotel near Government Street, fighting headaches that threatened to drive him mad with intensity and grovelling in the putrid odor of musk.

There was no need for Andrew Durnford to pray to God and ask why he was made to suffer so. He knew the answer. He fell into a deep depression with a sure and clear understanding of just what he had become. And in that state of mind he decided that he must free his slaves at all costs. Immediately, the roaring headache and the noxious aroma left him. He had endured more than a week of torture.

When those searing symptoms cleared, he collapsed into his mattress in total exhaustion and slept for thirty-six hours. He awoke in sunshine and learned that the Pensacola schooners had returned and would sail again the next day for New Orleans by the route through Lake Ponchartrain and Bayou St. John. It was, he said to himself, a great relief to be going home. His first concern was the trial that took place in less than two weeks. He and McDonogh must win. Not for the reason that he wanted to cling to St. Rosalie, but because he was determined to put into immediate operation his plan for freeing the slaves.

Durnford boarded a schooner, which ran along the Gulf Coast from Pensacola harbor until it reached Mobile Bay. There, the small ship entered with the tide. Almost immediately the schooner turned hard to port and slipped into the little harbor at the east end of Dauphin Island. The small harbor was sandy with a good growth of pines. The island itself was about three miles long, but less than a half-mile wide, and was home to a small settlement and a fort, which protected the entrance to Mobile Bay. The schooner had made a late start, and with the seas running high and the wind strong, the captain announced they would anchor until morning because the protected passage they were about to enter between the islands and the mainland was full of shoals and too treacherous for a night run.

There were no accommodations for passengers on the schooner, other than what space they could find among the bundles and boxes and kegs of deck cargo, and Durnford had settled down with his back against grain sacks to eat the supper he carried with him, when a white man sat down next to him. The stranger was a sturdy man with a large red face, almost hidden by a floppy hat and a full beard.

"You look as though you could use some company, I reckon. Mind if I settle in here for the night?" the man asked.

"Not at all, sir. And I will gladly share what I have."

The man slouched to the deck and wedged his back into a comfortable position against the grain sacks. Then he pulled a canvas back pack around to his front and pushed it down between his legs. "No need, friend. I have more than enough to last my journey." He lifted from his bag a small bread and dried meat, which he cut with a knife and stuffed into his mouth with great ferocity.

"You are not from this coast?" Durnford ventured.

The man shook his head. "From the hills of Alabama. On my way to Texas to try my luck there. I hear there are a great many Germans in the western part of Texas."

"So I understand," Durnford answered. "There are a great many west of the Guadalupe, more Germans than American born, I believe."

"Has they got many slaves?"

"I believe not."

"Well I reckon they'll break off from Mexico and make a free state down there by and by."

"There has been much about that in the papers."

Then the man fell silent and said little more while they each ate their suppers.

"What land is that?" the man asked after a long silence.

"That is Dauphin Island." Durnford told the man that the first settlement in the new French Colony of Louisiana was at Dauphin Island, and it became a major port of call for merchant ships and ships of war. A town of considerable size grew up on the island. But then a hurricane dumped so much sand in the harbor that it was unable to hold anything but the smallest ships, and then only one or two of those at a time. The settlement was abandoned and the colony moved to the banks of the Mississippi and founded New Orleans.

"New Orleans holds no interest for me," the man said. "I was raised in Alabama, but I would like to go into a country where they has not got this curse of slavery. And I don't want to move to the cold climate up north either, so it is Texas for me."

"You object to slavery?" Durnford asked cautiously.

"Slavery is wrong and God will put an end to it. When the end does come, there'll be woe in the land. In the meantime, we do nothing but make it worse and worse. That's the way it appears to me. You must agree with that, since you are of that color."

"Yes. I agree with that."

"I'm getting out of these parts before it all comes to a horrible end. I had as good Nigras as anybody, but I never could depend on them. They will lie, they will steal. Of course they will if they are slaves. Sold the lot, I did. Going to start out all new and send for the family when I'm settled."

"You did not set them free, then?"

"Nope. Thought about it. Where would they go? Can't take care of themselves or their families. They'd all end up shot and dead for stealing and cheating. And I couldn't live long enough to see 'em turn out any different.  You see, it would take generations before they'd be able to make it on their own.  I can't wait that long. I've got a family of children, and I don't like to have such degraded beings round my house while my children are growing up.  I know the consequence to children that way, growing up among slaves."

Durnford glanced nervously around and satisfied himself that none of the other passengers were within hearing distance.  "I'm not entirely sure it is safe to utter such sentiments among these people," he said in a low voice.

"Hell, I've been told a hundred times I should be killed if I were not more careful in my opinions.  But I never came the worst out of a fight yet since I was a boy. I'm not afraid to speak what I think to anybody."

"Nevertheless, I caution you to be more prudent until you reach Texas."

"You, sir, being a Negra, and from the looks of your clothing and manner of speaking, a man of some standing, may still need to watch your tongue a bit.  But I'm as good as the next white man, and all know it."

"Well, I venture there are not many Southern men who have as bad an opinion of slavery as you have."

The stranger nodded slowly.  "And what is wrong is making slavery so much worse than is necessary.  I believe Negras will improve, if they are given incitements to improve."

Andrew Durnford knew that he had done very little to improve the chances of his slaves succeeding as free men.

"Of course it is not wrong to hold slaves," the Alabama man continued, "that is what I hear all the time.  Don't drive them too hard, and stop work three times a day for meals, give them plenty to eat of good food, and good clothes, and from Friday night to Monday morning to do what they like.  Now really, my friend, who does that?"

"I had hoped there might be a few."

"Well it just won't work.  Slaves must be forced to work, and they must be held back from a reckless destruction of life and property.  And the gain from their labor is little more than enough to pay a man for looking after them—not if he does his duty to them.  And there is no answer to the problem."  The man paused and poked a finger at Durnford.  "The slaves are given better food and better clothing now than twenty years ago, but it would not be a bit safe to turn them free to shift for themselves.  Those Nigras are not any more accustomed to working and contriving for themselves than they were before."

Having said that, the man leaned back against the grain sacks, pulled his hat down over his eyes, and promptly fell asleep.

Durnford knew the man had spoken the truth. It was the way things were. He believed that slaves never felt any moral obligation to work or obey their masters. It really was necessary to use the lash occasionally. So what was the answer? Even this strange Southern man who was so opposed to slavery found it necessary to sell his people rather than set them free, because they could not survive a free life and would be soon dead. Perhaps it was the better plan to send them off to Africa after all. But Durnford decided he could never do that. He would free his people some day and give them the land they worked. What happened to them after that would have to be God's responsibility.

When Durnford awoke in the morning, the man who had spent the night beside him was returning from a stroll around the ship in the dim light. "Well I have to go to Texas," he said upon spotting Durnford searching in his bag for a breakfast roll. "I can't go North. Imagine, having your ground all frozen up and foddering your cattle five months in the year. I don't see at all how they live up there. I think I'll buy a small farm near some town where I can send my children to school. The Germans must be learning English, certainly they teach the children English in their schools."

"I am sure they do," Durnford said with encouragement.

"And what is your trade?"

"I...I am a physician."

"Good. Good. And where is your practice."

"In New Orleans."

"Well I must visit you there for a day or so before I go overland to Texas."

"I am afraid, dear sir, that would not be possible. I am a physician to the plantations about the countryside and am seldom home. And having been away, I must go on horseback immediately upon my return."

"Well, I can understand that. You are a physician to the slaves then?"

Durnford furthered his lie and nodded agreement.

"Well my good man, do not converse with any of those plantation owners on the question of slavery, there is an epidemic insanity on the subject."

Late in the afternoon of the next day, the schooner carrying Andrew Durnford nudged up to a long pier which stretched out from the swamp far out into Lake Ponchartrain. Having decided to free all of his slaves, Durnford himself felt freer than he had in years. The sky was bluer than he remembered, and the sail along Lake Ponchartrain had been a day of splendor, the sun bright, the water clear, and Durnford's heart light and full of song.

He stepped off the ship and sucked his lungs full of the fresh, sweet air. The bearded man from Alabama jumped down next to him, shook his had, adjusted his backpack, and sauntered down the peir toward shore.

The pier, built of piles and planked over, was lined with sloops and schooners. Men bustled around the ships, taking on and taking off cargo. The pier lay at the foot of the new railroad running to the City of New Orleans across land that was low, flat, and marshy.

It was still possible to go into the city the old way, on one of the little sailing vessels, which carried their cargo and passengers along the brown, sluggish waters of Bayou St. John to the basin at the rear of Toulouse Street. There, five or six miniature sloops and schooners could always be found along the pier, loading and discharging passengers and cargo. Durnford remembered when the basin held up to thirty smart-looking vessels busy in the coastal trade across Lake Ponchartrain to Mobile Bay, Pensacola, and beyond. But within two years the new railroad had nearly superseded the water route.

Many people of all colors were fishing from the pier, and Durnford stepped gingerly around them as he glided across the rough planks, carrying his traveling bag. The water along the shore on each side of the pier was filled with swimmers. Two long, white bathing houses stretched along each side of the pier at the shore. Beyond the bathhouses, blacks in flat-bottomed canoes fished for crabs. Farther down the shore stood the large Washington Hotel, with its long galleries and green shutters, where gentlemen from New Orleans came to eat, fish, and bathe.

Behind Durnford, out beyond the pier to the north, the blue water of the lake met the sky to form a horizon as broad as any ocean. In the West, the sun was low in the sky, promising not more than another few hours of sunshine. Durnford paused and watched the small pleasure sailboats skim over the lake, while other passengers pushed and struggled around him on the crowded pier.

Farther out on the lake, a steamer, bearing the United States mail from Mobile, stood out against the distant horizon, rolling clouds of black smoke from its stack.

It was a grand scene, a scene of peace. Durnford enjoyed it immensely. But then his thoughts turned to the business of meeting with McDonogh. There was the matter of defending St. Rosalie from his English cousins. And finally, Durnford yearned to be home at St. Rosalie, where he must talk with Marie-Charlotte about the future of the plantation. He would not even spare the little time it would take to visit Thomas at his boarding school in New Orleans, Andrew had decided. Life rushed him along.

Near the shore, Andrew stopped again to savor the moment and to gaze at the small village of beautiful, white-painted houses and hotels, cafes, storehouses, and bathinghouses. It was a scene he would come back to paint some day, he decided.

Stepping off the pier, Durnford passed a lively cafe with ornamental iron and glass windows. The huge doors were open and from within came the clatter of dominoes rattling on every table, and glasses ringing against glasses. Loud voices in all languages, mingled with laughter and oaths, came from the crowd of men in the cafe.

Another cafe on the opposite side was equally crowded and the adjoining billiard rooms were filled with spectators and players. Clouds of heavy, blue tobacco smoke rolled about the multitude and the rooms rang with shouts: *"Sacre bleu!" "Mon Dieu!" "Diable!"* "Son-of-a-bitch!"

The first bell for passengers was ringing as Durnford rushed for the ticket office and threw down seventy-five cents for the fare. White smoke screamed from the small engine, behind which were ten passenger cars, and behind those a long train of baggage cars, already heavily laden. The passenger cars, looking like elongated stagecoaches, contained four benches seating six people each. Behind the engine was a platform with a wooden canopy to protect the engineer and fireman from sparks, rain and sun. Durnford sprang into the only vacant seat of the first coach he came to. All the cars appeared to be full. The train lurched forward, then pulled away slowly and steadily, and then faster and faster. Soon they were in the fenceless, uninhabited marshes, where Durnford saw nothing but dwarf trees, tall, coarse grass, and rank undergrowth. The trees, heavy with gray Spanish moss, grew larger as they went toward the city through the cypress swamp. Vines twisted and wound around their trunks. Andrew took out his pocket watch and noted that they passed a milestone every three and a half minutes, and with a quick mental calculation, determined they were traveling at the fantastic speed of seventeen miles per hour. In less than twenty minutes, the train was in the city, where it ran for about a half a mile along a broad street with low detached houses on each side and then came thumping and bumping to a stop at the levee under a long roof which covered the end of the railway.

Durnford spent the night trying not to think about Henry Spaulding and pretending and drinking with Captain Gentry aboard the old *Creole*. They were both still awake at dawn, when the little steamer put out into the Mississippi on its weekly run to supply the plantations up and down the river.

During the morning ride to St. Rosalie, with the steamer stopping at most of the plantations along the way, Andrew drank black, strong coffee, not to keep awake, his mind churned with thoughts of what he must do for his slaves, and he never thought of sleep, but he did not want to arrive drunk. Marie-Charlotte would think little of him in that condition. He sipped cup after cup and watched the shore as they went along with the current. When they reached the cane fields of his plantation with the sun high overhead, Durnford strained to see a familiar face at work in the fields. But the fields were empty, and Durnford was puzzled. Noel should have the slaves out hoeing the cane, as well as the corn and peas planted between the rows, and digging ditches. The cane itself required little work once it was planted, but spring was the time to get the fields in shape. But nowhere was a slave working, not in the fields, not in the gardens, nor at the sugarhouse.

The little steamer swung around against the current and hardly stopped long enough for Durnford to jump to his dock and for his bag to be thrown down after him and was off again, out into the stream in a wide turn to the south with its catalog of plantation necessities.

Spring was everywhere and it was warm again with a comfortable feeling in the air. Birds sang. The livestock bellowed. But there was not the sound of a living human being, nor was anyone in sight. There were no slaves around the cabins. No slave children played in the dirt. The door to the sugarhouse stood open and inside all was cold and dark. St. Rosalie Plantation was deserted.

# Chapter Twenty Four

Durnford barely noticed the scent of the lemon trees as he turned through the gate and hurried along the shell-paved drive to his mansion. "I should never have given Lewis that gun," he said to himself. "All my people have revolted and run off and God knows what's happened to Miss Remy."

The doors to the mansion swung open as Andrew rushed up on the gallery. He stopped, and dropped his bag. So certain had he become that everyone on the plantation had been massacred or run off, that he was startled and stunned when the door opened. And then Marie-Charlotte came out the door, walking very slowly. She also stopped and stared curiously at Andrew Durnford. The house servants came out behind her and they too stood, staring at Durnford.

"Thank God you're alive." Durnford could say no more. Hot tears came to his eyes. "I thought I was going crazy," he said and threw his arms around his wife in a fierce embrace.

Marie-Charlotte struggled free and stared at him. "Andrew, what in the world is the matter with you?"

"I thought...I thought.... Oh, Miss Remy, where has everyone gone?"

Then Marie-Charlotte told him what had happened. Noel had taken the entire slave force north along the river to work the Stanton plantation. Old man Stanton had gotten the silly notion that he could run his plantation without slaves. He sold them all and hired Irish and Germans to cut and grind his cane. Well everything went wrong, Marie-Charlotte told Andrew. The hired workers knew nothing about processing sugar cane and the harder Stanton pushed them the more surly they became.  Finally it came to a strike.  The workers closed down the plantation and insisted on doubling their wages.

At last, Stanton came to his senses and realized he would never get his cane through the sugar mill or the new seed cane into the ground without help. Fortunately, there had been no hard frost, and the cane standing in the fields was still worth something, although not the sweet quality it had been.  But nowhere could he buy slaves with any field experience, and his entire work force had been sold at auction in New Orleans and transported to the cotton fields to the north.

"Noel was clever," Marie-Charlotte said.  "He handled all the negotiations. Stanton is paying $400 the week for all our field hands, men and women.  Why, that's more than five dollars for each, and giving them sleeping quarters and feeding them at that."  She stood with her hands on her hips.  "Now isn't that a bargain, Andrew?"

"But our fields?  The ditches?  What will happen to them?"

"It was only for two weeks, Andrew.  Noel has everything in hand. They'll be back Monday, in plenty of time to do our fields right."

"Monday?  What day is today?"

"Why, Andrew, its Friday.  What's the matter with you, Andrew?  You are shaking so, and your eyes are red and you look so tired and worn out.  And where's Henry Spaulding?"

They went into the parlor and sat down and a servant brought them both a cup of hot molasses and corn bread, which they ate while they talked.  Andrew told his wife how Henry Spaulding had died, and with each labored sentence he drew a long breath.

"The man should have had more sense," Marie-Charlotte said.  "And more appreciation of your efforts for him, too.  You are an honorable man, that I know, Andrew Durnford.  What man takes better care of his people.  You had promised him his freedom. Why could he not wait until then?  It makes one wonder if we shall ever be appreciated for what we do."

"I have decided that we must free all of the slaves," Andrew said suddenly.

"Andrew, are you sick?  Has the fever taken your senses?  Surely you do not mean to run this plantation with hired labor.  The foolishness of Ethan Stanton has proved that unworkable.  And what would I do with this house?  You know I need my servants, Andrew.  Who would do the cooking?  Goodness knows you can't expect me to do that."

Durnford wiped a tired hand across his brow.  "My plan is quite simple. We will set them free, all of them, and they will work for wages. I have had enough of this plantation business. As you have just proved to me, Noel is a capable man. He can run this sugar plantation without me." Durnford sat up straight and moved forward in his chair. "My plan is give the entire management of the plantation to Noel with the thought of selling the land to our people. Each slave will receive a portion according to his position...and someday our slaves will own it all, although I had thought of keeping the house here, and---"

"Andrew, how can you think of doing such a thing? These people can not be expected to look after themselves. Why, you know every little money they come by is soon gone for tobacco and liquor and silly little things. You have said that yourself, many times, Andrew."

"Yes, and it's all true. But this is something not to rush into. Little by little is how it will be done. With instruction, I believe every man, woman, and child on this plantation can overcome their deficiencies." He paused and fell back heavily in his chair. "It is something I must do."

This was a heavy blow for Marie-Charlotte who had seen them rise through the social classes as the plantation progressed. They were on the very verge of acceptance even by the best in white society. "I don't have the patience for these kind of jokes, Andrew. You can't be serious."

"I have thought about it a long time," he said quietly. "Peace has come to me at last."

"Think for a moment, Andrew. What would we do for an income."

"I am a physician." Durnford stirred, and sat up in his chair again. "I can hire out as plantation doctor. Planters are paying now $3.00 a head for their slaves up in the cotton country. I can easily handle three thousand, and that comes to $9,000 a year. A very good income, considering we do little better than that with the entire plantation."

"You are a dreamer, Andrew Durnford, a dreamer. Once it is known you have a plan for setting our slaves free, my servants included, who will want you administering to their work force? You will be like a pariah, a leper, persona non grata...what you propose is completely unrealistic, Andrew."

Durnford rose slowly from his chair and stood before her firm and straight. "You do not understand, Miss Remy. I have thought this over very carefully. It is a decision I will not, can not, retreat from. The slaves must be freed. My plan is one that will succeed."

He turned then and started from the room, allowing no time for contradiction, although he expected none, as Marie-Charlotte had always known when she could no longer challenge him.

"You have a letter, Andrew. An urgent message from John McDonogh." She got up quietly, walked slowly to the fireplace mantle, and picked up a sealed envelope, which she then handed to her husband, the master of St. Rosalie.

Durnford's fingers shook as he broke the wax seal. His fingers did not shake from nerves, but because he was now exhausted from his travels and lack of sleep and the tense conversation with his wife. He stood in the doorway reading silently, then folded the letter and looked up.

"The trial has been postponed," he said. "The judge was run over by a team of horses. He's dead. And there is to be a hearing on Monday next. Another attempt to place St. Rosalie in trust pending appointment of a new judge."

John McDonogh had little doubt they would prevail again in court. His riches were prone to work against him when he came before the law, as he so often stated, but in this particular case, it was ultimately the interests of Andrew Durnford that were in question. Since the sympathies with the Louisiana courts were more in line with the interests of the less fortunate and local citizens, and Andrew Durnford, even though he was a free man of color, when stacked up against his English cousins, fell within the definition of less fortunate and local citizen, McDonogh could only be optimistic.

However, the unexpected death of Judge Chollop under the hooves of a thundering team pulling a heavy dray changed all of that. Judge Rene Dufouchar, a skeleton of a man dressed all in black, with black, greasy hair, parted up the middle of his head and hanging down upon his coat, spoke no English, and he was the man appointed by the Louisiana Supreme Court to hear the motion for a trustee.

The legal system of Louisiana held a unique position. It was the only one among the states of the United States that was not based on the English common law. When the territory became a state in 1812 French was the accepted language. The Code Napoleon, the entire body of French law, was the law of Louisiana. Neither the Code nor the language changed when the territory became a state.

"I will make it clear at this time," Judge Dufouchar said in impeccable French at the opening of the hearing, "that all proceedings shall be in the French language, as shall be the record."

This was not a statement which surprised anyone, as the courts at that time conducted hearings in both English and French, and the judge had the option of keeping the official stenographic record of proceedings in either language. But then

Judge Dufouchar appointed the lawyer representing Durnford's English cousins as the court interpreter for the purpose of translating English into French. McDonogh's lawyer protested vehemently, to no avail. Strange as the practice seemed to outsiders, it was quite common, especially in the outlying parishes where it was either impossible or inconvenient to obtain the services of a qualified translator.

"I am, to say the least, incensed at your opposition to my ruling," Dufouchar screamed from his high perch on the bench. "You impugn the integrity of Monsieur Benet." The judge waged a bony finger at the attorney for the defendants Durnford and McDonogh. "His father is a good friend of mine, and a trusted and honorable man, as is the entire Benet family. And you impugn the honor of that noble family. You impugn the honor of this court. And I will hear no more of it."

The proceedings began, and it was immediately clear to Durnford that Judge Dufouchar's sentiments lie with the Plaintiffs, Durnford's English cousins. The English cousins, children and grandchildren of Colonel Elias Durnford, were not present in court. Their presence was not necessary, they were ably represented by their lawyer, Benet, and to the despair of Andrew Durnford, by Judge Dufouchar.

Monsieur Benet eloquently set forth the position of his clients in his opening statement. The English Durnford family estate consisted almost entirely of investments in the New World. First, there were real estate holdings in Quebec, where Colonel Durnford had so ably served His Majesty's government until his transfer to Pensacola. Then came the Colonel's acquisitions in British West Florida and New Orleans, made while the loyal ancestor served as Lieutenant Governor at Pensacola. The Plaintiffs' claims to those assets were undisputed. But in addition the heirs were entitled to the substantial holdings of Thomas Durnford whose only true heirs were his distant cousins. These assets, pleaded Monsieur Benet in the hearing before the Orleans Parish Probate Court, had in large part been illegally transferred to Andrew Durnford. The scheme, according to Benet, was carried out by John McDonogh as curator of the Estate of Thomas Durnford. And then Monsieur Benet went further. He claimed that the holdings of the deceased Colonel Elias Durnford were involved as well.

Felix Marchant, the fat and balding lawyer representing the defendants, John McDonogh and Andrew Durnford objected to the argument. Marchant was a huge man, and it seemed to Durnford that he puffed himself up to an enormous size every time he rose to speak. "The holdings of Elias Durnford are not relevant to these proceedings," he argued, "And all references to the same, I respectfully submit, should be stricken from the record, your Honor."

"May it please the Court," Monsieur Benet responded, "I give you my word that the affairs of the late Colonel Durnford are most important to my clients' case."

"You are promising a connection then, Monsieur Benet?" the judge asked.

"Most indeed, your Honor."

"Well we have no jury here, Monsieur Marchant. I am willing to allow both parties great latitude. You may proceed, Monsieur Benet."

Marchant puffed himself up even larger. "Your Honor I must take exception and ask you to reconsider. I see nothing in the petition to warrant an exploration of the estate of the late Colonel. We are, I believe, concerned with the estate of the late Thomas Durnford and the disposition of his assets."

"Monsieur Marchant, the Court has ruled."

Marchant slowly settled his great bulk into his chair, whispering, "I do not like this, Mr. McDonogh. Our Benet is a sly fox."

The attorney for the plaintiffs concluded his argument with a statement that his clients had lost a great fortune in West Florida, both through seizures of property by the Spanish authorities and through mysterious handling of properties by Thomas Durnford, properties that were now claimed by Andrew Durnford. And when Benet stated that all of the real estate of St. Rosalie Plantation rightfully belonged to the Plaintiffs', Andrew Durnford was dismayed to see Judge Dufouchar's head nod ever so slightly in agreement.

Benet began his case by introducing birth records to prove the lineage of his clients, and when the boring details and documents had taken up a good share of the morning, Judge Dufouchar suddenly slammed his hand on his high desk. "Really, Monsieur Marchant, can we not have an agreement on these matters? Surely you do not dispute the pedigree of Monsieur Benet's clients?"

"No, indeed I do not your Honor. I am more than happy to so stipulate."

"I might have thought you would have done so much earlier, Monsieur Marchant, and without the necessity of a request from me."

"I apologize for the inconvenience, your Honor."

Benet smiled at Marchant and then bowed to the Judge. "Thank you, your Honor." Then he proceeded with more direct proofs.

He introduced the sworn statement of Ann Gannaway of Kemmerson, County of Gloucester, England, who stated that:

"Henry Gannaway, this deponent's husband, had gone to Pensacola with Thomas Durnford, who was the same age as the said Henry Gannaway, being at the time fifteen years of age, and both said young men embarked in the year one thousand seven hundred and seventy six for Pensacola where they were employed in the office of the said Elias Durnford, at that time Lieutenant Governor of Pensacola."

Next, Benet put into evidence the deposition of Elizabeth Fontenelle of Yarmouth, County of Norfolk, England, who swore that Elias Durnford, "her said Brother-in-Law took the said Thomas Durnford out from England with him to Pensacola when he was a boy of age fifteen years, and Thomas Durnford, after his arrival at Pensacola acted for some time as clerk in the office of this Deponent's said Brother-in-Law at Pensacola, and whilst he was so acting this Deponent, Elizabeth Fontenelle, frequently saw him in her said Brother-in-Law's house and also in his office."

Then Benet offered the deposition testimony of Andrew Durnford, taken two years earlier in Richmond, translating both the questions and answers into French.

Being equally comfortable in both languages, Andrew Durnford saw their disadvantage immediately. Benet chose the French word or phrase which helped his client whenever possible. There were many situations where more than one word of French could be used, and other cases of questionable inferences, emphasis, and intonation. Clear and precise answers given by Durnford on his deposition in English, became hazy and confused in the French interpretation. Words of wit became sarcasm. And when Benet came to the question regarding Andrew's parentage, his answer, "It requires a wise man to know who is his father," was translated into something more akin to, "I am not wise enough to have determined who was my father."

It was at this point that Marchant repeated his earlier objection. "Andrew Durnford speaks and reads French. Can we not read him the questions in French and have him give his answers in French, in his own words?"

Judge Dufouchar threw down the pen with which he scratched notes to himself during the proceedings, spattering ink about his desk. "This is the second time, Monsieur Marchant, that you have questioned a matter upon which I have already made a ruling. You are delaying us unnecessarily, and shall be subject to contempt of court should you do so again. I thought I had made myself perfectly clear. The deposition of Andrew Durnford is part of the record in this case. Your client may not impeach his own testimony. What he said he has said." Then Dufouchar drew back and looked sharply down his long, thin nose at Marchant. "Surely you do not mean to impugn the translation of Monsieur Benet."

"No, your Honor. Not at this time."

"Not at this time, you say. I should think not, Monsieur Marchant. I should think that you would never do so. I further think you owe an apology to Monsieur Benet."

"Yes. I do apologize to you, Monsieur Benet. I meant no disrespect...I only sought to preserve my position on the record for a possible...a possible appeal."

"So, you are talking about appeal already, Marchant? Before I have even given my decision?"

"No disrespect intended to the Court either, your Honor. I seek only to serve my clients...to the best of my ability...within the law."

"Well, Monsieur Defendant, you are not serving the interests of your clients by incurring the wrath of this Court. But be assured, I am putting our personal differences aside, and shall adjudge these matters on the merits." And then with a final sneer at Marchant, Judge Dufouchar turned to Benet. "Monsieur Benet, please proceed with your case."

With great vigor and enthusiasm, Benet did proceed with his case. Document after document was stamped and initialed by the clerk and introduced into evidence. With each paper came from Benet a statement of its value and reason for consideration by the court. And each and every time, Judge Dufouchar said, "Most interesting, Monsieur Benet. You have a valuable point there." Then turning to Marchant, he continued, "What do you say to that, Monsieur Defendant?"

Now Durnford realized the tone of the trial had been cast. No longer did Judge Dufouchar refer to the defendants' lawyer as Monsieur Marchant, but simply as Monsieur Defendant. And he did so in a sarcastic manner that would never be refected in the record, while he addressed the Plaintiffs' lawyer respectfully as Monsieur Benet. So when Marchant began his argument in opposition to Benet, Durnford knew there was little chance of success. Marchant's argument was invariably that the documents were authentic enough, but the propositions of Benet were mere speculation, not supported by the evidence. Marchant objected again, when it became evident that Benet had taken a different tack, had, indeed put forth the supposition that the case turned not so much on a diversion of the assets of the estate of Thomas Durnford, but the misappropriation by Thomas Durnford of the assets of Colnel Elias Durnford of the Royal Engineers. Those asselts, Benet insisted, never legally belonged to Thomas Durnford. Therefore, those assets, including the land upon which St. Rosalie was built, could never have abeen sold by Thomas Durnford to McDonogh or anyone else.

It was, Benet maintained, a case of breach of trust. When the Spanish drove the

British from West Florida, Colonel Durnford was evacuated by the English fleet, but remained in service to His Majesty in the West Indies. The Colonel left behind to supervise his empire his young nephew and trusted business agent, Thomas Durnford. Copies of instruction from the Colonel in Tobago to Thomas Durnford at Pensacola were introduced to support Benet's contention. Most damaging was a letter of instruction to Thomas asking him to buy as agent for the Colonel the lands along the Mississippi which now constituted the entire St. Rosalie Plantation. Further proof was offered by way of letters of the Colonel to his wife and sons in England, advising that he would acquire the property and that upon his death the lands should be sold and the proceeds divided equally among his sons, separate provisions having been made for his wife. These letters were all dated a few months before his death on the island of Tobago in 1794. Thus, argued Benet, from the time the Colonel left Pensacola until his death, a period of thirteen years, his substantial business interests in New Orleans as well as Pensacola were in the hands of Thomas Durnford. And most importantly, the lands constituting the St. Rosalie Plantation were purchased by Thomas Durnford as agent for Colonel Elias Durnford, and the purchases were financed by funds which belonged to the Colonel.

So the trial went, that day, and the next day, and the following day, while Benet introduced documents completely changing the context of the case. No longer was Marchant defending a challenge to the disposition of Thomas Durnford's estate. It mattered not whether the land of St. Rosalie was given directly or indirectly to Andrew, or whether, as Andrew and McDonogh maintained, it was purchased from the estate for a full and fair price. The truth was that, according to Benet, the land belonged to Colonel Elias Durnford and his heirs. Facts which were known or should have been known to both Andrew Durnford and John McDonogh, one being the son of Thomas and the other being his partner in the very business which owed its existence to Colonel Durnford.

Unprepared to fight this battle, McDonogh did not have the documents to prove otherwise. "Clearly," Marchant argued to McDonogh and Andrew in private, "there were business holdings in Pensacola, both real estate and goods in warehouses, which belonged to Colonel Durnford." It was equally clear that Thomas Durnford had liquidated all of those assets when he moved to New Orleans. Colonel Durnford had been dead for five years at that time, and there was no accounting to his estate. There was no accounting at all.

Marchant argued that there must have been some understanding between Thomas and Elias. And it was patently unfair to raise these issues over forty years after the death of Colonel Durnford.

To further drive home his point, Marchant held high the petition filed by the heirs shortly after Thomas Durnford died in 1826. No where in that petition, nor in any subsequent petition did the heirs claim that Thomas had wrongfully converted the assets of Colonel Durnford to his own personal use.

The proceedings before Judge Dufouchar ended on Thursday afternoon, and he read his decision after lunch on Friday, having taken the time, he said, to review his notes, the documents and evidence, and to study the matter.

"First, I must remind you that the facts will be decided by a jury at some indefinite time in the future. My only concern is whether the plaintiffs have shown by sufficient evidence that they will likely prevail, and that the assets of St. Rosalie Plantation must be placed in trust and a receiver appointed to manage the plantation pending trial. Now, gentlemen, it is abundantly clear to me that Thomas Durnford did come into possession of a vast estate which belonged to Colonel Elias Durnford. What I see here is a repetition of the arrangement the Colonel made in Quebec. An arrangement, I might add that was respected and honored, for which I am sure the plaintiffs are eternally grateful since they now own the Quebec holdings without dispute. The agent in Quebec was worthy of the trust placed in him. The same cannot, however be said about the agent Thomas Durnford, or his illegitimate son, Andrew Durnford, or his partner, John McDonogh."

Judge Dufouchar paused in his reading, let his written opinion fall to his desk, and continued without glancing at his notes. "Monsieur Defendant," he said looking directly and sternly at Marchant, "you have ably represented your clients, but I must inform you that you have not prevailed. No doubt you will appeal, as you have threatened. But you have not failed entirely. I am not granting the petition of the plaintiffs' as presented. I am placing St. Rosalie Plantation in receivership, and I am appointing Andrew Durnford as the trustee. He shall make reports to the Court, that is to me, and to my successor, on the operations of the planation from month to month. To assist him, he shall engage the services of accountants satisfactory to all parties. And if you, Monsieur Defendant, and Monsieur Benet can not agree, I shall appoint such accountants, the same to be paid from the operations of St. Rosalie Plantation. Do you have any questions, Monsieur Defendant?"

After Marchant consulted with his clients, McDonogh and Andrew Durnford, he stood to address the court. "I am advised, your Honor, that Andrew Durnford wishes to free some numbers of his slaves. And since we are interested here only in the real estate, I assume—"

"You are greatly mistaken in your assumptions, Monsieur Defendant," Judge Dufouchar snapped. "The slaves are fruits of the lands. They were no doubt purchased from the profits of operations, and, therefore, my order, which is rather extensive, specifically prohibits any transactions of real or personal property, other than in the normal course of business. And slaves, as you well know, Monsieur Defendant, are personal property."

Then turning abruptly to the attorney for the plaintiff at the opposite table, the judge asked, "Monsieur Benet, have you understood my decision?"

"Yes, your Honor, I have, and a most wise decision it is."

"Good." Judge Dufouchar rose and slammed down his gavel. "This session is adjourned."

Andrew Durnford sat silent and stunned in the courtroom.

Marchant scooped up his papers and shuffled them into his briefcase. "There's nothing to do now but appeal."

"They can only say no," McDonogh said confidently, "but I think they will say yes."

"I would do anything to teach that fellow some manners," said Marchant. "I grieve to think of my continued treatment by Judge Dufouchar whenever I shall appear before the old goat. Appeal, yes. And the sooner the better."

Andrew sat at the table while everyone around him made ready to leave. Monsieur Benet bowed politely from across the courtroom, turned and left with his briefcase tucked under his arm. Slowly, the knowledge of what had happened fixed itself in Durnford's mind. He too, had become a slave at St. Rosalie. No longer was he free to deal with his property as he saw fit. No longer could he dream of his plan to free the workers. Monthly accounting must be made to the court. And a firm of accountants would be looking over his shoulder, questioning every entry, every expenditure. His voice was barely audible and rattled in his throat as he turned to Marchant, standing impatiently at the end of the table. "How...how long before we have the results of an appeal?"

Marchant spoke in a solemn voice. "Be assured, Mr. Durnford, it will be a speedy appeal, and in eight or nine months, perhaps less, we shall have overturned this unfortunate ruling."

"But for the time being," McDonogh said, "we must not think that all is lost. Andrew, you will have the burdensome accounting to deal with, certainly, but little else is changed in regard to administration of your plantation.  In the end, I have full confidence in Felix.  He will free us from this trap into which that sorry excuse for a judge has so painfully bound us.  In the meantime, Andrew, you have to endure...we have to endure."

"Courage, Mr. Durnford.  Courage," Marchant said cheerfully.  "This is, I understand, not your first excursion into the judicial system.  And as you know, not all goes as smoothly as one may wish, a predicament to which Mr. McDonogh can also attest.  But in the end, Mr. Durnford, you may expect that justice will prevail."

"Perhaps that is what I fear," Andrew Durnford said quietly.

# Chapter Twenty Five

The appeal motions came and went, and Andrew Durnford carried on the business of St. Rosalie Plantation without regard to the accounting requirements of Judge Dufouchar. No one raised the question of the missing monthly reports. As time went on, Durnford gained more and more courage. If no one acted upon his failure to abide by the court decision in one matter, he reasoned, perhaps he could extend his luck further. Thus, on May 20, 1839, Andrew set free the first of his slaves. As case Nr. 1578 in the Plaquemines Parish Notarial Book Number Seven, on page 359, it was recorded that André Durnford, free man of color, and Marie-Charlotte Remy Durnford, free woman of color, emancipated Harry, a Negro aged 45 years, as well as Harry's wife, Besa, aged 37 years, and their son Nelson, aged seven years.

Harry and his wife had been industrious slaves, and applied themselves well to raising rice and cattle on land that had been part of the Vachery to the south along the river. When Durnford freed the slave couple, he sold them the same land they had worked as slaves. Terms were six percent. Harry and his wife paid for that land within four years, and on March 17, 1843, Andrew Durnford sold to Harry his son Pomond for the sum of three hundred dollars. The bill of sale was executed before Gilbert Bernard, notary, and provided that Pomond was to be freed at the age of twenty-one.

Neither did Durnford neglect his own family. He was determined that his son would receive as good an education as Andrew himself. A week before his fourteenth birthday, Thomas was sent off to preparatory school. Andrew and

Marie-Charlotte put him aboard the packet *Alabama* at New Orleans. "You must do without money," Andrew told Thomas as they parted, "as it will not be a good companion to good studies." Three weeks later, Thomas landed in New York. In his pocket he carried a letter to the President of Lafayette College. The letter, written by Andrew Durnford, thanked the President, The Reverend G. Junkin, D.D. for accepting Thomas at Lafayette College in Pennsylvania. In his letter, Durnford stated: "I request, my Dear Sir, that no indulgence be shown to him. If he should not perform his collegiate duties, punish him with severity, it is my earnest wish. He has at times a disposition to be indolent, but with sufficient capacity to perform any duties imposed upon him."

It was through John McDonogh and Elliot Cresson that the door to Lafayette College was opened, and while on a tour through the Southern states, Cresson stopped at St. Rosalie Plantation a week after Thomas left. He was delighted with Andrew's plan to free his slaves, although disappointed to see Durnford still opposed to the mission of the American Colonization Society.

Thomas was met in New York by the Reverend Walter Lowrie, a supporter of the American Colonization Society and the son of a United States Senator. Thomas stayed with Lowrie a few days in New York, where the Reverend treated him like his own son.

Thomas and Lafayette College were the same age, both having begun life in 1826. Thomas did not enter the college when he was delivered to the new brick building at Easton, 160 feet above Bushkill Creek, by Reverend Lowrie's clerk. The primary purpose of Lafayette College was to train teachers. To further that purpose, the college ran a laboratory school. Thomas spent two years in the laboratory school in preparation for his higher education, and entered Lafayette College as a freshman in 1842. Thomas was then just sixteen years old.

Thomas was not the only black man from Louisiana at the preparatory school. David Kearney McDonogh and Washington Watts McDonogh, slaves of John McDonogh, were already studying at Easton when Thomas arrived. John McDonogh had sent Washington to prepare for the ministry, and David to study chemistry and science in preparation for medical school. Both black men, still slaves, were to complete their training and go to Africa as part of McDonogh's plan to construct a colony of freed slaves in Liberia.

Washington did go to Liberia and became a teacher among the Kroos, at Settra Kroo.

David Kearney McDonogh was graduated from Lafayette College in 1844. In

1847, this slave was further graduated from the College of Physicians and Surgeons in New York, and recieved an appointment to the New York Eye and Ear Infirmary. He practiced medicine in New York and gained a reputation as an outstanding physician. The first private hospital established in New York for Negroes was named after him. He died in 1893, never having joined his fellow slaves in Liberia.

During the six long years at Easton, two years in preparatory school and four years in college, Thomas Durnford never returned to St. Rosalie Plantation.

Andrew wrote first, on May 7, 1840, before receiving any letter from his son. Andrew's letter, written in French, was transcribed into the plantation journal:

"Mon cher Thomas," he began his letter to his young son, "I dare to hope that you have arrived long ago, my dear child, at your destination and that your stay in New York was most pleasant, and your reception in Dr. Lowries's home satisfactory. You were doubtless treated in a friendly way.

"Write me at the end of each month. I beg you likewise to write a letter to your godfather, John McDonogh, of thanks for the trouble he took in your behalf.

"Everybody is well here except grandmother Remy, who has been a little under the weather on account of her asthma. Your mother is well and embraces you most tenderly.

"I urge you, my dear boy, to do your duty well; be obedient to your teachers and make them like you, for if it is otherwise, you would cause me only pain, and I think you love your papa too much to cause any worry to him who loves you so much. Include in your letter details of your trip and of your reception at Dr. Lowrie's, and in your school; if indeed you have not done so in the letter I am expecting from you, for Noel is going to take this to the post office and see whether you have written.

"Everything is fine here. The river is very high and a flood is feared, as it seems that all the branches are bringing in a lot of water. The levee of the old munitions depot has sunk; fortunately, the levee behind the Mossy house at the upper ferry was there, or else everybody would have been flooded.

"Your mother embraces you with all her heart, as does grandmother, and as for me, I love you as I do my own two eyes.

Noel mailed the letter at New Orleans, but there was no letter from Thomas. Nor did a letter come the next week.

"Ah! My philosopher," Durnford said to McDonogh as they sat in his study on the second floor of the old man's bleak mansion, "you were right to send those two slaves."

Both David and Washington were older than Thomas, and in their second year at Lafayette. They were honor students. It remained to be seen whether Thomas would reach the same level of achievement. Andrew had yet to hear from him. Durnford had picked up his mail from the post office in New Orleans and stopped off to visit his old friend. And to Durnford's chagrin, McDonogh had received long letters from David and Washington. But again there was no letter from Thomas. He had not written since arriving at Easton. "I am at a loss to say what can be the cause of not receiving a letter from Thomas...he must have written and his letter miscarried."

Age had set its mark upon John McDonogh's craggy face. But a sparkle still came to his gray eyes. He leaned back from his desk and adjusted the band holding his long gray hair in a pony tail at the back of his head. "Don't worry, Thomas is doing well enough, Andrew. David writes that Thomas has even joined a literary society."

"What? A literary society?" Andrew believed in a sound education in the basics: mathematics, chemistry, science, the study of biology, all those subjects which trained one well for entry into medical school, which is exactly what Durnford had planned for his son. But not only must Andrew endure the knowledge that Thomas had failed to write him a letter, now it appeared his son was wasting his time in a literary society.

"Well," Andrew said, frowning deeply, "as to the literary society, it is probably a mere matter of form to put him on equal grounds with the other young men of the college." Andrew chuckled and shook his head. "If it were otherwise it would not be pleasing to my feelings, and Thomas knows that."

Now John McDonogh was beginning to enjoy the discomfort of his friend. "Well, whatever the reason, Thomas was accepted into the Franklin Literary Society, and I'm pleased. They bring in guest speakers, they hold debates, they build libraries. These are things more important than the study of bones and flesh."

"The study of bones and flesh, as you put it my dear friend, is of great practical use to us mere mortals."

And being satisfied he had agitated his prodigy sufficiently, McDonogh smiled and handed Durnford a letter. "This is for you."

The letter was addressed to Durnford, care of John McDonogh. It was from Walter Lowrie. Andrew read it eagerly:

*I would have informed you earlier of the arrival of your son, Thomas, but have been part of the time confined by a fever, and much pressed with business when I got better. Thomas came here on the first of May. I happened to be moving to a different house and could not keep him with us at night as none of our beds were up. He stayed with an excellent young man we have in the office, but spent most of the days with me. I became much attached to him, and my excellent wife took a great interest in him. We felt for him, away from his friends, and among strangers and he seemed to feel as if he had a kind of home here. I sent this young man, Mr. Stork, with him to Easton and I expect to go over sometime in June to see him. He expressed a wish to expend his vacation with us: I told him he would be welcome to come and stay with us, but it might remain till I would go over, and then we could arrange it. I think it would be a good thing for him. It would be a change and he would feel he had a home, besides the college. Thomas is a fine promising boy. He is now where he will become a scholar, and I think you will not have cause to regret his coming. When I go over to Easton I will write you fully respecting his situation.*

*I write in haste, but am respectfully & truly yours,*

*Walter Lowrie*

The next day, on his return to St. Rosalie, Andrew Durnford stopped at the New Orleans post office, and there was a letter from Thomas. His son reported the friendly treatment he had received at New York and at Easton, thanked his father for securing his education, and asked after everyone at the plantation. At a cafe just down the street, Durnford penned a letter to Lowrie at a table in the corner.

"I have this day received a letter from my son, Thomas, expressing in the highest terms the friendly reception he has met from you, and your good lady. Allow me sir, to return to you, and Mrs. Lowrie, my sincerest thanks and gratitude for the care and attention paid to my child. Such kindness will be forever engraved on my heart.

"If ever any of your friends be travelling up the Mississippi, it would afford me pleasure to do them any kindness that may lay in my power.

"I remain, sir, with Sentiments of Esteem, your obedient humble servant."

Life at St. Rosalie Plantation went blissfully on through the summer of that year. The winter sugar crop had been good and sold at $65.00 per hogshead, still much less than the $90.00 Andrew realized before the great financial panic of 1837. But his production was up, and plantation revenues of $15,947.00 were higher than any previous year. Nevertheless, by summer Andrew was financially pinched. There was the cost of Thomas' education, the expenses of rebuilding the boilers, and the numerous and continuing costs of maintaining the sugarhouse, the slave force, the machinery, the equipment, the livestock, and the St. Rosalie mansion itself.

"Two years ago I was in the habit of buying my people clothing at auction," he told McDonogh on one of his frequent visits. "But now I'm out of funds. I buy everything on credit. And that means the shoes I see going at auction for 75 cents, I buy now for $1.50."

"Well, Andrew, it's the hard times that make the man, not the good times. You must learn to manage your money better."

Durnford bit his tongue and remained silent. He would not, he decided, let his temper get the best of him. Several plantations along the river failed in the panic of 1837. Durnford brushed it all aside and pushed on, expanding his fields. He knew recovery would come. Now it had. Almost too late. The court order prohibiting emancipation of his slaves was a blessing, and Durnford knew it. Until his finances improved, he could not consider any further program of freedom.

He looked around the dingy study where he spent his visits with McDonogh in that decaying mansion. They ate their meals there on old and cracked plates, played whist there with old and bent cards. Talked there. Sometimes the old man slept there, upright in his chair under a mosquito net, and Durnford slipped off to his room on the second floor of the next building.

Through the years, weeds, brush, and now small trees grew up in the space separating the two wings of the huge mansion. The growth occupied the area planned for a splendid ballroom. Only the artists sketch of what was to have been attested to the dreamed of magnificence, the sweeping staircase and balcony leading to guestrooms above the dance floor. Now the artist's sketch neglected, dirty, and yellow from lamp oil and dust hung on McDonogh's office wall, next to the portrait of Susan, his former fiancée.

As time went by, Andrew watched his old friend grow older and reclusive. He suspected the old man now seldom washed and there was an uncomfortable odor about him. His fingernails were dirty and his clothing rumpled. How had McDonogh come through the panic of '37, Durnford wondered? It had cut down businessmen much faster than the planters along the river. The businessmen conducted all of their affairs on credit. When the banks called in the loans, they went down like those dying of cholera in the streets every summer.

McDonogh stood up behind his desk, a bent and awkward figure. "Come," he said, "let's walk along the river while we have light."

Durnford followed him down the unpainted steps in the rear, and as they reached the path at the top of the levee, McDonogh stopped, leaned against a tree and waved a hand toward the long, curving mound of dirt which followed the river's bank. "Do you see that section of the levee, there, just up from the oak tree, Andrew?"

Andrew nodded.

"That's where it gave way. Just started sinking late one day. The river had undermined it. George saw it happening. Never said a word. Organized a party. They worked all through the night by lantern, hauling up dirt from back by the old customs road and stopping up the holes where the river percolated up. By morning, when I awoke, they had it all under control. Now what paid hand would have been so diligent?"

Andrew felt the statement required no answer, nor did McDonogh expect one. The old man's slaves had always occupied a special place in his heart. And his people returned the affection. Everyone addressed him as "Dear Father," and he called them all his sons and daughters. Andrew strongly suspected that some of the slaves were in fact his biological sons and daughters, although he would never think of voicing his suspicions to the old man.

"I have been thinking of publishing my views on slavery," the old man said. "What do you think?"

"I think you would not want my opinion."

"You are a son to me, Andrew. I will have your opinion. What do you say to my plan?"

Andrew stared for a long time at the first lights of the city blinking across the river. "If you will have my opinion, I must not withhold it. Do not write on the subject."

"But I must, Andrew. What I do here is not enough. This country can not go on as it is. Every year the slave numbers grow. Fewer and fewer are brought to freedom. I fear we go backwards. Men of wisdom must take a stand."

"But publication will change the minds of no one, John. And it will bring you great notoriety. Perhaps ruin."

"I am not against the system, Andrew, you know that. Neither am I a foe of the South. I am a true friend of the South. But we must make changes. We owners must have limits on the boundaries of our ownership. We must establish how much is due the master from the slave. And anything beyond that should be credited to the account of the slave. Certainly it would require years of labor, but the slave would have hope. He should be allowed to accumulate sufficient credit for his master to buy a replacement for him. Then the freed slave would begin a new life in Liberia."

"John you are an idealist. No where up and down this great river, no where in this land of the South, is there another like you. And you do not understand that. World men will not work on such a plan. *C'est le system de laws tambe en deservitude.*" Durnford waved an arm up and down the river. "Will Duncan Kenner and others like him along here come to that plan? No. Not even the ones who have a well stocked purse as you have."

"When men stumble, someone must lead."

"Oh, John, sometimes you surprise me. You, who are considered such a good judge of mankind should see in the heart better."

"You know of course, Andrew that many great minds do not agree with you."

"Well, you speak of minds in the North, John, members of your American Colonization Society. They encourage you. They flatter you. But they know nothing of our planters. Self interest is too strongly rooted in the bosom of all that breathes the Southern atmosphere. Self interest is al la mode here."

"And you no doubt speak for yourself, too, Andrew."

"Yes." Durnford paused and nodded slowly. "I am afraid I speak for myself too. I could say otherwise, having the luxury of a court forbidding me implementing any such plan. But the truth is I am like the others. Financially, emancipation would destroy me. I hope for a better time. And then I wonder if it could ever come to pass. Mainly, I think the extinction of slavery can only come in future ages. It is something the government will have to do. I see a plan where the government will buy out the slaves, and perhaps be aided by a few emancipations now and then from rich and noble minded men...like yourself, John."

"And like Andrew Durnford?"

"Andrew Durnford is not a rich man."

"You have riches enough, Andrew. Give your slaves a chance to earn credits for the time when the court order is lifted. You could even pay them for extra work, and that would do you no harm. Perhaps such a plan would force you to manage your money better, as that seems to be your weakness."

Durnford had heard this argument many times before. And there was never a time when McDonogh was not critical of his accomplishments, even though St. Rosalie outproduced its neighbors. "Yes, I know my weakness. And I know that

Alexander of Russia died of a broken heart because his nobles would not free their serfs. I do not wish to die of a broken heart. I wish to be realistic."

"You are not being realistic if you do not look to the future. Think about your people. Give them a chance and they will show you what they can do."

"Alexander was not a complete failure. A Russian princess did emancipate 72,000 slaves at her death. But they all perished because they were ignorant and could not handle their affairs."

"We are not talking about Russia, we are talking about America."

"Of all your slaves sent to Africa, how many of them went away with anything at all?" Durnford asked angrily. "Nely, probably and her mother are the only ones, depend upon it, John."

"I do not inquire into their personal finances. That is something of a private nature."

"There is not one in a hundred that could save money."

"I know that is not true."

"They have not the moral courage to deprive themselves of luxuries."

"I think we have talked enough, Andrew."

"Ninety-five out of a hundred will not think of buying their freedom on that plan."

"Let us go to the house now."

"Will a master who owns a good slave part with him on that condition? I doubt it. Certainly, there are slaves that are particularly situated that can make money. Those working in hotels. Washerwomen. But can they save it?"

McDonogh stopped and turned in the path. "Are you arguing with me, Andrew, or with yourself?"

Durnford watched as McDonogh turned and went up the path again toward his half-completed mansion.

"When white men are starving can slaves prosper!" Durnford shouted after his mentor.

McDonogh stopped and turned slowly. "You, Andrew, are not starving. And I would think that you, among all men would give more serious condition to the plight of your slaves, because you, Andrew, are also not a white man."

"Yes," Andrew Durnford said to himself, "you are right old man, it is myself that I argue with."

Durnford carried these thoughts home to St. Rosalie the following day. And after a long October day in the fields, supervising the harvesting of the last corn, he sat at his desk in the library, composing a letter to Thomas. Many times he had started a letter, only to crumple it in disgust. In addition to an education, Andrew had hoped that Thomas would develop a social conscience at Lafayette College.

After beginning a short introduction anew, again in French, Andrew decided to raise the issue of the St. Rosalie slaves. "My dear boy, you know that I hope for a day that I will be able to do something for our slaves. It is not my intention to leave to you the burdens of this plantation, but that you should be endowed with a medical practice, which shall see you through your life. In this regard, I am in conflict. You have expressed a strong interest in our little enterprize here at St. Rosalie, and you have shown little sympathy to my plan of emancipation. Now do both of us the favor of being honest with me. If I am unable to complete my plans during the remaining years God shall give me, do you expect that you shall see your way clear to implementing my wishes, i.e., that the slaves shall have their freedom, and the lands and equipment of our venture on the Mississippi be sold to them?"

Marie-Charlotte wrote to Thomas on a regular basis and kept him advised of the family social activities, so Andrew avoided duplicating those efforts in his letter. "Nothing new to tell you," Andrew continued, "except that in two weeks I am going to begin to cut the cane for rolling."

And then Andrew added, "I notice that you are not using the name of Thomas McD. Durnford, which pays tribute to your godfather, as you pledged to me. You are young. There is still time to add these letters to your name and sign yourself Thos. McD. Durnford.

"I beg you to write me at least every six weeks, if not every month. In the meantime, I am sending to president Junkin a few piastres so he can give you a few cents from time to time so that you can play the young man. I exhort you, my boy, to conduct yourself well, for otherwise, no friendship between us and no more money for you to play the young man.

"Your mother sends you a thousand expressions of her affection and tells you that if it were possible she would send you the cake you requested in your last letter to her. But the thing is impossible for the time being. In two years we shall have a railroad which will take passengers from here to New York in five days. Then we can send you sweets. And visit you at the college. I make bold to hope that when we see each other you will show me all my letters, for I keep track of all letters that I send."

It was not until after Christmas that Noel brought home from the New Orleans post office a reply to Andrew's letter. Thomas wrote, "I must now acknowledge with gratitude the receipt of your letter of the 18th of October. You will please, Dear Father, accept my wishes for your prosperity through this life, a happy new year and an unusual good health. It is gratifying for me to receive your wise counsels, counsels which possess all that is righteous, all that is virtuous and good for my welfare both on earth and on high. Your motives in regard to those who so well serve you, Dear Father, are those of pure honesty. Although no flourishing words were used, one can not disregard it.

"A young slave holder from Virginia having borrowed it of me was astonished when he had read it over. And shortly after says he, 'Durnford, your father must be an uncommon man. I would like to know him.' He thinks like I do that it is true honesty in your part.

"We have had very cold weather here for the last three weeks, and the snow is at this moment nine inches deep. New Year's gifts I suppose are scarce, for my part I have received none as yet, and would as soon have a little extra money, if you can spare the same, for boots and a thicker coat."

Thomas described his life at school over the past few months, set forth his thoughts regarding his teachers, and complained that they were starving him and that the school motto must be "A starved head is a clear head."

"Now I pray you to present to mother my deepest love and affection. It has been impossible for me to come to a conclusion in regard to your plan of emancipation, for my studies have been pressing me, but before the month is out I will give you my opinion as to its merits.

Your Affectionate Son truly,

Thomas "

Andrew Durnford read the letter from his son once, then once again, and yet a third time. He sat at his desk in the dark library, staring at the crackling flames in the fireplace. A cold wind rattled the windows. He had not asked for the boy's opinion. He had asked Thomas for assurances that his plans to free the slaves would be carried out. From outside the library window came the dull clunk of a cowbell. "Noel, the cattle are lose again!"

No answer.

Durnford called out again, and when no one in the house answered him, he stepped up to the window, raised it, and walked out into the cold air. The distinctive clang of the cowbell now came from behind the oak trees near the cookhouse. Durnford headed in that direction, screaming out to anyone who might hear him, "Where in the hell is Sipion? Sipion! Noel! The cows are on the loose."

There was nothing but darkness at the corner of the cookhouse, and Durnford strained to see the silhouette of his livestock against the dark wall of night.

Nothing.

And again he heard the cowbell, then another, and another. Now he was enraged and he went around the cookhouse, swearing loudly. The cowbells, he could no longer count the number of them, were always ahead of him, seeming to come from behind one tree and then another, always from somewhere else when he got to where a sound came from. "Strange, indeed," he said to himself. And it occurred to him that he could be lured to his death by some of the slaves. Certainly, he decided, no cow was moving those bells so quickly and ghostly through the trees.

Cautiously now, no longer shouting, but moving as quietly and secretly as he could, Durnford moved from tree to tree until he found himself at the front of the sugarhouse. The cowbells, a whole chorus of them, were ringing inside the sugarhouse, and yellow light crept from under and around the door.

Durnford paused for a moment, wondering whether he should retreat to the house for his shotgun, when the sugarhouse doors were suddenly thrown wide open. He was greeted by a crowd of smiling faces, black and white, in the glare of several lanterns. "Happy New Year!" they shouted.

Durnford at first stepped back, then quickly returned into the light of the sugarhouse. "Oh, my God," he gasped. You people...Erskine, Pierre, Noel, Ms Remy...you, Carlos Reggios, Antoine Cagnolatte, Madam Cyprien Duplessis...? What are you all doing here?"

The crowd parted, and there was Sipion, proudly holding the reins of two magnificent black mares.

"Happy New Year, Doctor Durnford," William Erskine said. "You have served us and our people faithfully these many years, all without payment. And to express our gratitude, we present to you these horses, the best you will find in Louisiana."

Erskine took the reins from Sipion and placed them in Durnford's hands as he spoke. There were ten to fifteen white people there, some with slaves, and many of the St. Rosalie servants. Durnford fought back tears. "This is such a surprise," he said finally. "I do not know how to thank you."

"It is we, good Doctor, who are lacking in means of thanks," Pierre said in his ancient French voice. "For what you mean to us, these horses are mere nothings."

The glow within Durnford more than matched the glow from the several lanterns within the sugarhouse. He had now been the owner of St. Rosalie for almost ten years, and there was no time he had ever felt the deep satisfaction and peace of soul he felt that night looking into the smiling faces of his neighbors, the people he had nursed through sickness injury and disease.

" 9 Thomas left the city for New York on board of the Packet Ship *Alabama* addressed to W_{m} Uer Lamier Establi _ _ sion Rooms

May 2 I endorsed this day for John McDonogh four notes under date of the 3^{d} March of two hundred & fifty two dollars each payable in one, two, three and four years for lots or Squares in Huntsville bought at Public Sale

" " I Received as a present from John McDonogh a Gold watch, Marked Pemberton Liverpool N° 886. inside of the back case is Marked C. B. I. McD. [18]. 886. It cost 2 £ 0 in Liverpool

" 5 Elliott Cresson left here for Mobile this day.

the Ship *Alabama* arrived in New York on the 1^{st} may. Thomas went as passenger.

**Plantation Journal entries of 1840. On April 9^{th} Thomas leaves for New York and arrives on May 1^{st}. On May 5^{th} Elliot Cresson left the plantation for Mobile.**

*MEMORANDUM OF THE AGES OF DIFFERENT PEOPLE*
*ST. ROSALIE PLANTATION JOURNAL, AUGUST 4, 1841*

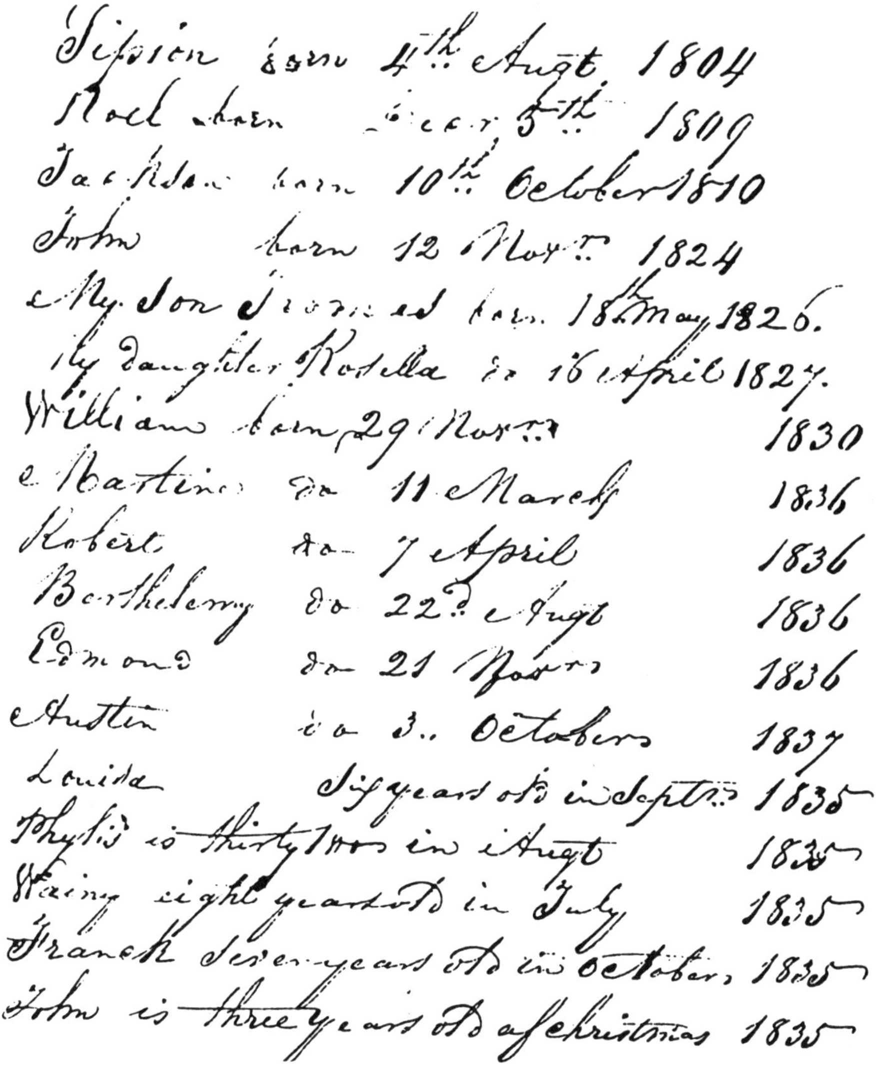

Sipion born 4th Augt 1804
Noel born Decr 5th 1809
Jackson born 10th October 1810
John born 12 Novr 1824
My Son Thomas born 18th May 1826.
My daughter Rosella do 16 April 1827.
William born 29 Novr 1830
Martin do 11 March 1836
Robert do 7 April 1836
Berthelemy do 22d Augt 1836
Edmond do 21 Novr 1836
Austin do 3. October 1837
Louisa Six years old in Septr 1835
Phylis is thirty two in Augt 1835
Wainy eight years old in July 1835
Franck Seven years old in October 1835
John is three years old at Christmas 1835

**Note that the fifth line is "My son Thomas born 18 May 1826," followed by Rosella, born April 16, 1827. In the middle of the page are entries showing the ages of Phylis and her childeren, Wainy and Franck. Noel was born Dec. 5, 1809.**

MERORANDUM OF AGES (CON'T)
ST. ROSALIE PLANTATION JOURNAL, AUGUST 4 1841

It would take four pages to show all the entries from the
ledger. It is interesting to note that Andrew Durnford lists his
children and slaves all under the heading of "people." He did
not enter his age or the age of Marie-Charlotte

*Copys of Letters to Thomas.*

Mon cher Thomas

J'ose espérer que tu es arrivé il y a long temps mon cher enfant, a ta destination, et que ton séjour a New York, a été des plus satisfaisants, et ta réception chez Mr. Louis satisfaisante, tu as sans doute été traité avec amitié, écris moi a la fin de chaque mois, a l'adresse de ton parrain comme suit, John Mc Donogh, Esqr. for A Durnford à P Othl. je te prie également de lui écrire une lettre de remerciment pour la peine prise en ta faveur pour t'avoir envoyé ou tués.

Tout le monde se porte bien ici il n'y a que grand-mère, qui a été un peu malade, de son asthme, ta mère se porte bien et t'embrasse bien tendrement; Clémence et toute la maison de Remy se porte a merveille je m'engage, mon ami a bien faire ton devoir, sois obéissant a tes professeurs et fait toi aimer d'eux, car s'il en était autrement, tu me causerais que de la peine, et je crois que tu aimes trop ton papa pour lui faire de la peine, lui qui t'aime tant. je te prie de me donner a ta prochaine lettre des détails de ton voyage, et ta réception chez Mr. Louis, et dans ton Collège, si toutefois tu ne l'as pas fait dans la lettre que j'attends de toi, car Noel va apporter celle ci a la poste, et voir si tu as écrit. le vieux Sharphead est toujours ici, il se rappelle a ton bon souvenir tous, ou ton cher David John Robot, et le fameux Toni avec son ventre de Batracien, tout se porte bien ici, le fleuve est très haut, il y a a craindre une inondation, car par les rapports des hauts, il paraît que toutes les rivières donnent beaucoup. ta mère t'embrasse de tout cœur ainsi que grand-mère, et moi je t'adore comme mes deux yeux tout a toi d'amitié       A Durnford
Paroisse Plaquemines 7 Mai 1840

**Letter to his son, *"Mon cher Thomas"* from Andrew Durnford**

# Chapter Twenty Six

Sugar, the lifeblood of St. Rosalie, became a matter of speculation. Drought followed flood. Wind flattened the cane in the fields. Durnford's slaves put it straight, only to have it blown down again. The market spiralled downward. Andrew Durnford bought more slaves and expanded his operations. Expenses went up. Revenue went down.

In 1841, St. Rosalie produced only 158 hogsheads. The selling price fell to $55.00 per hogshead, and Andrew barely met expenses. The following year was worse, the price fell to $40.00 per hogshead. In 1843 it went up to $42.50, still not enough to meet expenses. The next year, 1844, St. Rosalie produced a record crop, 304 hogsheads. But at only $39.00 per hogshead, Andrew Durnford faced financial collapse. He had borrowed from the New Orleans banks each year. Now they were asking for their money.

Deploring the relentless demands of the New Orleans bankers, he wrote in his journal on January 12, 1844, "Poor mankind! How it has become degraded." And as if foreseeing the novel *Les Miserables,* the Victor Hugo masterpiece of almost twenty years later portraying the plight of a noble peasant imprisoned for stealing a single loaf of bread, the philosophic black man continued, "He who steals a loaf of bread while he is dominated by hunger is punished, and he who is harmful to society becomes more and more numerous. I think society is made up of two distinct parts. On the one hand wolves and foxes, and on the other hand lambs and chickens providing food for the former. In the forest a lion recognizes another lion, tiger does not make another tiger its prey, only man is man's enemy."

Accident and illness besieged him. Noel, kicked by a horse, lay in bed with broken ribs, coughing up blood. Two slave boys and one man died of the fever. Silvie, the woman who had run away with Lewis a month after he bought her, and then had become his nurse, battled the fever that swept the plantation, and then Silvie herself fell in the battle. Marie-Charlotte went to bed with cholerine, the first stage of cholera. Water and mud were everywhere. Rain pounded the land.

"Can't dig ditches," Andrew wrote to McDonogh. "And the rain is flooding everything. It is impossible to work in the deep water without catching a dangerous fever. The three Germans you sent me gave up and left. One I paid off with some change I had. The other two I am sending to you with the request that you honor my account with the wages due them. Send me more Germans to work the ditches. I can not risk my people for that work. They must work at $10.00 a month, but I will go to $12.00 at most, for I am desperate."

Durnford continued his letter of bad news to McDonogh. "I am in need of wood. The batture wood we cut along the river is too rotten to last. I can get no wood from the back acres because my roads are damaged and broken up. Nor can the horses and mules to haul carts survive under these terrible conditions.

"I do not know when the rain will stop. From my window I see the river rising. To ship any sugar or molasses now, it is impossible. The river is over the batture, and to haul anywhere else than in front of the sugarhouse is out of the question now because of the mud."

In the depressed market of 1844 Durnford had decided on a gamble. He held his crop, waiting for a better market. What had been rolled and shipped now sat in storage in the McDonogh warehouses on Julia Street. McDonogh was nervous. "You say you don't know what to advise as to the sale of the sugar," Durnford continued in his letter to McDonogh. "I say wait. It will sell better when drained, and molasses will be at least 2 cents a pound, therefore it is worth saving. I have about forty empty barrels made and will make more as my cooper has time to spare. After rolling I will be able to send every two weeks, say 25 barrels of syrup, which quantity Petroni will be able to make with only an additional expense of $10.00. Two hundred barrels more or less will take the crop. The price must improve. Depend on it. The sugar brokers live on the sweat of the hard laboring planter. Larose wrote to know if I would sell him my crop of molasses, saying the crop will be large, and offering 15 cents to take it here. But I know better. He is a rascal. He has cleared $15,000 in one year, crushing the sugar with his augers to make it appear bad to sponge the poor planter."

Durnford blotted the paper to dry the last ink, slid the folded letter into an envelope and sealed it with wax. He then went up the stairs to the second floor of the mansion and out on the gallery facing the river. The rain had stopped. A silver moon, bright and full, broke through the clouds, illuminating St. Rosalie plantation as if it were twilight. And as he absent-mindedly stared out at the phosphorescent river churning south, Andrew heard the plantation bell clang wildly. Hastily running into the bedroom where Marie-Charlotte slept in spite of the noise, and pulling on the boots he had kicked off, Durnford tugged on a jacket and ran down the stairs and through the luminous night to the levee. Slaves streamed from their cabins, heading for the bank of the Mississippi as if their very lives depended on speed. Everyone knew what the bell meant. At that hour of the night it could only be one thing. The levee was giving way.

Durnford had watched the water rise all during the afternoon. Now it flooded the batture and surged and gurgled and swirled just a few feet below the top of the levee. Behind the sugarhouse, three slaves worked furiously, aided by the yellow light from lanterns hung on poles, shoveling soil from all around them into a bottomless pit that bubbled mud. Andrew needed no report from Petroni, who had sent a slave to sound the alarm and now directed operations. Andrew looked quickly around and the blood froze in his veins. The mighty river had crested well above flood stage. The top of the levee itself, built upon the higher ground behind the batture, was about twelve feet above the normal river level. But the water had risen, flowed up and over the batture, that gently sloping, spongy land that was home to myriad scraggly trees and shrubs. And then it climbed up the side of the levee. The levee was a fortress wall, almost thirty feet wide at its base. All along the Mississippi, the levee was built to hold in the river. The police jury, a committee of citizens, specified the dimensions of the levee in each parish, supervised its maintenance, and inspected its condition throughout the year. If any planter failed to maintain the levee, the police jury contracted labor to repair it and charged the delinquent, usually an absentee-owner, with a lien. This was a necessary practice, because a breach of the levee anywhere would soon flood neighboring plantations for miles up and down the river. Andrew Durnford, like all the other planters who lived on the land, needed no coercion from the police jury. They all lived in fear of that immense body of water swelling up on the other side of the dike, sometimes as high as the second story gallery of the mansions along the river.

The danger Durnford saw that night was not from water coming over the levee, it was from water percolating under the levee. St. Rosalie plantation occupied land along the inside curve of a bend in the river. The full force of the raging river pounded and surged against the levee, which deflected the stream back to the south.

The sugarhouse sat about ten feet back from the River Road, which ran north and south behind the levee. A second road, the shipping road from the sugarhouse, ran up the levee then down the other side to a dock at the river's edge. That dock was now under ten feet of water. And just where the plantation shipping road crossed the river road was a bubbling mass of mud and water. If any man slipped into that muddy cauldron, he would disappear, never to be seen again.

The water gouged out soil from under the levee and percolated to the surface on the other side. Unchecked, it threatened to undermine completely the levee and carry it away. Then they would be at the mercy of the unmerciful river.

"Damn it Noel," Andrew screamed at his loyal servant, "I have enough to worry about without you here. Get yourself back to bed!"

The tall, slender slave, still recovering from his broken ribs, stood and stared wide-eyed at the bubbling hole along the edge of the road.

"I'm sorry, Master Andrew, if we don't stop this now my bed won't be there long." Noel coughed blood into a handkerchief from his punctured lungs. "Dirt will not do the job, sir. We have to plug this hole somehow—planks, stumps, rocks, even the bagasse will help. But dirt will just wash away."

As Noel spoke, a piece of the River Road, three feet wide and over ten long, slid into the sucking hole.

"I understand what needs to be done, Noel. And you dying out here will not help. Go back to the house. Go back now, Noel, and do not aggravate me more. My problems are a plenty without worrying about you."

Andrew turned back to the nightmarish sump, and shouted out to Petroni and the other slaves who poured in from all sides. "Get the carts. Gather up all the bagasse and pitch it in here. You, Petroni, you stay with the hole. I need several men, you and you, and you four over there, get shovels. I want the dirt to go in with the bagasse. Stop shoveling Petroni! Wait for the bagasse. Noel is right, you're just wasting dirt."

Durnford organized the slaves into teams: those shoveling bagasse into the carts on the other side of the sugarhouse, those shovelling dirt into the same carts, mixing it with the bagasse, those driving the carts around the sugarhouse to the sinkhole, those shoveling the mixture of dirt and bagasse into the ever-widening hole, and those along the levy, scooping up the sod and tossing it after the bagasse into the bubbling mud.

He sent two carts after wood far back from the river, with five slaves to help the mules drag the carts through the deep mud. When the carts returned, Andrew watched as whole sections of tree trunks were rolled from the carts and disappeared.

Cartload after cartload disappeared into the boiling mass. They had been working for over two hours, when another section of River Road slid into the sinkhole. An hour later, the remainder of the River Road at that spot fell in and the edge of the bottomless pit was less than six feet from the base of the tall chimneys of the sugarhouse.

Noel was still there, shoveling alongside his master. Andrew said nothing more to him. Unless they stopped the river, the entire plantation would die that night. Retreat to the mansion was useless. Once the levee went, the force of the rushing water would bring down the big house too. And now Marie-Charlotte, sick and weak was there, and the old woman, her mother was there too. Every black man and woman on the plantation, master, mistress, slave and servant, was there fighting the cancer that ate away the land from behind the levee. Some flung dirt with pots and pans, others with garden tools, some with their bare hands.

Andrew handed his shovel off to a slave boy, and stepped back for a moment. They were losing the battle, he realized, and he needed a plan. Just then, Harry, the big man he had purchased in Virginia, came up with a cart of bricks Andrew had been saving to build a wall between the boilers in the sugarhouse. Durnford nodded his assent. Yes. Dump it in. Sacrifice everything. Stop the river.

Harry was the best driver Durnford had, and Andrew watched as the big man flicked his whip while standing on a narrow platform at the cart's front, deftly pulling on the reins with his other hand, turning the mules around and backing the cart toward the sinkhole. Already, two slaves were tossing bricks from Harry's cart into the muddy chasm. Dirt and bagasse flew from carts on each side of Harry.

The heavily laden brick cart inched back, and with a margin of safety to spare, stopped near the edge of the boiling mud. Then the right wheel started to sink. Harry, looking over his shoulder, saw the cart tilt. He yelled at his mules and cracked his whip. The cart lurched forward, then settled back and now Andrew saw both wheels sinking in the grass. "Let the cart go! Jump!" Andrew shouted.

The two men in the cart jumped as the mules pawed and pushed against the ground, only to be dragged backward. Harry cracked his whip furiously and swore at his team.

"Jump, Harry! For God's sake, jump!"

Harry glanced at his master, then at the sinkhole behind him. "Heave! Pull!" Harry shouted to his team. "Pull." And as he shouted he leaned forward and cracked his whip across each beasts' rump. The cart slid relentlessly backward and the swirling mud licked at its axle.

"Jump!" Andrew pleaded. "Jump! Jump for your life, Harry."

Then Harry dropped to the ground between his team and struggled forward, as the cart went completely down to the ground. Durnford watched as Harry seized the mule harness and urged them forward, even as their feet sank into the soft ground. And then they all went together, quickly, silently, man, cart and team of mules. The dark mud closed over them. The two bagasse carts on either side of Harry pulled away as the brick-laden cart, its team and driver sank into the depths.

A great moan went up from all the slaves.

Andrew shook his head. He looked up at the silver clouds in the moonlit sky. "Why? Why?"

All the slaves stood open-mouthed and stared at their master. When Andrew looked around, he saw nothing but fear in their eyes. Even Marie-Charlotte and her mother, both sitting in the grass on the side of the levee, looked at him wide-eyed with fear. And then he realized the importance of his leadership. He could not, dared not show fear or despair. His people were ready to run now. Another few minutes of indecision and they would bolt.

Anger swelled within Durnford. He was furious. Angry with the river which threatened all he had worked for so long and hard. More angry yet with himself for letting his emotions show. Then with a stony, hard, and intense face, he scolded his workers. "This river will not beat us! It can not beat us. We will beat it. We will beat it back. Now double your efforts, all of you! Work! Work with a fury greater than the river itself or I'll put you all to the lash, every last one of you!"

The impact upon the slaves was instantaneous. "Massah Andrew," one of the slaves from Virginia, the other Harry, shouted out, "if der a man beat ole Missip he you for sure! And you knows I afraid ob you more den dis ribber."

The horror of the lost cart and driver was forgotten. Some of the slaves grinned. A few laughed out loud. And Andrew knew none of the slaves were really afraid of the whip—the threat of a lashing was not taken seriously, but the spirit of his outburst was the spark they needed to overcome the paralysis which had seized his people.

Dirt, sod, bagasse, old bricks, timbers, good wood and rotten wood went soaring through the air and disappeared into the growing mud hole.

Andrew sent the carts after more material, and urged everyone to work yet faster. But in spite of determined efforts and high spirits, they were losing, Andrew realized.

The hole, which had been about five feet wide when Andrew first saw it three hours earlier, was now twenty feet across, and growing. Durnford ordered two of the slave cabins torn down, and those timbers and planks tossed in. But nothing satisfied the river's appetite. The river wanted St. Rosalie. Perhaps it would even change its course, no longer take the bend, as it had many times up and down the Mississippi, and there would be nothing left to witness where Andrew Durnford and his people had labored for the last ten years.

Then part of the levee itself collapsed into the widening gap of mud. Soon now, Andrew said to himself, the remainder of the levee will follow, and they will all be engulfed and drown. Swimmers could not save themselves. No one was strong enough to stay on top of sucking, bubbling mud, and then there was the force of the water after that. There was nothing left to do but retreat.

"Everyone up on the levee," he shouted. "Onto the levee, everyone! Look after your families and yourselves, all of you. And go north! Go north as fast as your feet will take you. And God help us all."

Durnford grabbed Petroni's arm as he passed. "You have no family, Petroni, stay with me. I have a plan."

"I have no fambly, Massah. I too will stay." It was Lewis, the slave who had run away and been whipped and put in irons, the slave who had thereafter lived up to his master's trust when Andrew made him the plantation hunter to replace Washington.

"Yes, by God, Lewis, I can use you too."

Durnford watched as the procession of slaves moved north along the levee, silhouetted against the moonlight and the silver river. Two women supported Marie-Charlotte, and two more supported her mother as well. Noel, at the rear, stopped and started back when he saw the three men standing halfway up the levee. "Go with them, Noel," Andrew shouted. "They are all in your charge. And take care of Miss Remy and Granmere."

Noel waved a sad salute, and turned to follow the St. Rosalie citizens trekking north along the levee.

"Now," Durnford said to Lewis, "you and Petroni fetch the powder from the storehouse, both kegs."

Inside the sugarhouse, Durnford lit three lanterns and in the bright light he opened the steel door to the ash collector on the first brick chimney. When Petroni and Lewis came in with the two casks of black powder, Durnford was busily shoveling ashes from the chimney to the dirt floor. He paused and took a sledgehammer from against the wall. Then he knocked out two bricks below the steel door. "Clean out the other chimney, right down to the dirt," he said, and knock me in a hole like this to run powder."

While the two men worked on the adjacent chimney, Andrew rolled one keg of powder up to the ash door, wrestled it over and into the empty chimney, and knocked the end open with the sledgehammer. Then he scooped black powder into a small pail and poured a trail of the explosive from the cask inside the chimney to the sugarhouse door. Closing the steel door of the ash chamber, he ordered Petroni to repeat the procedure with the other chimney.

Picking up one lantern, Durnford walked to the sugarhouse door with the two men. "Stand back," he said to them. And where the gunpowder trails from the two chimneys met just outside the door to the sugarhouse, Andrew tipped his lantern on its side and let the flaming oil ignite the explosive train.

"Run for the levee" he shouted as the black powder caught fire, smoked and hissed, supporting a small flame which marched along the dirt floor to the casks waiting in the chimneys.

The three men crouched on top of the levee and waited. It seemed to Andrew that an eternity went by before they heard the first muffled explosion. The chimney nearest them, forty feet high and massive, shuddered and swayed in the moonlight, then settled back into position.

They waited for the second explosion, which never came. Finally, Andrew said to the men, "Well, there's nothing for it now but to join the others. I had hoped to topple the chimneys into the sink hole." He shook his head. "But fate is not with us tonight."

Just as he finished speaking, there was a second explosion, much louder and stronger than the first, and the entire back wall of the second chimney blew away, sending bricks flying all around them where they stood on the levee. The massive chimney, two bricks thick, four feet square, and forty feet high swayed slowly. Bricks fell from the open wound at its base. Then the base itself collapsed, and the entire chimney, standing upright, moved back and slipped majestically into the sinkhole behind the sugarhouse. And as it went down, the other chimney, weakened by the first charge and set in motion by the second explosion, toppled in disarray, following its twin into the bottomless pit. Water and mud splashed higher than the levee, covering Andrew and his two slaves. When the dust, spray, and mud cleared, a pile of bricks covered the entire sinkhole.

"I forgot to tell you that first keg was only half full," Lewis said apologetically.

Andrew Durnford wiped the mud from his eyes and face, and smiled at Lewis. "Thank you for that explanation, Lewis."

As they watched, the pile of bricks settled about six inches. Then a few inches more. And then held firm. The three men stood and waited as the moon moved slowly to the west over their heads. The St. Rosalie population had long since disappeared down the levee. But there was Noel, coming very slowly. "I heard the explosions," he said softly as he approached. "I told everyone to stay and came back to see if you fools were still alive here."

"Well," Andrew Durnford said, "you can go back to bed now, Noel. Your bed is safe."

Durnford stood watch throughout the night with Petroni and Lewis, as all the slave force and servants returned to their beds. He gave strict orders to Marie-Charlotte's maid to stay with her during the night and remain awake. "I want a report every hour," he said. "If the fever gets worse, I want to know it. If there are any more episodes, I want to know it."

"I will stay with my daughter this night," Granmere Remy said in a wheezing voice.

"Well, my dear old woman," Andrew said, "you may stay with her but you shall sleep. I will not need my bed tonight and you have exhausted yourself. It shows in your asthma. I insist on this as your doctor. And you need not fear the cholera, Miss Remy has survived the stage where she could pass that to you. So open the windows, burn the incense I have on the nightstand, and rest."

Then near dawn, Andrew said, "Lewis, you go now too. You have an hour to sleep before dawn. Then I think it would be good if you could kill us a wild pig. Today we will not work. Today will be a day of giving thanks."

"I have powder left for only one shot," Lewis said.

"Well, Lewis, make it a good shot."

Thunder and lightning struck at noon, and with it came more heavy rain. Notwithstanding the weather, it was a day of good spirits. Lewis did kill a pig with one single shot, an act upon which Durnford marveled as Lewis was a poor hand with the gun and had never managed such a feat before. Thanks were given and short prayers. Everyone ate standing and sitting in the house, in the hallways up and down, on the galleries, and in the cookhouse. A Negro preacher, one of the slaves from Erskine's plantation, said a somber service for Harry, the slave who perished in the sinkhole. Deeply moving and slowly rolling hymns were sung by all. Andrew joined in with his off-tune bass voice. He always felt unsure of himself in matters of religion concerning the slaves. And although he would not think of leading a religious service, he could not help but sing along. He had lost a good man, that Harry. But God had spared St. Rosalie, for whatever reason.

In addition to losing a valuable slave, Andrew Durnford also lost the use of his sugarhouse. The cost of replacing the chimneys was beyond his means. And without the chimneys there could be no boilers to run the machinery or steam for the pans. Thus, he was left to grind by the old horse-powered mill, and to processing his cane juice by boiling in the old kettles, a slow and uncertain method. On the other hand, he could borrow more money from the banks.

In the end, Durnford went to the banks. And he did something he believed he would never do. He pledged the slave force, everyone, as collateral for a new loan. If he defaulted, Andrew knew, they would be taken from him by the bank and sold on the auction block. Nor could he save anyone from that fate, they were not people, they were property, chattels, including Noel and his beloved Wainy who was now eighteen and whom he had trained as a nurse to work with him in the hospital after Silvie died with the fever. Lewis, whom he now loved like a brother was pledged as collateral, as was Sipion, Petroni, Augustin, Phyllis, Wainy's mother and Frank, her brother. All of these people, as well as the old servants and loyal field hands, he had put at risk. But, he said to himself, what choice do I have? I can not free them because of the court order. I am already indebted, and if bankruptcy becomes my fate, my slaves will still be sold at auction, split up, sent north and south and east and west. "I will make it work," he swore to himself. "I will pay off this cursed debt. I will gain my footing once more, and then someday my people can have it all."

Thomas was doing well in school. He was in his second year of college. After that, three short years of medical school and Thomas would be set for life. In the meantime, Andrew Durnford was determined to rebuild the sugarhouse.

# Chapter Twenty Seven

Standing near the double doors which connected the drawing room to the parlor, Marie-Charlotte thought about just how she would give the news to Andrew. He sat in a wing-backed chair in the far corner, reading the New Orleans newspapers brought down by the steamer the day before. His back was to the open window, from which a mild breeze entered the room and carried away the smoke from his cigar.

It was Sunday, and the coolness of spring was giving way to the first hot and humid days.

"Listen to this," Andrew Durnford said, "taken from the Boston Morning Post. It is reported as a case of unusual cruelty aboard a whaling ship, reducing the poor victim to madness. It is a sad reflection on mankind—how we search for differences to set us apart, rather than what pulls us together. This, from *The Courier:* 'In August, 1842, the plaintiff, John C. Bull, aged 19 years, shipped as boatsteerer on board the whaler *Mount Vernon,* commanded by Captain Edwin Coffin, the defendant. Most of the ship's company and all the officers, with the exception of Bull, belonged to Nantucket, from which port the *Mount Vernon* sailed. It is surmised that the ill usage to which Bull was subjected on the voyage, originated from the fact that he came from a different section of the state from his shipmates.'"

Andrew paused and looked up from his paper. "Even in these modern times, we find brother mistreating brother simply because the victim is from a different region of the same state! How can we expect better behavior between people of different races?"

"These are but rough seamen, Andrew," Marie-Charlotte said quietly, "Now, if you have a moment—"

"On the contrary, Miss Remy. These officers are educated men. But it seems their prejudices got the better of them. They refused to let poor Bull, this lad of a mere 19 years, perform his duties of boatsteerer, even though he was the expert among the crew. And this is what happened. Listen to this: 'Bull was extremely mortified at being superseded in this duty, and in his manners exhibited the natural effects of his disappointment. When the *Mount Vernon* put into Tombez, Captain Coffin, as is the custom, entertained some brother captains with wine from the ship's stores. Subsequently, on the same day, Bull had some brother boatsteerers on board to see him, and he took an unfinished bottle of wine from the captain's room, opposite his own, and treated his company. Although it was usual for captains and mates to entertain company on the ship's stores, it was not customary for petty officers to do so. It was an offense, but a very trivial one. And for assuming he had the same privileges as the Nantucket men, the captain disrated Bull, put him to scrubbing decks, and ordered him to go aloft. Once he was kept on deck a whole day and a night, and not allowed any watch below. At another time, he was kept a whole night at the windlass, while it rained. This treatment affected his mind. He began to talk wild, and was regarded as sullen. In the morning he went below, refused to speak or eat, and lay in his berth till it was thought he was dying. The hands were convinced that he was sick, and so informed the captain. But Captain Coffin, suspecting that he was shamming sick, ordered him permanently out of his cabin, but would not allow any one to help him take his chest out and drag it forward to the forecastle. The officers, by the captain's orders, continued to treat him as shamming. He was confined in the forecastle and kept on bread and water by Coffin's orders.

"'In addition, he was struck in the face, and finally twice seized up by the thumbs and regularly flogged, till the blood flowing from the wounds on his back ran onto the deck. The "cat" used had four tails. On the first flogging he received 25 lashes. On the second flogging, 35 lashes. He was then thrown into the hold, where he had nothing to sleep on but a coil of rope. At midnight, he was hauled out and flogged again by a mate. In the morning, he was flogged by the captain, who not only gave his officers leave to flog Bull, but also extended the same privilege to the foremast hands, all from Nantucket.'"

Durnford paused and sighed. "These Northerners scream at us daily in their papers and admonish us for our treatment of our slaves.  But what do they do to their own?  As one might expect, the measures inflicted upon Bull failed to restore him to good health, so the newspaper reports, and Captain Coffin, an appropriate name don't you think?, transferred Bull to the *Potomac,* and told the captain of that ship that a good flogging would do Bull good and he could have him for crew. Well the captain of the *Potomac* looked at Bull's back and refused to take him. He suggested to Captain Coffin that he might want to seek medical attention for the young man and see that he went back on the next whaler.

"It appears," Andrew continued, "that Captain Coffin kept Bull for about a month, mistreating him all that time, and then put him ashore at Payta, where he was placed in a small grog shanty on the beach. There was no bed or domestic conveniences in this shanty, nor did Coffin provision Bull.  He was found at that place by officers of the *Potomac,* and, it says here, was conveyed on board in a 'state of lunacy.'

"Apparently, the *Potomac* took good care of the young man, but when he was returned on that ship to Boston several months later, not a glimmering of reason was perceptible.  His brother first awakened consciousness in him, by playing a familiar tune to him on the flute; and by degrees he gradually returned to a state of sanity, but with great physical infirmity.'

"Then Bull filed suit against Captain Coffin.  The trial dragged on. Examination of the plaintiff by Coffin's lawyer was furious.  Bull was forced to...." Durnford paused and followed the sentence in the newspaper with his finger as he read aloud. "'Was forced to retrace minutely the painful history of the facts, and so harrowing were they to the mind of Bull, that he became furiously and irrevocably mad, and was sent to the State Lunatic Asylum at Worcester as incurably insane, where he will probably soon terminate his miserable life.'"

Andrew shook his head.  "The plaintiff, of course, was unable to continue with his case.  That's when the defendant claimed justification on the grounds of mutiny, theft and drunkenness.  And since the Plaintiff was securely locked away, there was no one to refute the testimony of Captain Coffin and his Nantucket officers.  After being out some time, the jury came into court and said they couldn't possibly agree on any particular measure of damages.  The attorney for Bull pleaded with them that they should reach a verdict of some kind at that time, as another trial could not be had until next spring, before which time Bull would probably be dead.  The jury retired again, and after about an hour came back again and found in favor of Bull in the amount of one dollar. The attorney for the plaintiff was stunned, and asked them how they could possibly reach such an unfair verdict. They answered it was the only verdict they could agree on, and the attorney for Bull had insisted they come back with something, so they assumed it would at least finish the case, and Bull's lawyer could have a proper sum awarded upon appeal. The jury broke down in tears when the judge told them the case was over and their verdict was final."

Marie-Charlotte had waited patiently all through the long recital, but she could wait no longer. "Andrew, I have important news."

Durnford motioned to the chair opposite him. "Well, then, come sit with me and share your important news."

She sat down hesitantly. "I regret to say that Thomas will not be the only child come six months more."

"And you are certain?"

"I have all of the signs. Yes, I am certain."

Durnford fell back in his chair. "Shame on us to be guilty of such work at our age, old people of thirty-six and forty-five. It is not likely I will see him grow to be a man."

"Andrew you are robust and strong. You will live another twenty years and more. And who is to say the child shall be a boy?"

"You know," Andrew said with a smile, "I thought I noticed an unusual glow in those eyes of yours. A glow I had seen before." He nodded his head. The last time Marie-Charlotte was pregnant the child, a beautiful girl, died ten months after her birth. They now had only one child, their son Thomas. "A girl would please me."

"You are not upset, Andrew?"

"Upset? Yes. I am upset. But not with you, Miss Remy. I am upset with myself. The sugar from last year is not sold. It sits in the warehouse on Julia Street and has gone down by one-third. I sent Sammy up to fill up the hogsheads from the stock of sixty I keep on hand here." Durnford rubbed a hand across his face. "Now Erskine went with the market, got five and three quarters for his sugar last winter. I can't get five and one-half now, and already have lost a third of the crop through settling in the hogsheads. Where it will end, I do not know."

"Nothing lasts forever, Andrew. Not the good times. Not the bad times. You will see." She got up and went to his chair and slid onto his lap. "It has been so lonely for me here with Thomas gone, even though Mama is a dear. I think it will be pleasant for us to have a little one making some noise."

"This changes some things," Durnford said thoughtfully. "Now, if it is a boy, I must think of his education. There will be expenses I did not anticipate. How can I set our workers free when we face such obligations?"

"Andrew, you think too much on that subject. You are a good man, and my heart is heavy when I see you so tormented. But no one man can change the world, Andrew. Not John McDonogh. Not Andrew Durnford. You are good to our people. I think that is enough. Slaves can not expect more in these hard times."

"Perhaps I should give more thought to McDonogh's plan. Let the slaves earn their freedom and send them to Liberia. But then I think they know St. Rosalie as their home. Not one of our people are from Africa. This is their country, this America. Those who want should be able to return to Virginia, and should be allowed to go there with enough money to buy land. Those who want to stay right here, where they have Louisiana roots, should be allowed to buy a share of St. Rosalie. But how can I do that and be assured I will be able to fund our new boy's education?"

"And if it is a girl, Andrew, will you not think of an education for her?"

"Well you certainly don't mean Lafayette College, Miss Remy?"

"There are finishing schools in Paris where all the young ladies now learn polished manners that set them well in society, Andrew."

"I am relieved to hear you say that, as you know they do not accept women at Lafayette."

"There are some Colleges accepting women?"

"Where?"

"In the New England states. I have read of it in *The Courier.*"

"Strange that I should miss such an item. You must show it to me when you find it."

"Mrs. Stowe could be helpful in finding a situation for our new daughter."

"Mrs. Stowe? Do we know a Mrs. Stowe?"

"Of course we do, Andrew. Mrs. Harriet Beecher Stowe. We met her in Cincinnati as Miss Harriet Beecher, and her fiancé, Professor Stowe. It was some years ago."

"Yes. And a very talented young lady she was, too."

"She was educated in New England, Andrew, as you may also recall. So perhaps our little one could have the benefit of a sound college, and learn a little more than social graces and how to comport herself in a manner pleasing to society."

Durnford took note of the rough edge in Marie-Charlotte's voice, and smiled at her. "Sometimes, Miss Remy, I think you do not know me well. I would be as inclined to send a daughter to a good scientific college as I would a Paris finishing school.    Nay, perhaps more so inclined.    I think of myself as a progressive individual regarding the feminine sex.    Now Wainy, she does well in the medical trade.    And many times I think, 'Well, what a fine physician she might make if society were inclined to utilize a woman's services in such a science.'"

Marie-Charlotte stood up and looked down at her husband thoughtfully.    "Do you love me still, Andrew?"

Andrew rose from his chair and took her face in his hands.    "Of course I do. Yes.    Most certainly I do."

"You spend much of your time with Wainy.    I realize it is necessary in your practice.    And I did not think on the subject much until you bought here the armoire—it is such a splendid piece of furniture."

Durnford chuckled and embraced her warmly.    "Oh my dear sweet one," he said, "I love you truly.    And Wainy is a mere child."

"She is eighteen, Andrew.    And I was only sixteen when we were married."

"Eighteen she is," said Andrew, "And I am forty-five.    Old enough to be her father."

"But the armoire, Andrew, was it necessary to make such an expensive purchase for one of our slaves?"

"Dear wife now you must see this with reason.    The armoire is no more an expense than was Noel's desk.    And not nearly as splendid."    Andrew released his wife, then stepped back.    "And what's more," he said hurriedly, "Noel's desk was a much dearer purchase as I bought it when the dollar was stronger."

"Yes, that is true, and so were the finances of St. Rosalie stronger."

"Your condition is affecting your reasoning in this matter, Miss Remy."    Andrew stepped forward again and took both her hands in his.    "I am happy with Wainy. No, I am more than happy.    I am very pleased with her progress in medicine.    She is a great assistance to me.    I am able to more than double my efforts because of her."    Then seeing no favorable response in his wife's eyes, Andrew dropped her hands and stepped back.    "So it is only wise to reward her for her diligence, you see."

Marie-Charlotte walked away and sat down in her chair on the opposite side of the fireplace.    "I see that she is in love with you, Andrew.    I see it in her eyes.    A woman sees such things."

"Oh, Miss Remy, you amuse me so this morning.    I think you are feeling a little neglected.    Something I shall be sure to remedy.    And you do flatter me so, the old man that I am."

"You are not so old, Andrew. Who to know that better than me."

"Well, I think that Wainy has respect for me. That is a good thing. Perhaps that is what you see. Nevertheless, my good wife, it is you I love, and you alone. I shall not play the master and take advantage of our poor people who have not the right to say no to unwarranted advances. On that you have my solemn promise, Miss Remy."

Marie-Charlotte lowered her eyes. "Wainy would not say 'no', Andrew. It is her consent that I fear."

"I pledge you my word, you are my life's woman. Nor could I find it in my heart to think of another in your place. And so you have no need for concern in that regard."

Marie-Charlotte looked up and smiled for the first time that morning. "We shall call him 'Andrew, Jr.'," she said.

Andrew raised a hand. "No, Miss Remy, we shall call her 'Rosema'."

Marie-Charlotte laughed. "All right, Andrew. If it is a girl, we shall call her 'Rosema'."

All the women in Andrew's life were named variations of "Rose," Marie-Charlotte mused. First there was Andrew's mother, Rosaline. Then came Andrew's sister, Rosalie, who died when she was just three years old. The land of St. Rosalie was named after her. Andrew and Marie-Charlotte continued the tradition. Their daughter Rosella arrived one year after Thomas, and was gone before she was ten years old. The second daughter, Rosana, died within a year of her birth. So their third daughter would be Rosema, Andrew had decided. Well, she liked the name too, Marie-Charlotte said to herself. Then she prayed a silent prayer that perhaps this rose would live to be a comfort to her in her advanced years. Daughters could be depended on when parents aged. Thomas would always be busy with his life.

1844 was the worst year for selling sugar. Durnford went into the fall harvest without having yet sold the 1843 crop. It was a miscalculated speculation that brought near ruin to St. Rosalie.

Braddock Loring, of B. Loring and Company with operations at 7 Notre Dame Street in New Orleans was the agent for St. Rosalie then. And by September he had still not managed to sell the previous crop.

Durnford wrote to McDonogh, who had most of the sugar in storage on Julia Street. "You wish to know how many hogsheads I have on the plantation. I have

115. But to say what quantity there can be, I cannot. The hogsheads have gone down at least one-fourth.

"I request that you should put my sugar in the hands of F. G. Urquhart as a competent man for the business. He is the one who sold Erskine's crop nearly five months ago. Loring is not fit for that business. The brokers on the Levee just do what they please with him. Their object is to speculate on my sugar. The first man I saw when last in the city was Cucullu, who told me that he had told Loring he would not get the 6 1/2 he was asking for my sugar. It was a terrible mistake to hold out for that amount, and I would not have done so but for Loring's assurances. Now it is too late.

"And the brokers are too clever for Loring. He challenges their weights not. For the future not a hogshead of sugar shall leave my place without being weighed. I have found out all the secrets of their dealing on the levee, light fees and so on. You say, 'I am convinced that the only wise mode to dispose of sugar and molasses is get it into market as soon as possible.' I coincide with you in that opinion. Let me know if you think I must send my coopers to fill up what is in your warehouse in Julia Street again. This settling will be the further ruin of me yet, and it is clear the sugar must be sold as soon as possible."

Andrew Durnford, shaken by his failed judgment, looked to his father's old partner, John McDonogh for advice. McDonogh told him to sell the sugar in the Julia Street warehouse as it was, without further delay. When Noel brought him that letter of instructions, Durnford replied, "I observe what you say about selling the sugar as it is, and I agree. I wish I could do as much with what is here. But I am filling up. The savings in freight alone make the practice worthy of the effort. Larose's schooner, the *Augusta* is here, waiting to get the sugar, therefore, *la prudence est la mere de la suerte.* Please take out a policy of insurance on ninety hogsheads. I must not run any risk for the sake of a few dollars.

"And as you say it was my decision to hold for 6 1/2, and that you agreed and told Loring the same. It is all right. All has been done in my interests."

By fall, Andrew Durnford's spirits had lifted. The sugar in storage in New Orleans was finally sold by Loring, and the price he got was better than what Erskine's crop had sold for earlier that year, better by half a cent a pound. Andrew Durnford sent a letter to McDonogh expressing his enthusiasm. "By the *Fame,*" he wrote, "you will receive the second shipment of twenty-five hogsheads of sugar marked "AD" 26 to 50, which I consider as a superior article to the first twenty-five I sent up. Tell Mr. Loring if there is better sugar on the levee to send me a sample of it. It is dry to the bottom. I write in haste as my wife has unexpectedly gone to early labor. Please excuse my bad writing." Andrew Durnford handed the letter to Noel, who sealed it and delivered it to the captain of the *Fame,* while Andrew rushed up to the bedroom in the front corner of the mansion.

Wainy looked up and shook her head as Andrew came into the room. Her eyes were wide with terror. Marie-Charlotte screamed with pain.

Andrew's throat tightened and he swallowed hard. He had to stay calm. He could not run the risk of alarming Miss Remy any more than necessary, because it was important that she remain calm and listen carefully to his instructions.

"You must stop pushing for the moment, Miss Remy," he said with all the authority he could muster. Marie-Charlotte had been in labor for over three hours, and still her cervix had not dilated—it was two, perhaps three fingers wide then. Not enough. Not nearly enough, Andrew knew, because this was going to be a breech birth. And how many women had survived such an ordeal? It was less than one out of three, Andrew knew. He had no reason to believe his slender wife at thirty-six years of age had the advantage on the averages. It was quite the opposite. The great likelihood was that Miss Remy would not last the day. But he could not think about Cesarean. Although he might save the child, Marie-Charlotte would never survive.

Wainy had not had the misfortune of witnessing such a complicated birth, although she appeared to appreciate just how difficult things were going to get that morning. Andrew decided against taking Wainy out of the room to explain to her the procedures involved. That would cause too much alarm on the part of Marie-Charlotte. Better to instruct as they went along, he thought.

"Miss Remy, stop pushing. Take control of it, and stop. This is very important."

Marie-Charlotte screamed and pushed again.

"The child is doubled up, Miss Remy. Do you understand me? This is a breech child. You have to stop pushing."

"Oh, Andrew, Andrew, I simply can't."

"You can Miss Remy. You can. You must. The child is pressing on the perineum. Remember? I explained that to you. It is a reflex action that you feel. But you are not ready for the baby. I can feel that your cervix is not dilated. You have far, far to go."

The natural instinct was for the mother to push and push hard because of the pressure exerted by the baby on the perineum, and Andrew explained again, remaining as calm as he possibly could, the function of the perineum. He did so because it was important for Marie-Charlotte to understand what was happening and for her to fight the reflexive desire to push and push with all her might, which in another situation would be natural and beneficial. Now, however, she was killing her baby.

Andrew felt the cervix with his hand again and it was still hard and far from dilated. She had made no progress in the twenty minutes or so that he had returned to the room. It was, he realized, going to be a long hard day for all of them, Marie-Charlotte, the baby, him, and even Wainy.

Wainy wiped the mother's forehead and face and spoke to her encouragingly. Still, Marie-Charlotte pushed. She could not overcome that powerful natural urge.

"Marie," Andrew said sternly. "You must stop. Both you and the child will suffer if you do not. I can not speak of the outcome if you are not able to control this birth. Do you understand, Marie?"

Andrew's voice came to Marie-Charlotte through the searing pain like a whisper through a morning fog. Fear rose icily in her chest. Andrew never called her "Marie" unless he was very, very angry with her. But she knew he was not angry. Andrew was afraid. He was afraid because he knew she was going to die that morning. What then? Would the baby die too? If not, who would take care of the child? Her Mama Remy was much too old.

Just then, as she screamed and pushed in spite of her thoughts, Marie-Charlotte heard the stern voice of Wainy at her side. "Do you want to die, Miss Remy," Wainy said, "and leave the child and Master Andrew to me?"

The words fell upon her like a thunderclap on a dark night. That was exactly what would happen. She was going to die. Then Wainy would mother the child and she would have Andrew too. Andrew glanced up with a furious frown at Wainy's statement. What a foolish thing to say. My God, what could Wainy possibly be thinking. Surely Miss Remy was going to die, and the baby as well. Andrew himself had already given up hope. The child was being driven down unrelentingly, and there was really nothing Miss Remy could do about it. Already there was a terrible compression on the life-giving chord, chocking it off. And when the baby died there was a small chance he could still save the mother. If necessary, he would cut it out. He had done that before. But even then the mother died.

As he looked up at his wife's face, Andrew saw that she had turned purple with anger and determination. Her pushing stopped. The pressure on the child eased ever so slightly. Maybe there was a chance after all. Andrew ran his fingers around the baby's body, found the chord, felt a pulse there. The child was still alive. Slowly, carefully, he pulled gently on the chord until he had it out of the mother, and he felt its throbbing life-force. Wainy was talking very rapidly and earnestly to Marie-Charlotte. Andrew did not hear the words, just the tone, reproachful, almost scornful, but full of encouragement.

Having gained some control over the situation, Andrew carefully explained to Marie-Charlotte what was happening. The baby would be born doubled up, a full breech birth. He was going to have to cut, and all of that would be very painful. But there was a chance, a very good chance both mother and child would survive. First the baby must be turned, it was on its side and there was great risk to the child and to the mother too in that position. He must, Andrew explained, turn the baby so that the face was toward the floor. This position would allow the head to bend naturally and increase the chances of both mother and child.

Throughout that day, Andrew worked and sweated, calling upon all of his skills to keep both mother and child alive, and slowly, very slowly, Marie-Charlotte dilated. Andrew placed his fingers in the baby's hip joints and pulled gently and firmly. The movement through the birth canal was almost imperceptible. Throughout the afternoon and into the evening he worked to turn the baby into position, stopping and checking for the all important pulse in the umbilical chord.

Wainy wiped and stanched the blood, and the baby's bottom came into open air. An hour later the trunk was out, and Andrew reached around the child and pulled first one arm down and across its body and then the other. Except for the head and legs, now, the baby had come free. Andrew felt for the pulse in the umbilical chord again, nodded to Wainy, and then very carefully searched in the birth canal with his fingers. He placed two fingers in the child's mouth, and protecting its neck with his thumb and remaining fingers, slowly, carefully, he pulled. Marie-Charlotte pushed, encouraged and supported by Wainy.

"Quickly now," Andrew said to Wainy. "Take the towel."

Andrew instructed Wainy to pass the towel under the half-born infant. "Now lift up, lift the entire body up. That's it. Hold it high. Steady. And push Miss Remy. Push."

With his hand cradling the child's neck inside its mother's body, and two fingers in its mouth for leverage, with Wainy lifting the baby's body in a towel, and Marie-Charlotte pushing and screaming, Andrew pulled hard, but gently. Hard enough to move the baby along, but not too hard, not so hard as to break its neck.

With the three working intently, mother, doctor-husband, and nurse, a fourth soul was brought into the world.

The baby lay quietly, very quietly, much too quietly, in Andrew's arms. It refused to breathe. Refused to cry.

Wainy took the child and held it up by its feet. She slapped its buttocks and back. Nothing. The child was dead. Andrew sighed and shook his head. Just then a small, determined voice cried out, and quickly burst into a lusty yowl.

Wainy smiled at Andrew, then looked down thoughtfully at the baby cradled in her arms. Tears came to her eyes. "Your breath has the sweetness of freedom, Sugar." And then she continued in a soft voice as if neither Andrew nor Marie-Charlotte were in the room. "Black as me, black as any baby of mine will be, but the air you breathe is free."

Durnford sat back and watched as his young nurse wrapped the child. He had never heard Wainy speak of freedom. Her dress was soaked with sweat. Her face was lined and tired. She was exhausted and overwrought, Andrew decided.

Then when Wainy presented the child to its mother she smiled again. "You did right well, Miss Remy. Right well indeed."

Andrew walked around the bed, kissed his wife on the cheek and brushed her hair. "I have never seen a woman more determined," he said to her and then stopped abruptly, remembering the statement Wainy made which brought about his wife's resolute will. Well, she decided she wasn't going to die and leave the child and her husband to Wainy. Andrew chuckled quietly to himself. Women know women, don't they.

Andrew Durnford sat down again heavily at his desk in the library. He stared for a moment at the flames crackling in the fireplace. Then he picked up a pen and addressed another letter to his friend up the river. "This is the second letter I write to you today," he started. Then he looked up at the tall German clock standing in the corner near the window, crumpled up the sheet he had begun, and started anew. It was a quarter past one of a new day. "Dear John," he wrote on a fresh sheet of paper, "yesterday I advised Miss Remy was in labor. I can not describe the difficulties we have had here. But mother and child have survived and appear to be in fine health. I will be up to get a cradle for our little heiress, Rosema, as soon as I am confident both are in the clear."

# Chapter Twenty Eight

The sinkhole behind the sugarhouse was but a memory in May of 1845. With the River Road again graded and finished, only a small cross attested to the terror of that night when Harry, his team of mules and the huge investment they represented disappeared from the earth.

It was early May, and an unusually hot day, when Andrew and Marie-Charlotte, carrying the infant, Rosema, came down the front steps of the mansion to the carriage waiting in the drive. The magnificent carriage Marie-Charlotte had been so proud of years ago had finally seen its end when a hurricane destroyed the carriage house. Andrew had no thought of repairing the old carriage. Worn out and rotted, it had served them well.

The sugar plantation operated again on a profitable basis. There was even a little money left over after expenses—although not nearly enough to pay off the enormous debt to the bank which held a lien against the slaves. But enough for a few luxuries. One of those luxuries was a new carriage. Noel had found just the item, not a new carriage, to be sure, but one with sound wheels and axles and all of the wood completely without rot. He had seen it in a warehouse on one of his visits to the city as the plantation manager. Although free from the ravages of damp weather, the carriage suffered extensively from the opposite condition. All the leather, inside and out, approached a state of dust from years of neglect.

When Durnford learned of the purchase price, he wrote out a draft in the amount of $100.00, and sent Noel straight back to buy the carriage, relying entirely on his manager's assessment of its condition. Noel brought the carriage back by steamboat the next day. It was run into the new carriage house, and restoration started immediately. Andrew had hired a saddler at a dollar a day to make up the necessary bridles, breeching and cart saddle, with leather Durnford bought in bulk. When the cart saddle was finished, Andrew put the man to work on the interior, replacing the trimmings and upholstery, all in hand-buffed green leather imported from England. The body of the carriage was painted jet black and the fenders and gear a dark Brewster green with gold stripe. When finished, Andrew believed the restored carriage was the finest equipment on the West Bank.

Noel, in an ivory linen suit and matching top hat, mounted the front of the carriage and took his position as driver. Replacing the lost Harry with Noel, Durnford calculated, was a wise decision of economy, for Noel served in a dual purpose on trips to the city. Not only was he the carriage driver, he was also the plantation manager, and used the conveyance to continue on in his business of securing supplies and provisions for St. Rosalie.

Andrew and Marie-Charlotte took positions in the seat facing forward and laid their sleeping infant on the seat across from them. Marie-Charlotte unsnapped the ribbons holding the side curtains, and lowered them against the morning sun, as the carriage went down the white, shell-paved driveway and tuned north on the River Road.

On the floor of the carriage were three blackberry pies, which Marie-Charlotte had herself baked, as well as fresh butter, and plum pies made by the cooks. Marie-Charlotte planned on a short lunch appearance with Andrew at John McDonogh's house, and then she would be off with Noel and the carriage, across the river by ferry, to purchase summer clothing for her and the baby, while Noel searched for bargains in straw hats and provisions for the slaves.

John McDonogh, the millionaire, long the richest man in Louisiana, the Croesus of the South and the largest landowner in the United States, stood at the end of his drive when they arrived at his decaying mansion five hours later. He was an old man now, but stood tall and straight, with determined features. His eyes remained brilliant and piercing. His gray hair, as always, was combed back and gathered into a knotted pony tail. He was dressed all in dark clothes, the fashion of a half century earlier, and for protection from the sun he carried an ancient blue silk umbrella.

He greeted his guests from St. Rosalie almost absent-mindedly, and his gaze seemed to look beyond them, Marie-Charlotte thought, as if fixed upon some far-away goal.

The lunch awaiting them had been spread out on a table under an oak tree. Marie-Charlotte handed off Rosema to a nurse, and they sat down to a meal of green gumbo, a jellied ham, and peaches. The slaves Nellie, Ti Annie, and Joe cooled them with huge fans mounted on long sticks, and drove away the flies.

All around them was a scene of disorder. The estate was once a sugar plantation of 2,500 acres and 75 slaves. McDonogh bought it from Desiree Boisblanc, a lonely widow about twenty years older than he, buying at a bargain with flattery and a little cash, all entirely on credit. The dark green rows of lightly waving cane had gone long ago, along with the wooden sugarhouse. There was still to be seen the remnants of the shingle fence which enclosed the yard of the gray residence Susan had rejected.

Having taken up construction to build the new mansion for his fiancee, McDonogh found that business even more profitable than merchant trading. More and more, he was out of the office, leaving the daily affairs of the mercantile trade to his senior partner, Thomas Durnford. For his real estate speculations, McDonogh formed his own company.

The city stopped at Canal Street when McDonogh first came to New Orleans. After the United States purchased Louisiana, the small town exploded outward. McDonogh was ahead of the crowd, buying up all the plantations around the city and far out into the wilderness. But before he bought any land, he always went to the site in the wet season. He sold off the slaves and rented out the lands. As the city expanded, he built warehouses and retail stores, office buildings and residences, all with his own slave construction crew. Nothing was sold unless it returned a good profit. The shrewd businessman preferred to rent out everything.

The plantation across the river from New Orleans was too large for a vegetable farm, so McDonogh subdivided a large portion, forming the city of McDonoghville. The first lots sold quickly. Even Andrew's mother bought two lots. But few people built, and then it all came to a standstill. Now most of the land was used in McDonogh's construction business. All around the tree, under which they ate ,lay building materials: beams, both wood and iron, framing lumber and wood for floors and rafters, shingles and kegs of nails, and old lumber and windows and old doors from buildings McDonogh had torn down. Rusty boiler iron lay at the end of the driveway between the two wings of the uncompleted mansion. Bricks were stacked in piles all around, and sheds with metal roofs jutted and slanted at all angles around them, providing protection from the weather for equipment and materials.

"How goes our young man, Thomas?" McDonogh asked.

"President Junkin sent me his grades for last term," Andrew answered. "He has managed 81.5. And with that I am well satisfied, although he did miss eight college exercises of which only four were excused."

McDonogh nodded. "He is a young man. His absences can be forgiven."

"Perhaps," Andrew said, "but you will not be happy to learn that he also missed prayer thirty-two times. Religion does not seem to be his major concern."

"I have often said, Andrew, it is an affliction of our times."

"His lack of interest in that department causes me some distress though," Andrew said. "Contrary to your opinion of me, I believe religion is the cohesive fabric of our society. Without such guidance, man can but blunder aimlessly."

Marie-Charlotte put down her spoon with a clatter. "Thomas gives no reason for such fears." Then pulling an envelope from her bag and speaking in French, the language in which Thomas had written and which McDonogh also spoke fluently, she said, "I will read you but a part of his last letter. It is dated at Easton on March 24th. And after his normal affectionate addresses to us, Thomas writes, 'Another session has rolled around and the vacation has set in. The time will soon arrive for me to once again enjoy those sacred privileges of home. One year and six months more and the battle is won. I, like others will stand upon the broad platform on which man has to act, in fears, in doubts, in hopes and restlessness. The world! Mighty name of a creative power! What presumptions if I, so young, would say that I have a perfect acquaintance with the nooks and windings of this vast world. But experience I have in some small respects, sufficient may I be permitted to say, to act my part in life.'"

Marie-Charlotte folded the letter and looked up. "We need not overly burden ourselves with a boy who writes with such understanding."

"More insight than I had imagined," McDonogh said.

She was about to return the letter to its envelope when McDonogh leaned forward and tapped on the table with a bony finger. "Finish the letter. You can't cheat this old man out of his portion of news from Easton."

Marie-Charlotte unfolded the letter and continued with a softer voice, "'But let us return to our next session with vigor. It, like others, will pass with hard and difficult studies, indeed much harder than any previous ones. Our studies in the Junior class have always been intriguing to the student's brain. And may I add that our responses are not altogether relished.'"

Andrew stirred uncomfortably in his chair as Marie-Charlotte read, and at this point he reached out quickly and grabbed her arm. "Let's not bore John further, Miss Remy. I am sure he wishes to get to the point of explaining why he called us up here with such urgency."

"Andrew, you surprise me," McDonogh said. "Of course I want to hear it. I said I want to hear it all. Every word our dear boy has written warms my heart. And he uses the French so effectively. His letters are a symphony for these old ears."

Reluctantly, Andrew Durnford settled back in his chair.

Marie-Charlotte hesitated, then returned to the letter. "'Dr. Yeoman having made his exit, Dr. Junkin took his seat as president again. It seems to me like it was before his departure for Miami University. The circumstances of his return are somewhat peculiar, and it seems to me by the reports here that Dr. Junkin was forced to relinquish his station as president at Miami for having engaged in a controversy with the Synod of Ohio on the subject of abolition. Dr. Junkin advocates the cause of slavery and appears to prove it from scriptural documents. It is an able discourse and is worthy the perusal of the slave-holding many, although I am certain that my presence here, as well as that of Washington and David who have gone before me, being all descendants of Ham, are an embarrassment to his theology." Marie-Charlotte lowered her head, her voice unsteady, and read on. "'And what of you, my dear mother and father? And what of the many other free men of color who hold our brethren in bondage? Surely it is error to base this peculiar system of the South on scripture. Nay, it is but the way of nature, as borne out by history. Someday I shall no doubt join the ranks of the owners of mankind. And when I do so it may be with a clear and settled mind.'"

There was a complete silence at the table as Marie-Charlotte paused, and then she read from Thomas' letter in a stronger voice. "'I had the honor to be elected Orator for the Franklin association of the institution, to represent them at a contest between the two rivals. I had but very little time to prepare against my opponent, Mr. Stewart, but everything went off in good style and fine order.'"

She quickly put down the letter and looked up. "Well, that is about the extent of the news from Thomas."

McDonogh frowned. "But there is yet another page. Read that."

Marie-Charlotte read faster now, as if the speed of her voice would soften the words. "'There are various reports here concerning David. I am sorry to say that his pride will lead him to no good end, for he has not a noble spirit of pride, but arrogance and effrontery. He wrote some very abusive letters to an aged woman of color working on behalf of the American Colonization Society here. It is derogatory to his standing as a pretended scholar and Christian. He needs a reform and that before he gets older. His career alone will not insure him success no matter where his lot may be cast. But we must ever hope for the better from him in the future.'"

Marie-Charlotte said quickly, "Thomas has a question whether Andrew will be able to pay for his medical studies, and then comes the usual wishes of good health, including you, John, and with that he ends his last letter."

The old man gazed out over the river. "David tells me he will not go to Africa," McDonogh said sadly. "Nor will he return home. I told him I would honor his wishes and would free him if he so desired. David wrote back. It was a very short letter. Not done in a friendly tone. David told me he did not want his freedom to come from my pen. He said that before God and all right-thinking men he was already free and I should exercise no false charity in his regard."

Andrew Durnford was eager to move the topic. "What have you heard from our friend Elliot Cresson? Does all go well with the Colonization Society in Philadelphia?"

McDonogh sighed and put down the spoon with which he had been lazily stirring his cold gumbo. "He has written to ask about the religious instruction of the slave population here. He wants the names of those who do the most in that good work. My pen has laid dormant since. I am unable to give him the name of one, single individual who does anything in that way. With the exception of myself, there is no one, Andrew. Nor could I give him your name."

"Well of course I do not discourage religion at St. Rosalie. Just last year, when we lost Harry—"

"Andrew, you who are a son to me, said nothing at that service. Yet your duty of imparting religious instruction to your servants can not be doubted."

"Now, John this discussion can only lead to hard feelings. My Catholic background holds me back, I don't have the stomach for evangelical work. But I believe strongly in religion, and you know in my heart I wish only the best for my people."

"You are happy with your state of apathy, Andrew. The little still voice does not work within you. I understand. I am not happy with you. But I understand. Were our other planters even in a state of indifference or lukewarmness on the subject, like you are Andrew, we might hope for some progress. But that is not their state. Ninety-nine out of a hundred, and I fear even the hundred are diametrically opposed to the introduction of religion among their slaves. They cannot even speak of it with calmness."

It was the same old lecture Andrew had listened to countless times before.

"As you know, Andrew, our population are principally French, who generally speaking laugh at the idea of religion. And the Americans who are settled amongst them forget, if they ever had any. In the City, we have some professing Christians, but even there—"

It was the same thing the old man had said before so many times, and Andrew was impatient. "Well now I think we should get at this blackberry pie!" he said loudly, interrupting his mentor. "And you will appreciate, John, the labor of Miss Remy in making that a delight to the senses."

When they finished the blackberry pie, McDonogh whispered to a servant near him, who then ran off to the wing housing McDonogh's office and returned shortly with a packet of papers.

"I have often pleaded the case for the American Colonization Society," McDonogh said to Andrew Durnford. "And now I can read to you of some of the successes we have had. The first letter is from James Gray. You may remember him as the foreman of my construction crew."

The old man read slowly, carefully, and without glasses, although it was apparent to Andrew that McDonogh's eyes were failing. The first letter, from John Gray, gave reasons for his remaining at Monrovia, rather than moving to Sinoe, as McDonogh had requested. Gray stated that Monrovia was visited by the American Squadron on a regular basis, delivering supplies which were used in trade by the colony and generated a profit for the inhabitants, all of whom were sincerely grateful for the assistance McDonogh and others had provided. Gray, a slave who had been freed by McDonogh and later chose to immigrate to Liberia at his own expense, requested that McDonogh sell his property at Gretna and send him the proceeds, as he would not be returning.

McDonogh rolled the letter up and pointed it at Andrew Durnford. "So, you see, we have here a man who has the financial means to return. He invested wisely and could live comfortably upon his small farm at Gretna. But no. He asks that I sell his property here. Now what do you say to that, Andrew?"

"That letter is under date of January of this year?"

"January 28th."

"And Gray had just arrived not ten days earlier, John, so I still reserve my judgment and suggest you not be too hasty in selling his little farm at Gretna."

McDonogh then produced another letter, this one from Galloway Smith at Sinoe, Liberia, in which the former slave stated that he believed Liberia a fine place to live. Next, McDonogh read a letter from George R. Ellis at Monrovia, addressed to "My Dear Father," which notified McDonogh of his family's recovery from the African Fever, and that he had settled near St. Paul's River and planted twenty acres and that all were grateful for what McDonogh had done for them. Then McDonogh read from several letters, one after the other. Augustine Lamberth, who had settled at Monrovia, also addressed his letter to "Dear Father," and stated he too was willing to relocate to Sinoe, if McDonogh insisted. Another letter, from James McGeorge, acknowledged receipt of McDonogh's letters, and stated that they had not attained the expected prosperity, but they did grow enough to sustain themselves, and would move to Sinoe if McDonogh desired it.

"Sinoe," McDonogh explained, "is my own, personal project. I believe the land is fertile and ideally suited for the production of sugar from cane. That is why I think my people should go there. But of the last ten people, only one has gone on to Sinoe. The one succeeds and the rest fail. You see, they are still my children and I must treat them so, even across the water."

Next, there was a letter from Washington W. McDonogh who had gone to Settra Kroo upon graduation from Easton. "Dear Father," Washington began, and then he gave an account of his travel to his final destination at Settra Kroo and news of other immigrants. He stated that Settra Kroo was a healthy part of the country and believed Africa was a fine place to live. He desired to remain in Africa, he said, and he stated that a colored person can enjoy his liberty free of prejudice in the colony. However, he also reported that some immigrants behaved immediately like natives, unwilling to work and resorting to stealing. Washington felt it unwise to reveal the names of the lost ones, as he still held hope for their future. Most of the people at the Mission were well, he said. He lived among the Kroo people and was making great progress in their language, and found the natives very peaceable, although generally very ignorant and superstitious. In concluding, Washington stated that he was deeply indebted to McDonogh for the education he had given him. He desired to be married, however, and asked that McDonogh send him a few dollars for financial assistance.

McDonogh read from several other letters, most of which addressed him as, "Dear Father," stating that Africa was a fine country, that the land was rich and produced numerous crops. Others stated that they had been industrious and lived tolerably well, that the African soil was rich, the climate healthy, and Africa's laws were just and equitable, and that they enjoyed the same rights as their white brethren in America.    A few reported that they made their living from brick-making, farming, and building houses.    Almost all of the immigrants asked for more seed, or more working tools, and financial assistance.    One individual, George Ellis, asked McDonogh to send him two dogs, stating they were much needed in Liberia.

"I am disturbed by these constant demands for capital assistance," McDonogh concluded.

"My dear friend, John," Andrew said, "we are talking about people in a colony only recently settled.    I confess to you I am amazed at what they have accomplished.    Do not deal so harshly with them, John.    You can't take your wealth to the grave.    Send them what they want."

McDonogh sprang forward in his chair.    "Exactly!    You are perfectly correct, Andrew.    I knew you would agree when you heard what my people had to say.    The American Colonization Society and this project in Liberia is a success."

"Well, I—"

"And the really good news, Andrew, is that you can now join us."

"Would that I could, John—"

"Well you can.    There is no longer an impediment."    McDonogh pulled a paper from an inside pocket of his worn coat and waved it about.    "This is the decision of the Court of Appeals.    We have won, Andrew.    The injunction has been lifted.    You are free to do what you want with St. Rosalie and your slaves."

Marie-Charlotte beamed with excitement.    "You mean it is all over, John?"

"No," Andrew answered for McDonogh.    "It is not over.    We will still have a trial.    Only the interim injunction has been voided."

McDonogh said with a smile.    "It is, indeed, over.    I also have a letter from Benet, the lawyer for the English plaintiffs.    The case is withdrawn.    They are quitting—giving up.    Provided we agree to let them go without costs, and only a fool would insist on that."

"But why?    After all these years?"

"Well, Andrew, they can easily see that victory will be ours in the end.    And without St. Rosalie, there is nothing left to your father's estate."

"Nothing at all."

"No.    Not a penny.    It has all gone for my services and lawyer's fees over this long period of almost twenty years."

A broad smile broke out over Andrew Durnford's face.    It mattered little to him that there was nothing left in his father's estate. He was never an heir, not entitled to even the last penny, and the joke was on his English cousins. McDonogh, the Scottish fox had spent their inheritance defending St. Rosalie against their claims. And now, at last, the plantation was Durnford's, and his alone.

"Well," McDonogh said, "since you have just admitted the success of our Colonization Society, when will you be sending the first of your slaves to Liberia?" Then without waiting for an answer, McDonogh pressed on. "Oh, I know you are thinking it would take fifteen years or more for a slave to earn his freedom, but there are other ways. Your people who have family can select a relative to go now, and vouch to spend all their off time in earning his freedom. A debt which can be easily absolved in five years by the work of two or three slaves. It isn't much, but the idea is to start now, to give the remainder of your work force hope. Hope for a future in Liberia. Now what do you say to that, Andrew? ...Andrew?"

The smile disappeared from Durnford's face. He lowered his head while McDonogh talked. "John, I have permitted a charge to be placed against my slaves. I needed the money to rebuilt the sugarhouse."

McDonogh jumped up from the table and slammed a fist down on its rough surface. "Andrew, you are such a poor businessman! I wonder sometimes how you will ever succeed. Why did you not come to me?"

"If you gentlemen will excuse me," Marie-Charlotte said as she quickly got up from the table. She had witnessed many such arguments, heated and vehement. Both Andrew and McDonogh would soon be shouting at the top of their lungs. The next day all would be forgotten. Her baby, Rosema was in the good hands of the house servants. And immediately she was in the carriage and speeding down the long drive, Noel driving, and still she heard the raised and angry voices.

"You treat me as a child and I am a man of forty-seven years!"

"Andrew, you do business like a child—"

"John, this time you go too far!"

"How much did you borrow?"

"None of your business!"

"Less than $30,000?"

"How I conduct the affairs of St. Rosalie is my business, John!"

"Ah, how lightly you forget your mortgage to me, Andrew. Hence my interest in St. Rosalie!"

"Your interest in St. Rosalie does not extend to dictating my business affairs, John. When will you ever learn that?"

"Andrew, you could have sold me the house on Tivoli Square.  $30,000 I will give you.  Twice what it's worth!"

"You would love to steal that house from me, John...."

Finally the voices of the two contestants faded as the iron tires of the carriage noisily rolled on to the planks of the ferry to New Orleans.  And as the heavy workhorse on the ferry stepped forward to endlessly walk the squirrel cage connected to a gear and chain pulling the ferry across the river, Marie-Charlotte leaned back and closed her eyes.  She had seen the city from the river many times. Now she rested, thinking of the exclusive shops she would visit on Royal St. Then there was the advertisement of L. Binoche which she cut from the *Picayune* and carried in her purse.  Binoche had announced that at No. 30 Chartres Street he carried the last arrivals from France, printed cashmeres, *Mouaseline de lane* and woolen serge. She also planned to visit the American stores across Canal Street, especially the ones that advertised select stocks of imported silks, and then on to Magazine Street where she would look for a new Chesterfield driving coat and perhaps a satin vest for Andrew, and even a pair of doeskin pantaloons to go with it. At Magazine Street she would finally meet up with Noel again, who would have completed his purchase of straw hats and other provisions for St. Rosalie.

# Chapter Twenty Nine

The following year Thomas received his degree from Lafayette College and started home to St. Rosalie.

On the day of Thomas' unexpected arrival, a warm Saturday in late April, 1846, Andrew Durnford stepped from the door of the plantation hospital and stretched in the sunlight. He had spent that morning treating patients: his slaves, slaves from other plantations, white neighbors, free blacks, and Baptiste, the overseer from Erskine's plantation, with a dozen boils on his leg. He had dictated to Wainy instructions for medications and treatments for the patients and left them to her care. Unless some emergency arose, Wainy and her assistant would have sole charge of the hospital until Andrew came for his rounds on Monday.

He walked under the live oaks, whose heavy branches, streaming silver-gray Spanish moss, hung down all around to within a few inches of the ground. The trunks of the trees were huge and gnarled. The heavy limbs were thick and knotty. The sun streamed down through the old trees and danced upon the grass.

Durnford inhaled the fragrance. Spring Magnolia blossoms. Grass freshly cut by the slaves with scythes. He listened to the slaves singing in the distant fields. His people seldom sung when at work. But on a Saturday, especially a Saturday as splendid as this, when they knew they would be off work at noon, they sang with a rich and mellow harmony the spirituals that were so dear to them. They also sang songs of freedom. The freedom songs were not openly rebellious, they were coded in words and language the planter class was not meant to understand. But Andrew understood what the songs meant. He smiled when he heard the words. His people didn't really want freedom. They sang those songs because that is what slaves on other plantations sang; songs brought home to St. Rosalie by men visiting wives and lovers.

Andrew leaned against a low-lying branch and took a carefully folded letter from his pocket. The letter was from his Thomas. It had been sent to John McDonogh a few weeks earlier. McDonogh had sent it on to Andrew, as it was their practice to share letters from Thomas. Andrew turned to the second page of the letter and began reading to himself:

*I assume you have not talked to my father recently, because Dr. Junkin told me that in your last letter you asked whether I ever considered the legal profession. I suppose he has already informed you by now of my intention of studying medicine. The study of physiology has always been a favorite of mine, either because it is one of the most perfect and complex studies, or the interest I have seen my dear father take in it.*

*The advantages which one has in pursuing medicine far surpass those of the law. The law, permit me to say, sir, is too much hacked up by pettifoggers and men of little wit. It is not made an object to improve the intellect, but a mere money-making scheme. I think this should be as foreign to an individual's mind as possible, for it is impossible to improve the intellect when such an object is made the chief pursuit. Gain is mere nothing, if one does not gain what is useful. For many, indeed, have this in mind when they launch themselves upon the world, and alas, how many are forced to beggar the public? It is wrong, and should not be indulged in too largely. We live not for ourselves, but for God and mankind.*

*Where I shall study and when, is of course left to my father's discretion. I presume not to say, but leave it to his own proper judgement. You are aware that it is my last year in college, when I suppose I shall pay you a visit after so long an absence, and to those parents whom I so heartily love.*

*We had on Tuesday last a snow that fell to the depth of fourteen inches, but the weather after that began to get warmer, which causes the snow to melt very fast. The winter with us has not been very cold—*

At that moment, Andrew heard a long, piercing whistle, looked up and saw a steamboat coming around the bend. It was a boat he recognized immediately, the *Fame*. Durnford felt energy surge through his veins. All the care, trials and work of the plantation which had borne upon him through the long winter faded away.

And when the steamboat let out another long blast on its whistle, followed by a succession of blasts without end, he knew the premonition he'd felt was true. His heart raced. It was Thomas. It had to be Thomas coming home at last.

"It's Thomas!" Marie-Charlotte shouted from the veranda. At her side was her mother, who guided her steps. Andrew knew Marie-Charlotte required no assistance, she was neither infirm nor ill. But the old lady, as Durnford called Granmere Remy, would have none of that. Marie-Charlotte was pregnant again.

The suspense at St. Rosalie grew from minute to minute, and Andrew's curiosity was no less aroused than Marie-Charlotte's. Thomas was a boy when he left, barely five feet and weighing not more than one hundred pounds. Six years of growth to manhood had transpired. What did their little boy look like now?

Thomas had beaten home the promised letter stating the date of his arrival. His trip from St. Rosalie to Easton had taken over a month by ship. The trip home by the railroad less than five days.

With Marie-Charlotte in the middle and Andrew and the old lady at each side, the trio hurried to the landing. Already they could see a tall Negro at the rail. He was well dressed in a dark suit and tie, clothing too dark and heavy for the Louisiana climate. The boy's rugged features were barely recognizable. Andrew stopped and pulled the two women to a halt. He could scarcely believe what he saw. It was Thomas, certainly, and he was a head taller than his father. The gangplank was run out and chaos followed. Slaves, men, women and children ran from the fields and cabins, shouting and screaming with joy. Thomas rushed down the gangplank into the arms of his mother who shouted, "Oh my Thomas, you are the most handsome man I ever saw!" Andrew clapped his son on the back and declared he was the most solid individual he'd ever known. The old lady pulled at the boy's arm, shrieking and crying, and all around them circled and swirled servants and field hands and children of all sizes. The long absent son had come home to St. Rosalie.

The mass of humanity, Negro slaves and Negro slave owners, streamed up the sloping dike, down and across the river road and along the seashell-paved drive into the big house. Everyone came into the house, servants and field hands alike. No one was excluded or felt they should be. A son had returned. Noel took charge and ordered food from the kitchen and wine from its shallow, cool cellar. Marie-Charlotte laid immediate claim to her son and never let him from her grasp. Andrew drew back and let the circle of admiring relatives and slaves have their turn with his son, but he never took his eyes off Thomas. Indeed, he could not, for Thomas stood not just a head taller than his father, he was a head taller than the entire throng, only Noel came within a few inches of him.

Everyone ate and drank on their feet and marvelled at what a magnificent young man Thomas had become. Finally, Andrew took a deep drink from his wine glass and called for attention. "In honor of our son, Thomas, and his return to St. Rosalie, I declare everyone shall have off the remainder of the day."

Silence and quizzical looks followed.

"Why Andrew," Marie-Charlotte said. "It's already past noon. This is Saturday, and the people have the freedom of the day."

Durnford laughed. "So it is. Well then I declare a holiday until Tuesday morning. Even the servants are freed from duties. Everyone will have to forge for themselves. Our son has come home to us safe, healthy and, I believe, extremely wise."

The celebration lasted all afternoon and into the night. The doors were opened and windows raised and oil lamps taken out on the galleries. Laughter and gaiety flowed from the house along with the light as the citizens of St. Rosalie went freely in and out of the windows and doors and under the old oaks, singing, laughing, dancing, and eating and drinking.

Finally, Andrew steered Thomas into the library and closed the door. There was no fire in the fireplace as it was a hot and humid night, and the only light came from the oil lamp on Andrew's desk.

Thomas spoke before Andrew could bring up the subject of medical school. "When may I expect my little brother?"

"Well Thomas, that event should take place in late August."

"You do not seem to be pleased, father."

"Well I am not pleased. And neither is your mother. Your little sister was surprise enough. And I can remind you again that her arrival was not an easy thing for your mother. No, I am not at all happy. And I'm afraid this is the end of our marriage bed. I hardly need shake your mother's hand, and she is with child again. At her age, childbirth can be exceedingly dangerous."

Andrew picked up the bottle of wine Noel had strategically placed on his desk, and poured two glasses. "To the future," he said to Thomas.

"To the future, Papa. To the future of us all."

They drank and Andrew motioned to a chair next to his desk. "Well, sit down now, Thomas and tell me how it feels to be home again."

As they sat down on each side of the desk, Thomas said simply, "Good. It feels good to be home, Papa."

Andrew folded his hands on the desk. "John McDonogh sent me your last letter. I was reading it again as you arrived." Durnford paused and leaned upon his folded hands. "So you want to be a medical man, a doctor?"

"Yes, so I have said. But now that I am home, I wonder if I hadn't made a mistake. I have been gone from St. Rosalie for six years. And I am overwhelmed by the warmth and love I find here at home. I was a good student, Father. For six years I was a good student. I did not stay out all night, did not get drunk, did not carouse around town or spent my time idly on women and pleasure. And there is one thing I can tell you, dear Papa, if I had it to do over again I still would not go carousing about, but I'm not so sure I would leave St. Rosalie, even for an education."

"Oh, Thomas, you are just tired and overcome with emotion upon entering again the family fold. You must leave. You can't study medicine at St. Rosalie."

"Papa, I could study medicine at St. Rosalie. What better teacher than you? We have the infirmary here. Books, well those you don't have we can get. That should be much cheaper than three years of room, board, and studies in New York."

"You are thinking that I can not afford your medical studies, Thomas. And to some extent that is true. But it's not as bad as that."

"Well, you have the mortgage to John McDonogh and the charges against the slaves to pay off—"

"No, Thomas. This fall I shall pay in full the lien against our slaves."

Thomas smiled. "Oh, Papa, that is indeed good news." Then the son frowned. "But now that you can free the slaves, it is no longer possible."

"So, bad news travels fast."

"A copy of the new legislation arrived at Easton a few days before I left. Dr. Junkin in particular was pleased to learn that it had become illegal to emancipate a slave in Louisiana."

"And the worst thing, Thomas, is that any slave freed is subject to the first man to claim him. Emancipation is treated as an abandonment of property."

Andrew shrugged his shoulders, downed his remaining wine, and poured another glass. "They can't touch the slaves McDonogh sends to Liberia. But I still can not bring myself to that. As you know, Thomas, I had resolved to free all of the slaves, sell them St. Rosalie Plantation as well. The value we have here comes from the work of our people."

"And the work you have done, Papa. You have worked harder than any slave, field hand or servant, or even Noel."

"That I will not dispute with you, Thomas, because it is true. And I mean to be an example to you in that regard. I have not lived a life of idle pleasure. I have worked cutting the cane. I have spent hot nights in the sugarhouse. Now it appears I will spend my life as the sheppard of our slaves. But that is not a fate you need resign yourself to, Thomas. I'll find the money for your medical education. We have a good crop this year. It will sell at a handsome profit. In the meantime, Thomas, I would like you to be the overseer at St. Rosalie. I am an old man now, forty-seven years old. Too old to be chasing about the fields. So, if you can relieve me of some of the burden, I can devote a little time to my medical practice. And for your studies, I suggest we try a program where you will look after St. Rosalie one year and study medicine the other."

"Father, I could not ask for a more generous plan. And when I have finished my medical studies, I would like to return to St. Rosalie and work with you, both in the fields and in the hospital."

"Thomas you have a career ahead of you. St. Rosalie can offer nothing compared to the bright future you would have in New York."

"And just who would be my patients, Father?"

"I don't understand."

"Do you think the white citizens of New York will have the young colored man, Thomas Durnford, for their doctor?"

"Yes. I had thought they would."

"Things are not like that in the North, Papa. Perhaps they were once, but even David finds his practice limited to the Negro hospital he set up. When I first arrived in New York, Papa, I experienced a joy I had never known before. That joy was because of freedom—freedom to be whatever I wanted to become. And everyone treated me as an equal. I say everyone, but in reality, I must say the white citizens treated me as an equal, because there were no colored men of any stature that I met. But, Papa my joy did not last. My joy was like a fire in the forest, Papa, blazing and beautiful at first, but consuming everything and leaving nothing but charred trees and desolation behind. I soon knew that I was not in the promised land. I never wrote you of these feelings, father, because I wished to offend no one, but a sense of great loss and loneliness, and insecurity came over me in my junior year at Lafayette College and never left. It was at Easton that summer that I met a fugitive slave. He told me all about how he had run away and how many times he had again narrowly escaped being taken back to slavery. The North is full of Southerners, even at New York, who are hired to capture and return slaves to the South. And this fugitive slave who poured out his heart to me because I was but a youth, told me that the colored people in New York were not to be trusted either. Many of them were hired to be on the lookout for fugitive slaves, and would betray him to the slave-catchers for a few dollars."

Thomas paused and stared absently into his wine. "I have been home but a few hours and already it seems so far away and so long ago." He sipped his wine and leaned back in his chair. "I saw this slave again at Easton. It was a year later, and I was just entering the senior class. He had been gone all that time to Ohio and Michigan, looking for work and a place to call his home. But he had given up. He was on his way back to Virginia. He had decided to live in slavery. The rule of his master no longer seemed so harsh when compared to the life of loneliness, hunger and fear that he had known in the North. He also told me that it was perhaps as much his fault as anyone's. He had been a slave all his life. Had he been a free man he might have felt differently. But he had become accustomed to regard every white man as the friend of his master and every colored man as under the control of the white people. And so perhaps he imagined more discrimination than what was actually directed toward him. I never answered him, Papa. I was too overcome with emotion to reply. So I watched him walk away down the street, toward his home and Virginia, knowing that it was really no different for me in the North, even though I was a free man, and the son of a slave owner.

"You are a young man, Thomas, and we have never talked of such things. I agree that change is coming to Louisiana too, and not for our advantage. I find it increasingly difficult to go the city. The hotels I once stayed at are closed to me now. The taverns and restaurants I freely visited will no longer seat me. And this has been the course of history. Thomas, it will surprise you to learn that at one time the black man in England was the equal of the white citizen. I am speaking now of times not long past. Right up to the early part of this century there were in England black gentlemen. And this at a time when the white working class, considered loathsome creatures, could never enter into the class of gentlemen.

"But at the same time, Thomas, there were black slaves in England, as many as thirty thousand. These slaves lived mostly in London as domestic servants, and almost all of them received some education. A few gained their freedom and entered the social ranks. They could do that because of the education and manners they had acquired as servants. Slowly, over the years, the black man fell behind. And do you know why?"

"Well, Papa, they probably became a threat to the whites—started competing for jobs."

"No, Thomas, it was because of slavery."

"Father, I find that difficult to accept. You told me that slavery has existed throughout history, that even blond Englishmen were held as slaves by the Romans. And in all cases, slavery was not a stigma. Freed slaves rose in the social ranks. Now you tell me the same was true of black slaves in England. So, I think you must be wrong, Papa. It must have happened because of inherent racism among the whites."

"Not at all, Thomas. It was assumed human nature was universally the same. The best example I can give you is the law of marriage. In England there was no prohibition against marriage between the races, while it was against the law for Irish Catholics to marry English Protestants. The greatest social event of 1731 was the marriage of an African prince to an English woman. Members of both races served as attendants. The marriage took place in England, and the couple settled there and lived among the highest classes. And there were many other examples of such marriages. But, as I said, slavery existed too. And in response to rising attacks on slavery, its defenders made the first attempt to support the system by claiming the Negroes were an inferior race. Never before had such an idea been proposed. More and more, articles and essays appeared in the scientific journals, claiming inferiority of the black race. It was even claimed that the offspring of a white and black union could not reproduce, just as mules cannot reproduce. In 1772 slavery was finally abolished in England, but the outpouring of unscientific articles continued, because it was still necessary to defend the system in the colonies. It took a long time for prejudice to develop. As late as 1811, Paul Cuffee, a black American ship captain, reported that even the slave traders of Liverpool showed respect to him as a black man of some standing. And as a free black child in New Orleans, long before Louisiana became a part of the United States, I can remember going everywhere without discrimination. But by the time I was your age, Thomas, Louisiana had long been a state and all that had changed drastically. And it has been getting worse every year."

Thomas rose and walked slowly back and forth in front of the cold fireplace. "It is the fault of the North. If they would leave the South alone we could work out our problems. But no, the abolitionists preach hatred of the South and freedom for the Negro slave. The reaction in the North has been terrible for us. The more the abolitionists scream for freedom the more the common man in those cold counties turns against us. And the more the white South is pushed, the more the white South turns against the Negro as well, free or slave. And the more the South defends the system of slavery, the more the South is alienated from the North. There is already talk of secession. New England claims that if this country insists on maintaining slavery, then those pious free states of the North must leave the Union. And that, Papa, we can not permit. And if it happens, Papa, there will be war."

"Well, now, Thomas, those are things we can do nothing about. We were talking about you and your future as a doctor. If New York is not open to you remember that one-fourth of the population of New Orleans are free people of color. These are not poor people, Thomas. These are the people who could be your patients, and so this is where you must start your medical practice. Do not make the mistake I did. Do not let St. Rosalie be too strong a temptation."

"But, Father, I love St. Rosalie. I want to be the good master who works with his people in the fields and as their physician. I want to—"

Just then the door to the library burst open, and Marie-Charlotte, along with her mother, and half a dozen other celebrants pushed into the room in a noisy crowd.

"Andrew, you have had our boy long enough," the old lady said. "And now he's going to tell his granmere all about that school up North."

The celebration did indeed last the weekend and through to the next Tuesday. That morning, in answer to the five o'clock bell, Thomas rode to the fields with his father. "Papa, I have been thinking about the things we discussed. Everything you have done here at St. Rosalie is just the beginning of a long tradition. St. Rosalie will be here a hundred years from now. Both you and I will be long buried. And the plantation will be operated by my grandchildren. Your portrait, the grand patriarch, will hang over the mantle in the library. And that painting I think we must commission soon—"

Andrew Durnford stopped his horse and wheeled about. "Follow me, Thomas. I will show you something."

Father and son rode silently back from the fields and stopped under the oaks on the north side of the mansion, where they waited in the dark.

Finally, as the sun rose over the river and long shafts of light penetrated the darkness, Andrew raised an arm and pointed to the side of the house. "Do you see that, Thomas. It is a long, deep crack, running from the roof to the foundation, and now almost half a foot wide. Look carefully, as you must know it has been patched and painted many times. But it can not be hidden. The crack comes back every year. Each year I fill it in. Noel sees that it is painted over. There is a reason for the crack, Thomas. It is quite simple. The walls are thick and made of heavy brick. But this land floats on a sea of mud, constantly threatened by the river. The land will not support the weight of the building, and soon, within a very few years perhaps, this crack will widen beyond structural integrity, and the building will collapse. Look there, farther along the wall. Do you see those other cracks? Smaller now, but growing too."

Thomas nodded.

"I made a mistake, Thomas. This delicate land will not support such a massive and burdensome structure." Andrew paused for a moment. "And so it is with our peculiar Southern institution. Yes, Thomas, I once said that slavery would last another hundred years. That was about the time when I built this house and thought it would last that long too. I was not much older than you, Thomas. I was mistaken."

Thomas Durnford stayed on at St. Rosalie. Near the end of summer his younger brother, Andrew Jr., was born. The cane was harvested and produced sugar and molasses worth almost $17,000. As Andrew predicted, the loans from the bank were paid and the lien against the slaves discharged. There was money enough. Thomas left to study medicine in New York.

The following summer Thomas returned to the plantation as head overseer. He supervised a renovation of the sugarhouse and installation of new boilers, each twenty-eight feet long. New fields were added to the plantation inventory and planted with corn and peas and other vegetables. Germans were hired on a regular basis, the strongest Andrew could find, to supplement his slave force.

In the fall, St. Rosalie sent to John McDonogh a cart of sixty pumpkins, the best the plantation had produced, and a barrel of the best and ripest oranges. Thomas added two pair of water hens (*poule d'eau*).

Then Thomas took the train to New York to begin his second year of medical studies.

The week that Thomas left, Dr. Dumont of Algiers came down to St. Rosalie with his family and was soon followed by Judge Marian of New Orleans and his wife and three daughters. Dr. Dumont came as a convalescent to spend a few days. Judge Marian came with his family to escape the fever that plagued the Cresent City. Both families were white and members of the French Creole class in Louisiana. Both families were also long-time friends of the Durnfords.

Financial disaster struck St. Rosalie in 1848. Andrew blamed the cold and wet weather and wrote Thomas that it had ruined the sugar cane, which yielded only 45 hogsheads. The truth was, however, that the weather was not the only cause of the failure. Andrew suffered from a great depression after his son left. He made mistakes, and misjudged the time for cutting. Then he let the cane lay in the mud and water too long before grinding. Since there was no shortage of the crop, the price of sugar fell to $40 per hogshead, and the plantation received only $1,800 for the entire crop.

The corn survived Andrew's neglect.

Andrew Durnford made a special trip to New Orleans and purchased twenty barrels of the cheapest cuts of pork jowls he could find for the sum of $105.00. And all the residents of St. Rosalie, the Durnford family and all the slaves, survived the winter on hominy, corn meal, and pork jowls.

The next year was not much better. Andrew Durnford had lost all interest in the plantation and his attitude affected everyone. With no one to push them, the labor force made only the motions of work. Weeds grew with the cane. The weather, however, was kinder. But still, St. Rosalie produced only 55 hogsheads for a total income of $3,052.00. The cracks in the aging mansion spread. Andrew ordered them patched with stucco and painted to match. The few dollars Andrew had, he spent for a bundle of whitewash brushes and cheap paint, and a few necessities. The entries in the plantation journal show that St. Rosalie purchased on account with the steamboats plying the river that fall: 2 bags of shot, 1 box of cigars, 5 barrels of flour, 2 barrels of lard, 4 ploughs, 2 bags of peas, a coop of chickens, 1 bundle of red ochre, 2 oil candles, 1 box of soap, 1/2 keg of powder, 1 basket of sweet oil, 2 bologna saussengers, 1 bale of cotton ecru, 1 bundle of chocolate, 5 barrels of mackerel, 1 box of bananas, a coil of rope, brooms, and chewing tobacco.

But there was no money for medical studies, and Andrew sent Thomas a letter, telling him to come home.

# Chapter Thirty

With only a year remaining to complete his medical studies, Thomas Durnford left New York to again become the overseer at the plantation. Arriving by train in New Orleans on a rainy morning in February, Thomas rented a bay mare from the livery stable, crossed the Mississippi on the ferry, and rode hard down the River Road to St. Rosalie. He entered the plantation through a gate at the north. A few slaves wearing long coats roamed aimlessly about the wet fields. Others leaned on their hoes in the light rain. Thomas shouted to them and they waved back as he cantered along the narrow plantation roads between the weed-covered fields.

The main ditches along the roads were clogged with brush and debris, and the smaller ditches running from the fields were completely filled in with dirt and refuse from earlier crops. Dead weeds stood everywhere in the muddy fields.

Thomas took his horse straight to the stable, gave orders to two sullen slave boys there to wipe down the mare, and then went to the main house, and searched the empty rooms and halls. Finally entering the servants' parlor at the rear of the house, he found Noel working on the plantation accounts before a crackling fire in the fireplace and smoking a thin cigar. Noel, the frail old slave, manager of the plantation accounts, a man of light skin and caucasian features, and Thomas, the young Negro with rugged features, a free man of color and son of the plantation owner, embraced as friends and equals.

They sat down together around the desk, and Noel explained that Marie-Charlotte had gone with her mother to visit the Remy family up in the Cane River Colony. She had taken little Andrew, Jr. and Rosema with her. Thomas was not expected at

St. Rosalie for another week.

Noel continued with his work while they talked. "You went right past your Papa, Thomas. He's up at the Knox property. A slave there fell on the saw at the sawmill last week. Cut his arm pretty bad, and Master Andrew returned last night to finally amputate the limb."

"I came down through the fields, Noel." Thomas paused and shook his head. "I see a great deal of neglect. No drainage. These rains will ruin all the crops."

Noel laid down his pen and closed the journal into which he had been entering figures from a pile of papers at his elbow. He took a long, careful puff on his little cigar, and leaned back from the desk. "Yes. I know. My responsibilities end at the door of this room, and I seldom go to the fields anymore. But I can not help but see the direction in which everything is going. Your father has little interest in St. Rosalie, Thomas. I, his old and humble servant, am not the one to criticize. But unless things change this year, and change quickly, St. Rosalie will not survive. We can have no more years of these heavy losses."

"What has happened to Papa, Noel? He was always such a hard worker."

Noel took another careful puff on his cigar, and replied slowly, "Never repeat to anyone what I tell you, Thomas. Do you promise me that?"

"Yes, certainly."

"One day just before Christmas, when we were still rolling some of last year's cane, your father went with the wood cutters to collect firewood. He said he needed the exercise and wanted to swing an axe. When he came back his clothes were covered with mud. He told Miss Remy that he'd slipped on a log and fell down. I think she believed him. But I did not. Master Andrew's face was ashen, Thomas, whiter than the face of his own father. And he breathed with great difficulty. For many nights after that, he could not sleep. I think he must have pretended sleep to fool your mother, and then he would slip down to the parlor where I often found him slouching in a chair. He did not sleep well in that chair, and his breathing was hard and rough. Sometimes his eyes would snap open and he would be awake, and yet he never recognized that I was in the room. Then he would drop his head again and doze off. For weeks he seemed to be utterly exhausted, Thomas, but always bracing up and putting on a good show whenever your mother was about."

"Noel, Papa is an old man, and he has had a stroke or a heart seizure."

"It's his heart, Thomas. One day, I went to see him at the infirmary...we needed some iron to patch one boiler. He'd left his coat on a peg in the outer office, and while he was at one of the beds, looking after a patient with Wainy, I searched his pockets. I found what I was looking for. It was a small, capped bottle I'd seen him with many times. I tasted it and in it was the bitter powder he extracts from the stems and leaves of the Foxglove plant. It was the same medicine he'd made up for old Pierre Jean Pierre, just before he died."

Thomas nodded. "Of course, it is his heart then. But how is he now? You said he is at the Knox place, to do an amputation. It takes a great deal of strength to hold down a man, and strength and speed to cut through the bone, even with others helping."

"Wainy is with him. She knows his condition, even though she says nothing. She has become very protective of him, Thomas, and because of her, the way she looks after him, I think we can be assured that he has the best possible chance of a good recovery. Already now he has shown much improvement. I no longer find him in the parlor at night. Although I am not certain that he...."

"Not certain about what, Noel?"

"Ah.... Not certain that he will ever become his old self again."

Thomas studied Noel's face carefully, then said slowly and deliberately, "As I said, he is an old man. We can not expect him to be restored to his prior vigor."

Thomas took over again at St. Rosalie and using Irish labor, which had become cheaper following a wave of immigration to Louisiana, Thomas had the ditches dug and cleaned. One of the Irishmen, digging in the cold mud, water and rain, came down with the fever and died in the plantation hospital. The dead worker was buried in the plantation cemetery and the $11.00 due him for wages was given to his family. Had a slave been used in that dangerous work and died, St. Rosalie would have been out at least $800.00.

Thomas watched his father gain in strength. He was certain the old man had suffered a heart attack, massive and severe. He rested whenever he had the opportunity, and let Thomas run the plantation. Wainy ran the hospital. She covered for him while he took naps in the little cot in the medical office at the front of the hospital.

As Thomas suspected from Noel's unintentional slip, Andrew no longer slept at night with Marie-Charlotte. Both parents understood they were too old to risk any further pregnancy. Andrew took one of the guest rooms for his bedroom so that he would not disturb his wife, and this move was kept a secret from the house servants, all of whom soon knew the true situation, as house servants always do, and the house servants also knew when Andrew moved one bedroom farther, into

Wainy's room. Wainy, a child of seven years when Durnford bought her in Virginia, and now twenty-three years old, had become the mistress of her master.

Each day since his return from New York, Thomas rode to the fields at the ringing of the five o'clock bell, without his father. He returned each day after dark with the field hands. By summer, Thomas was satisfied that the plantation fields were once again in good order. In August when Andrew suggested a short respite from the oppressive heat and humidity, Thomas agreed. The planting had been done. All the hoeing was done. The slaves could manage under the care of the field drivers for a week.

The family boarded the steam packet *Doswell* at the St. Rosalie dock. Under the command of Alphonse Larose, a free man of color, known to be young in years but old in experience, they sailed up the Mississippi River to New Orleans. After landing in New Orleans, Andrew took his family straight to the Whitehall, an oyster room and coffeehouse at No. 44 St. Louis Street, just opposite the Exchange, one of the few saloons in the city still open to people of color. It was owned by an Englishman who avoided no sacrifice that would contribute to the enjoyment of his patrons. The Whitehall consisted of two large rooms. The first was a billiard room and bar, and connected to it was a dining room. Both rooms were decorated by local artists who painted scenes from the city and river on the white plaster walls. Although it was two o'clock in the afternoon when the Durnford family arrived, the restaurant was still cool because of its thick masonry walls and brick floor. There were no windows to let in the August heat. Gas lamps illuminated the interior and reflected from the white ceilings.

The waiters were polite and prompt and soon the Durnfords had consumed a sizeable quantity of the best oysters that could be had in Louisiana and were well fortified with liquors of the finest quality. Neither Andrew nor Marie-Charlotte were fond of liquor or any of the whiskeys for which Thomas had developed a taste, but in view of the ordeal they faced at the next stop, both parents drank well beyond their capacity. Thomas, on the other hand, remained quite sober, and with Rosema and Andrew, Jr., in tow, he led his parents to No. 196 Bourbon Street, where he left them, and took the children for a walk around the old city.

Andrew held Marie-Charlotte's hand, and they stood there for a moment on Bourbon Street, between St. Peter and Orleans, and finally, with each taking a deep breath for courage, the two entered the door of Dr. Duperon.

Dr. Duperon was a small man with a small moustache, and extremely large, muscular arms. He bowed to them with his large hands clasped in front as they entered.  "Durnford?"

Andrew nodded.

"And then who should be first?"

"I shall be the first to submit," Andrew said reluctantly.

"Well then good.  Now if you will just remove your coat and shirt and take a seat here in this chair.  That's it.  Good.  Good.  Lean back.  Ah.  Only a moment, you see, let me get this buckle here."  And as Dr. Duperon spoke, he pulled straps across Durnfords chest and arms and lap, and cinched them tight.

With his foot pumping furiously, the dentist leaned over Andrew with a drill connected to a long shaft held tightly in his hand.  "Now open wide, Dr. Durnford. This won't take but a moment."

The promised moment lasted nearly forty-five minutes, and during that time Dr. Duperon, who had learned the new method of drilling and filling teeth, patched three of Andrew's molars and pulled two others he finally pronounced beyond hope of salvation, all while Andrew screamed and withered.

When the good dentist had finished, Andrew staggered out the door, leaving Marie-Charlotte to battle alone, and swore never to return.  In the past, the plantation blacksmith, the biggest and strongest man at St. Rosalie, had simply pulled any decayed tooth with a pair of tongs. Andrew now knew he preferred that short and swift procedure to the unbearable grinding of a steel drill against the raw nerves in his mouth.

Marie-Charlotte emerged stunned and dazed about twenty minutes later, and announced that she had two teeth filled but would never undergo the procedure again.  Hand-in-hand, husband and wife went down Bourbon St. to Esplanade, where they turned toward the river to meet their children.

They boarded the train for Lake Ponchartrain at six o'clock.  That evening they stayed at a cottage near the waterfront and ate at a small restaurant serving free black people.  At eight o'clock in the morning, they left with the steamer *Olivia* and enjoyed a fish breakfast while they crossed the lake to the north shore.  Their destination was Bachelors' Hall at Mandeville, opposite the Main Wharf.

Bachelors' Hall was an odd name for the resort, Andrew thought, because it was really a family resort, open to both whites and free people of color.  Originally, it was a fashionable resort with accommodations for single gentlemen.  It had a restaurant, saloon, and billiard room, and was frequented by the highest classes of society.  It was also rumored that Bachelors' Hall had at one time provided escort service for bachelors, both real and pretended, who so desired.  But now with the railroad running at almost forty miles an hour, most of the city's gentlemen preferred to escape the August heat and humidity by traveling farther along the coast or even to the cities in the North for their entertainment.

Andrew had suggested the family vacation on Lake Ponchartrain as an escape from the oppressive heat down river. But the reason he wished a retreat had nothing to do with the weather. His affair with Wainy had taken a turn he had not expected. He had fallen in love with her. Then she asked him whether a child of theirs could ever be free. He was struck down almost immediately by that terrible searing pain which came with the overpowering odor of musk and had been unable to give her the answer: any child born to a slave, even the child of the master, could never be free.

On the afternoon of the second day at Bachelors' Hall, while Marie-Charlotte walked the beach with the children, Andrew bent over the billiard table and banked for the lead. Thomas followed, and announced that he had won since his ball had rebounded the closet to the starting edge of the billiard table. Andrew took his cue stick to check the distances, when a voice behind him said, "Juz so. The young man wins."

"Jules. Jules Toussaint. It is you, isn't it?"

"You is juz right, Misty Andrew. It is I, Jules. And this young man is the Thomas?"

"Yes. Yes. This is my son, Thomas."

Thomas and Jules, the agent who had sold Barba many years before, shook hands.

"Jules, it has been many years and your hair and your mustache have gone all white, but still I can recognize you by the light in your eye," Andrew said. "How do you come to be here?"

"I thing I see again Bachelors' Hall am dream of old times. Hof course, nothing as it was, 'cept for perhaps theze billiard."

"Join us, Jules. You can play the winner."

"Am to what number do you play?"

"Eleven."

"Yass," said Jules, "dat is sure-sure good number. I play."

Thomas chose the white as his cue ball, and placed the black at the foot of the table and the red ball at the head of the table to begin the game. Thomas took careful aim. He fired his ball at the far cushion, where it rebounded and struck the red ball, driving it into the black.

"Thaas one point for Thomas," Jules said.

Thomas carefully lined up his cue stick. A second time he hit the red ball, forcing it off a cushion and into the black. Now he had two points. Carefully, cautiously, Thomas continued, and luck was with him. He drove the black ball into the red, then the red ball into the black. Before he finally missed, he had nine points.

Then Andrew took over and scored a point. He missed the next shot, and Thomas shot two quick points to win the game.

"Now I know what you did with your time at college," Andrew said.

As Thomas played Jules, both men shooting alternately and being careful not to leave the other a clean shot, a man walked up behind Andrew and watched the play. When Thomas had won again, the man spoke up. "Jules, you fox, let us teach these people humility." The man who spoke was thin and dressed in a light gray suit and tie.

Jules introduced the new man as James Wagner of the *Lousiana Courier*.

"We subscribe to your paper, sir, and a fine publication it is, the best in the city," Andrew said.

"Well I'm glad to see our circulation extends to the West Bank."

"You know of St. Rosalie?"

"Certainly, Dr. Durnford. There are only a few Negro plantation owners of any substance in these parts. How many slaves do you have now at St. Rosalie?"

"Eighty-six."

Wagner nodded. "Yes, that is a good number. And what do you think of this hue and cry against slavery coming out of the North?"

"Mr. Wagner, you are talking about a subject I seldom discuss, and would never engage in for publication."

"Oh, Durnford, now you should know better than that. I am not about to publish what I discuss with you, I could not even admit in print that I talked to you. A Negro slave owner? No. No. We would never print that. In fact, no one on our staff, no one in our free-thinking city, for that matter, will ever admit that such a person as you exists."

"Less us not to waste the day," Jules said. "I choose the boy, Thomas for my partner. Because he the moz good shot I ever see. Ha! ha! I swear I thing you both fools to play uz fo the money."

"I am sorry, I could not play for money," Andrew said. "Even though it might stay in the family on this paring."

"*Mais bien,* you moz smart man, Andrew. We juz play to make fun the game."

Andrew Durnford and Thomas were given the honor of banking for the lead. Andrew won. But he missed the first shot, where it was necessary to drive the red ball into the other player's cue ball, a shot Jules made look easy. But when Jules finally missed after seven points, Wagner took over and ran up fourteen straight points. They had agreed on one hundred as the goal, a number which Andrew thought unreasonably large, but now admitted was not out of the question, as his partner, James Wagner was clearly the best of the four players.

They talked for a long time about the weather and the history of Bachelors' Hall, and how the city had grown and would grow further, avoiding politics and issues of race or slavery, when Thomas finally said, "If the growth of our city is tied to the Mississippi River trade, you must have some strong opinions about the Union, Mr. Wagner."

Andrew winced. Thomas was again in areas he should steer clear from.

Wagner, who was about to take a shot, rested his cue on the floor and looked up at Thomas. I am as strongly opposed to the dismemberment of the Union as anyone can possibly be. And so is everyone on the editorial staff of the *Courier.* We have constantly advocated preservation of the Union. Yes, as Old Hickory said, 'The Union must and shall be preserved.' But, what the North does not understand is we do not desire to maintain the Union at the peril and expense of the South." Wagner's voice rose a little higher in pitch and he tapped the floor with his cue stick for emphasis. "We do not believe in compelling the South to give up its rights to the tyranny of the North...to...to prostrate itself to the Yankees until the South is despoiled of every inch of ground where slavery can be preserved. No. No. We are in favor of the Union, young man, but as Southern men, we have some duties to perform—some sacred rights to defend—rights guaranteed by the constitution of the Untied States, the palladium of our liberty! We know our duty—and as Southern men, we understand our rights."

When Wagner stopped talking. He took a deep breath, fired his cue stick, and missed his shot. Thomas, next in line for his team, studied the table carefully. "And what is your opinion of the Clay compromise, Mr. Wagner."

Andrew Durnford spoke up quickly. "Thomas was a member of the Franklin Society at college, Mr. Wagner. It was a debating team. At times his competitive nature gets the best of him. Now I think we should enjoy our sport here and—"

"Oh no. No, Durnford. I am interested in your boy's opinions. I want to know what the new generation of free people think of our slavery issue."

Thomas, still studying the lay of the table, glanced up and said, "We are the sons of our fathers'. But I am not certain the fugitive slave bill is a good idea."

"The passage of the fugitive slave law has created panic among the blacks in the North. This I know from our correspondent newspapers. Upwards of three hundred fugitive slaves left Pittsburgh alone for Canada within a few days. But, Thomas, I think after six months have lapsed, all the excitement will be gone and forgotten. By that time, most of the runaways will have been captured or fled to Canada. And in the future, there will be but few attempts to abscond, as the slaves are already well aware that the thing cannot be accomplished. And that will be so much the better for the slaves themselves, their masters, and the people of the northern states."

Andrew Durnford stepped back from the table and rubbed his face. "Thomas, please, it is enough." His old headache, massive and over-powering, was returning. "Mr. Wagner, I am sorry, but all this talk of slavery disturbs me. Can we not just have our game, here?"

"Yass, yass, Misty James. *C'est* very true. *Mais,* we talk not pleasant things, den de game not so pleasant more."

"So you wish to escape the truth by ignoring it?"

"Misty James, why you wanting talk 'bout miserabl' tings like dat? Me, if I should talk such miserabl' tings, den I would kill meself."

"Well, Jules, it is the talk of the day. And Durnford, here, must have some interest in these important questions. Right now he is a free man of color. Rich and powerful. If the North would have it's way, all his slaves would be free. St. Rosalie plantation would perish. Durnford and his boy would no longer be free men of color. They would simply be colored people, along with thousands of others."

Andrew Durnford had never thought that way about a South without slavery. The picture Wagner had just painted, a picture of the Durnford family wandering the countryside with thousands of other Negroes, all poor and equal, was a description of the future he could not accept. "Thomas, take your shot," Andrew said sternly.

"Just remember the toast that Jackson made when he was installed in the presidential office," Wagner continued. "Jackson said then, 'The union of the States—it must and shall be preserved.' There were plotters and disunionists there at that dinner. Old Hickory's toast fell upon them like a shock of thunder, and it showed he was aware of their scheming mischief and determined to suppress them, cost what it might. And I, like all good people of Louisiana, Thomas, prize the

Union.  It is for the security it has afforded us, and you and your father, as Southern slave holders.  It has proved its faith and strength for seventy years, and if the great mass of thinking men in this country will, as they can, control fanaticism and disunion, I will trust it for seventy times seventy.  Twenty years have passed since that nullification assault on the Union, Thomas.  We were told then that it was a curse; that we were slaves in it, and we could never prosper until the Union was dissolved and the South went its own way.  But at no period of our history has the South prospered more than during the last twenty years.  Our Union has been bound together by the railroad, Thomas, and made literally one body.  The southern limb that would be severed from it will surely wither and die."

Thomas carefully took his shot and missed.  "The Fugitive Slave bill is the worst thing that ever happened to this country," he said to Wagner.  "We got along for years without it, and the few slaves who escaped to the North were never really missed.  But now North turns against South, South turns against North, and everywhere white people turn against black people.  And all of this is a direct result of this stupid bill of Congress which allows allows us to go north, swear out a complaint, and force the local sheriff to arrest and return our slave."

"My God, boy, what would you have us do—abandon our property?"

"But in the North they do not understand slavery as we understand it.  They do not consider an escaped slave to be property!"

"Not property!  Those hippocrates!  More than twenty-five million dollars of the public debt of the United States has been collected by levying on slaves as property! Not a year passes in which creditors from the North do not coerce payments of their debts from Southerners by executions upon slaves—they buy them—separate them from their families–remove them to distant markets to command higher prices—one of the most cruel of all the exaggerated ills imputed to slavery, Thomas!"  Wagner had thrown his cue stick on the table while he railed against Thomas, and now he wagged his finger in the boy's face.  "Over the last twenty years of anti-slavery agitation there have been thirty thousand abolition petitions submitted to Congress—thirty thousand, Thomas, and not one of them asked for repeal of the law permitting executions against slaves for the satisfaction of debts!"

Jules threw his hands to his head and retreated from the billiard table.  "These is moz distress," he said, "Pleez, pleez, Thomas—Misty James—talk no more on these."

Andrew also backed from the table and sat down in a straight-backed chair with his cue stick in his lap.  His headache was overpowering and thundered against his skull. He felt weak and sick. The voice of his son banged against his brain.

"But we must do something before the entire white race turns against us and drives all Negroes from the country," Thomas said to Wagner.

"Well, that is indeed a joke, Thomas. What would you have us do?"

"Why can't Congress buy the freedom of the escaped slaves—spread the burden among all the citizens?"

"Thomas, what did you learn in college? That is precisely what the northern states did not do. Slavery was abolished—but the existing slaves stayed. None of the northern states bought them freedom. With all their pretended abhorrence of slavery—and what they profess to regard as the revolting admixture of free and slave labor in the same State—behold! They would not vote a single dollar for the riddance of their States from the crime and curse of slavery! As late as our last census in 1840, there were thousands of slaves still in the North, in New York, and New Jersey, and Pennsylvania, and elsewhere. And why? Because they had not died yet, Thomas. Only death liberated them from slavery in the free North!"

"Thomas," Andrew gasped. "Thomas...." And then he fell from his chair to the floor.

# Chapter Thirty One

Thomas rushed to his fallen father and put his hand on the old man's head. Andrew's face was pale. Thomas felt his pulse—weak.

Just then, Andrew opened his eyes. "Thomas, take me upstairs."

"I will, Papa. As soon as I can rig a stretcher."

"No, Thomas, you will not carry me upstairs on a stretcher. Now help me to my feet."

"Papa do not be so foolish. This is not the time to tax yourself."

Andrew leaned on an elbow, than sat up. "I am getting up, Thomas, whether you help me or not. And if I fall, it will be your fault."

"All right, Papa. Here, take my hand."

"Good," Andrew said when he was on his feet. "Now if you gentlemen will excuse us, my son will help me to my room."

"No *bien,* Misty Andrew. It is meestake. Listen to the boy."

"Good bye, Jules. Good bye Mr. Wagner. I'm sorry to leave you in this condition, but I will be fine."

With Thomas supporting his father, the two men struggled up the stairs of Bachelors' Hall to the Durnford rooms.

"Papa, you are going to kill yourself for sure," Thomas said as they reached the landing. "At least have the wisdom to rest here."

"Thomas, I will ignore that remark. Now get me through the door."

They shuffled down the hall and into the room, and Thomas sat his father on the bed and lifted his feet from the floor. "Now lie down, Papa. You are lucky to be alive."

"What do you know?"

"I know more than you think. I am on my way to be a medical man too, Papa."

"Well the first thing you should learn is that a little knowledge can be a danger-ous thing. It was necessary to get me up here as soon as possible. Now reach into my bag over there and bring me the small bottle in the side pocket."

Thomas pulled out the bottle, uncapped it, tapped white powder into his palm, and tasted it. He recognized immediately the bitter taste. "Foxglove, Papa. So, it is your heart."

"Thomas, you take too many liberties with me. Now give me the bottle."

Andrew took a pinch of the white powder from the bottle, slid it under his tongue, and lay back on his pillow. His breathing was very shallow and his face still ashen.

"You have all the symptoms of a bad heart, Papa. I know at least that much."

"Then get the sounding instrument from my bag and bring it here, Thomas, and we will continue your medical education."

The stethoscope was made of rolled paper with leather cups on each end, and lacquered for stability. Andrew made it himself at St. Rosalie. "Put the instrument on my chest, Thomas—right here." And when Thomas did so and put his ear to the instrument, Andrew asked, "What do you hear."

Thomas listened for a long time. "I do not understand, Papa."

"My heart is as strong as a mule."

"Then why the Foxglove for these many months?"

"Ah, you have been listening to that old rascal, Noel. He doesn't think I saw him snooping in my pocket at the infirmary. Well, Thomas, I do not take the Foxglove for my heart—it is for these terrible pains that sweep through my head. For many years all I needed was a bleeding now and then. But it no longer has much effect. I have tried every other remedy mentioned in the literature. But only the Foxglove seems to help. My problem is too much water in the blood—it expands the volume beyond my capacity, and that is what the Foxglove relieves."

"How long have you had this condition, Papa?"

"More than these past twenty years, Thomas. For a long period, I was free of the condition. But now it has returned."

"And you have no idea what causes it?"

"None. The attack starts with a strong aroma of incense, and I believe that is from pressure at the rear of the nose. From there, the massive and relentless pain takes over. Sometimes it lasts for a week, and I just do my best to go about business in spite of it. At times it's worse than others. This one is a major attack. The strong smell of incense overwhelms me. The pain hammers behind my eyes. But with the Foxglove, all will go slowly better now."

"I should get Mama."

"No, you should not get your mother. And she is not to know. Understand?"

Thomas nodded.

In spite of the pain which surged in Andrew's skull, a condition he kept well hidden from his wife, the Durnfords stayed on at Bachelors' Hall. They enjoyed the cooler climate of the north shore of Lake Ponchartrain, and rented an open carriage for excursions into the countryside. They visited Madisonville on the Thcefuncte River, Covington to the north, and travelled east along the lakeshore to the town formed by John Slidell, a lawyer from New York City. At the end of the week, they returned to St. Rosalie, where, in the warm embrace of Wainy, Andrew's massive headaches retreated at last.

Though there was peace at St. Rosalie there was turmoil throughout the nation. The Civil War was still more than ten years away. But already the northern resistance to the fugitive slave law had fanned the flames of hatred throughout the country. "It is happening," Andrew said to his wife and son in the parlor of their mansion on the river that fall. Listen to this from the *Courier:* "The Abolition fanatics, failing in their efforts to destroy the Union through legislation, have gone home from Washington to stir up rebellion among their particular friends and allies—the Negroes. The Free States are filled with runaway slaves who are encouraged in their insolent and rebellious course by men with white skins, but whose hearts are blacker than the skin of the verlest Congo. Men high in office openly encourage opposition to the laws of the land. We are no disunionists. We have stood by the Union. We have battled for it with all our souls, looking to it as the great palladium of our safety—" Andrew paused. "Does that sound familiar?"

"Yes," said Thomas. "Those are the very words of our good friend Mr Wagner."

"Mr. Wagner?" Marie-Charlotte said.

"Oh he is a man of no consequence, Miss Remy. Just a man we played a little billiards with at Mandeville."

And then Andrew continued reading from the newspaper: "We have battled for the Union with all our souls. But, if this spirit of abolition is tolerated by our people—if the Negroes in our midst are encouraged in rebellion, it requires no prophet to foretell the disruption of this mighty empire, and scenes of strife and bloodshed. Our hearts are filled with sorrow and shame at the bare thought of it."

Andrew put down the paper.

"To God we never had the Fugitive Slave Law," Thomas said. "I no longer see any hope for this country. The more the abolitionists rave against the law and block its enforcement, the more determined is the South to see that slaves are captured and returned under it. It was far better to have a few slaves escape our grasp than to have North turn against South and South turn against North, and white men everywhere turn against the Negro, free or slave."

"Thomas, you should be ashamed of yourself to talk so," Marie-Charlotte said sternly. "How are we to ever get our property back without such laws?"

"Mother you live here at St. Rosalie as in a cocoon."

"Do not talk so disrespectful to me, Thomas. Is that what they taught you at college? " She shifted her penetrating gaze to the master of St. Rosalie. "Andrew, set the boy straight and show him the error of his thinking."

"Thomas is right, Miss Remy. Because of this law, war between the North and South will come. It is already too much in the air. And the effect is as Thomas states, the more the abolitionists support the plight of the slave, the more the white man turns against the Negro, slave or free, North or South. But it goes beyond the Fugitive Slave Law. It is the institution of slavery itself that is splitting our nation."

"Well, Andrew, surely you are not against slavery?"

"Yes, Miss Remy. I have reached that level of understanding of humanity. I no longer embrace our beloved system, but I know not how to escape it."

"I am sorry to here you speak so, Andrew. My family have owned people for three generations. The entire Cane River Colony, over fifty black-owned plantations, owes its existence to slavery. And I might let you know, Andrew, that a few of them were once slaves themselves. It hurts me so for you to attack the memory of my father, and his father, and his father before him."

"I know, Miss Remy. It hurts me too."

Andrew Durnford was careful never to discuss the issue in the presence of Marie-Charlotte again. She was related to almost every slave-owner on the banks of the old Red River. They were her cousins and her uncles, and her brothers too. Most of them owned as many slaves as he did.

Throughout the month of October, the *Courier* continued its attack upon the abolitionists, who continued their attack against the Fugitive Slave Law. In the issue of October 17, 1850, the *Courier* stated: "The Abolition papers are lashing themselves into convulsions over the Fugitive Slave bill. The movements of the South indicate a growing purpose on the part of the Southern people to submit no longer to this perpetual war on their institutions. The Northern agitators perceive this with gratification—Southern resistance to their insolent schemes, they expect, will precipitate a dissolution of the Union. But before this shall happen, they and their fugitive slaves, and every African within our borders, will be driven from the country."

Andrew was in the library, reading to Thomas.

"Damn those abolitionists," Thomas said. "They have ruined what little good will existed between the races. Why can't they just leave us alone?"

Andrew looked up from his paper. "But then I wonder, Thomas, will there ever be any change without strife? Can that fellow in Cincinnati who sold his plantation in Kentucky and set free his slaves to take up the cause of abolition be so wrong? It was a great sacrifice, Thomas, it cost him his life when a white mob burned his office and threw his press into the Ohio."

"And we escaped, didn't we, Papa?"

"Yes. We escaped."

"We escaped with all our slaves."

"Thomas, are you mocking me?"

"No, Papa. I am not mocking you. I am only thinking out loud." Thomas stood up and slid his book back into its place on a shelf next to the fireplace. Then he turned to look at his father. "Papa, we have been good to our people, and they have been good to us. I go through the fields without fear, because I know they love me as they love you. What will happen if you sell them St. Rosalie, my rightful inheritance? Noel is too old to run it. He knows nothing about leading the field crews. And you certainly don't expect me to work for them as overseer."

"Well, Thomas that is what I had in mind. Without your cooperation, how can it work?"

"Papa, I can not believe you are asking this of me!"

"But I am, Thomas. And I must have your pledge of support."

"Father, I will support you to the ends of the earth in anything you want to do— but not this—I can not become a slave to our own people. Yes. Yes. I know you think that is a strong term. But it is what you ask. I must stay on as overseer, or field manager, or general manager, or whatever it shall be called. That is what you ask me to pledge. I would be no freer than Noel is today."

"Noel can buy his freedom any day. He has had the money for years, and the cheap rascal refuses to make the expenditure."

"Well, then I would be worse off than Noel, for he has that option which you would deny to me."

Andrew Durnford sighed. "I am sorry that you feel this way, Thomas. It makes me very sad."

Andrew said nothing more to Thomas about the subject until a week later when they were returning from the fields on horseback. "Well, Thomas," he said, "have you read yesterday's *Courier?*"

"Papa, I am no longer interested in reading about the Northern attacks against slavery."

"Well, I am sorry, then, Thomas. But if you would read it, you would learn that even God is on your side."

When they returned to the house, Thomas went to the library, lit the oil lamp, and unfolded the newspaper on his father's desk. On the front page was another article on anti-slavery fanaticism. The article contained the usual blasts against the abolitionists and Negroes in general, and then, about half-way down the page, Thomas saw what his father had meant: "Anti-slavery denunciation wages perpetual war against the very prophecies of God. God's Bible records the Divine ordinance which instituted the condition of slavery among men, and decreed it to extend and endure down to the remotest generations; how can the same mind believe that slavery is a sin, and that God who established it is sinless! Christianity teaches that in these great truths originated the memorable African slave trade several centuries ago—and all Christendom was reconciled to the extradition of the slaves, because, while fully concordant with the scriptural prophecy—it civilized, and christianized, and greatly bettered the condition of the enslaved—and no one has ever denied that the conditions of slaves here is ten thousand times better than that of the heathenish and God-forsaken natives of Africa."

Andrew came into the library while Thomas was reading. "Well, Thomas, what do you think of that?"

"I agree with it, Papa."

"You can't agree with it, Thomas."

"But I do. It is the same thing Dr. Junkins taught us at Lafayette College."

Andrew shook his head and sat down in a chair in front of the fireplace. "Thomas, the Old Testament cannot be taken literally—"

"It is the word of God, Papa."

Waving a hand at the newspaper on the desk in front of Thomas, Andrew said,

"Well, Thomas, if you believe what's printed there it would not surprise me to hear you say you are a member of an inferior race."

"Do you refer to the scientific studies on brain size?"

"Exactly."

"Well, Papa, I am half white and half black, as are you and Mama. I owe my intelligence to my Caucasian heritage, which is dominant, and I owe my strength and agility to our African races. I am the best of both races, and superior to each."

Andrew burst out laughing. "Thomas, you talk nonsense."

"No, it is true, Papa. I am the tallest and strongest man on the plantation. I contested our smithy and put him on the ground in minutes. And yet I have a superior intellect from our European ancestors."

"Oh, Thomas, you can be such a fool."

"Laugh if you will, Papa. But you can not deny the scientific studies on intelligence."

"Oh, yes I can," said Andrew, as he got up and walked to the library door. "I can prove them wrong. I am tempted to do so. But it would require cutting off your head and emptying it of that jellied mass to establish that the capacity of your cranium is less than the volume held by the skull of our dear departed Barba." And having said that, Andrew left and slammed the door behind him.

It was only a few months after the birth of Andrew Jr. that Marie-Charlotte had closed her door. She knew it would come to that. Andrew had pledged fidelity forever. But Marie-Charlotte knew that with a man like Andrew fidelity forever would never last.

Almost fifty, Marie-Charlotte was yet a woman of natural beauty. Her body remained strong and trim. She was still capable of child-bearing, but the risk of another birth was out of the question. Although not the near-death experience she'd had with Rosama, Andrew Jr.'s birth had been extremely difficult.

The mansion on the river was as silent as the oak's shadow on the lawn during the fall nights. Every whisper, every cough, echoed down the halls. Late at night she heard the boards creak under Andrew's weight, and then the soft sound of Wainy's door closing behind him. Before dawn, the floor creaked again as Andrew returned to his bed.

For months, Marie-Charlotte had spent those nights in silent tears. But then came acceptance. At least Andrew was cautious, if not successful in hiding his nocturnal adventures. Marie-Charlotte realized that if she knew, then all the servants knew as well. None of the night sounds escaped the household. Late at night, Marie-Charlotte had even heard Noel's pen scrape paper as he bent over the small desk in his room, writing to his love in New Orleans. She was married, Noel's love, but would never leave her husband. What did Noel, a slave, have to offer a free woman of color married to the owner of a dry-goods store on Rue Dumaine. And how silly these secret lovers were, Marie-Charlotte thought, what they did was plain and simple for all to see, but they went about their imprudent business as if the world were blind. Every time she and Noel went to the city, she to shop and he to buy provisions for the plantation, Noel always stopped at the bookstore where he first met his lover. And although Noel was a prodigious reader, she never believed he read every book he bought, they were merely the vehicle used to pass to the clerk a letter or note for his beloved. There were those rare times too, when the object of Noel's interest was also in the bookstore, and at those times Noel was all feet and clumsy and nervous and bought the most inappropriate titles such as the *Secrets of Gardening in Southern France*, a topic which Marie-Charlotte knew interested the scholarly Noel not in the least.

People were people, Marie-Charlotte believed. They were not made of wood. And so she was jealous of Wainy, so many years younger, and she was angry with Andrew for being nothing but a man after all. But she understood her jealously and understood her anger and understood them both. She was also happy it was Wainy, and not one of the common slaves. Wainy was intelligent and uncommonly simple. She had also survived her own tragic love.

Wainy's first love had been a slave on one of the plantations across the river, the estate of Christian Pollerian. The slave's name was Reuben and he fell in love with Wainy while recovering from a fever at the St. Rosalie hospital. But his passion was too strong for the few times he was allowed to cross the river to visit his woman, and so he deserted the Pollerian plantation. One night, as he lay sleeping in the hospital where Wainy hid him, Pollerian's overseer came to arrest him. Just as the overseer stepped into the boat behind him, Reuben struck the man down, seized his pistol, and shot him in the chest. Now a murderer as well as an escaped slave, Reuben fled to the swamp. Marie-Charlotte knew that the St. Rosalie slaves kept him alive. They took him bread and milk and butter and cheese, not because they liked the man, but because they loved Wainy.

Then a young hunter from the interior stumbled across Reuben late at night on the River Road. After a fierce battle, both men fell into the bayou, and while in the water, Reuben wrestled the hunter's knife away and stabbed him. The wounded hunter crawled home and died. Two murders were enough. Overseers from all the surrounding plantations organized a hunt and tracked Reuben down. They burned his hut one night and then shot him as he bolted from the door.

These were the things Marie-Charlotte thought about late at night when Andrew was in Wainy's room. Was it love, she wondered? Andrew claimed he loved her still, foolishly believing that Marie-Charlotte knew nothing of his nighttime wanderings. And what did God think of it all? Marie-Charlotte believed in her religion. She believed in Adam and Eve and the snake and the apple. But she also believed in forgiveness. Nevertheless, she was an angry woman. Why did it have to be this way? Her heart beat furiously. The blood went hotly to her head. Her breath came fast and hard. Then she would look out the window of her room and see the many stars, small and large, sparkling in the black sky. Soon it would be morning. And she would fall asleep thinking about the books she could read that day.

# Chapter Thirty Two

With Thomas as overseer, the year 1850 saw St. Rosalie return to prosperity. 163 hogsheads of sugar were produced on the plantation, more than three times the amount produced in each of the two previous years. But it was also a year of change and sadness. On Saturday, October 26th., late on a cold and rainy night, Sosthene, John McDonogh's old body servant, burst into the lower hall of the Durnford mansion.

The entire family and all of the servants ran down the dark stairs in response to his screams of anguish. When Andrew finally calmed the old man, he learned that the trusted servant had ridden hard down the River Road until his horse collapsed, and then ran the remaining three miles.

"Now tell me what has happened, Sosthene." Andrew said.

Sosthene screamed and wailed, and finally blurted out, "Oh is terrible, Massah Andrew, it be my old Massah John. He daid!"

John McDonogh, age 71, had died at half past two o'clock, Sosthene told the Durnfords. "He say he tired and would lie down some, and then close he eyes and gone," Sosthene said.

Andrew called for the carriage, put Sosthene inside to rest, and sat down on the opposite seat, while Thomas mounted the drivers seat for the thirty-five mile journey to McDonoghville. It rained throughout the night, and was still raining steadily when they arrived at daybreak.

The body of John McDonogh lay on a small cot in his office, where he usually slept.

Andrew made the sign of the cross. Then he carefully stitched shut his old friend's eyes and tucked the thread in so that it would not show. He stepped back. "You lived longer with fewer friends than any one I ever knew or heard of. My family and your slaves here, are the only people who were close to you. The richest man in Louisiana had no white friends at all."

Sosthene stood at the door, ringing his hands.

"Do you have people to prepare the body?" Andrew asked him.

"Yassah Massah Andrew. They waitin down on us."

"We will carry him down, Sosthene, and then you can have him laid out in the front room, where it is cooler. Make it up like a parlor, and that is where we will have the funeral."

After they took the body down, Andrew and Thomas returned to the McDonogh office, where Andrew searched the old man's desk until he found what he was looking for. It was a small envelope, too small to contain a will, Andrew realized, sealed with wax, and addressed to McDonogh's lawyer. On the envelope the old man had written in a beautiful scroll the words, "Directions upon the death of John McDonogh, Jr."

McDonogh's lawyer for many years, Felix Marchant, the man who had defended against the claim of the English Durnfords, had died the year before. The old man retained as his new lawyer Christian Roselius, a brilliant German immigrant who began life in America as a printer and later became an attorney. Roselius had just completed a term as Attorney General of Louisiana and was one of the law professors at the University of Louisiana. His firm, consisting of himself and three other lawyers, had its offices on Custom House Street.

That same morning, Andrew sent Thomas across the river with orders to deliver the letter to Christian Roselius, purchase a casket, and take notices of the funeral to the offices of *The Louisiana Courier* and *The Daily Picayune*. They would keep the body cool with ice and the funeral would be Sunday afternoon.

Andrew sat down at McDonogh's desk while he waited for Thomas to return with the casket. After a short while, Sosthene rapped lightly at the open door.

"Massah Andrew," he said, "when de casket come we take Massah John to de church—dat wat he say."

"Yes, of course, Sosthene. We will do that." Andrew knew then he should have asked Sosthene about the funeral arrangements. It was only natural that John McDonogh, who had lived so closely with his slaves for so many years would want his funeral at the brick chapel he built for them.

"Thank you, massah," Sosthene said and bowed his head and left.

Andrew looked absently through the papers in the old man's desk. He did not expect to find McDonogh's will, that, he knew, would be someplace safe, to be revealed in the envelope to his lawyer, Roselius, containing directions to be followed upon his death. Nor did Andrew have any interest in the will. He knew that he would not be included among those who would inherit. John McDonogh had always made that very clear. Andrew could not rely on receiving one penny, McDonogh had emphasized. It was the best gift he could ever give him, the old man said, the gift of independence. He would not have left his own children a thing, McDonogh maintained, had he ever had any children, because that would surely ruin them. Nor would he leave his slaves more than what was necessary to transport them to Liberia and provide the bare essentials. What the old man proposed to do with the remainder of the estate was never mentioned, but Andrew assumed he would give it all to the American Colonization Society.

What Andrew thought he might find in the old man's desk, however, was a personal note to him. A letter of good-bye and well-wishes, perhaps. But then, according to Sosthene, John's death came on rather quickly. The old man had either a stroke or a heart attack, and had acted perfectly normal up until a few minutes before he told Sosthene he felt tired.

So Andrew was not surprised when he found no note.

In the bottom of a drawer, with miscellaneous scraps and discarded ribbon, he found a sheaf of wrinkled papers. Andrew spread them out on the desk before him, and examined them one by one. They were old invoices and shipping orders, and then Andrew came upon a document stamped and executed by the Collector of the Port of New Orleans. The document certified the genuineness of an entry of foreign merchandise imported by John McDonogh Jr. & Co. in 1804. "Oh, my God. I can't believe this," Andrew said quietly. The McDonogh Company had imported from Sinoe, West Africa, forty-eight slaves at a total value of $4,800.00. "There must be some mistake," Andrew said to himself. Sinoe was the very place which later became part of Liberia and where McDonogh urged his freed slaves to establish a sugar plantation. And then he examined the document again. It was true.

Looking through other papers, boxes and boxes of them, Andrew Durnford realized how John McDonogh got rich. He made his fortune early—in the slave trade. On November 22, 1804, McDonogh sold at auction 84 more slaves imported in the ship *Sarah,* Captain Kennedy, Master. The cargo sold for $20,984.00, plus another $20.00 for two Negroes who were listed as "almost dead." Expenses were sales commission of $524.60 and advertising of $37.00. After freight, the new entrepreneur from Baltimore had made a profit several times his investment.

John McDonogh, the young Scotsman expanded his slave-trading operations to include purchases from Virginia and the Carolinas. McDonogh then took his huge earnings from the slave trade and invested heavily in land speculation. He was careful, prudent, and exacting, and his wealth multiplied. No one else had the immense fortune McDonogh had accumulated. No one could compete against him when he scooped up immense tracts of land all around New Orleans and up and down the Mississippi Valley.

Andrew was still going through the old man's papers later that afternoon, when Thomas returned with a handsome casket, for which he had written a St. Rosalie draft in the amount of $5.00. At the same time, Christian Roselius, Esq. appeared before Judge Buchanan of the Fifth District Court and informed him that McDonogh had left his will at the Union Bank. The Judge issued an order requiring the cashier of that bank to bring the will into court by Monday morning at 10 o'clock.

The funeral notices appeared in the morning and evening edition of the Saturday papers, and on Sunday afternoon there was a short and simple funeral in the brick slave chapel attached to the back of the house. The church was filled to overflowing with all the McDonogh slaves, the Durnford family, McDonogh's lawyers, and bankers and businessmen who had never acknowledged the old man as a friend. Prayers and a short sermon were said by each of the church's preachers, both McDonogh slaves. Then the slaves closed the casket, and carried it out to the adjacent cemetery McDonogh had set aside for his Negroes, where his coffin was placed in a plain oven-shaped brick tomb no different than those around it.

After the funeral, Andrew helped Roselius gather up the papers McDonogh had collected through fifty years of business and living in New Orleans, including the items documenting McDonogh's slave-trading years. When Andrew came across a folder containing all the letters he had ever sent his friend, he frowned. Included among them were his letters from Virginia in 1835, documenting his own slave-buying expedition.

The next morning, the Durnford family returned to St. Rosalie. The John McDonogh chapter of their lives was closed.

While the Durnfords drove home in their carriage, the Cashier of the Union Bank appeared before Judge Buchanan, as ordered, with a tin box containing the will of

John McDonogh. Roselius presented the will, the signature of McDonogh was proved, and the Judge read the will to the packed courtroom. The will consisted of twenty-four pages, closely written, in the old man's own handwriting. After leaving $6,000 and some land to his sister and her children in Baltimore, McDonogh gave $400,000 to the Protestant Male Orphan Asylum of New Orleans and other amounts to local charities. He gave another three million dollars to the City of Baltimore for a school farm. He gave the remainder of his estate, consisting of several million dollars, one half to the City of New Orleans and one-half to the City of Baltimore for the purpose of establishing in each city free schools for poor children of all classes.

McDonogh also left a large sum of money to the American Colonization Society. Then he liberated all of his slaves and provided for their passage to Liberia. And because of the immense wealth of his estate and influence of his trustees, McDonogh's wishes were honored, notwithstanding the Louisiana statute prohibiting manumition of slaves.

In his instructions to his executors, McDonogh stated that: "And whereas Dr. Andrew Durnford, a free man of the Parish of Plaquemines is indebted to me by a mortgage on his Sugar Estate (he being a worthy and honest man and my friend) my Executors are to wait the payment of said debt with him, and give him time to pay it off at 6%. It being well understood, however, that the amount of the crop which he will make on his plantation he will annually pay over until the whole amount is paid."

The amount Andrew Durnford owed to the McDonogh Estate was $38,000. Andrew Durnford had no desire to deal with those men, cold and distant, who administered the holdings of his old friend. He also wondered what John could have been thinking in requiring that Durnford pay the entire sales price received for his crop each year on the mortgages, leaving nothing for expenses. He could not run the plantation without revenues, he knew. Immediately, he sold off six acres of St. Rosalie river frontage to George Urquart for $25,000. The sales price was a bargain, because that soil had long been exhausted. Even without that land the Durnford plantation produced one of the largest crops ever, 197 hogsheads in 1851.

Other plantations did not fare as well, and the price of sugar rose to $60.00 a hogshead. Durnford sold off a few more acres and paid off his debt to the McDonogh estate. He could have avoided selling any of the St. Rosalie land. The property on Tivoli Square would have brought more than the entire debt to McDonogh. But that property was in the middle of the expanding business section of New Orleans.  It would, Andrew predicted, double in value in a few years.

So Andrew sold off the least productive land of the plantation.  And as Thomas took upon himself an ever larger share of management, Andrew withdrew more and more from the everyday affairs of St. Rosalie and turned his attention to his medical practice, which grew and grew, until he was providing free medical care to a majority of Plaquemines Parish, white and black, free and slave, on both sides of the river.

# Chapter Thirty Three

Over the next few years talk of secession and war between the states grew louder, as the cracks in the big mansion expanded. *Uncle Tom's Cabin* was published by the young lady the Durnfords had met in Cincinnati, Harriet Beecher Stowe. The anti-slavery book sold one and a half million copies, surpassing any other publication of the Nineteenth Century.

Andrew Durnford bought a copy and added it to the St. Rosalie library. "I'm putting it right here, over the fireplace," he said to Thomas, "so that I won't forget to mention to everyone how we met Mrs. Stowe in Cincinnati."

"Papa, I don't think we should display that book. It is an insult to the South and can only upset our guests."

"Have you read the book, Thomas?"

"No, Papa, I have not read it. But I know it does not show up slavery in very good colors."

Andrew rubbed his chin and looked at the book displayed prominently over the fireplace. Then he looked over at his tall son standing next to the fire. "Well, Thomas, it does indeed show the evils of slavery rather thoroughly, I think."

"But it isn't a fair treatment, Papa. Mrs. Stowe takes extreme cases and presents them as the general condition, and that puts us in a very bad light."

"I thought you hadn't read it."

"Well, I sort of browsed through it."

"Where?"

"In the city." Thomas shook his head. "I just happened to see it in the bookstore when I was looking for *Gilbert's Atlas*. I wouldn't lay out my money for it."

"So, you formed your opinion upon casually glancing through the book? Thomas you surprise me."

"All right, Papa. I did read the book. I spent the afternoon reading it from cover to cover. And it seems to me that Mrs. Stowe doesn't understand the difference between discipline and cruelty. A certain degree of discipline is necessary to manage a work force, slave or free labor. And it is not true that slaves are generally ill treated."

"Well, Thomas you can't deny that there are cases in which slaves, the people of our own blood, are badly used."

"Papa, you talk like an abolitionist lately. And in answer to that challenge, no, I can not deny there are cases of cruelty. Abuses exist in any system. You yourself, Papa, have said that children are worked to death in the English factories in conditions far worse than endured by any slave."

"True. I have said that. But at least the law forbids whipping them, and they are free to leave."

"Now Papa don't start that. You know flogging is necessary. You have done it."

"Yes, Thomas, I have. And the punishment was administered judiciously. But the point you have missed, is that the law allows us to whip our people. Now if we allow bad men to own slaves, and we also allow them to whip their slaves, and at the same time deny the slave the simple privilege of resisting cruelty, even you, Thomas, must admit that we have an institution that legalizes cruelty. Thomas, slavery is evil. I know that, and I think you know that as well."

"Well, Papa, now that the law denies you the joy of freeing any of our people, you have taken a most pious attitude toward the ancient system that built you St. Rosalie."

"Thomas, you will not address me in such a tone. We may have our differences, but I am still your father, and I insist on respect."

"I apologize, Papa. I don't know what comes over me when we discuss this damnable subject. And as soon as I said that, I knew I had said too much." Thomas shook his head. "Papa, I never again want to talk about the slavery question. It divides the nation. It makes me irrational. And it brings about harsh feelings between us. Please forgive me, Papa."

Andrew Durnford did forgive his son. His son had expressed the very same views he had held until very recently, and he knew Thomas was still struggling with the same rationalizations that Andrew had struggled with for so many years.

St. Rosalie plantation continued to prosper under Thomas' management, producing a record 280 hogsheads in 1854. But then the soil was finally showing signs of exhaustion, as it was on all the neighboring plantations. Downriver from St. Rosalie, many plantations were turning from sugar production to rice. Upriver they were converting to raising cattle. When Thomas suggested they do the same, Andrew agreed to turn a few acres over to rice and to experiment with livestock breeding.

Thomas said, "And if we can get along with fewer people, we can always sell some slaves to get us through the bad times."

Andrew was stunned. Thomas had talked about selling slaves as casually as he talked about the price of sugar. Andrew Durnford would never sell a slave. He had sold only the insolent slave he was forced to shoot in the buttocks years ago and his old friend and body servant, Barba. He would never do that again. His people belonged on St. Rosalie. The plantation belonged to them. Some day, he repeated to himself, he would free them all and sell them the plantation, no matter how much Thomas objected. But for now, it could not be done.

To free the slaves in his will was no solution, Andrew realized. He did not have the power of a John McDonogh. Under the law, such an emancipation provision would not be recognized by the courts. Only if the law changed before his estate was closed would the slaves go free. But there was very little chance of that happening. So his children would inherit the slaves with full rights of ownership, no matter what Andrew said in his will. All he could do was hope that some day in the future, when emancipation again became legal, his children would honor his wishes.

Thomas was a good manager. Andrew admitted that readily. But Andrew knew he could not trust him to carry out his wishes and free the slaves. And Andrew was getting along in years. Lately, he felt a hollow pain in his chest. It was getting worse every year. At fifty-eight, Andrew Durnford began thinking about death. He also thought about his two other children. Andrew Jr. was too young still to give any indication what his philosophy might be when he came of age. But Rosema was an angel. Although his only daughter was only fourteen at the time, Andrew thought of giving her the slave Wainy, then 31 years old. When the law permitted, Rosema would free Wainy. Rosema had promised Andrew that much. But Wainy despaired when Andrew told her of that plan. Rosema was still just a child, Wainy reminded him, legally a minor and powerless before the law. So Andrew struggled over his trusted nurse. He could not free her. To do so would have put her at risk of being seized by the first man to come along and cast her back into slavery under terrible conditions. He could not rely on Marie-Charlotte. The good wife was growing old, too. And then Wainy had been his mistress and Andrew would not insult his wife by asking her to take the slave and free her after his death.

So what was Andrew to do with Wainy, the woman he loved, but gave up for Marie-Charlotte, whom he finally decided he loved even more? He would no longer embarrass her in his old age, he told Marie-Charlotte, and he would act the fool no more.

Then there was a child of Wainy that was more of a problem. Andrew had promised Wainy that her child would be free. It was a promise he meant to keep. And for this child, Andrew gave up his dream.

The agreement was made when the old man and his son, Thomas, were riding along the river, inspecting the levee that held back the high waters of the Mississippi. "All right, Thomas," Andrew said, "I will not emancipate the slaves on those conditions."

Andrew stopped his horse and peered out over the muddy water. His face twitched and he felt the pain of a beginning migraine. "But you must promise me one more thing, Thomas."

"Yes, Papa?"

"If there comes a time when the Federal Government shall offer a plan to purchase freedom for the slaves, you will then let our people go."

"Oh, Papa, that I would gladly do. Even you have said it is unfair of the North to ask us to carry the burden of emancipation. But if we are given the opportunity to see our way clear of this burden, then surely I would do that, and my promise is not necessary."

"But you do promise me that?"

"Of course, Papa."

"There are some who would not free their slaves even under such terms," Andrew said. "But even if half the value of a slave is to be given, I think then good conscience obligates us to emancipate."

"Papa, I see your reasoning there. But a good field hand today is worth a thousand dollars. If I were given that money and invested it on a ten percent return, I could hire an Irishman for a period of fifteen years. But to receive less than full value would leave me without any capital in a short time. How can I be expected to survive?"

"Thomas, this is a matter I can not negotiate with you. I must have your promise that you will participate, no matter what the subsidy might be."

Thomas thought for a long time before answering his father. Finally he said, "To tell you the truth, Papa, I don't think such a plan will come about in my lifetime. But nevertheless, I agree. No matter what I might be given in payment for the slaves, I will go along with such a program."

And so the bargain with Thomas was struck. If Andrew would not write into his will provisions placing upon his heirs the moral obligation of freeing the slaves when emancipation became legal, then Thomas would carry out Andrew's wishes in regard to Wainy and her baby. Thomas would free both Wainy and her son as soon as Louisiana law permitted.

Having secured Thomas' solemn promise, Andrew returned alone to the mansion and sat down at his desk and wrote into his will, "I hereby order to be emancipated my slave Wainy and the boy of my servant Wainy born the 2d day of January, 1857, and should emancipation then not be legally permissible, I hereby bequeath to my son Thomas said servant Wainy and her said boy upon his promise to free them both when that shall become legal, and when the said boy shall be ten years old, I hereby give him two thousand dollars ($2,000) to contribute to give said boy a good education, and hereby request my son Thomas McDonogh Durnford to see that said disposition be carried out in respect to said boy."

With that provision written into his will, Andrew Durnford sighed in relief. Wainy's baby boy, Albert, was his own son, and would be a slave until the law permitted his emancipation and Thomas was legally able to carry out Andrew's wishes and free him and his mother. There was nothing Andrew could do to prevent his own son, Albert, from being a slave, because Albert was born to a slave, and neither the mother, whom Andrew loved, or the son he also loved could be freed under the law of Louisiana. The system which made him a wealthy and respected citizen of the West Bank had finally entrapped Andrew Durnford.

Two years after executing his will, Andrew Durnford left the plantation hospital late one day and walked through the evening shadows toward the big mansion. He thought about the slaves, and hoped that he would be given the right to free them before he died. He hoped that the day would come when he could avoid the bargain he made with Thomas. He'd said nothing to Thomas about freeing them in his lifetime, only that he would not bind Thomas through his will.

Then he looked up and noticed that the fracture in the north wall gaped wider than ever before. Several cracks spread out from the main fissure like a spider web. This time, there would be no simple patching and painting to hide the damage. The soft soil had given too much. He stopped under an oak to get his breath, looked out over the muddy river where it surged against the levee, and sighed. Currents ran under the levee to bubble up and further weaken the mansion's foundation.

As Andrew leaned against the old oak tree at the end of that long day in his medical practice, he thought of a plan to defeat the river. Why not drive down pilings? They were doing that around the city. Drive them down twenty feet or more. Build the new house on that. It would be entirely of cedar, he decided. Framed, floored, and sided with that remarkable hardwood, the new mansion would last forever. So even if the law changed and permitted freedom for the slaves they would have to wait now, wait until he finished the new mansion. After all he had done for them, they could wait another year or two.

Andrew Durnford pushed himself away from the oak tree. I must tell Miss Remy, he said with a smile. She will finally have the biggest house on the river. All with magnificent columns and porches and painted white.

He took a step toward the old mansion, and a terrible, crushing pain ripped through his head, followed by an overpowering smell of incense.

Noel, with the yellow light of his lantern, found his old master lying on the lawn under the oak tree. He called for Thomas, who came running with the house servants. They carried the master of St. Rosalie up to his bedroom on the second floor.

Andrew Durnford lay there for hours, looking out the open window at the river, silver in the moonlight. Several times, he tried to talk, but the words would not form in his mouth. Neither could he lift an arm or leg. The pain in his head was completely gone now. He was at peace. Without the pain, the aroma of incense was rather pleasant, he decided.

On July 12, 1859, at half past four o'clock in the morning, Andrew Durnford died.

# Chapter Thirty Four

The old master of St. Rosalie was put into the earth at the plantation cemetery north of the sugarhouse. It was a plain ceremony attended by no priest or parson. The details had been prescribed by Andrew and adhered to by his family.

Facing the hot July wind flowing down from the levey, Thomas, addressed the throng around the grave. He read from papers his father had prepared for his funeral. The words came slowly but strongly, masking the emotion boiling within him. He recognized the theme from Ecclesiastes.

"I lived my time among you, seeking what makes mankind happy, and doing what men do in the few days they have to live. I did great things: built myself a mansion, planted cane; put in gardens and orchards. I bought men slaves and women slaves; and had a few home-born slaves as well. Then when age laid a heavy hand upon me I wondered about all that my hands had done and all the effort I had put into my dreams. What vanity! It all comes to nothing more than the wind blowing through the house!

"In my old age my reflections also turned to questions of wisdom and folly. The wise man sees ahead while the fool walks in the dark. But both are soon forgotten; wise man no less than fool must die. Wisdom too, then, is nothing more than vanity

"All I have toiled for, I now bequeath to my successor. He will be master of all that was my vanity. Who knows whether he will be a wise man or a fool?"

Here Thomas looked up and along the levee. Wainy had left the graveside and strolled along the levee, her head held high, the hand of her young son Albert in hers.  Thomas continued his recitation from memory, while he watched her:

"This, however, you must know: God made man simple; man's complex problems are of his own devising."

When he had finished reading Thomas looked around at the faces of his family and slaves, and the white neighbors and friends of Andrew Durnford surrounding the grave.  He looked into the eyes of Noel and saw wisdom smoldering there.  On the old slave's face was a seasoned smile.  Thomas smiled.  Only Noel understands Papa's meaning.  And he will explain it to no one, because that would be vanity.

"And now," Thomas said, "My father has asked me to read a poem he wrote long ago."  Thomas paused for a moment and sucked in air between his teeth, fighting back tears that threatened.  He began in an unsteady voice:

> I was the fool of time and terror.
> Days stole o'er me and stole from me;
> Yet I lived,
> Loathing my life,
> Yet dreading still to die.

> Knowledge is not happiness; and science
> But an exchange of ignorance for that
> Which is another kind of ignorance.

> To give birth to those
> Who can but suffer many years and die,
> Is merely propagating death
> And multiplying an unforgivable lie.

As Thomas completed that stanza, Marie-Charlotte slumped to the ground, her hands covering her face.  Thomas waited while Noel knelt beside the mistress of St. Rosalie and comforted her, and then Thomas continued in a determined voice:

> I knew what I could have been; and felt
> I was not what I should be.
> Now it has come to an end.

> There lurked a wish within my breast

Not to feel the consciousness of rest.
Now my fate that wish does fulfil,
And now I sleep without the dream
Of what I was and would be still!

Marie-Charlotte moaned uncontrollably.  All the slaves, sobbing and groaning in deep-felt pain and sorrow, joined her.  Tears streamed down the faces of the whites who stood mixed in with the crowd of Negroes, slave and free, family and friend, who came from all over Plaquemines Parish, the Cane River Colony, and New Orleans to attend the funeral.

The *Picayune* noted the passing of Andrew Durnford, stating simply that Dr. Andrew Durnford, a respected physician of Plaquemines Parish had passed away to the great loss of the citizens of that region.  No mention was made of the fact that Andrew Durnford was a free man of color, that he owned one of the largest plantations in the state, or that he was a slave owner.

Marie-Charlotte Remy Durnford filed the will of her late husband for probate in the Second Judicial District Court of Plaquemines Parish.  As Andrew had directed, she was given control of the assets of the sugar plantation during the administration of the estate.  For inheritance tax purposes, the plantation lands were assessed at $30,0000, machinery and implements at $20,000, livestock at $1,500 and the seventy-seven slaves at $71,000.  The total value of the plantation was $122,500. Adding to that the value of the house on Tivoli Square in New Orleans, the Estate of Andrew Durnford exceeded $150,000 of assessed value and was worth approximately twice that figure.

Life continued at St. Rosalie much as it had before Andrew's death. Thomas took over his father's duties in the plantation hospital with Wainy as his nurse.  Thomas also continued as plantation overseer.  Noel kept the books of account and made all the necessary purchases in New Orleans.

The year following Andrew's death was another good year for sugar production, with 165 hogshead produced at $82.00 per hogshead for gross revenues of $13,530. The year after that the plantation produced another 150 hogsheads.

Under the law in Louisiana, it was still a crime to free a slave.    Thomas continued to believe that what he told his father would always be true. There would be no change in his lifetime.

But change did come. Along with a bounty crop, the year 1861 brought Civil War.

The free man of color, Thomas Durnford, heir apparent to St. Rosalie Plantation, was not drafted into the Confederate Army. Nor would he have been accepted had he volunteered, since the law prohibited free men of color from regular military service. However, his cousins and uncles at the Cane River Colony moved to support the Confederate cause. They were Negroes. But their hearts were with the South because they were also slave owners. So they formed a calvary squadron called the "Augustin Guards," after the family patriarch. A second company of infantry was organized as Monet's Guards, and the citizens of Natchitoches at Cane River appropriated $600.00 to defray the expenses of those Confederate Negro volunteers and their families while they went off to the defense of New Orleans.

Thomas Durnford stayed on as overseer at St. Rosalie. When the Union Navy blockaded the Mississippi River, cutting off all exports including sugar and molasses, Thomas turned the plantation into a producer of rice and vegetables. A portion of those new crops from St. Rosalie Plantation were packed into carts and hauled by mule down river to the forts protecting the City of New Orleans from Union attack. Fort Jackson on the west bank of the river had been taken over by the Louisiana State Militia, as well as Fort St. Philip on the other side of the Mississippi. The Confederate Army mounted over 50 new cannons and huge mortars in each of the two forts, all strategically trained on the river to block Union passage north. Then a chain connected to logs and other floating obstructions was stretched across the river from bank to bank. Derelict schooners were placed in a line behind the chain, and behind them, a little farther upriver, a small fleet of the Confederate Navy took station to assist the forts.

When Thomas first saw these defenses, he believed the assurances of invincibility appearing daily in the *Picayune*. New Orleans would never fall to the Yankees. Nothing on the river could survive the withering fire from the two forts.

On Saturday, April 12, 1862 Thomas delivered his weekly load of supplies to Fort Jackson, received a Confederate voucher as payment, and mounted the wagon driven by Petroni, one of the plantation slaves. As they went out the gates and along the River Road, heading north toward St. Rosalie, Thomas turned to see a black hull crawl from beyond the woods down river around the bend. The ship, puffing smoke as black as its hull and flying the Stars and Stripes, rounded up in the middle of the river, broadside to the fort. There was a flash along the black hull, followed by a puff of smoke from one of the ship's guns. The shell came hurtling through the air, a distance of two miles. Thomas realized immediately it was a well-placed shot, passing critically near to those men of the South who stood on the ramparts watching its course. The shell passed over the fort and fell between its walls and the river, smashing a small foot bridge and throwing up mud and water. A second shell followed and landed a few feet beyond the outer bastion facing the river. Thomas watched, caught in the spell of men at war, as a total of twelve shots came from the sole ship in the middle of the river.

The Yankee ship seemed to be playing some type of strategic game Thomas did not understand. The ship backed and turned, placing shots all around the fort. Two shots came dangerously close to a small excursion steamer docked at the landing in front of the fort. It was packed with sightseers from New Orleans. One shot passed directly over the pilothouse of the little steamer, and another dropped into the water just beyond the stern. None of the near misses seemed to affect the group of spirited citizens on the steamer who pointed and shouted and waved their arms.

Finally, the Federal ship turned its attention to the fort across the river, St. Philip. Several projectiles were sent whizzing over the river, to land all around that fort, with one shot passing completely over it and landing far out in the prairie.

Then there was a louder, rumbling explosion from beyond the woods at the bend of the river. A huge projectile came sailing up from behind the trees—a mortar shot. The shell came in a lofty, aerial arc and exploded in mid-air high over Fort Jackson. Then a second mortar shell came sailing up from the deck of another Yankee ship hidden behind the trees and landed squarely within the fort, tossing up a huge cloud of earth as it exploded.

Finally, Fort Jackson returned fire with its seven-inch guns, sending water splashing short of the black hull in the river. And just as suddenly as it had appeared, the Yankee gunship turned and disappeared behind the woods again. Except for birds singing in the trees, all was silent up and down the river. Cheers and jeers rose from the fort and from the little excursion steamer as well. Then passengers went streaming from the pretty little white boat to pick up pieces of shells that lay about for souvenirs of the event.

Thomas felt a lump rise in his throat as he watched the unruly crowd. This was not a picnic. This was war. He had seen a ship flying the flag he loved, the Stars and Stripes, fire upon his countrymen in gray, and they in turn had fired upon that flag.

A week later, Thomas returned with another load of provisions. As he approached the fort, he heard heavy cannon fire in the distance, much louder and stronger than the week before. On the road behind the levee, he ordered Petroni to rein in the mules and then Thomas stood up in the wagon. A mile downstream, on the other side of the chain stretched across the river were Federal ships, big warships, gunboats, and mortar ships, all enveloped in clouds of smoke, with guns blazing. The Union ships had already passed Fort Jackson, leaving that bastian to fire vainly at their rear guard. The Yankee flotilla bore steadily down on Fort Philip, farther upstream, where the chain and obstructions blocked the river.

As Thomas watched with tears in his eyes, the Union ships continued upstream at full speed. Shells from Fort Philip bounced off the water all around them. Then the forward ship, large and heavy rammed the chain, and was followed by a second to port and a third to starboard.

Suddenly, the chain parted and the entire Union fleet sailed on past Fort Philip, the last defense post of the city.

Thomas watched and under the fierce barrage of the heavy guns on the Union ships, the small Confederate fleet exploded before his eyes. Suddenly the Union ships were right there, on the other side of the levee, guns silent now that the enemy had been vanquished. Thomas stared at the dark-uniformed Yankees hanging in the rigging who starred back at him and Petroni.

Quickly Thomas dismounted from the wagon and ordered Petroni to help him unhitch the mules. Then, leaving the loaded wagon standing in the road, he mounted one mule while Petroni mounted the other, and together they rode off toward St. Rosalie, passing all of the Union ships, which plowed slowly north against the swift current.

The two black men, slave and young master, rode on into the night, and arrived at St. Rosalie when everyone was asleep. Marie-Charlotte heard him come into the house and went down to the parlor where her son had lit a cigar and fallen, exhausted into a chair. Lamps were going on in the slave cabins as the St. Rosalie work force learned from Petroni that the Yankees were on the way.

"Thomas, why are you back so soon? And at such an hour?"

"The Yankees have broken through, Mama. They will reach the city in two days."

"My God, Thomas, you can't mean that?"

"It's true, Mama. I saw them. There must be more than twenty ships, all heavily armed. They broke through the chain. They sank our Navy in minutes. Nothing will stop them."

Marie-Charlotte looked out across the grounds to the slave cabins behind the sugarhouse. A light shone in every cabin now. And she heard wails and moaning, and laughter and shouting too.

"What are we to do, Thomas."

"There is nothing to do, Mama, except go to bed and sleep."

"Surely our Army will protect us. They will come with cannon and sink the Yankees, one by one."

"No, Mama. Nothing will stop them."

"But our brave men from the Cane Colony will repel them, Thomas. Mark my words. Those Yankees will see what fighting is all about when our Negro soldiers face them down."

"Mama, there is no one to defend New Orleans. Monet's Guards are days away. The Augustin Cavalry has not yet left for the city and would never reach it in time. Besides, they are no match for the Federals. It is all over, Mama."

"And our regular soldiers left last month for Virginia. What will the city do, Thomas?"

"The city will surrender, Mama. As shall we all. Now it is time to go to bed." And saying that, Thomas put out his cigar, rose from his chair, took his aging mother into his arms, and led her upstairs to bed.

A little after noon the next day, Thomas, Marie-Charlotte, the other children, Noel, Wainy and all the St. Rosalie slaves watched the Union ships steam majestically up the Mississippi toward New Orleans. No one went to the fields. The excitement of the prior evening had worn off, and now even the slaves stood with sour and worried faces as they watched the Yankees on the ships. And when the Union men waved gaily at the black population of St. Rosalie, only little Albert, Wainy's son, waved back.

As the Union Navy surged past St. Rosalie, the morning edition of the *Daily Picayune* reported that: "A week ago we gave some account of the firing of the first gun by the enemy at Fort Jackson, the commencement of a bombardment which has lasted ever since Sunday, the 13th inst. Advices from the fort, as late as 8 1/2 P.M. Saturday evening, showed that the enemy's fire had very much slacked, and was very slow compared with what it had been for several days previous. Within that space of time it is estimated by an experienced judge that the foe has thrown at and into Fort Jackson a thousand tons of iron, in the shape of shell and ball, at an expenditure of some three or four hundred thousand pounds of powder—and this occasioning no greater loss on our side than five killed and ten wounded.

"The enemy keeps his mortarboats out of sight of the fort, behind a line of thick woods, only his gunboats making their appearance, at intervals, beyond the point. Yet two of their mortarboats, we learn, have been sunk by our fire, and one of their large steamers disabled.

"This certainly is a most remarkable bombardment, and we think history hardly supplies a parallel with it. The officers in command are confident of being able to hold the fort, and its nearly opposite neighbor, Fort St. Philip, besides. The latter has not yet been assailed, being beyond the range of the skulking mortarboats of the enemy. It is quite ready to do its part in the defense when its turn comes."

But the citizens of New Orleans knew differently. Long before the dawn of that morning they had been awakened by the tolling of fire bells. Twelve peals repeated four times over—the signal that the federal fleet had passed the forts. Throughout the city families everywhere were fleeing, with their children screaming in terror of the Yankees, and their slaves bent to the ground carrying heavy bundles of precious belongings. The mayor issued orders to destroy all ships and supplies to keep them from the hands of the enemy. Every vessel on the wharf was set on fire and pushed out into the river to drift down on the hated enemy. Miles of corded steamboat wood and huge pyres of cotton blazed up and down the levy, lighting the scene as bright as day. Horses and wagons came galloping up and down the streets carrying more cotton and goods to the levee to be burned. Smoke choked the city.

People, black, white, free and slave, looted everywhere. Men smashed open boxes and crates on the levee, stealing everything, while their women and children broke into stores and collected groceries, salt, meat, charred bits of cotton and anything else they could carry away. Hogsheads of sugar and molasses were broken open on the levee, spilling a river of thick sweetness which flowed onto the street and into the gutters where it was ladled up with pails, cups and shovels, or even scooped up with bare hands.

Women ran through the streets with their hair flying and waving pistols in the air and firing randomly. They screamed, "Burn the city! Never mind us! Burn the city!"

At the corner of Common and Magazine the crowd ran down a poor man, pale and trembling, and strung him up on a lamppost. The crowd looked on and jeered the suspected Yankee sympathizer, and just as his face was turning black, a small detachment of the Foreign Legion, which had been formed to keep order, came running down the street in quickstep, and its officer drew his sword and slashed the rope in time to save the wretch's life.

Later that morning, a great multitude crowded the levee in silence to watch Farragut's squadron round Slaughter House Point in an implacable, grim line. The decks of the Federal ships were black with silent sailors, and the Stars and Stripes snapped at every masthead against a background of leaden clouds.

The Union Flagship *Hartford,* bearing the blue pennant of Admiral Farragut, the steamships *Brooklyn, Pensacola, Mississippi* and *Pocahontas,* nine gunboats, and several other Federal ships came up through the burning wreckage in the river and dropped anchor, all guns trained on the town.

The mayor claimed to have no authority to surrender the city. For a few days messages were passed back and forth between the city administration and Admiral Farragut. Finally, Farragut sent ashore a detachment of sailors and marines to haul down the flag of Confederate Louisiana, and without any means of defense and no army to protect it, the city surrendered without firing a shot. At 11:30 A.M. on April 29, 1862 the Stars & Stripes of the United States of America was hoisted over the Customs House.

# Epilogue

Not long after the fall of New Orleans, Baton Rouge, Natchez, and all of the lower Mississippi River fell into Union hands.  But Federal occupation did not bring an end to St. Rosalie or slavery on the plantation.  The Emancipation Proclamation when first issued by Abraham Lincoln did not apply to St. Rosalie, because the plantation came under the clause excepting lands in Union hands.  Slaves who mistakenly thought they had been freed, found themselves returned to the plantation by Union troops.

It was not until October of 1862, six months later, that a second Emancipation Proclamation was issued by President Lincoln.  This time there was no exclusion.  The St. Rosalie slaves were, at last, free people.  None of the slaves left.  They stayed on and worked the plantation as they had before, but for wages.  The plantation records of 1864 show that Noel was still there as manager of the accounts, and all of the men were still there, earning wages of $8.00 per month, while Wainy and the other women earned $6.00 per month.  All groups, field hands and house servants alike, were paid the same wages, regardless of the work they did.

The last available records of St. Rosalie are for the year 1867.  Most of the slaves from the prior years were still carried on the books as wage earners.  However neither Noel or Wainy remained on the plantation.

Thomas Durnford married Elizabeth L. Robinson after the surrender of New Orleans and stayed on at the plantation with his mother, sister and brother until after the end of the Civil War.  The only child ever born to Thomas and Elizabeth,

Marie Ida Durnford died at age 13 months as the Civil War ended in 1864.

In 1866 the Durnford family moved off the plantation to New Orleans and leased the entire operation to Edgar Marin, a white man.  Upon leaving the plantation, Marie-Charlotte reapplied for the administration of her deceased husband's estate, which had sat dormant because of the Civil War.  On June 10, 1866, shortly after filing the new petition for administration of Andrew's estate, Marie-Charlotte died.

Thomas had no interest in the plantation, and William Erskine, the white neighbor to the north, himself an old man at that time, took over administration of the estate.  Within six months, the house on Tivoli Square was sold and the estate readied for settlement.  Thomas immediately sold his interest in the estate to Edgar Marin, the man who had taken over operations under lease.

On April 27, 1867, the final account of the estate was filed by George Urquhart, another old neighbor who succeeded Erskine as executor when Erskine died.  The Durnford heirs, Edgar Marin substituting for Thomas, along with the Durnford children, Rosema, and Andrew Durnford, Jr., filed opposition to the final account.  They would not approve the claim of $2,000 to be paid to Albert, Wainy's son fathered by the deceased master of St. Rosalie, Andrew Durnford.  Hearings were held, at which the Durnford children and Edgar Marin took the position that the gift to Albert was illegal.  The grounds for this position were simple.  Albert was a slave both at the time Andrew Durnford executed his will and at the time of the master's death.  Louisiana law at both those times prohibited emancipation of slaves.  Since the emancipation was illegal, and it was also illegal to give a slave $2,000, the bequest could not be honored by the court in 1867.  The court ruled in favor of the Durnford family.  Wainy, who had filed the petition on behalf of her son, Albert, lost the battle. Because he had sold his interest in the estate to Edgar Marin, Thomas had no legal standing to carry out his father's wishes.

Andrew Durnford, Jr., and Rosema continued to run St. Rosalie Plantation with Edgar Marin, each owning one-third, until 1874.  In that year, the plantation was sold to John Dymond, who converted entirely to rice production.

After selling his interest in his father's estate, Thomas became a man of leisure, dividing his time between Paris and New Orleans.  In 1891, Thomas died in New Orleans at the age of sixty-five, leaving as his widow, Elizabeth, the woman he married during the Civil War.

The last Durnford heir was Sarah Mary Durnford, the daughter of Andrew Durnford, Jr.   Sarah Mary Durnford died on Sept. 16, 1954. She was a graduate of the Normal Department of Straight University in New Orleans and had been a teacher all of her life.

The land once occupied by St. Rosalie Plantation is still shown on charts of the Mississippi River as St. Rosalie Bend. The site is now the home of a grain loading operation. All traces of St. Rosalie have disappeared, including the mansion, the sugarhouse, and the plantation cemetary.